ANDI JAMES CHAMBERLAIN.

ONE MAN AND HIS DOGMA

- a novel -

Andi James Chamberlain

Published By CYMprint

ONE MAN AND HIS DOGMA

Copyright © Andi James Chamberlain
First Printing September 2015
Design - Matt Young Design & Illustration
Edited by Paul Martin

ISBN - 978-0-9934016-0-2

DEDICATED TO JAE.

The Original Mr Edmunds.
The inspiration, the influence.
Him who told me it should be a book...

Thank You.
x

SPECIAL THANKS:

All of the brilliant people who pledged toward the Kickstarter.
The Book you hold in your hands exists only because of your kindness.

You are - each of you - my hero.
x

PROLOGUE
Catalysts and Origins

I'd thought that when someone said that they had seen everything, it was just a silly, little turn of phrase, a meaningless boast, made in the passing of some silly, little occurrence in a silly, little life.

People throw sayings and phrases like that around all day, every day. They think nothing of it and then one day, you are stood, staring at the most beautiful thing you can ever claim to have seen and all of a sudden, the silly, little turn of phrase, the throw away comment takes on so much beauty, so much resonance.

And you think to yourself;

"I have seen everything now, and I can die, knowing that nothing will compare to this sight before me."

The line of the arm, the tiny, little fragile fingers that top off the wonderful, simple yet brilliantly minute hands. The body a light, purring shade of pink that is untouched, unsullied, perfect; the legs that kick gently at the air, and wave around in hopeful abandon; the smile and gurgle of the squat, squashed little face; the eyes, catching the light in an array of perfect blues and greens and browns; the lips, soft and pink, warm and tender; the nose, a button sniffing and sneezing with wonderful amazement at all that is going around it.

Laying there, in a small plastic and glass cot, tubes feeding in and out, supplying life, supplying dreams of yet-to-be-told futures, a little monitor beep, beep, beeping along with each precious heartbeat.

My Son.
My flesh.
My blood.

Imagine, if you will, this vision of absolute perfection. Wonderful, crazy, biological perfection. This being that was once nothing but a *"twinkle in your eye"*, something so tiny and perfect to you, and you alone, that looking upon it is like looking upon God himself.

Imagine looking down on this being that you created, and knowing that - in your heart of hearts - though you love him more than you could ever love anyone ever again, more than you have ever loved anyone before, knowing all of this, imagine then the realisation that this boy, this perfect baby, YOUR baby, YOUR son, this being of pure love, created by the uncompromising pureness of true love, has killed the only other thing you have ever cared about in your bitter, insignificant life.

Imagine looking upon your son, your baby, your boy, and knowing that he is responsible for your wife's death.

"*Murderer,*" your mind whispers, taunting you.

"*He's not a murderer,*" you argue.

"*Mur. Der. Rer.*" It persists.

"HE IS NOT A MURDERER!" You scream.

With tears streaming down your face, you look around, horrified, that everyone is looking at you.

And they are. Horrified, shocked, mouths agape in disgust. Imagine that you look down on your boy, your beautiful baby boy and he looks back, you could swear that he smiles – impossible as that may seem - and then he, too, dies.

Just like that...

CHAPTER ONE
The Box and Other Stories

"Before I spoke with people,
I did not think of all these things because there was no one to bother to think them for.
Now things just come out of my mouth which are true."

— Bernard Pomerance, *The Elephant Man*

The way that the sun is shining outside would make you think it was the middle of summer. Bright, cloudless skies and a smart golden sheen to everything you can see outside the window. The treetops, the road, the cars that zoom up and down the street full of busy, little people going about their busy, little lives, oblivious to the other lives they unsettle with their smog-filled vehicles.

But the trick is, the minute you step outside, you get caught short by that curt, nasty, late October wind. Not strong or blustery by any stretch of the imagination, but bitter and biting and deeply, deeply penetrating as it hits you unawares and burrows deep into the core of you, the breath evacuating from you in sudden shock. Damned, October wind.

I sit in the window of this house, staring out on the world I see from my safe, tiny haven. And I smile at the banality of it all. The sad looking people are hurrying here, there and everywhere in a mad, verminous stampede – like giant bipedal insects, I imagine them like human cockroaches, scuttling around in the way cockroaches do.

Three hundred and twenty-five days now. I have woken up, showered, had my breakfast and sat in this window, with my tea, and my notebook and just watched the world unfold, never getting involved in any measurable way… simply sitting, watching, and noting the things I witness and see.

"Agoraphobia."

That's what they call it, the doctors and the care workers and suchlike, all the busy little people who come round here, bringing the outside in to me, *agoraphobia,*
an almost pathological fear of wide and open spaces.

Selective interaction is what I call it. I'm not pathologically scared of anything, I argue, I just don't particularly like people.

Not anymore, anyway.

But they won't accept this. They keep coming round here, probing me, delving and digging and bothering, and I tell them every day, "I don't like people."
But do they listen?

Do they fuck.

Three hundred and twenty-five days. Day in, day out, morning 'til noon, 'til early evening. I sit, I watch, and I write.
I find it takes my mind off the bothersome little things, the bothersome little worries, the thoughts and the whispers and the...

You get the point.

Three hundred and twenty-five days. I have sat and watched and noted. Doing my little entomology tests and experiments. Watching the neighbours like a hawk. Watching the postman, the milkman, the repairmen and the blah, blah, blah, every day. Going about their headless routines, and all the while they look, and smile, and wave and pretend that I am not scaring them – and mostly I know I don't, but every now and then I catch a glimpse of hostility, a flash of terror, a spattering of utter fear and trepidation in their eyes, and I have to leave my window and entertain my thoughts elsewhere.
After all, I don't intend or want to scare anyone; I just like to watch. The whole world is my fish tank, and each and every person who walks past my window play the fish in my aquarium of life.

Golden. Orange. Fins.

"*Murderer.*"
Leaving the window always brings the whispers back, and they only upset me, and as the doctors said to me,
"*We can't be having you get all upset again, can we?*"
"*No,*" I'd say, "*we can't.*"
And I knew I meant it. I don't handle getting upset well, all sorts of things happen.

A knock at the door.

I have many people call on me.
The doctors and the nurses we have talked about, the day carers and
the social workers who call once a month and make sure I am safe
and well, awkward talks about feelings and my past – conversations
about love, and loss, and motion – painting on smiles and answering
questions as passively as I can.
Then there are the relatives who come and make pleasant small talk,
but who always have to leave - and good job too, as the small talk
with relatives always brings the pain flooding back to my head, and
the rage burning again behind my eyes, and the words play over, and
over, and over again inside my mind.

"YOU. FUCKING. PARASITES!"
Or…
"COME AND TAKE A LOOK THEN, COME LAUGH AT THE
SAD LITTLE MAN IN HIS SAD LITTLE WINDOW!"

And I don't want to upset anyone, but it gets stressful and
mostly they only check on me to placate their bitter sensibilities, and
not because they give two shits. As harsh as it sounds, with them
having lost someone too, I see how they try and handle the memories
and the grief, but it just makes me angry. I am an afterthought, and
somewhere deep down I know they blame me for her not being here.
They blame me for not having a chance to see their grandchild.
I don't blame them. I really don't. Grief is a funny thing. You handle
it like an angry, unbroken horse. That is to say delicately and with no
small amount of fear.

But do they LOVE ME? Hell no, it's all about twisted loyalty as a
fucked up badge of social duty. I feel sick to my stomach, and it
takes everything I have to not let them know this.

"FUCKING, PARASITES!"

But no, we must play nice, they mean well, in their own special, little ways.
So this knock on the door. It's not a normal knock, it's not a regular knock, it's a single thud. Dead and heavy. When I go to the peephole, I see no one, and I get that sickly flash of anticipation.

Three hundred and twenty-five days. Every knock, every ring, every rap upon my door I have memorised, and memorised, and memorised. I now know every person uniquely from how they knock. But today, I don't recognise the knock, and for the first time in forever, I feel a disgusting rush of adrenaline. I realise that my uncomplicated little world has just taken a turn for the melodramatic and new.

I hate new things.

I open the door, and there on the doormat, staring at me, if that were even possible, is a box. A brown paper-wrapped, cardboard box, bound with strings and tape. A label is written in a ragged, capitalised, stickman scrawl, 2nd Class postage and left idle on the doorstep.
Just a box.
Mocking me.

A quick look around the street, leaning out with one hand grasped firmly on the door frame, so as not to fall into the big wide world and thus suffer the death of life sneaking up on my isolation, I see no one who could be responsible for the box being there.
No delivery truck, no post van, no postman, nothing.
A dog barks as a mother walks with her child gurgling in a pram down by the old social club. An old man steadily washes his car, even as the first drops of rain start to ruin all of his great work, as droplets land in the suds on his windshield.

I look down at this box, sat solitary, alone on the doorstep, and pick it up in a hurry and carry it into the lounge. I place it on the table, sit opposite it, and stare at it for a good hour and a half.

Waiting for something to happen.
Waiting….

Three Years Previous.
It was a warm day. He remembered it was a warm day
because the memory of children playing around by the park in shorts
and t-shirts was pretty enduring in his mind. Everyone was expecting
the frost that had been teasing all week, and no one dressed for the
warmth – scarves and jackets everywhere – even as the sun shone
above. The screech and giggle of the five and six-year-olds on
swings and roundabouts and slides. Playing silly buggers down by
the waters edge, all on that unexpected warm day in the park.
　　　He was sat with his usual awkwardness on the bench just off
the bandstand, the birds were singing, the sun was shining and he
was letting every sensation flutter over him as he sat half-reading his
daily newspaper, thinking himself an intellectual with his Guardian
open on the arts section, people watching. He was happy just to be
out and about and off work. Of course, there was the phone call he
was expecting… But…

Lazy days and all that.

　　　He recalls that the first time he saw her was about an hour
earlier, as she strolled past him in the Shopping centre. She made her
exit out the back entrance and into the Abbey gardens, toward the
war memorial with the copper-tinged soldier staring out over the
park, down towards the river. She was singing away to herself,
quietly, not quite making a spectacle of herself, but all the same, he
can still hear her singing that song.

"I'M FEELING GOOD."

14

She smiled as he caught her eye, and he smiled back, trying and failing at keeping his composure after being so blatantly caught in the act of stealing a glimpse of her. He nodded slightly, and shuffled off dizzy and confused, a laugh painted on his lips that smiled as wide as the river. She smiled wider still at the fact that such a brief but glorious flirtation was made so easily and carried on her way, singing and walking.

The next time he saw her was just before the moment that almost solidly set his life in stone from that point forward.

At the top of the hill, as you come past the old Bangladeshi restaurant and turn toward the multi-storey, a young man is stood waiting for some unseen friend. Now and then he looks around, adjusts his hoodie and checks his phone, no messages have come through, but that doesn't mean that there isn't one on the way. Suddenly, with little warning, a car screeches to a halt at the bottom of the hill, half-abandoned in a pedestrian zone. A man gets out; profanities and screams explode from him as he runs at the Hoodie, his arms flailing, angry and uncompromising, as he reaches for the hooded man.

The argument and fight break out almost instantly, with little in the way of traded words or banter. Instead the guy from the car, indignant and angry, throws a punch that cracks on the face of the hoodie.

Through a constant barrage of punches, the hooded man doesn't punch back. Instead, he just clings on to the arm of the attacking man - blood trickling from his cheek, arms up as he tries to block the torrent of blows...

And then.

Suddenly, with no grand orchestration, there is nothing but silence. A silence both cold and deadly.

The man from the car staggers backwards. His arms suddenly by his sides. His legs are weak as they give way under him.

"What did you do, man?"

The man in the hood stands against the wall, breathing heavily, bruised and battered, unsure what fury of circumstance he had just unleashed.

The man from the car slumps to the ground. Still, silent, dead.

The knife apparently entered just below his solar plexus. The twist, however, was what caused the guy from the car to stop raining punches down on the prone hoodie, as he clung on to avoid falling heavily and unguarded to the floor.

There is a crowd now gathering as the man in the hood looks down at the victim, and then kneels by his side. Something happens, someone says something, there is a flash of some sort, and then the whole world comes crashing down around him.

Whatever the flash was – it slapped him into life – his body aching from the beating, his mind on fire from shock, he sees the spurt of blood that has sprayed on him from his attacker. Who then, as if turned off at the mains, collapsed downwards, softly holding his newly-ventilated wound.

The hoodie straightens himself up, his clothes all pulled out of shape, his hair ruffled and the cut on his cheek swollen. He is bleeding from the blows, bruises already showing on his face, and after one brief look of terror at what he has just done, he looks at the silver-handled pocket knife and recognises it immediately as his own. Confused how it ended up here, as he lost it months previously, he bends down and grabs at it. Managing to pull it free, he sets off hurtling down the gangway, in blind panic, towards the river.

The girl is stood alone, a short walk from the river's edge, next to the swings and park a pedalo pond is separated by a small decorative bridge. The girl stood quietly at the pond's edge, watching as the swans and ducks quack and snarl for breadcrumbs. The young man with his paper, sat on the bench just off the bandstand, is still sneaking the odd look down at her.

"She's beautiful," he thinks, and she is, he's right...

Tall, with slender legs and arms, wide heeled platform boots that stop just short of her knees and stretch her calves into oh-so-desirable shapes. Long black hair, that waves in the gentle breeze and flows down to her elbows. A slight heave of her breasts as she breathes in. He is still looking at her as the youth in the hoodie hurtles down the gangway and, in trying to avoid a small gaggle of joggers training in the park, smashes straight into the beautiful, beautiful woman innocently transfixed on the water.

The sudden crash, of the man into her, sends her tumbling. As she falls, her head ricochets off a canal boat post, and she is knocked unconscious. She falls – as he recalls – ever so dramatically into the murky waters of the pond, built for pedalos, for kids and families, to laugh and enjoy the summer sun.
The man on the bench, just off the bandstand, is halfway towards her before he knows what he is doing. The hoodie is gone, back into the park, blood-stained and guilt-riddled.

Not from the thrust you understand.
The thrust would not have done any significant damage.
No, the twist of the blade as it entered that was the culprit, opening up the wound and leaving the outside to get in and the inside to get out.
He bleeds out, on his back staring at the last few gaggle of geese as they fly in squadron formation over the multi-storey and down toward the river, their incessant honking and bleating the last thing he hears before Death grasps hold of him and he dies in a pool of warm metallic scented blood.

The attack was nothing more than a moment of insanity brought about by the heavens, a situation no one was in clear control of – a series of horrible and un-needed catastrophes – based on angry assumption and lack of clarity.

The man from the bandstand is now at the water edge, the small group of onlookers are sent scattering as he flies through their throng, diving straight into the murky water beyond.

He regrets this later; his phone damaged beyond repair. There was a
call he was waiting for that was incredibly important.

With one hand stroking the dark water, and one searching for
life, he finds the woman within seconds and pulls her out of the
water,
"God, she's beautiful."
And then he sets about making her live again: deep breath, share it
with her, rub her heart… Breathe!
And she does and he sobs and the crowd cheer before the man
shouts:

"Call a fucking ambulance!"

The situation snaps back into the present again… after having been
playing at what seemed to be half speed before.
But this was a long time ago…

* * *

\- 3 -

I sat staring at the box for another hour after bringing it in the house.

The fucking thing rested motionless on the table, not moving,
not doing anything, just being a box, serving its lack of purpose with
apparent ease.
I sat opposite it, on my green sofa, sipping lukewarm tea and
becoming hypnotised by the sound of my wheezy breathing, all the
while staring at it.

Just staring and doing nothing more.

If you asked me now why I did not open it there and then, as
you would any delivery – with no second thought or pause for any
discernible or considered reason – my answer would be the same
now as it was then.

18

I could not – I DARED not open it. I can recall the feeling of muted discomfort, a buzz of angst that emanated from the damned thing that set my hairs on end and a weird shiver of chill that ran through my bones.

The same way one feels when you walk into a house and feel the buzz of a TV you were certain you had turned off, or the magnetic and zealous strike of the static that hits from nowhere in a house with heavy carpets.

I dare not open it.

I know instinctively that the box is not right in some way, I am not expecting a package, no one cares or loves me or gives two fucks about my existence in any real way to have sent me anything – The postage is oblique, 2nd class and no area code, the address label a capitalised, ragged stickman-like scrawl.

There is no return address, no other clues to where it came from and its packaging is so neat and tidy it looks like a prop from some strange TV fiction.

There is a compulsion which tells me that I SHOULD open it, but a voice of reason wins through and allays my rash curiosity, stating that if it is important, it will find a way of opening itself.

A stupid thought, as irrational as the rational voice has ever been. This is the advice that calms me and leaves me happy to leave it alone.

The sounds outside start seeping back into my world, and I snap back to reality. I walk over to the window; one eye remaining transfixed by the box, resting on my table motionless, not doing fucking anything.

With the occasional sip of my tea and the sporadic look at the box, I carry on with my daily routine of nothingness. Staring, watching, note taking and whiling away another dead afternoon.

The box rests there, motionless… I catch myself now and then looking at it, a seductive spell that it carries over me being fought tooth and claw by my fragile sense of self.

19

I would open it.

But the thing is, if I do, I know I am allowing the outside into my world, something cold and unexplainable and new – and I am so happy being unhappy in my world of old and familiar and I dislike the idea of my fragile status quo being upended by this ridiculous delivery. With its weird vibration and its strange enigma I try and tell myself it's just a brown paper box, wrapped in brown string, and it's just resting on my table.

Motionless, not doing fucking anything.

But it's no good – I am drawn like a moth to a flame at irregularly lengthy intervals to stand over it, often with a cup of cold and flavourless tea in hand, to simply ponder it.

Tonight the bins need to go out. So, with no second thought or hesitation, I decide rather than to be put out in my home by something I had no hand in having delivered, and never invited in the first place, I shall throw the damned thing away. Out of sight, out of mind, and done.

I pick up the box, so curious and heavy, so nameless and annoying, and I dump it in my waste bin, tie the thing up, and wait until the sun has set, before leaving my secure, safe surroundings to dump the crap and useless waste at the end of the garden path. From where it will take the four and a half mile journey to the town waste dump, which can be smelt from here on a hot summers day.

"*It's gone now. Put it out of your mind.*" I think as I walk back inside, ignoring my pleasant neighbours hello as he returns from work.

"*It's gone… fucking forget about it!*"

As I walk inside, door slamming behind me, and no longer a care in the world, I switch on the news and see what I have been missing all day.

Whether the item in the box was important or not, I care not, as it's now consigned to a fucking tomb of used condoms, tinned foods and fucking old tabloid rags… unopened, unimportant, and unneeded.

A plain brown box, with brown string, and ragged, capitalised, stickman scrawl…
No return address and no reason to be here.

"It must have been a joke." The voice of reason in my head says. *"Something someone we once knew sent for some anniversary of some event we forgot because we don't care about remembering."*

It's true as well… It must have been a joke.
Well, fuck you, the joke's now on a one-way journey to the landfill.
Congratulations.
Joke's on you.

It's dark outside, the bustle of life and the world outside has become muted and feeble. The streets lights, one by one light themselves and become an orange herald of the Sandman. It's time to go to sleep…
I have a busy day ahead of me tomorrow, hating the world and watching it go about its scurrilous way… Panicked and confused.
Mad like ants doused in boiling water.
It's a hard job – being the avatar of fury and indifference. It takes a lot of energy.

So, I brush my teeth, and I shower. I fold my clothes neatly in a pile and throw them in the corner of the room on the hamper, which is my only visual reminder of her, and which has remained unopened since she left and I go to bed.

That night I dream of cars crashing and fires, and I smell the horrid stench of decaying and burning human fat. Of purifying infernos pouring and washing down entire roads, incinerating the world on touch, of human bodies bursting into uncontrollable, raging, green-flamed cyclones of fury and heat.

I dream of me. Standing alone atop a hill, orchestrating this madness and destruction like some stern-eyed, trance-induced conductor.

21

The entire world burns. Trees, houses and little insignificant ant-like people - exploding into flame as the tongue of fire licks each one.
Seduced and destroyed by fire as great and vast as the ocean is deep.

My last abiding memory of the dream is of a postman, stood on my doorstep, flames engulfing every part of him, his hands outstretched as I open my door to him, and in his hands is a box, wrapped in brown paper and string and tape, with a small label written in scrawled, chicken-scratch capitals – he holds it toward me, a smile on his melting face and he whispers:

"Special delivery."

Before he explodes into a ravenous ball of flame and fury, transmuting from a person into a pile of ash and dust.

It's one of the best night's sleep I have had in weeks. Months maybe.
I sleep like…
Well, God help me.

I sleep like a baby.

* * *
- 4 -

The light creeps in a slow crawl from one side of my window to the other, as the world turns, a shaft of sunlight cuts like a sword through the gap in my curtains and I lay there in bed watching as this obscure laser draws across my wall. How long I lay there I cannot begin to tell you, but, it's some time as I watch this bright shaft stretch out. Finally, it reaches my face and scorches a warm line across my eyes like some mask of enlightenment.
It is the prompt I have waited all morning for to get myself out of bed.

The bed itself is vast and cold. Usually, I am lonely as hell in its embrace. The feng shui of the room is off. I have been aware of this for as long as I have lived in the house – she would tell me often that I had to sort out the alignment of bed to the window. I am sure she would have done it before she left, but since she has, it has remained in the awkward corner, where we dumped it and left it after moving in.

I remember falling about on top of its bare mattress, me and her together, out of breath, exhausted and giggling, having just negotiated the stairs in a semi argumentative way. She told me which way to pivot and which way to parry, where to lever and where to rest. And then we carried it through the whole house - from the hallway to the bedroom. Before collapsing in a heap, sweat pouring from us, gasping with laughter as we looked at each other and then – with a moment of sweet rapture and pause – we kissed, deep and passionately, threads of saliva between our lips when we broke – each big kiss followed by two or three little kisses on the forehead, her way of signing her love, something she did since our first tryst.

We made love on the bare skeleton of a bed, in the corner of the room – bodies wrapped together in weird and seemingly impossible contortions – blood and flesh and bone becoming one, her breasts heaving and rising with the rhythm of her heart and glistening with a fine perspiration – a smell of strawberries and vanilla – the smell of her permeating into my skin, lingering. Together we smelled like a cake factory, a sweet, intoxicating bakery smell. Taking me deep inside her.
She had a way about her that was gentle, but deeply passionate, when I was inside her I felt like I was merging with her, every breath, every thrust and every moan – we were one and the same, lost together on some heady wave of elation and pure pleasure. Her on my lap, grinding hard and bringing me to an awesome, breath-taking climax.

I remember her staying on me, with me still inside her, for minutes afterwards, as she pulled me closer and gave me more of those signature kisses, her tongue probed and licked and sought sanctuary in my mouth, her body a sticky, sweet dough, moulding and forming around my strong arms.

Married for six weeks. Our first house. Our new bed. Everything such an adventure.

I look around the room now and I don't recognise the "me" from those memories, much like the life I had, that person is erased and all that is left is this bitter and lonely, scabrous shell of a man.

An echo. A ghost. A memory of a man that used to be.

All that remains is the chest where my clothes from the night before lay.

I stared at the clock on the bedside table, its red LED had a nauseating shimmer that meant looking at it could be both hypnotic and sickening, it made you feel woozy and ill with suggestion – the shimmer and flicker a Morse code feeding your mind with dark ideas and invention.

11:37am.

A recognisable knock at the door.

I only recognise the knock as it was the same as yesterday, a rap and a half, the second knock almost sounding like the caller had given up, or their hand had evaporated upon contact with the red paint of the wooden door.

I was unaware at the time, but I would come to hate that knock, as surely as I hated the world and everyone in it. As surely as I was alone and broken and blackened to my core with negativity and self-loathing, I would come to hate that knock.

I pulled on some pants and trousers – catching a glimpse of my flabby, pallid self in the mirror: hint of a belly beginning to appear, the horrendous mid-morning shrivel of my penis, a faint illness in the colour of my pale and waned skin.

A weak specimen for sure.

I casually walked downstairs, pulling on a sweater, its V-neck showing the nape of my neck and collarbone, a tuft of chest hair morosely pouring from the arrow of the stitch.
As I reached out to answer the door – the knock came again.
A rap and a half.
I grasped the handle and opened the door immediately to an empty world.
No one there. Nothing to suggest anyone had knocked at all.

Nothing except a brown box, wrapped in brown paper and sealed with string and tape with a label written in the now familiar, capitalised scrawl.

Now though with a bow on it.

* * *

- 5 -

Miniature explosions of rainbow were falling in diamond formations across the walls as the rain came down, hard and menacing, outside the huge arch of the window. The sun snuck in and out of the clouds, playing hide and seek with the world, occasionally penetrating the dark and dingy sky with a vast shard of brilliance that would smash through the stained-glass architecture and bring the ancient facades and murals in the glass to life. If only for a fleeting moment.

There were three panes, separated by a three or four-foot lead partition, splitting the window into three distinct murals of dizzying size.
The first of an angel lying dead before a ring of fire. The second the naked, pert-breasted Eve tempting Adam into life with a dazzling red apple, and the third the angels Lucifer and Michael embroiled in a strange and fascinatingly erotic embrace as Michael cast Lucifer into the pit. All grew from stationary, colourful barrier into life-like reality played across the walls of the great hall with each new shard of light that cascaded from behind the epic nimbocumulus clouds.

Then, they were gone, switched off as more clouds covered and muted the sky with a miserable grey hue, dampening the mood all around.

The gaunt, dark figure of a man breached the peace, his clothes were of a colour that looked like the sea at night-time, sinister swells which rippled with a sentient peril, velvets and silk, smooth yet so heavily worn it seemed like some pliable armour. The colour had appeared to be black, but as the clouds broke and the dull light did come into the room, it took on a more clearly identifiable green shade, a rich dark jade with a thin vein of silver in the lining and the stitch.

The figure stood with one pale, white hand touching the marble of a table that rested below the window, the tip of his index finger absentmindedly stroking a fissure within the rock. With his eyes closed the man imagined he could feel every finite detail and infinitesimal imperfection. It was a meditation of sorts, calming his mind of the clutter the windows and strobing sunlight had brought on in him.

The room itself was a circle. The stone a clean-cut, polished marble, inherently beautiful and grand, but infused with a sad melancholy that permeated the stone. Its thin purple and grey-blue veins taking on a varicose feel, which leant the room a strange organic isolation. At the wall directly opposite the window was a line cut into the rock. A door of some sort?
No handle existed. No perceptible means of opening the portal with which the man could use to exit. Instead, just a deep crease inside the wall that went in a foot or two to the stone itself, but did not allow any light between rooms. A thin vein of light occasionally pulsed and flickered from the bottom of the door, as if people were walking backwards or forward. It gave nothing away of the environment or geography of where this room was found, and the light could well have been a reflection of what was happening outside the window. Bleak, empty, strobing cloud and shy sunlight hiding for eternity.

The man circled his finger deep within the crack and let out a faint laugh of sorts. The room was tall, the ceiling a dome, twenty or thirty feet high at the tallest point. It echoed any noise made within the circular walls eerily, and the echo would resonate and fade like a musical note being dealt a slow and agonising death. The man laughed because he realised that he had been toying and probing the fraction on the desk now for an inordinate amount of time, and that the task of doing so was a form of madness in and of itself.

He looked at the line, to him cavernous and wide, though tiny and barely noticeable to normal eyes, and then at his finger – examining the dusty tip with humorous madness. He shook his head and turned to see the stained-glass window quickly flash a projection of colour and image, briefly and fleeting once again, on the wall.

He smiled and placed his hands on each other, resting them on his stomach, in elegant repose, as behind the creased line in the wall, something stirred. A groan could be heard, and then a shuffle, as a piece of parchment neatly folded, and upon which was some stained ink, slid smoothly across the floor to the man's feet.

He looked down, confused and vacant, trying to discern what was happening, what this could mean? The second turned into anxious, absent-minded aeons until he finally leant down and picked the paper up with long, thin fingers.

So long he had been inside this room now with no contact or connection with the outside world, apart from a window that reflected parts of his past, and the arc of a weak sun that came and went in such wanton haste that the man could barely drink the glory quick enough. Barely sipping at its meagre offering.

He regarded the parchment patiently, turning it around in his hands, as he examined the material and scent of the paper, before finally taking its delicate fold in his fingers, and with shaky hands, weak and thin, he unfolded the yellowed note. Aged or dirty paper, it was impossible to tell, but its content clearly perked the man's interest.

To describe this man would have been a task full of paradox and confusion. A beautiful mess he was. His skin the mottled off-white of a person who had been terminally scared of the sun; dirty-blonde, thick, lustrous hair tumbled over shoulders that were broad and yet thin; a perfectly triangular torso as the musculature gave way to an unashamed thinness that bordered on anorexic. If not for the muscle tone and tautness of the flesh around the muscle, or the way that every one of his ribs was hidden behind a tight layer of skin - that gave shadows and echoes of muscle that used to exist – you would swear the figure had been starved for decades. A skeleton which only when looked at closer reveals to be a bodybuilder.

The figure swayed where he stood, a vapour, a ghost. The parchment paper was fixed to the figure's grip as he continued to read intently; his gaunt face maybe pouring over the words twenty or thirty times. Finally, with a confident gesture, his fist squeezed shut and he rolled the paper into a ball which was greedily grasped and kept out of sight, the mottled parchment now useless to man or beast. From behind him, the crease groaned again, and then heaved a heavy sigh, as the marble of the wall cracked and then broke. The wall gave way to a hole – arched, deep and jagged.

From the hole, a glorious shard of pure light poured through and illuminated the man.

His skin prickled and fizzed, a stream of dust and vapour oozed from him as his muscles became taut and tight again, his flesh visibly grew around the new frame that was born with the touch of the sunshine and light.

His dirty-blonde hair evaporated into an incandescent and beautiful mane of tangled, beautiful, golden and white blonde trusses and locks.

He shed himself of the cloak and stood naked, bathed in the light, and with two clenched fists at the end of two muscular arms, spread his palms open wide.

He glowed with radiance and joy in the warmth of the sun.

From his grip the parchment, now rolled into a ball and desecrated, fell free and landed with a tiny thump upon the floor.

The words were chiselled now on his mind. Freedom was restored.

Lucifer Morningstar.

God's firstborn son had drank of the grace and light of creation for the first time in a hateful, isolated, exiled millennia.

"Finally." The first words uttered by the man in all that time.
A cavernous, hateful whisper full of majesty and menace.
Majesty and menace… And celebration.

* * *

- 6 -

A little about our man in the house…

James Edmunds had been a lonely child. The middle of three children, his elder brother Malcolm and younger sister Jenny were mollycoddled and given far more attention. His brother because he was a careless, adventurous and fearless child that needed protecting from himself, as he climbed trees and rode go-karts down steep hills, jumped barb-wire fences to chase cows and sheep and other sundry livestock. His sister to stop her from acting like a princess and annoying or bullying other children, poking fun and hiding behind big brown eyes and pigtails and always denying any wrongdoing when collared for pulling other girl's hair, or tattling on boys who used secret curse words. A shallow, selfish girl, she was never far away from some rumour or another, always quick to make one up where none existed if bored.

James - by contrast - was bookish, quiet, and obedient, never causing controversy or trouble. He did his homework without being told. Usually the minute he got in, picking at dinner as he completed the Maths and English work set by his teachers – whom he actually liked.

He would read quietly in his room, listening to the radio his parents bought him for his twelfth birthday – where his elder brother had demanded a BMX or his sister a party full of balloons and cake and entertainment and MORE presents, James simply wanted something on which he could listen to music. The radio was always on in his own Fortress of Solitude as he poured over book after book in the mountain of paperbacks and hardbacks that seemed almost to appear organically as if created by mitosis.

He was never seen far from a book. He was always reading, or pouring, his thoughts, ideas and stories into the pages of some leather-bound tome.

His friends, of which there were few, seemed to like him in spite of the fact he was neither the strongest boy nor the fastest - though he was by far and away the cleverest, this mattered little when climbing a tree or throwing stones into the swamp at the top of the fields, where legend had it hundreds – possibly thousands – of cows had died, like some strange suicide spot for cattle.

He was never outspoken, he never lead, barely followed – he simply existed. Never doubting, never believing, just *being*. His was a life of the other guy; the group would barely ever even notice if he were not with them. But his presence always bloated them with a feeling of ego, each one knowing that he was there simply to make up the numbers and by doing so, he was always helping others feel better about themselves by his being so terminally ambivalent and temporary.

James preferred solitary moments in the playing fields - hiding in dens, reading and making forts, where others would pour over found pornographic materials stolen from father's secret stashes, or pages torn from lingerie catalogues – James would be reading from whatever book he was dedicated to at that time. Where others were climbing rope swings, James was always making sure the knots were of a sufficient standard to hold his and the others weight – he was never happy just following the trend. Instead, he looked before he leapt, he walked before he ran and he sat wherever a seat was available, because in his mind, this was the way the world worked and why make life any harder than it had to be?

The only day James did go against the grain of his nature was the day the fight broke out between him and the gang's de-facto leader. It was the first giant leap into the shaping of the man the boy would become.

The lives of children are as complex and tribal as any subset civilisation, where the Incas and Romans and Egyptians had their funny little traditions and ways of getting things done – that made anthropologists and psychologists crazy - these were nothing compared to the traditions and tribal customs of children. The bigger and meaner you were really didn't mean anything to children. Big and mean meant you were a bruiser, not a leader, a bully, not someone to be followed. Big and mean was reserved for Goliath-like shock tactics. A final resort when your biggest, ugliest guy hit the other team's smallest and weakest. No, big and mean never meant LEADER. Leaders were cunning, were clever, were devoid of morals and had impressive little skills to twist and manipulate. Machiavelli himself would have been a leader when he was a child, a sinister, dark-minded, blackly-hearted tactician, as uncaring and as unfeeling as any despot. The children who were in charge were not usually the ones who joined the police and army, but those who had high-powered jobs in businesses and influence, who could stare down the fear of not knowing what your next action would be, and who didn't give a single thought to the bad consequences of what was about to happen.

The leader of James' little child posse was Michael. Michael was twelve, slight in physique, slender and delicate looking; his hair was an immaculate hazelnut brown, his eyes dark circles of deep brown. With his big pupils and the dark, rich colour of his iris, it seemed as though he had pure black eyes, no emotion rang from them. When he smiled it was the smile of someone who painted brushstrokes across his own face and just as quickly wiped them off, no register of truth ever passed his lips, he was a liar in face, feature and voice. What he lacked in physical size he more than made up for in his unrelenting swagger.

A perfect leader.

Michael would command the creation of forts – built into gaps in hedgerows that divided the fields that surrounded their estate. Using string and scraps of wood, they would stretch out the nascent holes in the hedge and create doorways, perfectly arched openings that would have structural engineers scratching their heads in wonder at how they were created.

They would take salvaged planks and make chairs and seats in between boughs and branches using tools they surreptitiously stole from their father's toolboxes, nailing them into place in haphazard ways that belied their youth – yet highlighted their abundant enthusiasm.

The dens and forts would be dotted around a half dozen areas, the whereabouts crudely drawn on a map that showed where hidden treasures were kept, marked in big red X's where they could escape at any one time.

Each member of the gang had a map, and each X was numerically organised, as the forts were divided into seven designates. In Michael's street-facing bedroom window, visible from all the other boy's houses or easily from the road, he would blu-tac a scrap of paper up when he wanted a gang meeting – on it would be nothing more than 5 digits.

51300 was showing on the day that James could not make it to the meeting.

5 – The Fort.

1300 – The time they had to meet.

James was eating his late breakfast, picking at a slice of toast his mother had cut into soldiers for a boiled egg, cooked so the yolk was runny, and he could dip them inside.

He took his food to his room, his mother smiling as he did, this being the usual routine.

"What book are you into this time?" She asked idly, a flutter of warmth in her voice.

"I'm reading Cosmos by Carl Sagan… it's about space and that." James didn't turn to look at her, as he carried on right up the stairs, trudging in his half-shoe-shuffle kind of way.

"Seems a bit grown up isn't it?" His mother, a kind and light-hearted woman, had seen the book on a library shelf once, all she remembered was the bold image of Jupiter on its cover.

"Was it Jupiter… which was the one with the rings?" she would think, a thought that would drive her mad for days in the silly little way that she allowed things to do, her mind always obsessing over the inconsequential. Always mulling over the correctness of tiny details that only she cared about.

"I like the pictures; it's never too grown up to know where we come from Mum."

His reply having a fine edge of reason and earnestness that Margaret Edmunds had grown accustomed to with her middle child. Wise beyond his years, a shy and lonely child he may appear to be, but he was fiercely intelligent – and if shy and lonely did not bother him, so in turn she would not allow herself to be bothered either.

James was gently dipping and gobbling his toast soldiers as he sat in his window. He was sipping noisily from a tepid cup of tea his mother had made him to go alongside the breakfast when he saw Michael put the signal in the window. James looked down at his little Casio wristwatch, noted the time as 11.37, and thought no more of it. Michael was not one of James' favourite people. He hung around with the other kids mainly to pretend to his parents that he was interested in having friends. To show that he was trying to be a normal child – running and jumping and climbing trees – but really, they were so ambivalent about his presence, and he in return to them, that he sometimes wondered why he was wasting good reading time hanging around in cold, muddy fields. Playing games he cared nothing about with people who were barely his peers, as much as just being people his age stuck in this prison of geography.

Michael saw him from his bedroom window and waved a curt, explosive little wave at James as if to say "You'd better be there!"

James ignored the gesture entirely and instead hopped down from the window, placed his breakfast on the bedside table, and with a stone-faced look of utter disdain looked directly at Michael and shut his curtains.

"No more pretending." He said to no one but himself.

"No, no, no."

And he went back to his book, his egg and his neat, little toast soldiers, slurping a gulp of nearly cold tea, just the way he loved it.

The Box was back.

    How it had returned, he did not understand, and who had brought it back was an even bigger mystery. James stared at his doorstep in perplexed and growing bewilderment. Added to this was a twitch of anger that was slowly crawling up his core, as if affixed like a caterpillar to his spine, slowly shuffling up each vertebrae towards his mind, where it would poke all his buttons and make him a ball of furious indignance.

    James gave the box a poke with his foot; it did not budge. It was like kicking a concrete block, his foot recoiled in shocked pain, he threw a face like someone who had just been told to watch a video of his own parents having sex, a disgusted, sneered lip grimace that showed the world just how unhappy and put out he was by this turn of affairs. He gently used the side of his foot to try and move it an inch or two to the side but again it refused to budge as if glued to the doorstep. As if it had grown from the step as a solid growth of paper, string and cardboard.

    From the street, he heard a whistling, an out of tune warble, full of joy and dizzy ignorance. A whistled version of "O, When the Saints" that was barely recognisable in its abject refusal to stay in tune or adhere to any real structure of music at all. Betrayed for the song it was by nothing more than the man whistling it giving up the ghost of his whiny whistling and instead breaking into a happy and even worse rendition of the song in a sung little moan.

    He rounded the corner of the small hedgerow that surrounded James' immaculate garden. Immaculate due to James' insistence on paying for a gardener and landscaper to tend it, even though he would never venture more than to his hedge's edge to put out bins. His feet never touching the grass for fear of disappearing in a puff of smoke and sulphur.

The postman had in his hands two small, white envelopes, circulars of some description, a brown envelope that looked like some form of bill and a larger packaged envelope, with special delivery notes on it. "Morning, sir! And what a fantastic morning it is as well, eh?"

He affixed a smiling, cheery little grin on his face and pointed it at James like a deadly weapon. James, in turn looked up from the box, still in his mid-morning stupor, still mesmerised and confused by the box and its unwelcome return, he looked directly at the postie and said "What the fuck is this?"

The postman looked down at the box, his smile for a flicker of a second entirely dropping from his face before looking back at James and firing that smile back with blind ingenuity.

"Well, that looks like a parcel, innit?"

"I know it's a parcel, I can see very bloody well it's a parcel. What is it doing there?"

The postie regarded the box, then James and gave a little look around his shoulders to check there were no cameras, that this was not some TV show where he was being pranked. Happy this was indeed just one of those people he was always warned about on the TV and in the Daily Mail, he smiled wider and replied:

"Looks like it wouldn't fit through the letter box, hey?"

James stared at him sharply, his eyes snapping up from the box to the postman's returned gaze, and he regarded the man for a second – the fires of eternity burning incandescently and righteously behind his eyes, he looked directly at the red-jacketed moron in front of him, took a small half step forward as the postman retreated the same distance and whispered in a white-hot voice that could cut steel, "What is in it?"

Silence filled the air as the postie looked down again, then back to James, then the box – and finally decided on:

"I haven't a fucking clue, pal. Now please sign here, I have a dozen or so other mentalists to visit today."

James automatically took the board held towards him, signed his name in a clean swooping cursive and handed it back. The postman gave him the letters and the special delivery and smiled a bigger, wider, broader smile than any he would do that day.

"Why can't I move it?" James said absently.

"What do you mean? You can do whatever you want with it," postman said.

"It won't move, it's solid, how am I supposed to pick it up?"
The postman looked at the box, wondered again if this wasn't indeed some form of joke he was not getting, and bent down. Gently picking up the box with consummate ease, it seemingly weighing less than a feather, he handed it to James.

"There you go, sir. Maybe see a doctor about your back if you were having trouble lifting it, terrible thing it is to have back pain."

"Why did you leave it on my doorstep?" James queried, confused by the postman's ease at picking it up when it wouldn't move a centimetre for him, puzzled by why the postman had left it and then double backed with more post.

"Why didn't you deliver the other post when you dropped this off earlier?"

The postman for a second lost a half of his smile; his face cracked as if his façade of happiness was slipping off and nothing was left but the true person behind the mask.

"What are you talking about? I didn't deliver it. This is my round; I come from number 38, all the way down to number 112. Then I cross over and do the odds over there," pointing at the houses across the road "then I fuck off home. I started twenty minutes ago; I'll be done in 3 hours. Then I get to go home, kiss my wife, have some tea and chill out until I do this all again tomorrow – joy of fucking joys!"

James' face was one of abject confusion, like a dyslexic trying to spell any one of the ridiculous town names in Wales, like a numerically challenged child trying to multiply Pi by itself.

"But, the box... it was delivered this morning."

"Not by me, pal and Parcelforce don't start 'til 2 pm, so whoever did bring it, they ain't wearing a red tunic, and they ain't pushing no Royal Mail trolley. Now have a lovely day... And really, I'd see someone about the back."

And like that, the postman carried about his way, the horrible whistle starting again with aplomb, the street abuzz with his discordant dirge.

James walked a zombie-like shuffle into the lounge. He dropped the envelopes and special delivery on the sofa with a cold and distant thump, and then placed the box on his glass-topped table.

The glass cracked immediately, then smashed and the box fell through, cracking the under shelf in two before resting in a heap, angled on the sharp shards of wood.

James gave a sudden start the second the glass ruptured and the box fell through, he jumped back in wide-eyed terror when the wood creaked and then gave. A vaporous, smoky waft of dust plumed from the coffee table as fibres and glass settled, a slight, creaky awkwardness still resonated as the remnants of the table took the weight of the box. For a second James did a mental double take, trying to remember if he had a basement, as if the floor were not concrete over solid foundation, he had absolutely no doubt the box would have found a way through this too.

He took a step toward the debris and devastation of what was his late grandmother's vintage coffee table. The glass was a good quarter inch thick and was reinforced, it had taken a lump hammer and several boots slamming against it in its time and never even registered a smudge, yet the box that was picked up by the postman as easily as a coin or a feather would have been, had smashed the glass almost entirely. Nothing really remained, a few large shards here and there, but it had done a good job of crystallising the bulk of the glass and making a powdery glass haze.

He attempted to lift the box again, despite all his efforts, a good grip and proper lifting posture, it would not move even a tiny little bit.

It was Mjolnir; It was Excalibur – and James was very much not worthy of the weight of the moment.

He looked at the whole sorry affair for a few seconds, stroked his beard with absent indulgence, dabbed his sweaty, beady, mottled brow and then retired to the kitchen where he made himself a ham sandwich and a cup of tea in silence.

He took the time to eat the sandwich in small, deliberate bites, wiped his mouth with a tea towel, and then slurped heavily on the tepid milky tea.

He swallowed it down heartily, noisily and fast. Then sat at the table, without warning, without thinking about it at all…He burst into tears and cried for a good half hour.

* * *

CHAPTER TWO
Waiting Backstage, Our Supporting Cast.

*"Faustus: Stay, Mephistopheles, and tell me, what good will
my soul do thy lord?*

Mephistopheles: Enlarge his kingdom.

Faustus: Is that the reason he tempts us thus?

Mephistopheles: Solamen miseris socios habuisse doloris.
(It is a comfort to the wretched to have companions in misery)"

- Christopher Marlowe – Dr Faustus

Static shadows were painted upon the cold stone wall, and there was a throb of intense discomfort permeating the room. The only light was from a half-dozen, oil-burning torches, lining the entire length of one wall.

A lonely, thin and weakly-framed man stood by a window looking out over a blank domain. Black was all that could be seen on the horizon less for one pinhole of light that stood at the northern most point of the sky. A slight, tender, blue-glowing aura circled it, a solitary star in the sky devoid of anything other than impenetrable darkness.

The man had his hand folded behind his back, the skin like a waxed paper stretched out over bamboo bones – so thin and so porcelain that he at first looked like a waxwork left in a position of repose in some museum of horror.

But, the man flexed and closed his hand behind his back into a tight and taut fist, the sound was that of a wet clump of leather being wrung out of water. The click and grind of bones were that of birch sticks breaking under clumsy feet. And the veins, blue, green and deep, dark purple became lengths of tough, gristly rope. A strength existed behind the intense weakness that was on the surface, deep below a strength of some significant and terrifying power dwelt and in the simple gesture of a hand being opened and closed it was evident that it was as honed and ready to be unleashed as a whip in a slave trader's hand.

A door opened with a heavy effort, the static shadows lit up and shifted as if they were alive and trying to hide, for an instant the figures imprinted on the wall burst as if a flock of blackbirds at a gun report, and sought the sanctuary of anywhere that was not in the gaze of the man in red who entered.

Standing easily at seven feet tall if he was a foot, the man had a beard as big, busy and thick as a lion's mane, a deep strawberry-blonde, streaks of white bled from the corners of his mouth, down. The beard followed the line of the man's chiseled jaw up into a messy burst of golden-red hair, the flame's light caught it and it too looked like it was bursting at the seams with terrific fury and flame-borne sentience.

"My Lord, we have word." His voice a boom of bass-heavy intemperance, an undulating feeling of immediacy, lacking any subtlety or patience, his voice was a one tone bark of indifference, you felt that if he had spoken to you a question it would sound like a command.

"He is dead," not a question, but a statement came the reply, The man in the window did not move, his pose remained calm and still, his voice a gentle crackle - distinguished and full of fertile authority. A regal timbre.

"I know. Of course, I know."

The man in red went to reply as if to ask how, caught the words in his mouth, and swallowed them deep down. Of course, he knew. Of anyone in creation, it would be him who knew before anyone else.

"Ready the Tribunal, tell them we are overdue a conversation. Tell them to assemble every councilman and woman, every single member of the board, there is much to discuss, and there are other things stirring. I see now that we are behind schedule."

The man in red clipped his heels and barked an affirmation, what he said would be understandable to maybe three people in the entire history of the universe we understand and can comprehend. The man in the window, still stood impenetrably still and calm was one of them.

The red man turned and held the door to close. It was easily three or four feet thick, oak-sandwiched between iron and gold, with thick, iron bolts and hinges and a handle that was fashioned like a horse' head; sinewy and angular, strong and proud.

As he was almost out of the room, the figure in the window turned calmly, hands still behind his back.

"And War." The red man stopped and fixed the pale man with an unsteady gaze, a solitary bead of sweat prickled on his forehead and was allowed to roll down past his eye, the fear of showing weakness preventing him from wiping it away.

The figure in the window had deep-set eyes that seemed to be almost perfectly black, but for when the light of the torches caught them, then they were the pale blue of the horizon when it meets the ocean,

the intense crystal blue of ice, fixed in a face that looked like it would shatter should it dare carve a line of any emotion, not so much a skull, as much as a waxy, porcelain, china doll mask, young and beautiful, but affixed with a shiny, unsettling hue of the dead.
"My Lord?"
"Ready the horses." The Pale man allowed himself and the man in red a sly, almost non-existent smile, his lips turning maybe a quarter of a millimeter in both corners upwards, a cruel joke of an inflection. The red man caught the smile and returned it with a bright, toothy gape. He nodded curtly and exited, closing the door as if a giant bank vault. A gentle pop sounded as the lock snapped shut, and once again the room was returned to its previous stillness. The shadows, one by one, crawled out of their hiding places and found their homes in static silence upon the wall again.

The pale man raised one thin, slender and febrile arm with hand outstretched. A single finger and thumb reached for, and grasped, the light from the sky, holding it between his digits, its pale blue aura emanating a warmth and hum as it throbbed in his cold and waxen hands.

It had been a long time coming, but finally the moment was upon them, they were about to name their fourth, and the stories were about to become a reality. A million lifetimes of work was about to be brought to fruition, and the world was about to learn a new destiny.

The pale man smiled deeply, as he gazed longingly at the pale blue dot between his finger and thumb, rolling it gently back and forth, before he closed his fist around it so hard his skin seemed to light up. Waxed paper skin became an amplifier for the light and life, as he closed the window with a gesture, and sat in front of a fire that burst alive in flame as if by magic in his presence. As he paid regard to his hand, a pale blue glowing fist, he smiled slightly wider, a sick movement that shook the room with giddy revulsion. Some things were not meant to smile.
Crocodiles and misery were but two. This man was the third and the

worst of them all. His smile was a hammer to everything good about the world.

A vicious stroke of a butcher's knife across naked flesh would have made a better smile.

* * *

- 2 -

When they went to view the house the two of them could not believe how perfectly it matched and fulfilled all of their silly little criteria: the hidey-holes, the nooks, the little shelves here there and everywhere that allowed them places they could put all the many trinkets and things they hoarded together and individually.

The kitchen that was open plan and just large enough for a table and chairs and which opened up to a back garden that was just small enough to be on the right side of quaint. Blocked from view by a high fence, strategically planted fir trees and a large Willow that wept and bowed straight at the bottom of the garden it made a den of secret shadows and occasionally burst into light as the sun pierced and ricocheted through the sweeping branches.

The bathroom was deliciously tiny but filled every need a bathroom could. Two people could just fit in snugly, making it just right for the tactile and touchy feely lovers. A fact they smiled at and shared a tender, fleeting, teasing kiss about, before exiting with childish giggles.

The estate agent was good at reading people, knew when to do a hard sell and soft sell and when the house would sell itself. She had been in the game long enough to have become a layman psychologist and anthropologist, and had taken great care in selecting houses for her clients that she felt would fulfil needs from their list of, sometimes outlandish, demands.

She was not really a people person, but had flunked out of architecture colleges and had taken what she felt was the next best job, someone who shows the features and finery of architecture and someone who got to sell the benefits without having to worry about ever building it.

She much preferred this role to the one she had failed at university.

She had seen the house on the road, not three streets down from her home, driven past it most days, in fact, and always eyed it with gluttonous, covetous eyes. When she had overheard at the school, picking up her two darling children (*note the sarcasm, her real thoughts were "her two great mistakes"*), that the house was on the verge of being put on the market, she made the odd decision to go and call-in directly to the homeowner. Inside her a buzz of excitement knowing that she could sell this house and gain a better commission for herself than allowing it to go to some half-arsed agency who could care less if it sold quickly or not, one more house for their overflowing book in a saturated market. Estrella knew this area and wanted this house for herself, it was sure-money in her greedy bank account.

She called in on one Thursday morning; the homeowner was a sad, lonely widower named Gerald Passby whose wife Patricia had died quite suddenly in childbirth where the baby had also sadly passed away.

She turned on her voracious charm and handed over a card. She stated how she had heard the house was to be put up for sale and had mentioned how she felt as a neighbour, and a valued member of the community. She could help the man get exactly what he deserved from the sale considering how terrible the situation was and how sensitive the circumstances he had been left in.

Of course he had agreed to let her be his agent, it saved him from having to do anything to sort it out himself and left him time to grieve. Truth be told, the man would not of cared if someone had come and taken the damned house and its memories away for free – but this way, the money could go to good use, to the right places, before the man did what he had been planning to do, retire to the coast and a quiet life by the sea, closer to his remaining family. Sisters and nephews.

She had called the young couple, James and Kay, not a day later after contracts for her management had been confirmed, and she was certain, this being the fourth house they had looked at, that it was the one that nailed the entire and lengthy list of needs, wants and demands they had handed to her.

She was certain - so much so she had already put the deposit on the holiday away with her girlfriends she had been bleating about to her put-upon husband for months on end about – In her mind it was already booked, already sorted and she was already tasting the fresh Mediterranean Sea air.

The young man – James - and his wife, Katherine (she preferred Kay) were hand in hand, walking around and busily touching all the fixtures, running fingers across door edges, fingering all the lights and sockets, and noseying around things that other people would have entirely missed.

Occasionally a silent nod to each other, or a subtle grin and giggle would signify approval, or they would exclaim "That's lovely" or "Oh Jim, Look at this!"

And he would run over in an odd little waddle, and they would examine every angle and inch of whatever they were crowing after there and then, giggle and come up smiling and nodding.

Estrella, the Estate agent, would smile back, wiping away the look of disdain for one of abject class and naïve charm, turning the screw with a little "OK!" sign with her fingers or a sage nod of approval a silent *"yes, that's exactly what you think it is"* look. She had not spoken once during the entire visit past greeting them at the door. She was already locked inside a daydream of the holiday, mentally three thousand miles away sunning herself, and her cosmetically enhanced attributes, being doted on by a golden-skinned waiter. His arms look like bronzed Adonis's, his chest wide and barrel-shaped, his body cascades into a perfect triangle-shaped toward the waist - she would no doubt later suck off this waiter behind the bar, as was her dirty little peccadillo, her guilty secret.

The couple finished the tour by entering the lounge, with its big bay window, its wide sill that you could sit on and while away afternoons watching the world go by, it was a beautiful final selling point for the house. If they had been holding back any doubt about the house until now, it was exhausted and expelled upon seeing that lounge. It was wide and long, with *that* window overlooking a garden in need of attention - but which clearly once had had a woman's touch. It was now overgrown and in need of a day of vigorous weeding, but its ample charm and quirk was still bursting through in fleeting dribs and drabs of colour. Like a masterpiece painting that needed restoration, it was under there, you just needed the tools and time to release its hidden beauty.

A gentle hedgerow had grown around the perimeter and was green and full of future growth, and the road was quiet and still and controlled.

"We'll take it" Kay had said, her mouth an arc of engaged and dizzy joy.

Estrella also smiled widely.

"I thought you may" was all she said, teeth white and deadly as a shark hungrily probing a beach full of paddling children. The grammar of the sentence all wrong, but fulfilling all the right purposes nonetheless.

Kay looked out the window toward the garden again, made an excuse and wandered out. James looked at Estrella, who smiled that great white smile and said,

"Let's talk numbers."

It was a good day for Estrella. The sun on her skin was warm and refreshing, the Margherita on her lips was cool and tangy and the waiter would later slide into her with ease and power and remind her that she sometimes didn't mind not being in control. As she stood there in the lounge, opposite the bay window, opening her folder to start discussing basic terms needed and required by the homeowner, she could already hear the tide rushing in, the almost impossible sound of the sunscreen boiling on her already too-tanned skin. She could smell the cheap and wanton sex of the waiter from the night

46

before all over her…

The beach had never been so close.

* * *
- 3 -

Seven days to create a universe was propaganda neither
wanted nor appreciated by the gods in the multiple Heavens. It was a
lie, a myth and a fairy tale.
It is true, there had been seven days at the start – but as time in those
days was something like treacle, seeping and oozing, rather than
running like the water we have nowadays – days could seem like
months, and months like years.
Yahweh had always seen his position at the beginning of creation
taking a prominent and important role, and this was good and true.
He had been the first to take the emptiness by the scruff of the neck
and paint upon it impressions and ideas that had been pregnant in his
mind no sooner had he woken up. However, though he took on a dual
capacity as Creator and Destroyer – his role was just one of many
hands and many gods.
No one could doubt his importance as being both Doter and
Carer of Mankind and the universe. Nor his voracity and speed in
being the vicious Corporal dishing out punishments and lessons both
miserable and glorious. At the end of it all he was trapped within
those rules he had had a good hand in creating.
One of many, one of a council of gods who had all taken a share of
the eternal oblivion, witnessed from their thin shard of existence, and
given to them all with carte blanche to build what they may.

The abridged version had it that at the beginning there was
nothing, darkness. And from the darkness born was the word, and the
word was the light and the lie of it all. From the word came the
planets and the stars and the truth, and the heavens slowly but surely
began to take shape and form.
From this was born a countless aeon of infinite possibilities and

consequences. God had crafted this from nought more than from the air in his lungs – unfolding a handful of dusty breath onto a table cloth of night and shadow and upon which he unpacked his smorgasbord picnic of life.

Or at least it was in his little corner of creation.

The thing about God was, no matter how much he argued to the contrary, he was just as lost in this sea of uncertainty, in the mystery of this ephemeral existence and life as any one of his flock. One day there was nothing, no light or creation or being, the next a pop and there was God. Full of wonder and memory and idea and confidence, his hands huge powerful tools which could build form from nothing and could work on a design so infinitely small in scale to himself it was scary to even him.

But, He was *not* the first.

When God opened his eyes that first morning there was a plethora, a literal superfluity of others like him who were just as confused and lost, yet, just as powerful. All looked just like him in the flesh, but their shadows would tell different stories – animating differences that were infused in their souls. Some had heads like nothing yet known in this wide expanse of nothing, others had multiple arms, others were naked and chiselled in shapes he was confused and aroused by, others still were not constrained by shape or conscience instead were mists of idea and emotion.

Each one was conjured from the space between spaces, born of the breath before idea. Each staring at the other and each looking for a leader amongst the throng.

God spoke first.

"I am Yahweh," he said.

How he knew his name was beyond his ken, he just knew instinctively that he was.

"I am he they will call Allah, Jehovah and The Lord."

A silver-haired man, whose skin emanated an aura of steely warmth stood, he looked around and helped the other men and women around him to their feet, looked at Yahweh and bowed gently.

"I am Zeus." Was all he said, as he helped more to their feet, creatures of every shape and size, every colour and creed.

One such man, a huge, bearded boulder of a man, one eye missing in his head, a blank of scared skin had been placed where the eye should have been took Zeus's hand, and gave a laugh, loud and boisterous.

"I am Odin. He they will call Allfather."

A creature, not man, not animal, a strange tusked beast whose frame was made of multiple arms and a long trunk appendage on his face stepped forward and spoke in a language and timbre that would be impossible to emulate using mere human voices, he stated he was Ganesha, and that he was one of many gods, that *"This is a grand day, the beginning is now and even though the end is now in sight because the beginning is here, at least,"* (he said with a smile as ugly and impossible as anything seen then or since) *"That the beginning is now here. Little blessings."*

Yahweh was the first to ask the question that made them more than lost husks with a name on their tongue, and elevated their minds to a new plateau – one of thought and reason and question.

"Where did we come from?"

Odin looked at him and smiled.

"Who knows? … Is it not enough that we are?"

Odin was right. It was enough they were there. This multitude of lost, confused and infant gods. Each full of raw power and energy, each hungry to stretch and flex the creation they had within themselves.

There was time enough for this. At this point, there was only time. Time and space and void.

There was only the thought and the space in between.

Time was a true concept then, a malleable and melting concept of liquid and shape, manipulated easily and controlled with idle gesture and annoyance.

It was also a creature of its own right, invisible to these gods, but witness to the day they woke. Working and pulling infinite cogs and strings in shadows and isolation.

The gods were hungry and restless, and something inside screamed of them that they work. Before them was the beach, and beyond this the plan. Between them, they made the plan, to divide the world and the creation, and they made an accord upon which they could begin their duties... whatever they showed themselves to be. In the time that followed, the gods, so many and so varied, so powerful yet so childlike, decided that they were family, born together, they would live together.

No harm from one God to another could ever be dealt – their cardinal rule.

The second rule, that the part of creation that was taken by them was theirs and theirs alone. Others of their kind could not take the land upon which they built.
They would live and let live. Or thus bring into question the first and cardinal rule.

This was not to say in future times they would find ways to damage each other using their own flock – sometimes with control, other times purely at random with the flock deciding this action against other gods purely of their own reason.

The final rule – given to them by someone not of their Ilk, but of something far greater and stranger – was this.
Gods found they could die.
No matter how much they wanted dearly for this to be contrary to reality, it was not – they died just like men died, sometimes easier. When these creatures had woken, having shaken the first stirrings of sleep and confusion from their minds – after they had spoken their names for the first time – they found there was One who had been awake long before them. If indeed he ever had been asleep. Someone and something that stood amongst them.

Mayhaps he was a god himself.
He would never be so bold to suggest or promote this idea. No.

Instead, he perfectly lacked in pride, lacking any self-righteous ego; he was a creation of muted indifference and utter ambivalence.

So much so it was terrifying.

His name was death.
When language came into being, people would learn to capitalise him and make him Death.
The hard D always capitalised, always prominent.
Always unnecessary. He was purely and simply "death" - no pomp or ceremony, much like the act itself when filtered down to its pure essence.

He, Lord Death, sat amongst them.
The gods shook the webs of sleep from their heads and eyes and began to take the first tentative steps toward the bright white luminescence of birth. He touched each one deep inside with nought more than a thought, and he said clearly,

"You are gods and you are born, each a creator and destroyer all, yet, remember – whatever you do from here on out there was once darkness and nothingness from which you came, and in that I was king. I was here before you came, and I will be here long after you leave – and one day, we will meet face to face again, and we will not have quite such as pleasant a chat as we did this day. I am Death. And you are all my children."

Gods have little to fear, but one day, worship and tribute will dry like a riverbed in a heat-wave, and the tokens and the gifts and the ceremony will die like a fish out of water. The feeling of imbibed love and attention will calcify in the veins of the god. Blood will crawl like desert sands across plains, edging slower and slower into despair. All the goodness of the praising and love of their minions will end as one after one their people die and forget and lose themselves in chaos and apathy. The god will turn around, and the dark, ice-blue eyes of death will be before them, staring deep within their souls. Death will hold out a thin white hand, and the god will

follow him into oblivion, never again to be seen and spoken of, except only as a hushed whisper, once a brother or a sister, now a fleeting burst of dust on a passing wind.
As forgotten as a wink or a yawn.

So it was that Creation was made, not a one-man affair, but a labour of many hands and many minds and painted many colours and using many tools. To say there was a grand calculated design, a "Master plan" would be a bold-faced lie. What there was in spades was an observance, that there would be order, and from the ordered chaos of a more natural kind.

The gods came together and carved the blackness into slices of fabric which they could wear and could toy with. Each creating a plane for their own senses and desires. Odin ripped his fabric into nine sheets and thus was created the nine realms; some gods came together and built as a team, sharing duties and strength, pooling ideas and intuition. Others still carved the fabric into images of themselves, mirrors of their Godhood and hung it loose in the darkness, alone and free. When they were done, this first Pantheon brought all the fabric worlds together and shared what they had created. It was stitched together into the Cosmos we know now. Eclectic, eccentric and real – different pantheons joined to breathe life and form into different areas of the universe, and the vast blueprint was the result of many hands from many deities. Mankind was Yahweh's own contribution. There would be other attempts from many other gods after. Some copying the template, some experimenting in ways that would birth monster and beast. But Yahweh was first – this much is undeniable.

At first was only the beach and the lapping tide.
From whence all gods woke.

Now, thanks to Yahweh, built from this tiny fragment of land, he had built Eden.
The infant Earth.

He made the garden from elements of other gods' ideas and inside the garden, this lush and perfect green circle of life, he placed the first two humans.

Adam and Lilith.

At first Lilith, the first Daughter amongst the new world, who lay down with animals and roamed free amongst the many hills and rivers, plains and mountains, showed signs of subservience. She was a wife to Adam; she lay with him too in the shade of the vast oak that sat in the forest. She bathed in the waters of the lagoon that sat at the top of the mountain, with its massive waterfall cascading clear, blue waters into the lagoon and drying naked and beautiful on the banks of the lagoon steam rising from her in the warmth of the early sun. But soon, without ever having been designed, she took a fancy to curiosity and question. Looking at things in a strange skewed way, head to one side, a notch of puzzle on her brow and she would point and ask "why is this?" and "why not like this?" One day, whilst in the forest following a stag that was bounding across the mud and moss and darting between trees and bush, walking side by side with God she dared to ask the question that she had been obsessing after for so long, she dared to ask him that which he was struggling with.
"Who made *you*?"
"From whence did *you* come?"
"When you are gone – *what* will be left?"

In Lilith, God had found his first and most significant mistake – a mistake that would follow him always.
He had imbued her with just as much soul as himself, with this came intuition and promise and adventure – she tempted, and she seduced. She spun yarns and stories, and her constant questioning was a revelation to him - it being all of her own making. As well as also becoming a thorn in his side.
Questions he would never be able to answer, questions that plagued and bothered him - questions, questions, questions – buzzing and berating him, the wings of flies boring into his expansive and omniscient mind. Permeating every neural pathway and vein, a deep,

brown poison drip, drip, dripping into his very being.

But, he was on the whole in the early days, a mostly merciful creator. Before he knew what vengeance or retribution or anger or hate or violence was (because these were man-made constructs he simply adopted later, as one would an accent or a mannerism) God was, above all else, also curious.

One evening, Lilith came to the mountain. Her flowing golden mane of hair, the only protection she had from the elements, she sat cross-legged and quite naked amongst the lonely roses that grew upon the mountains peak, amongst barren patches of grass and a gentle stream and waterfall, the lagoon alive with fish and light. God's daughter came and sat and silently, wantonly, Lilith called out to God.

She had a way of bewitching him.

Watching them together – Lilith was born of the dust and soil of the world and the breath of the ocean's wind. As much a child of Gaia as himself, she being the designer of the ground upon which the garden grew and the winds which moved his Trees and flowers. If God was the father, she was surely the Mother of the Earth and the life born from the seed of it.

Adam, created second, was born from God's own hair, twisted and manipulated into shape and life. Ignited from a kiss from God's own lips.

Yahweh could see the vast gulf in difference between the two of them. Adam so dull and dutiful, so blindly optimistic and full of vacant charm. Lilith with her sultry stares and her serpentine figure, her breasts that rose and dropped in dramatic and energetic fashion when she ran in the rain. Her long slender arms that contorted into strangely spellbinding shapes when she danced in the waterfall. The wildfire that existed behind her eyes, sparkling and bursting into vivid and voracious life when her mind fixated upon a detail or an idea.

The life that emanated from her, like an aura, of rich, invigorating energy.

God found that he cared little for Adam's moronic love. So constant, so bothersome, so annoying – constant wasp stings whenever he prayed.

Never allowing a moment of peace.

Adam who would watch the animals in dumbstruck wonder, patting their backs and guffawing and laughing as though it was the most wonderful thing in the entirety of his little slice of creation.

His eyes so distant and dull, never showing an iota of the curious and beguiling fire that Lilith hid behind her pupils. Adam, who would wander naked and cumbersome around the garden slowly touching the trees and the grasses and giggling in imbecilic chuckles and barks of laughter for no specific reason or spur. Just laughing his redundant and indifferent laugh at the surroundings, unaware himself why he laughed – but carrying on regardless. How could God love this creature when his attention was stolen by the Nymph that was Lilith?

Adam's smile was a blunt, unusual slash across his square jaw lacking any real engagement or understanding. God looked upon his son as being a functional creation, but one that he was rarely proud of.

Lilith was different. She rarely – if ever – prayed. She never mentioned God in name or verse when she did. Instead thanking nature for its beauty, passing grace to the weather for its clemency and offering appreciative murmurs towards the deer that Adam had struck down and cooked, forever grateful for its sacrifice.

Lilith was a different being than God had hoped or dreamed for, something he watched and regarded with odd pride and a pang of perpetual, curious lust.

When he met her atop the mountain, her nakedness was betrayed by the lily-white tenderness of her beautiful skin, her hair the same colour as a fresh carpet of snow. When he was in her presence, he never had control and felt like *she* was driving *him*. Like her being was entwined around his being, her every smile, her every sway in the cool, indifferent air of the mountain was in and of itself a beckon and a nudge to lose himself. His mind a heady drunken mess of confusion and impulse, his clarity dipped in misty, murky instinct. Daring him, goading him into surrendering to his appetite and hunger rather than standing as the pious and steadfast Deity he would want to be seen as.

Inside his mind, he could hear the begging of surrender to his instincts and emotions.

And then, one day, he did.

"Father, I do not covet Adam anymore," Lilith said when she heard God appear behind her. His silent, preternatural ability to exist in the spaces between spaces, and, therefore, move unseen around the garden was never something that worked around this white-haired beauty. Her skin prickled and came to shuddering, shivering life in his presence and she was always aware when he was around, often before God himself was aware she knew.

"His skin is weak, shallow; it does not warm me as I wish it too. His heart is so full of folly and bemusement, he cares not for a woman such as I. He is happier to wander the fields and forests, picking fruit and making fires, than he ever does with my flesh, with my heart. How can I learn to love him if he does not know who I am if he does not care?"

Yahweh shifted again, folding in on the space and dimensions around them, and came from out of the waterfall. His nakedness shimmering with a silver ripple as the water evaporated from him, wafts of platinum steam circling his aura and dispersing into nothingness. He reached a huge, welcoming hand out to Lilith. She regarded it and its strength, smiled, and lay her dainty, delicate hand in his palm and allowed herself to be pulled into the water, led by him into the waterfall.

Yahweh took her gently and rolled her into his chest, she reciprocated by throwing her arms around his waist. Her head squeezed tightly against his breastbone, as his hand circled her shoulder, gently cupping her neck and hair.

"Adam is Man. His attention is on that which is unknown, that which is fleeting.

His mind will slow, his body will hunger, his passions will find you, patience my daughter." He had to swallow hard on the *'My Daughter'* as the word bore some new significance.

Lilith's hand had found the small of his back, and she gently pushed away from his arms to look him directly in the eyes. She half smiled, a line in her grubby, yet so delicate and beautiful face, from where she had cried.

"If to love you is unconditional, and you are love, why then do we need to dress our praise of you in tribute and gifts and presents? Why can we not just be and shine out our love for you to see?" She held his gaze.

Yahweh stood silent, momentarily lost in her green eyes. He could not remember ever making them this beautiful or dazzling. They were a rich aquamarine. The colour seemed to sparkle with untold adventure in a way that stole him. Making his mind heavy with the sense of insanity and angry need.

"I love you with my everything; I am sure you can see that?" Lilith said, her hand gently stroking his cheek.

"I would do anything to show you my love, but surely the fact the love exists is all you would need for you to know. Am I not correct?"

Yahweh looked at her, her naked body glistening in the spray from the waterfall, her eyes a magnet of emotion and heady love. Her breasts still rising and falling. Rising and falling with each of her heady breaths.

He broke the gaze, dropping his head slightly to look away from her eyes. The colour was doing something to him. The waterfall cascaded around them in loud, warm torrents; the froth and steam made the cave behind the curtain of water a warm and welcoming retreat in which to have this conversation, away from prying eyes and minds.

Lilith was made from the dust of the Earth and brought incarnate by the breath of Oceans, but the spark that made her real was tempered with parts of creation he did not have a hand in, though

she was most definitely one of his toys, built by his hand, she was tainted with elements under the rule of other gods.
He realised; he had made a mistake in her.

Her hand was still on his cheek, he rested his head gently on her palm, gently stroking his electric golden skin, his hand framed and held her face gently, and he drew her to him. Their skin entwined in gentle static bursts, her hair became a fizz of life, as his ardour became elevated, and his skin shone brighter.
She held a hand around his waist and pulled him close.
He in turn, cupped a hand around her shapely rear and slightly lifted her toward him, the damp glisten of the waterfall on her skin fizzed and disappeared upon contact with his skin. The two of them were alive now in static ballet, light and water dancing in elliptical arcs around them.

"I love YOU. I want YOU; I do not want this half-man you made for me."
Lilith said this with her lips so very nearly touching gods, he – in turn – seemed to mirror her mouth moving. Swallowing her words as though they were rich and filling morsels of food, the taste of her breath invigorating him in the most delicious and wonderful of ways. So close to his flesh, her lips merely brushed his. In this lightest moment of contact images and emotions exploded in vivid colour inside her mind as God's mind also became awash with emotions he had had no part in creating. He was in no way controlling or expecting or ready for this alien side of her, born of nature created by the hand of some other God or Goddess. This imp, this demon he was no part of had filled her with curiosity, impertinence, adventure and defiance – she was a vampire, an animal, a hybrid of two worlds – and he could no longer help himself. He fell into her lips, as one would fall into sleep, simple and unexpectedly his lips and hers touched and the kiss became all that there was.

Her kiss was as beautiful and as revelatory as the day he was born, hacking and spluttering though he had, so naked and alone upon a plain of darkness. Before the sound of others dotted the collective unconscious and he was staring at a plethora of gods – his pantheon - all who had been brought to creation by an unknown hand, some unknown power and who had left them, alone, to figure their own way. A scary, incredible feeling of unknowing, of a future unwritten, of a beginning yet to come, the feeling of being able to do anything and knowing it was yours to make of as you wished.

The birth of the gods and this kiss was one and the same to him, his mind was sure.

Her lips and her kiss were as shocking and as terrifying as the day Death had told them he would one day come for them, one by one, and that even gods were mortal.
He was filled with a cocktail of unbalanced emotions, revulsion at his action, excitement and a need to know what would happen if they continued this path.
So…

As he lifted her up in his strong, taut, golden arms, she wrapped her legs around his waist as though they were tendrils of root. Unexpected strength squeezed him, and she sighed as her sex nestled on the electric golden edge of his. As he entered her in a single gesture, her face came away from his and her eyes took on a fiery aura around the brilliant aquamarine, her mouth a circle of surprise and desire, her eyes wide and staring at him. A single hand scratched at his solid, muscled chest, cutting and gouging a line of light into the flesh that healed in a dark, golden brown reminder of the deed. Her breathing rapid and ecstatic, the chest heaving in deep gulps of life-giving air, stifled by gentle moans and a warm giggle. Her hair fell in heaps across her face as she held his face lightly, squeezing him deeper into her with her thighs as He nodded gently in approval. God grew in power and passion inside her and drove on to an orgasm of such magnitude and power that the land around them cracked and broke. As it shook the waterfall lilted, and a great deluge came as they did. Lilith screaming and scratching two lines of four deep scars into his shoulders, as though the scars were the skeleton of wings. He pushed harder one last time and groaned a deep rumble of appreciation into her hair as he held her head against his chest. The two collapsing, laying upon the bank of the shadowy, warm beachhead inside the waterfall, the sound of the lagoon suddenly all they could see and hear around them. God allowed himself a single tear to run from his eye in silent abandon, the tear evaporating within seconds upon his beautiful, golden skin. His being twinned for a moment of pure, unquenchable joy with hers. He looked up, breaking from her grip, a fine sweat upon his brow. He was much like Man in those days: discovering new things, feeling in new ways – he was struggling to find the sense in what had just happened, and then he felt a sudden burst of a new emotions, feelings of shame and guilt and regret.

His previous ardour and romance for the situation was dying like an aging rose as he separated from her embrace. Instead of the heavy spell of her intoxicating skin and love, all that remained was the reality of his action, the shocking realisation of what had just happened.
He rolled away and regarded her.
Her naked figure lay upon the bank, the warmth of their labours still gently smoking off her skin, and the glow of her white hair and the lily whiteness of her skin for a second stained golden with his energy and his love.
He stood, and one hand raised to his mouth as he fully realised the horror of his actions, she looked at him with a curious and confused poise, her eyes slowly coming out of the spell of intoxicating lust, and instead awakening to what was about to happen. God looked at her with a look of disgusted and brutal judgment, his warm eyes falling into a deeper, darker look of disdain and his mouth curling into a downturned sneer of revulsion.

"How you bewitched me. How you tricked me with stories of love, of need, of desire…how you lie to me. This is not love."
He barked the last word, flecks of spit flying from his snarling mouth.
"Do you call this LOVE?"

Lilith, for her part, simply laughed.

A deep, rich, fertile laugh which shook the heavens and reverberated across the hills and mountains and valleys of Creation.

She stood up, stretching her limbs in a sultry and sensual way. Her breasts heaved again and fell. Her arms stretched high above her head, then came down in alluring patterns as though in a dance, the arms slowly curling into a cross low and lovingly in a cradle across her stomach. She smiled widely and with a smouldering intensity as she simply said.

"No." her hands squeezing gently across her stomach, nurturing her abdomen.

She smiled at God, and her eyes welled with tears and a look of victory.

"This is Love."

Her belly churned, there was movement there, and the flesh of her stomach swelled and shifted. The skin became pinker and warmer. It started to stretch and become swollen and round, and behind the flesh, there was movement.

Lilith smiled and held herself, tears rolling down her cheek, her eyes red with happiness.

"What gift is this?" She laughed, her lips contorted into a painful, happy grimace of surprise and adoration.

Yahweh stared, one hand still on his mouth, cupped, holding in his terrified guilt.

A dull but poignant understanding grew in him.

He pointed at the woman, at her belly, now full of the pangs and spark of birth – so quick, so sudden – and it dawned on him what he had done. Realising how easily he had been used, his own terrible pride twisted and used against him, his desire manipulating his sense.

He roared with unrequited rage and burst through the waterfall, shifting in on the space where water molecules met oxygen in silent alchemy, and disappeared to a place where he could be alone to gather his thoughts.

Something else within the curtain had been dwelling and had seen everything.

Hidden and contorted in the shadows of the cave.
Just as shocked, just as surprised.
This entity skulked further into the darkness to gather thought and plot.
Yahweh had not seen it, nor felt it, but as surely as the deed had been done – the entity had been watching.

Lilith was alone, behind the curtain of water, her arms slowly slithering out cutting a swath in the water as she left the cave, hands returning to her belly and a gentle, mournful laugh upon her lips. She looked to the clouds, and to the cliff face above where blue water tumbled into green lagoon.
Her laugh became a louder, more hurried one of frenzy and madness. She screamed at the heavens three simple, significant and powerful words.

"THIS IS LOVE!"

And she left the water, to make her way to the beach.
Something inside her mind was telling her that this was where she had to be.
The beach and the lapping tide beckoning her home.

* * *

- 4 -

The box was still in the centre of his lounge. It had burst through the table neatly and with minimum effort. James had managed with clumsy and panicked haste to clear the remnants of the table. Taking the broken shards and fragments he had put them in black bags and put them out in his garden - half for a bonfire, the rest for recycling.

He vacuumed the dusty glass and fibrous chips and then sat on his sofa, a pair of scissors in hand. He idly counted in his head to gain some control of his wits, waiting for the perfect moment of clarity to try and open the box.

As he was staring at it – ready to make his first move – a fly landed on the box and began to noisily buzz and flap its wings. The fly was the size of a thumbnail, it had a deep mottled green and blue hue, its eyes were oily and dark and full of deep illusion of filth, its hairy little legs were like fir pine, dipped in treacle and each carried a billion illnesses in James's head.

He stared and stared at the thing. Its translucent wings like petrol in a sea, so beautiful and cataclysmic, they fizzed a retort in fly language, as James sat forward in curious disgust. His glasses perched on the end of his nose, he moved slowly and calmly forward to regard the insect closer, and in turn, the fly hopped on the spot and looked at James right back. They met a glance at each other, and all was still for a second before the fly took off and buzz-bombed right at James's face.

James jumped from his seat, the scissors bursting from his hands. As he tried to catch them in mid-air, for fear they would damage the upholstery of the sofa, he grabbed them by a single blade and gouged a deep gash into his index finger and palm, the rich red blood flowed immediately. Instead of scissors marking his pale blue sofa cushions, the arcing drops of blood did the same job, only quicker. A dotted arterial spray left across the seat.

James rushed into the kitchen to run the gash under a tap, drips followed him, his injured hand was being squeezed tight in his other, the scissors were resting on his floor now, a fine line of blood settling under the blade.

The fly was gently buzzing around the stainless steel of the scissors edge and then rested in the blood, puckering deeply around the red elixir. Its wings seeped up the colour, its eyes glimmered as if in a stupor, drunk on its iron and tang. It took off, dizzy and loaded, and full of rich, fresh blood. Finding a dark corner of the kitchen to rest in, its many eyes all focussed on James washing his hand under the water and ripping off kitchen roll to stem the bleeding. The hungry, unquenchable thirst of the metallic blood was still on the flies' mind. It ripped into its very being, and filled the fly with new purpose and zeal, making it pregnant with new ideas and a single-mindedness.

James wrapped the towel around his fingers, bit open a fabric plaster and tightly wound it round the cut. Luckily it was not as deep as he had feared. Instead, it had just caught him at that perfect place where the vein was most vulnerable.

He threw the towel down, discarded and finished with. The fly saw it and its Rorschach of blood. As James left the kitchen, armed with an antiseptic wipe to clean the blood-soaked sofa and carpet, the fly landed on the counter top and got stuck into the blood on the kitchen towel… getting bigger and fatter with each pucker of his proboscis.

As James came into the lounge, the first thing he noticed was a second fly sat on the top of the box. This one was black, with bursts of brown and orange under its wings, a common housefly; a little, black, pea-sized dirt magnet. James felt a surge of revulsion and deeply miserable hate – he hated flies like he hated people. Parasitic, useless and bothersome, they were one of the few things he hated as equally as he did the general populace. He wanted to swat them all and kill them dead, a bursting sense of accomplishment filling him every time he did so.

He grabbed a nearby tea towel, drying on a radiator, spun it in a slow lasso and then let out a whip that struck with a snap at the top of the box.

He flicked the bow off in a single shot. The bow, which was a cheap piece of plasticized paper dressing available from almost any shop, flew off and smashed a vase that was sitting on a nearby side table near the window. As fragments hit the window with a thud, James honestly thought the window was going to give, but it did not. Instead, it just made that dull noise that assured him – strangely – of their quality.

The fly was now nowhere to be seen. Not entirely convinced he had hit it, he kept the tea towel with him, stuffing it in his back pocket as he walked over to the bow.

He gently and with a real reluctance, remembering how hard it had hurt to stub his toe on the box that morning, poked a solitary finger of his – now – good hand at the bow. Expecting, for the singular reason that it was easier to accept what was going on than question it, that the bow would weigh an extraordinary amount.

Instead, the bow moved as if made of plasticized paper and then, quite suddenly, the remains of the vase evaporated into a fine dust around it like the life had been dragged out of it with cool, dark efficiency.

It reminded James of Christopher Lee as Dracula, hiding behind his cape while someone pulls open the blinds and scours him with sunlight.

He looked at the dust for a second, a look of bemusement written all over his face as if the day could become any weirder. He turned to face the box. Now sat on top was now not one, nor two, but three flies, all of them looking at him with beady, buzzing and goading looks. Mischievous and full of mockery. They were laughing at him in their own little way, James was certain of it, and with a bilious rage in his throat, he burst a "GAH!" sound and swung his lasso tea towel at the box. The cloth immediately ripped into two fragments as it made contacted with a whipping crack noise. Like the velocity had done the damage, which James knew to not be true, where it was instead the box, and nothing more than the box. Its bold impassivity had ripped it in two, and he let out a little laugh. Seeing a half-drunk fly stunned by the tea towel crawling in a listless and stupefied manner toward the chair in the corner of the lounge, James's half smile disappeared entirely and he marched over to stamp on the thing, double time. His foot came down with a satisfying crunch, like a peanut being stood on, the fly left a mucousy splotch on the carpet. James didn't even care, he just felt a glow of happiness that he had got the bastard thing. As he turned around to leave for another wet wipe for the mess on his window sill, and now his carpet, there were four flies on his sofa arm, including the blue bottle. Its green and blue hue had doubled in size, and he felt sure he saw some strange luminescence in its eyes. It paced hungrily and angrily on the arm and hopped down onto the sofa, its head bobbing up and down on the splashes of blood. James felt a wave of sickness. Inside or outside of his body that was still *his* blood, and he felt sick knowing the unclean mess was crawling around his fluids. It felt like the worst kind of violation, the worst kind of betrayal of his body to allow itself to be used so.

He remembered that he had packed a box of knick-knacks and useless household rubbish into a box in his shed, and he recalled inside there was a swat. He shuddered with revulsion at the memory of all the wasps and flies he had swiped out of existence like a crazed Wimbledon tennis champ as a child. He could see the bright pink thing now, handle sticking out, a perfect tension in its surface, a handle that bent like a whipping birch, he smiled.

It was exactly what he needed.

* * *

- 5 -

I stir, not quite awake, indeed – I am never quite asleep, damned forever in a half world of insomnia, existing on a diet of idle restlessness, catching the brief moment of gentle peace on the wing. Like a swallow.

Then, just as soon as I rest my eyes and welcome the blank coldness of sleep, I am struck as if beaten or shocked by powerful bolts of electricity, blind agony crawling through my skin and I am awake, dull-eyed and desperate for the seconds to while away into slumber again.

In my slumber, I missed the sunrise, its fleeting arc across my skyline being all of a minute before it makes a dwindling dawdle back into the horizon again and drowns me once again in darkness… My grace of God and bath in light lasting no more than 10 minutes a day, before I am left alone in the almost perpetual darkness, and abject misery.

Such is my punishment.
Such is my spiteful regret.

I stand in front of the beautiful stained-glass window, now dreary and mute as the sun lingers behind the caustic clouds that

smog my view. Grey, dead and cold.
Full of pity and yet so full of self-righteous mocking.
I would laugh, but, you know what?
I outgrew it.
Laughter, I outgrew it - Many a good year ago, now I am serious,
hewn of pallid flesh that betrays my frustrations like a canvas
painting of Prometheus.
Laying chained to a rock and allowing birds of prey to eat my flesh
every day, as I watch it heal and then wait for the flesh and liver to be
ripped from me once again.

He is a cousin of mine.
He is dead now. Long gone into the Ether with the shadow of Death.
Another fallen and aged God fed to the Carrion in the darkness.

      The window is a triptych today - it shows an Angel, dead and
fallen. Laying at the circle of fire. Of the tempting of Eve with the
Apple, Adam taking the fruit from her hand and the desire for that
first tantalising taste.
The final stack of the window is reserved for the beautiful if
inaccurate, depiction me being cast out and thrown into this prison by
my brother. Of Michael and his fiery sword and his ridiculous piety
and his "heroism,"
Of his victory in the early days of this creation, as he threw me down
to the marble cell I now call home, also banishing the kin I helped
our father build.
Easy to be a hero says I when you have twenty scores of our brothers
kicking seven shades of faith out of me on the Elysian Fields.

      At first I could watch this window day in and day out. Awake
with a new vista every morning, fall asleep with a new one every
evening.
Now, it seems to be the same three or four frames and images every
day. Lots of my mistakes, lots of my errors, haunting me.
Back in my days in the garden, I would watch, and I would learn.
I did a lot of watching in those days. Of the children, of the land
forming and shaping to the west and of the plain and the land

forbidden to the husband and of the wife.

I watch still now, as mental pictures fill the gaps left by my three
window memory box painted upon the wall. My mind my prison
within my prison.
A constantly evolving maze of regret and despair and sadness,
fleeting glimpses of hope always just out of reach, just like the
daylight.
Hungry for the grace of the morning light.
So transient and vacant.
Much like my father. A glimpse, a burst of its light like a flash of his
smile, taken away by the clouds and the mood and the fucking
drama.

I, Lucifer Morningstar.
The Adversary, the Great Enemy, the Tempter, the Immoral.
I, Lucifer; The Lord of Lies, the Firstborn and Harbinger of the New
Day.
I sit here in my castle in the heart of a void and wait for the sun to
burst for those brief seconds soaking as much light as I can, as much
of the suns goodness as I am able and I watch you all.
It's a funny thing to know that I can never do all the things
that I am credited with. The tempting and what not... It's annoying
thinking that you all sit there and whisper hushed prays to ward me
off, and I am sitting here like a bitter exile from the promised land,
My father and siblings holding the keys to my freedom, left with
morsels of crumbs and scraps. My father telling me I will have feast
enough when I have learnt my lesson.

Only my father instead forgets about me altogether.
I am forever, eternally punished, and I am never let back, forever a
beggar at the gates of the dining hall.

That's what Hell is...
A big absence of a brilliant parental figure – you and your thoughts

and all the things you love - just one inch away from arms length and therefore, always seen never held, never adored, never touched.

A witty comeback two minutes after the target leaves.
Forever wasted and never able to be used.
It's the apple and pitch of water for a starving man, left to rot and spoil an inch away from his grasp. A bastard's practical joke for a bastard son...
The punch-line being it's NOT funny, but you are forced to laugh at yourself all the same.
By the window, there is a table, it is crafted of the same ageless, perfect marble as this prison, it has seen aeons of history.
My constant companion, stained dark with the scent of the open fires and shadows, one-half is bathed sporadically in light, the other the dark of the moon, its surface is rich and deep with silence.
It is perfect except for a line of fracture no more than an inch or two long; whose topography and shape I cannot stop obsessing over. The only solitary, unfixable imperfection within a room of perfect architecture and geometry.

As I absentmindedly toy with the crack with my index finger, running the pad of the digit up and down the fissure, I hear the sound of the object being slid under the crease of the door shape, scratched deep within the wall. Unable to be opened and unable to be moved.

I open the papyrus parchment with trepidation and fear.
The item in question is contraband, nothing is given to me ever, and I have never seen another living creature the entire time I have been isolated within this pristine, abandoned marble hell.

I open the sheet and gently flatten the crease.
Reading the paper several times, with hurried comprehension and a dawning realisation of what this means.
Upon the parchment are simple words in a neat, unfussy script.

open the door, you're free. it's time.

It was not the words that surprised me, nor the fact that it was left without me sensing or hearing or being aware of a messenger. No. This all made perfect sense when you saw the signature.
Indeed, it is the signature with which I am taken aback.
We did not always get on – and though he owed me a favour, I never once thought he would return it so…
The signature simply read.

ego sum mortis

"I am of death."

The crease behind me rumbles and shakes, and then folds, turning instantly to dust and rubble, as the pressure of space opening up in the atmosphere crumbles its matter to powder.
A shard of incandescent sunshine. Pure, white light of redemption, pours through the open wound in the marble and soaks me and my mind.

The green tunic is shed quickly, and every inch of my body and frame greedily drinks this bath of light.

My saviour, opening the door to Hell and freeing the number one son.
"It's time." The parchment says.
"It's time." The end of days.

      I take the first tentative steps toward the hole and daylight. I can see this scene play out in my mind like some overblown stage-show.
The curtain draws, I take the stage, the audience are going ecstatic, I take a dainty little bow… I hold it long enough to let the blissful shivers of adulation run over me. As my skin becomes alive with the presence again, I am imbibed with a new vigour, the colour returns to my skin, and I am alive once more.

In my mind, rampant imagination paints the picture…

The crowd carry on with the clapping and yahooing and whistling. I am a someone, and everyone wants to be associated with a someone.

My time is here.
I am finally free... And I can finally have my revenge.

* * *

- 6 -

What started as a persistent lo-pitch hum had soon developed into a constant, tumultuous whiny of buzzing.
He couldn't tell where they were coming from, nor why they were here. He had no pets, could not envisage a neighbour's cat or something bringing in a mouse or something similar to rot and fester under some cupboard somewhere.
He had scoured on hands and knees looking for the source, but nothing was found.
James lay a drooling mess of exhaustion and grime, he had not bathed in days, was in fact scared of entering his bathroom for fear of what would be in the tub.
He pulled the bed sheet higher over his head, and with the light of his mobile phone, curled up in a foetal position to hide from the cataclysmic drone that was outside his manmade, uteral fort.
He had used something like a can and a half of the Raid he had put away in his cupboard under the sink, and sprayed another two cans of air freshener to hide the fug and bitter tang of its scent.
He had swatted and smashed his way around the house for two whole days until he had broken the antique swat he had found in the shed by smashing it on a doorframe.
He had killed somewhere in the region of twenty or thirty flies, but still, they came. And the blue bottle, the big green and blue beast that had arrived as patient zero on the first day, was now bigger and filthier than ever. It had a vendetta in mind against James, James who felt he was being stalked by a bloodthirsty ghoul...
How close to the truth he was.

There was a housefly in the window, and as it rubbed its forelegs together, a harsh, caustic sound of industrial sandpaper being scrapped on shiny metal would pierce and shatter James's quiet. His wings fluttering, like two sheets of cling-film, stretched over a coat-hanger, so delicate and translucent, made the noise of a turbine stuttering into life. The two noises together sounded like a cruise liner starting its motors, a gigantic propeller starting on dry land, in a dock full not of water, but glass and scrap metal.

James had dealt with this all night. One fly causing nothing but irritation and noise that, in James's head at least, was amplified twenty or thirty times more brilliant than could ever actually be real. But he heard it OK, he heard it. Each rub of the leg, each flutter of wing, each lazy buzz, just as easily as if it was in the bed with him, and the fly was the size of a man.

A ridiculous thought.

A terrifying and ridiculous idea.

The noise carried on regardless – and with each new wave it sent those familiar and disgusting waves of fear, those ghostly shivers up James's spine, swelling like a fever and wave around the base of his neck, and shaking through his hairline. He felt like he was bathing in insects, their strange alien proboscis all over him – and a new wave of revulsion and sickness came over him.

He had not slept in some time, at least 30 hours. Instead, he had stalked between rooms; a rolled up newspaper in hand to replace his antiquated swat he was genuinely sad to have broken. His other hand wrapped in reversed tape, to make a sticky mitten, swatting at air and sashaying his paper at imaginary enemies, all the size of a pea, and all as black as slice of obsidian itself. All except Patient Zero.

He had seen the blue bottle bastard three days previously, sitting on a windowsill in the kitchen. Not unusual, with his little compost tub next to the sink, and the window always slightly ajar to allow the soft peat-like smell escape. But it was when he was sat on the toilet that it had really caught him unawares, when he was reading the newspaper, wistfully digesting a story about a foiled armed robbery in a post office in Kettering, when the fly landed on his hand. Not moving, not flying away or freaking out as is the way of flies in their transient nervous little lives, it was happy to stay where it was, sitting pretty as James brought his hand curiously all the way up to his face to get a closer look through his glasses. Glasses so thick, when they were removed James's eyes seemed a good quarter of the size smaller than they would usually seem through the lens.

The beast sat and gently turned to face James – and for a moment, a genuine moment of understanding came between the insect and the man, eyeballs on lenticular legion of eyeballs – they struck a moment of brief rapport and understanding.
The fly looked at James, and then buzzed his wings, and scratched his forelegs together, and then buzzed his little, see-through, oily wings again, and James for his part gave a little huff of curious glee. As he did so, the fly took advantage of the situation and darted into James's mouth. A mouth that maybe parted lips for all of a second in brief, happy idling, which was exactly the time needed for the insect to commit his mad dash for suicide-by-gullet.

James had been entirely un-expecting of the beast's inherent, kamikaze attack, the spring made for his open mouth, indeed, the idea of it did not register as anyway likely or something one could ever expect in a universe of possibilities that existed – the idea of a fly deciding off the cuff to kill itself by flying into your mouth would never have occurred to James – his being an analytical and scientific brain or not. It was beyond anyone's ken that a fly would willingly commit Hari-Kari in such a way.

James at first choked in wonder and surprise, the beast disappearing into the bowels for all of a second, before he span in his throne, and hacked and gagged and eventually spat the poor, bastard bluebottle out in a sea of vomit, all over his own morning shit. The fly gave a final indignant twitch of his legs and a buzz of his pearlescent wings, before James vomited again, and then quickly flushed.

He was left a heap leaning over the toilet bowl, his boxers around his ankles, the newspaper in ruins across the entire bathroom and his still unwiped arse staining the white, bathroom toilet mat.

He strained out one final hack of sick, and then cleaned himself as best as he could, before showering.

Twice.

Once to clean himself, the second (*so he told himself*) to clean his soul.

There had been other flies in the advancing days, admittedly none as big as the beast, but there had been others. One was watching him from the corner of his wardrobe as he changed. It barely moved, had barely been noticed until a brief flicker of the wings and a half turn three millimetres to the left was seen as James put on his socks. "*I see you, you fucker*" Had been all James had muttered as he carried on regardless – pulling his socks up, lacing his house shoes, before swinging wildly with a belt, succeeding in nothing more than chipping his wardrobe's beech-effect veneer.

The fly simply hopped on the light fixture and carried about his idle twitching.

"*Fucker.*" James had said, his belt dinked and dented with the impact.

There was another fly in the kitchen, which was soon joined by a couple more, all three were flying spirals and DNA shaped pirouettes around the compost tub, occasionally dive-bombing the Tea Bag Graveyard by the kettle, a drip tray ramekin James dumped squeezed bags into.

There were three or four – it was difficult to tell – in the bathroom, each one slightly bigger than the other, the largest of them another bluebottle that moved around like a lazy airship, its wings barely able to lift its bulk, but the noise that of a chinook transporting the SAS into Afghan killing fields. James was certain it couldn't be the same one who had dived into his bowels… But, it had a lazy insolence, a keen obsession with James that he found to be weird and disconcerting.

There were five in the lounge later that morning, as James went to drink his cold, flavourless tea and curse the passing world. The largest of which would constantly dive-bomb him as he sat in the window cross-legged, annoying him so much that - in a rare moment of all of his control being totally abandoned – he threw his tea everywhere in surprise, an arc of grey, milky water arching in slow-motion before impacting with a devastating Rorschach ink explosion upon the carpet. This was followed by James throwing his cup as hard and as fast as he could at the fly, the handle clipping the wings and torso like a coconut at a shy, and both cup and fly smashed with wild, chaotic precision against the wall. Fragments of dark putrid flesh and white bone china careening into a thousand, million pieces.

It wasn't the first time he had killed one, the pile of dead flies now resembled a pyre of filthy, black boogers – however - it swelled him full of pride and filled his insides with a sense of warm, curious accomplishment with every one he swatted, struck or maimed. Then the irritation became too much for him to bare. Their constant buzzing and dive-bombing saw James rechristen himself as a mythical fly hunter, resplendent with an arsenal of rolled up newspapers and slippers and a sticky, homemade sellotape paddle he made by stretched the sticky tape over two coat hangers he had bent and folded and which was now fashioned into a weird hybrid of swatter and tennis racket, a sticky baton of death.

The flies, however, would never just go away – they remained, and for every one he killed it felt like three took their place. Like an insect Hydra, three heads for every one dead. The toilet had never been flushed as many times in a day as when James had swatted and chucked the black, speckled bodies into the bowl. His sanity fraying with each new kill.

On the fifth day of the invasion of the flies, James had woken from a particularly bad nightmare – sleep had been in fits and starts for the last week, he felt like his skin was crawling with disease and dirt. He hated how the flies had made him feel unclean, a shudder of awful revulsion had stretched out over his nerve endings and flattened into a pulse that gleamed and dragged fine tooth, pin-bristled combs over his skin like his body was being dragged over red-hot coals and then doused with ice-cold jet-wash.

The dream had started in the kitchen. He had opened the fridge to get a beer, and upon popping the cap and taking a swig of the cold, bitter liquid, instead he had taken a deep and awful swig of nothing but bottle flies. Great buzzing, ugly, devilish looking monsters, filling his mouth and dancing and jostling over his tongue, hiding in every salival pocket, squeezing themselves into every filling and cavity and had not stopped pouring, even when the bottle had hit the floor and shattered into untrustworthy daggers splintered across his smooth, shiny, granite floor.

James had pulled open the door to the fridge, gagging and spitting flies out of his mouth, an abominable retch of puke had seen to a great deal of them, but the rest were now crawling out to escape the horrendous reek of bile and death and stomach.

He pulled open the fridge door to grab the nearest thing he could use to swill out his mouth, but, instead of finding sweet relief and tonic, he found a fridge full of flies and cockroaches and bugs. Teeming with black, irascible life, every item was being attacked, the cheese had turned to an unsettling green mulch, the meat had putrefied and gave a sweet, unbearable stench of death and rot. Maggots were writhing on every surface, a strange alien tundra had replaced his once largely normal fridge freezer – filling his mind with invasive, instinctual, caveman recollections, he gagged again, and another fly fluttered on soggy and saturated wings from his lips.

He opened the cupboard to see if any red wine was left, and this too was a hotbed of activity and terror – flies and mold and sticky, speckled, spit ravaged the cupboard's warm veneer. Flies poured out like molasses, and the counter top was awash with sinewy, throbbing buzz like the world had come alive.

Flies of every size and colour congregated in the kitchen, doors of every appliance and cupboard shuddered and then burst open as more specks of hate cascaded and flowed like black water from shelves and hidey-holes and nooks and crannies, and James was knee deep, then elbow deep, then chest deep, then neck deep in the sea of filth.

His eyes were now banging a drumbeat of confused agony in his skull, and then, like someone popping a champagne cork, they burst in milky gloops of ambivalence, as a magnitude of flies, an absolute hell-borne legion, rode forth from his sockets.

It was at this he had woken. He vomited hard at the edge of his own bed, the hardwood floor taking the impact with a colossal

76

splash, and he hacked and spat the remnants of his stomach lining , a bedraggled string of bile and spit bungeeing from his lips, he was face to face with what he knew was the Beast. Its mottled green and blue belly now easily the size of a bumblebee, its eyes were oily, oozing alien mirrors. The beast hopped greedily into the bilious stomach contents rubbing his forelegs, and probing hungrily with its proboscis and even then, James could hear his beady psychic laughter, as he guzzled on the vile vomit.

Like someone pulsing a blender, and crushing glass, a cacophonous and jagged sound that bore into his soul and clung to him like bitterness.

James had never felt such hate.

Such venom.

He fell out of bed, and slammed his foot down hard on the blue bottle, the beast popped with an audible crack, and a white, mucous membrane *spluched* over the floor, in amongst the creamy white fluid, poured a viscous red stream… Blood.

James' own blood.

James tried to back away from this mess he had inflicted upon his own bedroom. Suddenly aware of the evil stench of his sick and the thick, black speckling on his own foot, he shifted around, retching, and slipped into the bathroom. He barely made it; the vomit caught somewhere between his heart and his teeth when he collapsed into the bathroom and knelt by the toilet bowl.

As he raised the seat to release the jet-stream of stomach contents into the bowl, he was met with an absolute hive of thriving, buzzing houseflies.

An explosive mass of black and brown. Flashes of light reflecting translucent pearl from the wings. He could not hold it in any longer, and he released the contents of his stomach, a chugging hacking noise escaped his throat, and instead of bile and vomit, James coughed up a stream of angry black flies. At least five hundred of them burst out of his mouth and crashed with a violent pitch against the mass of flies inside the bowl.

From inside the bowl, a stirring took place, and James barely had managed to cough up the last dregs of his stomach - spitting a final fly out of his mouth - before the army of black-winged devils

swirled like a hurricane upwards and outwards from the bowl, filling the bathroom with a sound of thunder and destruction.
A cacophonous orchestra of darkness and disease.

James' psyche and his patience had been a fragile house of cards for days now, but this was it as far as James was concerned, this noise brought the foundations crumbling down and James finally lost any charade of control he had tried to maintain.
For days, buzzing and dive-bombing could be tolerated, but a maelstrom of insects exploding from his mouth and toilet bowl was the pincher.
Still wiping away the taste of chemical and crude oil and raid from his mouth, the cocktail of flavours that had burst forth when he was gagging out an entire hivemind of black death, he swiped and swatted wildly with his hands as flies invaded every aspect of his pristine and brilliant bathroom – such a small room, so intimate, just big enough for two people – he recalled the first time he and Kay had been in there smiling and holding each other so gently, laughing and sharing an innuendo or two.

"That shower would be good for a show or two," he had whispered.
"How on earth are you going to know when you'll be in there with me?" she replied.
"I have cameras... I can film," and she had smacked him good-naturedly on the arm, and he had pulled her to him and they kissed...
He had always done this when the estate agent was around, half to affirm his credentials as a lady-killer, and half because she always looked at him with hungry eyes, and it had made him uneasy. She wore too much makeup and skirts that were barely able to be described as such. Less material than one of his work ties he had said.
"Which is what she used to gag her victims." Kay had laughed, and snorted in that naughty, dirty way she was inclined to do.
It had always made him love her so much more.

He flung open the door and just as quickly shut it again. He ran through the lounge, careful – even considering his state of mind – to avoid the box, still there, still mysterious and still unopened, what with James' preoccupation with the flies.

He ran to the back bay-windows and pulled hard on the latch. It gave with minimum effort, and he ran outside, his pyjamas dirty and wet within seconds around his ankles from the damp grass.

His garden was a small square, long enough that it was a gentle walk toward the willow that bent and bowed and provided a hidden canopy for kissing or sitting or shade. He slung the door back shut, taking care to lock the dead bolt so it could not shut him out, and he paced back and forth. Shaking and swatting imaginary flies from his hair and body, kicking at the air like a lunatic scarecrow, spitting deep, phlegmy wads of saliva and stomach onto his shaggy, untamed grass.

It struck him immediately that this was the furthest he had been outside without immediately returning back in for almost a year. He suddenly felt very small and insignificant as his eyes became dizzy and his legs heavy. He fought the urge to throw himself back into the house, and instead, his mind simply uttered one word:

"SHED."

It made sense, a man with his peculiarities, whose agoraphobia had been a by-product of feeling trapped beyond his own control due to what had happened, sometimes, it just needed the perspective of a small room to steady his gaping, expanding mind, to drag him back into the here and now.

He opened the door to the shed and was met with a wall of flies. They went off like a house of fireworks in every direction, and as they did, James let out a yelp of terror and ran back toward the house. He threw open the bay-window, stamped in, and slammed it shut. As he did, the flies all smashed against the window, dropping down dead like someone had thrown a box of raisins at the glass. He laughed uncontrollably, pointing angrily at the glass and gave a triumphant *HA!* at the final dead fly. He put both hands on the glass and rested his weary head against the pane as a voice behind him suddenly made him start again, banging his head against the double-glazed glass.

The voice simply said, *"What's in the box?"*

James turned around slowly and sitting on the single chair, matching the sofas so well, in an impeccable suit of perfect onyx black that rippled in the sun with a muted but brilliant sheen of emerald green was a man, smiling at him, above his head a swarming halo of houseflies. His grin toothy and wide and full of sinister sincerity. He smiled heavily. A hard smile; a luminous smile of deadly, weird knowledge and creepy, good intention - like he knew a secret he knew you really wanted to know, and he was about to tell you with a salty half story peppering out the details.

"Who?... What?... Just who the bloody fuck are you?" – Was all James could muster by way of reply,

"I'm Lucifer. Firstborn Angel of the Host, King of Hell, Father of Lies."
His smile broadened, and he motioned for James to sit. When he smiled, there were too many teeth in his head, and his eyes burned with an intoxicating edge.
"And, I would like to know..." he smiled broader still, *"What's in the Box?"*
James looked at him, his fingers went to his eyes and rubbed, then to the temples either side of his eyes, and they massaged deep and slow circles into the tender flesh of his skin. He gave a long and burdened sigh of complete, confused retreat.
"The truth?" he half asked, half muttered, quietly, under his breath. His eyes were fixed upon the crown halo of flies that swarmed in a circle above the Lucifer's head. The droning humming like a fridge motor that was about ready to burn out and give up the ghost.

The man in the suit, Lucifer, smiled both broadly and menacingly at James.
He liked this question; it was one of his favourites.
"Always." He replied, keenly.

James looked at the box, heavy on the broken table fragments, and then to Lucifer, then to the insect halo over his unexpected guests head.

"*I haven't a fucking clue,*" and James melted into the sofa, hand over his eyes and rubbing temples with his thumbs.

"And right now... I can't say I give a fuck."

Lucifer looked at the bedraggled mess before him and simply nodded and smiled wider and more deadly than before.

"Gods love a mystery."

And he sat back in his chair and stared at James' nervous, exhausted face.

And he smiled wider.

This was going to be interesting.

* * *

CHAPTER THREE
Childhood,
And Other Disaster

"When you're young, you think everything you do is disposable.
You move from now to now, to crumpling time up in your hands, tossing it away
You're your own speeding car. You think you can get rid of things, and people too -- leave
them behind.
You don't yet know about the habit they have, of coming back

Time in dreams is frozen. You can never get away from where you've been"

- Margaret Atwood - The Blind Assassin

Growing up on an estate, like James had to, you soon find ways of making your own entertainment. Of course James' way was books and cold tea and reading – so completely happy was he when he was alone in his own company he often chuckled that he'd like to grow up and marry himself as he was never happier than by himself.

Even then, James was unhappy with the vastness of outside. His world was four walls and a good library of books borrowed, given and stolen from friends and family and the school library – the index card crudely cut out, or the page it was attached to neatly removed with his elder brother's craft-knife.

He never saw it as theft. Indeed, he was a French resistance fighter, liberating these books from a prison of solitude and confinement, ignorance and tragic loneliness.

These books would live on in splendor and triumph in his collection, not just read once, but multiple times, corners so dog-eared – as all goods books should be – spines so creased it was as if they had been to the ends of the Earth and back and seen adventure and life and experienced travails and journeys that truly deserved its attention and time.

Each book was a memento mori of a time in his life, and each page was a napkin upon which he wiped his mouth on this feast called learning.

The other kids on the estate were not the same. Essentially it was an island surrounded by green-hilled seas, trees were waves upon the vast ocean of nothing that they were placed in the centre of, the estate had roads and hills and cement garages top and bottom, but it was a dot in a vast nothingness of green fields and ploughed land.

A veritable adventure playground for the young minds and adventurous souls of James' peers.

Michael, the gang's de-facto leader, was a cruel mouthed whelp. Lippy, insolent and with a single-minded brutality of instinct, he saw problems as brick walls half finished to be kicked down and laughed at, before laying blame at the feet of others and smiling sweetly and innocently and getting away with murder.

Michael saw nothing wrong with shooting BB Guns from his dad's .22 rifle at cats, geese, birds nests – he did not see it as cruelty, rather youthful naivety.

He owned a bow and arrow that he had made for him by his father. Michael's dad was an engineer at the brick company, a technician of the kilns. He had found a big branch from one of the elms in the field that directly lay adjacent to the houses, and he took it home, stripped it and treated it with preserve, strung it with a tensile fishing wire, thick and tight, and then bent the branch into a near perfect capital D shape. He found some willow branches from the smaller field at the bottom of the estate, again, stripped and treated and cleaned the wood, fashioned some tips from Fimo, he had made supple and pliable with a hairdryer, and then secured using cotton thread, and made blunted and weighted arrows for firing.

In his garden, he had painted and set up a stall with thick-cut paper targets secured between two poles with a small slide hat you could slot the targets in. He drew a box for date and time and divided so you could say how many arrows were fired. A way to keep recorded how well you had gotten on and progressed.

He did all this for his son as his own father had done for him.

On his first attempt using it Michael had missed the target five out of five times. His face a portrait of barely controlled rage and upset, tears welling in his eyes, a dull roar trapped in his throat, it had taken everything for him to not snap the bow and throw it at the target, to scream and tear the stupid target from its mount, to sit and scream and slap at his father for humiliating him so.

His father had taken the bow and fired a single shot, and it went dead centre of the paper target. The arrow had rested dead and triumphant in the bale of hay that rest behind the target.

"It's not a lucky shot, Mike; that was three years of practice and hard work. Sore elbows *and* wrists. That's what you have ahead if you want to do it right, maybe it will be shorter, maybe longer, but you'll get it." Handing the bow back to Michael, he ruffled his son's hair somewhat and returned to his other little projects and toys.

Michael took what had been said on board with quite vicious seriousness. He used the bow every day for an hour burst, steadily trying to learn the mechanics of the tool, the weight and its science. The way it dealt with his grip, the arrow weight, how different ways of holding effected the spring of the line, how different releases of the arrow affected its flight. How the tension was not necessarily the key to its flight or power, instead, sometimes he could use a very gentle grip, a very suddenly pull and release and get just about as much power as he needed, sometimes, more.

He was an expert at the crude, homemade bow and arrow within 12 months.

Lined up across the mantle-piece of Michael's house were trophies from his success at the Swindon Archery Association's competitions and prizegivings. Rosettes and medals were in a cabinet in the corner of the room. Certificates of new skills learned, qualifications passed in his learning of the bow and art of archery. Michael was considered a prodigal, no one cared about his self-imposed discipline with his homemade bow and his blunted arrows and the little range his father had built in their long narrow garden. Little did they know of his rage-filled need to be better than his dad ever was, his desire to have mastered the damned thing to erase the memory of just how awful he was on his first attempt. How those first five arrows haunted and humiliated him in his dreams and every time he pulled back the string.

He was a burning knot of anger at those five dead arrows from so long back.

His leadership of the Estate's gang of kids was reinforced with each competition he won, and each trophy he brought home. His sport being so much more about skill and self-centred solitude and desire than a football win or an athletics medal. He was looked up to by all the other kids – all but James – with a gilded edge of awe and fear and giddy excitement; he was a someone. Someone they could all measure themselves against.

All but James, who did not see a point in measuring oneself against another's standards, and had such a lack of ego, he would laugh if anyone dare accuse him of plagiarism of another.

He was James – plain and simple.

Michael always looked at James like someone had rolled a poisonous snake into a rat's cage, something that was alien and strange and deadly, not because he was particularly a nuisance or a viper, but because he was quiet and detached and seemed to not want to be there with them. From the very earliest days Michael looked at the boys and girls he had around him, the people he climbed trees and kicked footballs and threw rocks with, and he saw James on the fringes, never smiling, never enjoying himself doing the dangerous things that kids were want to do. James always stood several degrees on the outside of every adventure – *present*, for sure – but not "There" - the look of absent boredom always spread across his face like jam on toast.

Michael could not control James, he could never manipulate this boy with his usual scare tactics, his bravery, his naivety in the face of common sense, his smile and his bravado did not impress James, in fact, it seemed to do the opposite. Every time he tried to show off or impress the gang, James would be at the back looking elsewhere, his mind on others things, his heart not interested or involved or giving a damn.

When Michael looked at this awkward, shuffling boy, slightly rounder than the others, not fat, but stocky, like he was wearing clothes that were a size too big on a frame that was broad but not bulky. This kid with his weird walk, like a two-shoe shuffle, a strange waddle somewhere between a man with a dead-leg and a penguin in a rush, Michael saw only one thing: a Usurper - and as such, he was also a possible obstacle, someone who needed to be shown his place. Letting him just go would be counterproductive to being the big "I AM" so Michael saw it as his place and his obligation to teach James some lessons of humility and status.

If he left the gang after, so be it, it would be because Michael had shown him the true hierarchy of life and not because James was his own man and had shown utter apathy toward Michael's illusion of power.

Where would the fun in that be?

Michael wanted to make sure that when he made his power move, to tighten his position amongst the youth of the estate, that it was done right, and it was big enough a statement that he would never have to do anything again.
He was not a cruel child, quite the contrary. He was well regarded in school, his teacher always commenting about his punctuality and his manners, his clean cursive handwriting so neat and well presented, his constant use of P's and Q's and his willingness to do anything when asked, often when not. He never came across as cloying, desperate or fake as the suck-up kids who only wanted extra credit and merits. Indeed his friends – the ones he would admit to being friends with – liked him a great deal. The most trusted of them would look at him as someone who they could rely on always, who would be ready with a hand on the shoulder if a game goes begging or a day becomes stressful, a laugh and a joke never far from his lips, always smiling and seeking new adventures. He was a fiercely loyal boy, always ready to stand up for a good cause and defend. But, circumstance and social environment had forced this lofty elevation of status on him, and he would be damned if he would allow it top be mistreated and used by someone who would never deserve the attention of these loyal subjects.

Such tribal thinking, for someone of such tender years.

Michael wanted nothing more than to keep the kids in a place of understanding, the estate was a small one, it had a very tight and understated power hierarchy, and some of these older kids who would take the younger ones under their wings were harsh, cruel and not to be trusted. All he wanted was to provide a calm before the storm of puberty, but, saying all of this was fine and dandy – deep inside though – when he saw James, and his blanket indifference, his vacant interest, his wandering mind and eyes, always living on some other cloud than the one Michael and the gang had created and decided to sit upon, James made Michael's blood boil, in ways he could never have imagined possible.

This calm, loyal, well-spoken boy was torn away and shredded to tiny fragments, and all that would remain was a husk of anger and unmanageable rage when he looked at James.

He would never be able to explain why.
His hand and eyes and mind were guided by something beyond his ken.
A demon inside his fibre, guiding and pulling strings and riding this poor, otherwise gentle boy into fits of spitting fury.

Michael just knew that when the time came, James would either tow the line, or he would not show his face amongst the kids again.

He knew that a reckoning was coming, and he would be the one that dealt the cards, and let fate decide where they fall.

* * *
- 2 -

On the bed was a body.
A horrible stench filled the room, and the skin of the body was a bruised and ugly shade of purple and brown, contusions and scratches, cuts and marks peppered the skin in a disturbing pattern of repeated abuse.

The room a deep cavernous hole of dark and damp chaos, full of shallow bursts of candlelight and decay, moss grew on the stone like spidery-green grass, a sweet smell of rot and warm tang of mildew was permeating on every surface.
This was a hole that people had forgotten about for a long, long time and which only now had been remembered. There was one door, at the very end of the arched tunnel that made room.
It was an access tunnel converted into a keep or a hideaway or something similar, used now as a makeshift morgue for a body that looked as though it should have been dead sometime sooner than today.

Pock-marked arms were riddled with track marks from needles; blood had dried and caked around each puncture mark. There were various awful fluids dried on the skin, and it had a horrendous sheen of wax that glazed it like it had been dipped into a fine honey and dried in sunlight. An unreal plasticity that made you think of mannequins and dummies, but, this was very much a real arm and it was very much a horror to the eyes.

The body lay covered in a damp sheet of cotton, the cotton had been dipped in oil and dragged over the body within minutes of it being brought in, however, not an hour later, the perfect tint of the cotton, its fine, white shine was now brutally plastered in sores and cancerous, seeping marks where the body had bled out, or leaked foul smelling and vicious looking bodily excreta. Yellow puss stains, red and purple patches of blood both fresh and congealed. The dark mold one would see in a damp bathroom. The sheet that was dipped in a fine lilac and patchouli oil was now a bedraggled, diseased slice of terror – dripping with stains and overwrought by the scent of illness, decay and sickness.

The body was that of the fourth horseman. Pestilence. And he was dead. No one could understand the situation that had lead to Pestilence – Lord of Sickness, Disease and Illness – deteriorating so quickly from his usual radiant darkness and dismay, to being a decaying slab of meat that was making the basement smell of rot and waste and absolute horror.

It has long been said that Pestilence was a byproduct of War, and a friend of Death – a brother of Famine, it rode a steed that was caked in dried blood, and sweetly scented sweat, dripping and oozing a fine sheen of horrendous tar.

However, where War was thriving in this modern world, where missiles could target a man from ten thousand miles away, and death was possible from the passing idle breath of a perfume, why the Lord of Illness had died seemingly a victim of the way he had reaped was a mystery only until he was looked at by Death himself.

Lord Death trudged into the room, his slender frame stooped over so low that he resembled a vulture grazing the desert for bones. His hands were behind his back, one hand held by the other at the wrist, a statesman gesture; his face was a picture of passivity. He never showed signs of exertion; it was effortless and ruthless with Death, the most minimum of effort having the most maximum of results. He walked to the body and pulled the sheet off slowly, uncovering the face of Pestilence.

Pestilence was caught in a mid grimace, his jaw had captured in a teeth-grinding portrait of utter pain, his neck muscles and shoulders, his collarbone and his chest were tensed as if they had been flash-frozen mid-choke, his eyes tightly squeezed shut and crow's feet and frown lines riddled his face, he was clearly in several realms of agony in his last moments and he had died, his light had expired, in mid seizure. His arms were tense all the way to the bicep where they – strangely – went limp and his elbows and forearms were placid and lucid and horrifically scared with the burden of a thousand razors and needle marks.

Death, in his effortless way raised the right arm of Pestilence, and took a deep breath of the skin, pulling the arm as tight toward his nose as he could, his pale, colourless features, blues and bruises on the flesh of Pestilence.

Lord Death knew that it was an evolution to the life of a horseman, having to deal with the changing world, but Pestilence really never stood a chance. Where War had become privatized and franchised in the most minute ways, and his stock was rising, way, way faster than Death had really liked as it was as if his brother was trying to vie for his position as head of the family and board.

Famine had always been guaranteed a good berth as long as bureaucracy was booming, and corporations could not agree just to lose the bonuses and pay the price to feed the world, Pestilence had to deal with a world that was choosing profit and innovation and exploration – privately and through big business – where everyone and their son was attempting, and succeeding, to find cures for all the world's ills.

Cancer, Aids, SARs, Ebola, Influenza - even the common cold. All had been more or less eradicated when cure after cure had been found.

Whether the cure was widely available, or safely under lock and key mattered not, because the mere fact it existed was a knife to Pestilence's heart.

No sooner had he invented a new superbug than the Apes had cured it, mass produced the cure and made massive profits from its creation. Where profit was not possible, war and conflict had taken shape, and from this his red-headed elder brother had grown further in stature and strength – not to mention arrogance. With each new conflict more displaced and starving people were left, and Famine had her day. Blissfully wandering amongst her throng, waving her brittle arms as if conducting some huge orchestra of suffering, when the word around her starved and died en masse from hunger, only then did she feast herself.
Pestilence watched his twin sister gorge herself on the souls of the dying and the famished, and he went hungry as international aid poured in, the food only so basic that it kept Death away, but Famine still clung on, Medicine was in abundance, though, each new corporation using the opportunity to test the after effects of its latest chimera. Each new pill and jab a million bucks or five in free tests and lab rats.

Pestilence felt every administered vaccine, each prescribed and overdosed tablet, his lungs burned from the tincture and potion, his heart wallowed in hungry need from each By-Pass in a clean, sterile hospital, where his bugs and his sickness could not survive.
In the end, Pestilence had died from his own business, only the suffrage had been inverted. His reach always out measuring his grasp, for every ten bugs or diseases he created and flung at the world the apes reacted twenty fold with determination – determination that The Horsemen had no hope of ever matching, lest they upset the cosmic balance – took effect and Pestilence always seemed to end up last and lost, brow-beaten and broken.
The day that smallpox had been eradicated from existence he had wept openly like a child with a scabbed over knee. His last vestiges of beauty, hidden behind the pock-marked skin and yellow,

jaundiced scars, had long since departed and all that remained was this broken and infected thing. This ruined soul of illness.

He struggled on, dragging himself to every council meeting, hacking and coughing and fitting, shaking like a leaf upon the tree caught battered on the edge of some unstoppable and tumultuous hurricane. Then one day, he could come no more. When the cure for cancer was unleashed from a corporate trust-fund, control tested on the most aggressive test subjects, clearing all and any malignancy within a couple of months and tumourless in less than a year – Pestilence decided enough was enough, and died of his own broken and weary flame going out when the thousandth cured Ape had paraded itself in glory for the world to see.

Cancer was cured. Pestilence was dead.

Like the gods, Horsemen could die. Unlike gods, it was relative to the business they were in. Throw enough distractions at a gaggle of God-bothering Apes and soon enough they will forget their deity. One or two may hold faith in higher accord and still pray, but as the age old adage says: "*Man cannot live on bread alone*" – so it was gods could not survive on the fleeting morsels thrown ragged across the table, like a dog begging for scraps.

It required adulation and worship and tribute and constant attention. The Horsemen required their business to be booming, their primary concerns and reasons for being were based upon stocks in trade: War needed conflict, Famine needs disaster and poverty, Pestilence needed unsanitary conditions and germs and death required…

Well, you get it.

Take these things away – as philosophically impossible and physically challenging as this may have been - and the Horsemen had no purpose, no substance and no longer were.

So it was, that every few thousand millennia, the chess game was braced in a delicate and gripping stalemate, where only one or two moves remained before cosmic checkmate.

Gods, Demons, Horsemen – all, convened around a table and set about discussing terms for the end game and last days…

Last days being relative to the time of course... There had been, in reality, LOTS of Last Days. Humanity reset so many times it was beyond the ken of even some gods' minds.

Let's just say, we are an ancient race, and dinosaurs – they were a practical joke that got out of hand.

There would always be other Horsemen, Death knew this. He had seen to over a dozen councils of his kin. Some shared names with siblings long since gone and dead, wiped out by lasting peace and food in abundance, only to be called again – the mantle passed to another willing servant to the Sword, the Scales, the Scepter and the Scythe.

Whatever vice was currently being ridden with graceless aplomb by the humans would vie and parry for the now vacant steed. But Death wanted something more, something different.

Pollution was too transient, and to be honest, a terrible loser – as soon as a new accord was signed he was like a teenager who had been dumped by a girlfriend of five minutes, crying and complaining and just making such a mess.

Global Warming was an unbearable bore, he appeared one day out of the ether, a wandering concept, dusty and sunburnt and dehydrated and parched, salt-cracked lips and sweating sweet lines of crystallized ice, a mess frankly and so awfully self-righteous. Lord Death hated him. War couldn't stand him, and Pestilence would just laugh in his presence, until, of course, he died... No, Death wanted something interesting to turn the favor in his direction; he had grown tired of gods and monsters and Demons and Apes. He was a God, in everything but ego, he walked Deities into the epic cosmic Diaspora and let them stagger into oblivion.

Zeus, Odin, The Roman Pantheon, The Greek Pantheon, more Indian gods than he cared to count, Sumatran, Sumerian, Persian and Celt... Gods had died by his hand on incalculable occasions, always fast and always fleeting – but they died.

Of course, like the Christian/Catholic/Islamic God – Yahweh, Allah, Jehovah – whatever other name he had chosen for himself and circulated amongst the plebian homo sapiens in his charge, some

Gods had learnt to bend the rules. He had created an avatar of himself as a young man, returned that to Earth to live amongst them, and then invented the loop in the rulebook of "RESURRECTION" gods could sometimes return. Odin was knocking on the door thanks to Rock 'n' Roll and comic books…
But it took more than this to have the welcome mat thrown out.

Lord Death knew this was the case with himself. People were getting older and older, death was being assaulted almost daily with stay young beauty treatments, new medical procedures, limb and organ replacement, immortality was a long way off, but time is relative for these creatures – and so what may be a million, million years for us humans would be a flicker of a candle flame for the gods. Lord Death knew his time, War's time and Famine's time was nearly up – and he wanted to play one last game and win.
He wanted the pot for once, not to fold his hand and sit in abject boredom as the Devil and gods gloated.
Just for once, Death wanted to fix the game.

He lay Pestilence's hand down by his side, pulled the sheet off of him, tucked his lank, dirty hair in a neat row behind his brother's ears and lay a single waxen, thin hand with glass-like fingernails an inch or so over his fallen brother's feet, and slowly gestured in a wave over the whole of his body from feet to head. His final gesture was to close the unnaturally blue eyes of Pestilence, and lay a single kiss plucked from Death's own lips to the temple of his brother. The sound was like someone dragging granite over flint, a scraping sparking noise.
From where the shadow of Death's hand had passed the sores and cankers and pustules on Pestilence's skin evaporated into tiny wafts of smoke and nothingness, his skin become a warmer, unblemished tapestry, the tight and muscled flesh underneath was beautiful and pock-free, and his features were strong, angular and edged with a beauty unnatural and unseen in aeons.
Pestilence lay upon this bed looking like the man he had started this world as, a creature of beauty and elegance, leaving this existence as he had came, unsullied by the duty of his role, and unblemished and

free of the burden of his name.

Lord Death muttered a single indecipherable prayer in a language not heard by anyone in ten thousand lifetimes and then he turned and left the room.
As he did, with each stride a light upon the mildewed walls extinguished and died.
The room was silent and empty, obsidian shadows on every plane the room had ceased to exist, and Pestilence was dead, gone and never coming back.
Lord Death had shepherded him into the Diaspora and erased the room from being.

Though he did not cry, he felt a momentary sting of sadness, as he had for his multitude of fallen brethren, every time he had to do this ritual of cleansing and chaperoning into the wide, forever expanse of the never after.
He breathed a silent lungful of repose and opened his eyes wide and alive.

Now, right now, there was work to be done.

* * *
- 3 -

Since the tryst with God in the waterfall, Lilith had been unable to return to the garden where Adam lay. He had barely noticed, of course, his spastic indifference was mainly due to his fascination now with the flowers and plants and grass, stolen away from the animals and their coats and furs by thorns and leaves and the berries and fruits.
Adam was none the wiser about what had transpired between his God and his Woman.
Truth be told, she did think it likely that he would care should it have been fully explained, his attention span was errant and transient, his eyes and his heart always fixed on something else than what it should

be, his life that of a wandering shell of curiosity and tactless fondling.

God too had disappeared, his warmth was absent from her life, instead, she felt the coldness of his shadow as he turned his back on her in displeasure and distrust, in pitiful anger at his own mistake and folly, blaming her even as he tried to absolve himself of any responsibility for his sin. Making her wallow in her accused betrayal of his love and life and bask in her somber, solitary pain.

Pain being what she had now, a beautiful and exquisite pain so soon after the event.
Her belly swelled and groaned with the fruit of their labour.
Her pregnant stomach now full of a new kind of life, hitherto unknown in creation.

God was absent, but, from his vantage point – in his way, greedy with curious need – he was watching, whatever was about to occur, he was part of it, he wanted to have it, but he would not help and he would not allow himself to be become victim to her power and witchcraft again. Enjoying her beautiful and deadly elegance, even now, in such a new form and shape – from a distance, God smiled and silently allowed the what and wherefore to unfold in front of him. His chest beat rampantly with giddy curiosity.

Lilith had found the farthest edge of the coast at the Eastern-most point of the garden. The tide of the Eastern Ocean lapping deliriously at the white-gold of the sandy beach.
Her swollen, sore belly was full and alive, a convulsive need pushed from her and a squeal of intense pain, pleasurable to her now electrically charged, nerve endings – but pain, nonetheless – flowed into pins and needles through her legs and spine.
She collapsed upon the water edge; the tide unending lapped the toes on her feet, and her white hair ran in ringlets of sweaty heaps about her face, framing her beauty. She pushed again and heard the bones of her hips give a creak and crack.
A damp, sudden wetness flushed from her, running warmly down her

legs, the clear fresh water now infused with a salty essence of blood and sweat. She grit her teeth as she felt the convulsion take her once again.

The breaching had begun.

There was already an unfair amount of blood, the strain and stretch of the skin on her stomach, swollen from the growing in her womb was dancing a quivery conveyance of life. Sweat trickled down her skin, pooling by her buttocks as she lay, legs apart, facing the ocean, to which she had decided to honour with her offering.

Lilith had decided this was how she would birth out the growing beautiful monstrosity in her belly, this Nephilim of God and woman and nature, born of lust and magic and malice.

She bore down, and more blood came, her teeth were sore from clenching, the sound like porcelain cracking, her face red from the effort, her eyes welling tears she forced her way through with sheer bloody mindedness.

The swell of her belly shifting and moving and writhing, her insides alive with hands and feet kicking and pushing. The barrier of her skin now a sheath which many hands imprinted upon from inside out.

She let out a tiny whimper, barely audible except to the winds that stroked and soothed poor green infant Eden. Earth was a young creature then, barely more than a beautiful garden, fringed by a vast, barren desert and the monolithic, lifeless plain. The west of the plain – far away on the horizon – stood the shimmer of Zeus's enormous mountains.

Lilith had wandered the entirety of this green haven, had grown bored within the first year or so, She would stare over the plain so vast and empty and inviting, so full of potential and so overwhelmingly unfulfilled. She would fantasize about conquering it and running away, herself alone in this vast playground of nothing and find a home that would be hers and hers alone.

This tiny slither of garden was not hers, it never would be. God had not spoken or seen her since the encounter in the waterfall, he would not answer her prayers, he would not listen to her cries for him, she could feel her worship dull and die upon no reception.

A radio-wave floating around a gulf of vast forever, never listened
too.
A dead broadcast.

Lilith looked out as the sun started its slow rise in the
distance, its corona bursting out of the ocean and a golden, blood-red
halo slowly set fire to the water and rose in stages toward to sky. The
beauty unbound, a bursting of colour and warmth and light from the
darkness of the cold blue water's edge. Lilith smiled then, a faint
smile, but it was there – God saw it – from his peak high above, and
he gave a groan of absent anger.
How dare she smile through this, how dare she enjoy this moment.
His fist clenched hard and taut, the muscles in his arm tight and
golden.
He carried on observing, nary another sound from his lips escaped.

She bore down again, another crack and groan from her pelvis
and a fleeting burst of what seemed to be naught more than light
came from her body. A shaft of unnatural whiteness momentarily set
free from her belly, the contraction lasted seconds, the light emanated
then was as quickly gone. Another push and another groan and the
light shone again, answering the pulse and wave of heat from the
dawning sun, she bore down again, a gasp of pain and an
exasperation of shocking agony, the tears were no longer held back
as she let them go, the smile giving way to a shocked expression of
utter anguish, her mouth fell from a kind and insolent V of a smile to
the surprise of an O ringed with pain and discomfort, eyes squeezed
tightly shut and red with the effort and exertions. God watched, he
now smiled at this turn in events, the pain summoning a smile of
sprite-like cruelty from his mouth. His fist loosened and he silently
stood sentinel watching as the salt from her eyes mingled with the
salt from her sweat, pooling in her back, mixing into the water of the
tide and as the sun popped out from the edge of the end of the world -
Lilith gave birth.
A gush of energy erupting from her bruised and torn flesh,
blood and water and life meeting a lapping ocean tide and becoming
one into a frothy soup of red sweat and red foam and blood and life.

The baby was here, the first baby.

God took two steps forward from his perch, and held his hand over his eyes, a visor from the now rising sun and a smile as broad as any in creation's history came across his face.
The child was a boy. His son.
The first of the Host.

Lay on the sandy beach, quite beautiful in his majesty was Lucifer.
The Morningstar Born.

* * *
- 4 -

The elbow had planted harsh and blunt into her back.
At first, as is the way of these things, pain was almost utterly conspicuous in its absence, more a trifling annoyance buzzed around Kay's head, even as she was toppling head first into the pole, ricocheting off and falling unconscious, headfirst, swooning into the cold embrace of the water in the pedalo pond. Even as her conscious mind was undone and lay out to rest by the impact of the bar, and even as the blood started pouring from her wound, a deep gash above her eyebrow now faceting claret at an alarming rate. Even as all this was happening pain was far away. All there was for her to feel was a bursting, fleeting vein of annoyance at having been so rudely dispatched.
The hooded boy was running at a rate of knots, his knife thrown into the adjacent pond as he stomped the curbs and walkway of the park, the gesture an afterthought and a reminder of the horrific moment of no control and panic.
Indeed, he had not intended to kill the man; he had barely been able to stop the attack on himself and could not even recall how his knife had made its way into the situation.
Such a petty misunderstanding, such an avoidable tragedy piled on top of such wanton mistake and misery. Some horrendous cog, destiny making each second a part of some grander machination he

was now certain would ruin his life.

The hooded boy ran.

He had not seen Kay, indeed, for the fraction of the second it took for her to take the step back from the pond into his path, he had turned his head and looked over his shoulder to see if the feeling he was being followed was correct or a paranoid delusion of emotion haunting him and spurring him into his escape.

He turned back and narrowly avoided the gaggle of runners making their way up the hill.

In the instant between this and turning his head, the connection with the woman was missed almost entirely.

The two people, who had never before met, impacting as both lives cruelly smashed headlong into each other, a car-crash of things entirely out of their hands to control, the incident that lead to this fateful meeting was simply a power play in a game of chess being played by Love and Fate, a gambit that will lead to one of two eventualities. Neither force cares or remembers which is theirs, Cogs they are of nothing more than Destiny – another force to which there is no origin but many questions.

As her head impacted with the pole, the universe slowed down to allow the innumerable variables to be calculated. The man on the bandstand watching the day pass slowly, waiting for his call – important and life-changing.

The phone he had been sitting and watching on the bandstand, waiting to ring.

Even as the man ran toward the bridge, and the girl fell headlong into the water, his phone chose that precise moment to ring.

A whining tone, piercing the air. But one lost on the breeze amid the frantic circumstance all around them.

The boy with the knife, a knife he had bought years before for a camping trip he had planned with friends, a Swiss Army copy bought from a second-hand market in the town. Once owned by a soldier who also used it to kill a man, its blade seeped in murder and history, drinking up the blood of innocents and living on in an

100

unknown spiral of never decreasing violence. A knife he could have sworn he had lost months previously.

The girl at the park for the anniversary of her Great Grandmother's death – the park being where she would go every afternoon from school on her Great Grandmother's birthday, she was 78 when she passed away a little way from here in the shade of the Cedar trees that line the riverbank, her heart giving out as the sun lit up the gaps between the branches, and the leaves showered light through the canopy.
Her birthday also the day she departed from this world, her Great Granddaughter there to hold her hand as ambulance men carried her away on a stretcher, covering her face as the light simply went out of her eyes.
Chaos sometimes seems the exact opposite of its nature when slowed down, so many strands all connected, so many threads interwoven into the fabric of the story – order hiding behind every random outburst, the whole canvas seeming to become clear as a giant, cosmic, quantum equation plays out to the beat of its own unique and fun-filled drum.
She was unconscious within a fraction of a second of the impact, blood was pouring in less time than that. Thick globules of viscous blood cartwheeling off into the fabric of her dress top and the grass, Kay tumbled rather balletically into the water, submerged for all of ten seconds before hands were grabbing her and pulling her out, dragging her – with a certain amount of care; of gentleness onto the bank of the pedalo pond. Warm, sweet lips over hers as unknown breath flowed into her, sharing life into her lungs. She can remember nothing of the day, save for the taste of cherry on her tongue.
Cherries that the man on the bandstand had been eating from a brown paper bag bought the day before at the self-same market as the knife was purchased at those years ago. Two stalls down from the other, the paths and connective tissue drawing another line in its monstrous tapestry of dense fate.

Kay had, until that moment, always hated cherries.
She thought to herself in the darkness, a barely active, barely audible

whisper telling her that some things change and that these changes
were good for life.

The taste of cherries all she could fixate upon in the darkness... The
dim light at the end of the deep corridor she seemed to be stood in
beckoning and welcoming – but the pull of the man whose lips tasted
like cherries was too much a draw for her to stay, so her attention
was on this and the slowly lumbering vision of the park, and the
sunlight and green trees and...

Breathe.

Her chest moved slowly up and down, and her hands gripped the
grass, blades between her fingers, and the feeling of burning inside
her lungs, a banging in her temple, throb, throb, throbbing away.

A voice was calmly but forcefully commanding the throng around
them, his voice croaked and dried. But no less in control.
"Call a fucking ambulance! Somebody get some help... Quickly!"

Lazily, her eyes opened, and the blurry image of a man came
into view, He leaned in, one warm hand on her cheek, and another on
her chest, holding her gently, his features came into focus surely, and
her perfect blue eyes grabbed onto his brown eyes, hidden behind
thin-rimmed glasses and she saw his lips move but heard no words or
sounds, the knock on her head had dazed her so, but she could see
what he was saying as clear as if it were whispered into her ear.

"My name is James." He said. His hand on her face, a gentle circle
being drawn by the thumb on her cheek, a pleasing and thoughtful
gesture that made Kay's heart flutter momentarily despite the pain.
"I'm going to make sure you are ok."
And she forced a gentle, beautiful, meaningful smile at him, which
he caught and returned.
And she passed out, his hand still warm against her cheek.

James for his part stayed with her until the ambulance came.
Staunching the blood on her forehead with his scarf. The sticky,
syrupy feel of the blood slowly congealing into a gelatinous solidity.

The scarf stuck now to the woman's head.

He had barely had time to register what was happening before he had bound off the bandstand to the pedalo pond's edge. There was a faint smear of blood on the hand rail where the woman had struck her head, he held his hand on the wound on the forehead, gently applying pressure, his other hand on her cheek, a warm, faintly tanned cheek, so welcoming and inviting.

It balanced delicately against his hand, as though sleeping, cuddled against his soft hands.

He had to shake his head back to the here and now to ignore how inviting it felt.

"Where the hell is the ambulance?" He shouted to no one in particular.

A lady jogged back over and waved her mobile at him, a bulky and ugly plastic thing, her face was grey and sallow. Lacking any trace of life.

"It's on the way, there is one up there on the hill in the market car park, but it's for someone else – apparently someone has been stabbed." She waved a hand behind her toward the walkway that cut through the hedgerows into the back entrance of the market, where the top level of the multi-storey car park met the street.

James gave a glance over his shoulder, at the place her hand pointed to, and on the top of the hill through the hedgerow he could see a commotion, and the blue lights of an ambulance and a police car arriving.

Thank God this was a small town, or the response could be hours.

He looked down at the pathway that ran parallel to the bandstand and ponds, winding down toward the river and through the meadows toward the old bridge.

Glimpses came to him of the boy, running, colliding, spinning and almost losing his footing into the pond himself. Panic stricken and sweating. His hood lending a low shadow on his face.

How he had not seen the woman, and the collision being one of those inexplicable moments of chance, both his and her world's colliding in perfect, chaotic synchronicity.

Two lives melting into one for a fraction of a second, her life and history imprinted on his future, her future so indelible in his present. The head hitting the handrail, the arch of blood, his hands reaching and throwing something, it landing… somewhere… James tried to picture the scene and piece the fragments of the moment together in some semblance of sense and continuity.

He raised his hand from the woman's cheek and pointed toward the bush that grew alongside the pond and that circled the playground – and he clicked his fingers at it, the woman who had called the ambulance looked at him in curious wonder, her face still so grey and lost, her eyes imploring him to use words rather than these Cro-Magnon gestures.

"In the fucking bush, look in the fucking bush – Whoever did this also did that!" He threw - his arm from the bush to the top of the hill. "He threw something over there, I don't know what, but go look – and don't touch, whatever it is, just look, and then get someone from up there down here and do it fucking now."

The woman looked at James, at Kay, at the bush and then behind her at the hill.

James clicked his fingers two more times and barked a solitary "OI!" She snapped to bright, alert wakefulness and did as she was commanded. James' hand returned to the cheek, to the safety and warmth of her skin, and she nestled against him and his touch.

"God." He thought.

Her eyes now open and a flush of life returning to her cheeks, her eyes focusing slowly, the colour suddenly coming to bright clarity. He stared at her, for the first time realizing just how real she was, how feminine, and he swallowed hard on his nerves and his panic, and looked at the real Kay, not the victim that he had rescued almost on impulse, his brain and muscles were in control; however, now his heart was driving and as he looked at her he realized one thing and one thing only.

"She is so, so beautiful."

- 5 -

Blood lined the entire shoreline. Frothing and lapping at the bank of the beach, a deep mottled crimson, dying the beachhead itself a pink cerise, each lap and swing of the tide in and out brought a new wash of pink.
The air was loud with the sound of crying, as the babies were nestled and placed in the grass that jutted from the top of the slip that led to the water.
Lay amongst the reeds and long grass were the first of the host, the eight children that would become the Archangel.
Gabriel, Michael, Raphael, Uriel, Raguel, Remiel and Saraquiel.
Sat by them, her face raw and puffy, her eyes red-ringed and blackened by the exertion, her hands and fingernails sullied from blood and sand where she tore the umbilical from her body with a retching tear, hair stained red and pink from the water and the labour, was Lilith, in her arms, was Lucifer. Silent, content, his eyes open even now fixated upon the mother and his mouth around her teat, suckling and taking in the life.
Each pucker of his lips brought a flush to Lilith's face that pulsed like a flux of energy throughout her skin.

She looked over her children and smiled a weary, longing smile, drinking in their beauty and their smell. Even now she knew her time with them would be short, and she glared at them burning the sight of each child into her retinas, onto the front of her mind.
Sweat still bubbled on her brow and left its mark in streams down her dirty face. Lines of salt in amongst the sand and brine. Lucifer suckled and stared, his fine blonde hair a wisp atop his head.
The other children gurgled and huffed fat and contented in the grass.
Lilith had no idea how she had managed to survive the exertion, the pain, the inexplicable power that flushed from her and her loins, now so raw and savaged by this unnatural birth.

Her legs were red with the effort, her feet stained as badly as her hands, with red and black, the sand and the blood encrusted on her skin. Painting a picture of the torture she endured.

God was behind her. The fold of the space between his perch on the mountaintop - from where he had watched and witnessed, smiling broader with each push and crack of her hips, the gush of her blood upon the oceans, that gluttonously swallowed her life and swelled in size with the offering – and the beach itself, where he now stood touched momentarily, and he was in one place, then both then the other all in a blink of an eye. Dimensions of space dancing and dallying with each other in a microcosm then just as soon parting company in different directions. Order and nature restored.
He smiled at her, the waft of dimensions touching as he suddenly appeared there gave off a stench of burning cotton and paper, a wisp of ash and fire, just as soon gone as it appeared.

"These are our children?"
Lilith nodded, gently, her head rested down on her chest. Her eyes welled with sad understanding.
"This is unexpected. I did not foresee you surviving… I thought the children would have ended in your womb and that you would have been taken by chance, I was wrong.
I have never experienced surprise at the hands of another before – so for this I should thank you, Witch."
Lilith raised her head at this, looking at Lucifer and at his golden, radiant beauty in her arms. His perfect pink mouth circling the dark of her nipple and feeding on her energy and love.
"*Witch?*" she whispered accusatorily.
"How can you call me this when you made me what I am?"
Yahweh looked at her, and his faint smile betrayed the cruel inflection of his thoughts,
He sneered at her, stared at the children. Then back at Lilith, who had shifted in her seat, and was slowly rising. As she did Yahweh threw out his hand, and she and the child flew to him and with a sound of painful, sickening surprise, as soon as she was on her feet she was in his hand, his grip on her throat tight and taut, his fingers deepening

106

into her windpipe.

His free hand stroking the forehead of the baby, which loosened its mouth from her breast and fixed the golden-skinned God with a look in brown and orange unblinking eyes, his nose turned up, and a faint line of a wail painted delicate and gentle on his mouth.

Lucifer stared at his father, and the father stared back – and there was hatred in both their eyes.

"I call you as I see you, Witch. You betrayer of my love, of my light, glutton of my senses."

His fingers squeezed harder into her neck, leaving bruises and welt of red in the skin beneath of his fingers.

Lilith's eyes were wide, her breath caught panicked and tight, trapped in her windpipe, now squeezed shut by God. Her beautiful eyes now startled and wide with shock, pain and longing for a gulp of the fresh ocean air. Her lank, blood-stained hair on her face in strands of matted imperfection.

"You are not of my hand. You are some broken half thing, a mistake. One of the few I have made since I woke on that plain of nothing and began work on this Eden. I do not know what you were made from that made you less of me and more of something else, but I will not be tempted by your witchery, your unnatural sensuality again. Never again.

I curse you, Witch, to a life of exile away from this Eden, to the plain you so wantonly covet.

You are free to reign on the nothingness that is beyond the garden's wall, but you are alone, and you are damned. You shall not step foot in this paradise again, you will not take a single step back from whence you came."

He still held her out, in his other hand, he took the baby and held it out from him and looked at them and then Lilith.

"Maybe I should just end these whelps here and now, smash their heads against the rocks and free them from a lifetime of being bastards in this world… Kill them and then you, so you can see what I do with mistakes before wiping out my biggest? Hmm?"

Lilith's eye opened in shock and terror; she knew he was capable of it. This God after all was a just but angry God, he would do it to prove a point and would be convinced it was the right thing to do, not batting an eyelid at the blood on his hands.

She choked on the hand squeezing tighter on her throat, and managed a gasped and rasping two words.

"P... Please. Don't..."

Yahweh pulled her close and regarded her bluing lips, her bloodshot eyes, the reddish and purple colour of her cheeks, he looked down at the baby Lucifer, still staring back with hateful intention.

"You love them?" He whispered, spitting the words slowly and with menace.

Lilith struggled a nod from her choke.

"Then maybe I won't. Maybe, there is a better way to punish you." He pulled her closer still until his mouth was resting tightly against her ear, and his words were audible only to the woman, teetering on the edge of unconsciousness.

"These children are mine, and I will see that they are never again subjected to your half-nature again... They will know nothing of you, I will never speak of your name again, there will be no word of you on their lips. No thought of you in their minds. It will be as though you never even existed. You are now no more a mother than you are my daughter, you will remain forever incarnate as the first lie in my garden and the most vilest of mistakes."

His hand dropped from her neck; she had been an inch or three above the ground in his effortless grip, and she fell hard, her ankle twisting as she hit the beach.

With Lucifer in Yahweh's arms, the other children were floating around him, suspended upon a golden halo that stretched out of God-like tendrils of light, their faces bright and warm and happy, basking in the nourishing light and life.

Lucifer was smaller than the rest, though he was the firstborn; he was clearly the runt of the litter, his skin a fine white and his hair a sharp, golden blonde, the colour of the mid-day sun.

Lilith looked at them, from her collapsed heap on the floor. She had no energy to argue, no power to fight; it was an effort to find simply a rasp of breath from her throat that was now torn in a sharp and exquisite burst of burning pain.

She sobbed hard, and with her dirty hand, she wiped away a streak of tears.

"I am your daughter." Is all she managed to spit out.

God clenched his fist again and the girl once again, like a ragdoll on a rope, flew toward his grip, he raised his hand out, and with the golden halo that enveloped the children following his reach, he stroked the air around Lilith's face, like a painter, or a sculptor, finding the shape in the mass of clay, or the picture in the canvas. God smiled a half smile, absently his tongue darted out and licked his lips, as he closed his fist, and Lilith now was suspended again, an inch or two from God's face.

She gasped and swallowed hard for air, trying hard to shield away from the furious light and heat from Yahweh's gaze.

He leaned into her, her ear mere centimeters from his mouth, and he whispered into it in a quiet, calm tone.

"Not anymore. Harlot."

She allowed the tears she had been attempting to hold back to flow now, harsh and heavy, down her face, her reddened eyes now so beautiful and delicate and heartbreaking.

God held his hand out in a clenched and tight, angry fist still – and then with a half-turn, a mere gesture of his fist opening to an wide open fingered palm, the space around Lilith shifted and then folded, she flew backward as though pulled by some epic invisible inertia – and the space in the air opened and she was taken, from this place to the place beyond the wall.

As the space folded back in, and she slumped heavy on the ground, ragged and broken, the final thing she saw was the sharp, fire tainted eyes of Lucifer, her firstborn, staring at her as she faded into the obscurity and oblivion on nothing.

Now exiled to the Plain.

Leaving God with the children and the open ocean and the morning sun.

He slowly walked into the waters, the halo still suspending the children around him, Lucifer still in his arms, and as he took small, steady steps into the water, the space around him folded and opened as well, then he too was gone. Babies, halo and all.

The landscape was once again quiet, lonely and serene.
Nothing remained, but the gentle sound of water lapping the cerise pink beach.
Empty once again of life.
Nothing but salt and soil.

* * *

- 6 -

   "All I am saying is that it is one thing to go there with our armour on and play the game, but the chips stacked as they are we are not ready to take on the Thrones."
The voice was a weak rasp; it rattled around inside the throat of the woman who spoke.
A frail, febrile arm was lay in front of her on a rich, oak wood table, its surface was a deep obsidian black with gilded silver detailing, it was a foot or two thick, and resting on a central pivot stand that was an unblemished, untreated oak tree stump.
She raised her hand once more; a thin, delicate porcelain finger raised to the sky, and she ran circles in the air.
"The fact he cannot hear us – that none of them can hear us – means nothing. He has slowly been losing his mind as the aeons roll on, and each generation of these apes he allows to breed dwindles his sanity further and further. Drunk on idolatry and confused worship, he has become a danger to us all, the great and good and God alike. This is a fool's errand you set us upon Brother, and one we will not see through."
She rested her hand again.
Her eyes wandered across the table to the vacant chair that lay dormant to her right "Have we not lost enough?"
The frosty silence lingered like a charge of electricity on the air. A simple buzz of nothing, anticipation and expectation joining in a frenzy of patient wonder.

Lord Death spoke then.

"We have lost nothing that can not be replaced." He gazed a stiff-necked half glance at the empty chair where so recently Lord Pestilence sat.

"As much as I mourn my brother alongside you, forget not I saw this coming a billion, billion years before you can begin to imagine. I was here at his coming, and I walked him to his ending, silent and borne heavy on my shoulders. And I mourn him just as you do, but rest assured, if he is gone, it is for a higher purpose. How lucky you are that these creatures are like as are – or it could have been you, not he, Lady Famine."

The thin lady could not look at him, instead, her long fingers picked at the silver on the table, brittle nails tapping the inset on the wood, the faintest pooling of blood behind the nails, her flesh weak and empty and lacking in any semblance of life, the voice she made breathing like a can of something collecting dust and kicking around in the wind.

She instead looked to her left, and the red armoured, bearded face of War stared back at her. His deep, auburn brown eyes ringed with fiery amber and red. His beard so big and angry and ginger. Flecked with patches and dashes of white.

His face a creased forehead grimace of attention, he did not move, just stared.

"Mort is right. We have to do this. Too long we have sat as lapdogs to the game, forever the middlemen between the black and white, and existing as a grey-clad indifference. How many of our brothers and sisters must we bury until we do something to protect our own existence?"

Famine shook her head, each move a creaky jointed horror, the movement looked like she would twist her own thin neck in two, and the head would fall and shatter into a dusty demise on the solid wood of the table.

"His proposal is sound - the idea is a good one. There are no rules being broken, this is merely a new move for us and one which will provoke for sure, but better we are honest in our intentions than hide behind cowardly acts.

"Gods forbid that we would upset your sense of duty and honour,

111

Brother." Famine laughed.

"I am outnumbered then. Would that Pestilence was here…"

"PESTILENCE IS DEAD," Lord Death said, his voice booming, his hands hard and sharp on the table top, leaving indented marks of his balled fist in the veneer.

He stood, and walked around the table, stopping at Pestilence's vacant throne.

"The end of days comes, and we go as we are beckoned, and we do our duty, and this world is wiped clean like a table being shed of the leftovers, and the apes are wiped out by whatever endgame the gods and monsters decide is vogue, and we start again.

The books and myths and legends are written, and the history of the place is put back to zero, and we start again and again and again.

I have walked so many gods, so many Princes and Kings and heroes to the place beyond this place. The beckoning darkness."

He rubbed the wood of the throne between his slender and strong fingers.

"I have seen the existence we are denied and the world beyond this, and I have witnessed the death of us all, myself included, and I have learned to laugh and live and like what I have in store for myself."

Famine looked at War, and War transfixed on Death, simply smiled a wider grin.

"Why? Why do we need to settle for this? All in the name of a broken, aged, useless accord, borne from the lips of a senile and demented gods? One of which, let us not forget, who has cheated his way to these lofty heights of monopoly, who has seen to the end of religions and deities wide and far, who has broken almost every promise Eden and creation allowed.

Why do we kowtow to this despot?

I say no longer."

His hands clenched the throne and pulled hard.

The wood gave and with a gesture he turned and threw the heavy chair to the wall.

It ruptured and shattered and crumbled to dust.

Nothing left but a fine silver mound of powder.

"I was here before THEY came, and I will be here long after THEY leave. I gave him his name!"

He did not gasp, or breathe heavily, his actions and words were not tainted with any exerted effort and tiredness, his strength was scarily incomprehensible.

Indeed, he was Death, beyond mere constrictions like strength or pain or effort his existence was guaranteed and was profound, for everything in this universe and the next died, and as this was true, so was the Lord in Black.

No, his anger was merely due to the fact he had grown weary of the games gods played, and his constant towing of the line...

He was beyond the reach and touch of gods – and though he never wanted to end the reign of Man – he had no intention of this folly...

He was very bored of the reign of gods.

The council of four was forever impartial and worked to clean the slate while the children bickered and fought and squabbled over the morsels.

Lord Death wanted the take the seat at the head of the table now and wanted to be listened to rather than be dictated to.

It was no longer enough to exist. He wanted to live.

"War. What do you say?"

The bearded giant stood. He walked round the table, circling counter-clockwise, and stopped when he reached his brother in black.

"The monkeys guarantee my place by your side. And we both know it will continue regardless of God or belief. Why do I need to pretend that the book and scripture are all that keep me in business? As long as blood runs in their veins, I am guaranteed a seat at this table. So what need do we have for cheats, liars and children? I am your red right hand, as ever as always, brother. My Sword is yours as it ever was."

He offered his massive hand to the dark-cloaked man, who took it and gently covered it with his other hand, and the two gave a curt and fancy bow to the other.

Death's hands were tiny when encompassed in War's giant, red paws.

Famine stood, slowly, and lay her hands on the table to hold her balance, she wheezed and she coughed, weakly, though there was clearly muscle beneath the skin, taut and strong, it was hidden and unused beneath skin baggy and worn and grey.

"My time will come, I am aware of this. But while I am here, for our brother, who has fallen, I offer my scales."

She bowed her head in courtesy and service

"But, we have always been four. And four is how we will remain. So... We need another. You know this."

Lord Death smiled, his pale, almost albino skin was like a fine Corinthian leather, so beautiful and so delicate, but so deadly. Like pallid wax. He nodded to his sister, and he sighed in agreement.

"And therein lies my gambit."

He walked to the window of the chamber and looked out over the plain, that made their tiny kingdom of creation.

"I think it is time we upped our stake in this creation, and made it clear and apparent we are not slaves to any god."

And he laid out to the two horsemen exactly what he intended to do. They listened, silently, their eyes alive with wonder and attention. Lord Death's mouth a dry line of amusement, as he realised his plan was a good one.

And his siblings agreed, heart, body and mind.

* * *

- 7 -

It had felt like she had walked for weeks.

Sore, cracked, bloody feet trudged on across the sand, shots of constant pain jolting through every part of her skin.

In truth, she had been trekking for days, deeper into the plain, dead and desolate and lacking in anything resembling life.

The compulsion to walk forced upon her by the hand and will of God, his vengeful and violent streak emerging. Having woken in the dust, her body aflame with agony and ache, her stomach swollen with the final pangs of her unexpected labour and the turmoil of birthing eight children she had gestated in a matter of days. Her body

114

a ravaged and wrecked vessel, cracked and lined with every tumultuous trial she had experience and endured these last few days. She wanted this plain; she knew this, and she welcomed the solitary existence where she could finally breathe unperturbed by the feeling of being watched and being studied. But, she had wished it on her owned terms, not expelled from God's grace and presence with force and torn from the children she had birthed not days before.

The eight beautiful creatures who crawled from her belly.

Golden and radiant.

She had woken with her face buried in the dust, the wall of the garden behind her, two or three miles back, and when she had tried to walk toward it, a force had stopped her, like a barrier of air cushioned her back when she tried to walk backwards toward Eden's confines. She could gain no ground, nor step one foot back the way she had been sent.

Instead, the cushion of air allowed her to walk only due west from the garden and no other direction. West, toward the mountains, across the barren, boiling plain.

So, that is what she did. She walked, and she walked.

Still she walked, the feeling was something akin to a constant trudge over hot coals, a searing and intense heat, discomfort and pain carved deep inside her legs.

Lilith walked.

The plain was a vast panorama of nothing, lacking all and any feature or character, but for the mountains that levelled out on the horizon that never seemed to be any closer. This was a vast void. One would find nothing unless one were looking for a nihilistic emptiness. The desert was an opaque and colourless hue of grey sand, no life grew there, a barren and haunted void of anything good or worthy.

A blank canvas of terror, one which Lilith had always pondered and wanted to carve into her own image with her own good hands.

Lilith was the first life to set foot on its heathen soil.

Even gods had not stood here.

The walk was slow and arduous, the heat bore down in ways that violated nature and reason, her breath was laboured and her steps unsure, and she lacked anything that would seem like confidence, instead, her steps were autonomous, each a mechanical process dictated by the feeling of certainty this was the only thing she could do, droplets of blood still came from her, the birth of the host had ripped her and torn her in ways that made her step in a shallow and unsteady hobble.

The whole time she did nothing but keep her eyes on the ever expanding horizon and hold her belly and the final pangs of the birth she had held back.

Lilith walked.

The horizon seemed endless. Vast, uncompromising and taunting, but she refused to look back – this she could do – but, to be able to look back and not step back, this was too cruel a punishment. Regardless how far she was from the garden, any attempt at taking a step back the way she came was met with the same cushion of air, and the same sense of being shepherded to her death, alone and quietly in the vast depths of forever.

For that was what the plain was. Forever.

Her eyes fixed the entire time on that in front of her, a future, whatever it may be, a new beginning, her own life now in her own control, mostly, but for the toying, hands in her back goading her forward.

Her belly ached and groaned, her arms cradled and pawed gently over the soft flesh that was still sore and delicate from her violent and exhausting birthing.

The skin sagging and lined with red reminders of the stretched belly she so recently had. The colour on her stomach now a numb, lifeless, grey hue, like ash had been rubbed into the skin. The pink of her skin so faint and hidden you would never have believed it had ever been there.

Her every cell glowed with pain and intense discomfort.

But still she walked.

Blood slowly trickled down her thigh and mingled with the sweat she seemed to exude, it dropped in thick splashes from her to the ground where she did not cast them a second thought, her eyes fixed straight ahead, not sure what she was looking for but trusting entirely when it was upon her she would know.
She held her belly and staggered forward, onward, progressing slowly but surely toward the place only she could understand, her eyes fixed and intent on a point somewhere ahead where she knew she had to finish her journey.

God, of course, could see all of this, and though he had power enough to keep the cushion pressing her forward even he knew he was as powerless to stop whatever was to happen out in the plain as Lilith was.
He sat cross-legged on the high mountaintop and he meditated on the barren, dead dustbowl that bridged his Garden to the lands of the Western gods his eyes like a hawk, seeing all that was happening, a keen vision of the walk Lilith continued to make. Not stopping for days, not resting, her relentless march toward whatever was ahead of her waiting.
His garden Eden was all he had created, the plain was unclaimed, and had never interested him until now, though it was bordering his domain, he had thought small and dealt with the material that was already there – cliffs that were raised plateaus of the earth, like that which overlooked the lagoons. The forests and the fields.
The plain was just empty, desolate, scorched – some curiosity he would get to if he had time. An inheritance of space from a committee of gods – one he had yet to develop or build upon, a no man's land bordering his land with the Mountains of Zeus.

And maybe he was hasty in throwing her to the vast unknown ground, Maybe he was responsible for everything that was happening. But, he was curious as well and so he allowed it to unfold

117

just to see what would occur.

His eyes were red from tears; he cried for a mixture of reasons. Firstly because he knew he was responsible for everything that was about to happen and being omniscient and omnipresent to a certain extent he could read the cascade of cause and effect and see an endgame that he was powerless to stop. Secondly, he had loved her deeply and what had happened to her was neither expected nor something he would have ever predicted, the nature in her had taken his breath away and left him cold with a sense of distinct loneliness. He was, for the first time, utterly powerless and not in control by something – someone - a feeling he was unhappy with and which left him feeling angry, full of rage. The first bitter cracks in Yahweh's veneer.

If nothing more his own nature of spiralling between poles of emotion continued, he was not yet a merciful and forgiving Deity, instead, he was naïve and immature and power had given him no control of his own self.

He watched Lilith stagger and lunge toward her fate and as she did he was mocked with every step once again by Nature and her wily, uncompromising ways.

Gaia was also watching, from her vantage at the plateau of the mountains to the west, an arm thrown around her by Zeus, God of the Westlands, Gaia's kin.

Gaia cried; silently wept tears running down her cheek, as she watched her first daughter continue her slow, pain-soaked lumbering ever west.

Every step Lilith took she bled a little more. Her arms tightened that bit harder, and her stomach throbbed with more frequent discomfort.

If she had of looked back - which her mind had demanded she never do, regardless of it being a choice she could make, even with the shadow and the gentle push of the cushion constantly on her heel - she would have seen what magnificent power she had been imbibed with.

Not only had she given birth to an entire host, each one golden and carved as if from marble, perfect and pure and full with incredible faith and pathos. Eight shining Archangels full of heavenly power, grace and spirit. But, each drip of blood she had lost with every step she had taken on the barren and dead plain had sprung alive with vigour and colour and life in her footsteps.

Flowers and grass and brilliance burst from every mark laid in the dust, and each drop of blood and sweat that had fallen from her broken body had borne fruit and trees and saplings. An entire world was being created in her wake.

Lilith walked on.

Oblivious to the brilliance of her wish being fulfilled behind her, to take the plain and tame it and carve her own world and existence in this place.

"I must carry this burden, I must carve a path, I must survive until I fall and then I will carry on in new ways beyond," the voice inside her bellowed and screamed this mantra over and over and over so much it had become a drumbeat that drove her further and further forward.

However, her legs were tired, her muscles were burning deeply inside and her drumbeat was starting to subside to a new repeated mantra of *"slow and rest and there forever live on,"* and these two dichotomies were battling and fighting, and one or the other was soon to give way to allow a victor. Lilith could feel each part of her give in to the second mantra, and her pace was becoming more glacial, more strained and less determined.

The blood was a constant trickle now, her legs were tanned with the redness, and her feet looked as though she wore red stockings. Each step was a wet squelch as sand noisily moved under her bare feet.

Her hands were still red and dirty from the beach, caked and cooked into her skin and flesh from the sun relentlessly bearing down overhead.

The ache between her thighs was now a perpetual throb of pain and agony, there was nothing left of the glory of the birth, instead, all she had was a pain that she was being slowly pulled apart, only her hands on her stomach warding off this feeling of imminent evisceration. She stumbled slightly.

God stood up from the rock that had been his perch as he overlooked this grand scene.
The look of dismay and doom on his face flickered for a split second into concern, and then just as quickly disappeared into a blank stare of passive aggressive wonder.
He spat.

How was she making this life?
Under what power and authority had she been given providence and permission to create from nothing? How could she so nonchalantly still stride toward the unknown, so coolly ignoring the life springing into vivid reality in her devastating wake?
His anger was inexplicable, his rage incandescent, for the second time in his existence he realised his lack of control and surprise washed over him like a cold, frozen lake pulling him down to a death of drowning and lungs full of ice.

Lilith tried to carry on, four or five more steps and then her knees buckled and gave way, she collapsed onto her side, a hard slap of flesh on the dust, kicking up a storm of dirt and soil, her face half-caked in the pebbles and grit, the pain deafening and draining her of all breath. Her arms still cradling her stomach as she wailed out a scream of defeat and a huff of exhaustion.
Gaia shook off Zeus's arm, and strode deliberately and panicked to the edge of the mount, her hand grasped out at the air as if to help Lilith up, but it was no use, she could no more stop this series of events happening than she could have stopped the events that lead to it. She was powerless, a mother watching her only child dying in front of her very eyes. Zeus paid more attention to Gaia than he did the plain.
This was a clear act of hostility from his sibling God, and Yahweh,

on his own cliff face at the highest point of the garden, was starting a crack to form that would only become wider and more expansive. Zeus did not want to see where these cracks lead.

Lilith could not hold it anymore, whatever was happening was happening now, here, this immediate new burst of pain and horror had to end. The hateful stab in her crotch and the pangs of unbearable agony in her abdomen were now all she knew. Her legs dead and completed devoid of life or strength, they lay like broken matchsticks connected uselessly to her hips. This pantomime was drawing to a close. Whatever it was she had so adamantly strode toward and whatever had driven her for these last few days had run its course, and the decision had come to pass that the end was nigh for her, she knew, and as cold as comfort could ever be she smiled a strained grin through the gritted teeth and unrelenting pain from her every cell.

God now was struggling to see her through the green and beautiful shrubbery and undergrowth being borne from every flick and fleck of sweat, blood and drop of fluid. He strained and twisted in his rock nest to see beyond the nature that burst and exploded like fireworks around her, but he could not.
His limitations had been met, and he screamed a terrible rattle across creation, which all the other surviving gods heard and smiled coyly at.
The biggest bully in the playground had been bested by his favourite, and they all marked this as a day to remember, yet a day to also fear.

Lilith bore down hard, holding her stomach, the final remnants of birth came from her in a bloody and awful crack, a wet, sickly sound heralded the afterbirth that remained inside her from the Host born. With a single push, hard and determined, there was a visceral and horrendous mass of viscous muscle and sinew expelled from her body, her sex torn again, the muscle around her most intimate area lit up with sensations untold, it pulsed with a weak yet potent heartbeat, she screamed as way of relief the pain was done, but, then realised there was movement from her groin and looking down, could see tendrils flickered and whipped from her, a cable of bloody, muscular tendon came from her and connected to the mass of black, oily, blood splattered afterbirth that crawled and writhed and wriggled from her as a snake would slide from a pit.

Lilith gave a final guttural yelp of terror and was split in-two by a final push, the umbilical that connected her to the afterbirth strained, tight, taut and solid, before flexing and then snapping as one would unleash a bullwhip, the movement exploded from inside her, a throbbing mass of gristle and flesh, a seam opened right the way from the crease of her sex to the top of her head – she gave an honest, gentle sigh of surprise and relief her eyes wide and terrified, soon relaxed in a sensational look of inevitability and understanding, finally she smiled gently and let out a gentle, harmonic sigh of release.

The line that cut from groin to the crown of her head gently peeled, and she gave a laugh, as quiet and gentle as ever heard to that day in creation before she opened like a blooming flower and the mass of tendrils and gore became her new shell; Each tendril flashed and slashed and whipped around looking for some clean air for it to be alive within, before stabbing hard into the plain's once dusty and dead surface, which now bristled with life and livery and growth. The tendril became a root that bore deep and hard and wound around the earth like a twisted knot, anchoring into place and allowing Lilith's new form to pull itself up and stand tall.

Shreds of her old form now ripped, torn and flagged in branches as terrible red strands. Like clothes snagged on a thorn bush flapping in the wind.

The sinewy monster stretched out, and the blood and gristle slowly coagulated into rivets of deep and serious brown and grey. The tendrils at the top of the monstrosity stretched and spread and formed into spirals of branches, the length of serpentine body solidified and became a trunk the same colour and solid stature of the branches.

Lilith had finally fulfilled her destiny, and her birthright, born of a God who was selfish and cruel and wanton in his desires she had been, but torn from the earth and from the Mother of Nature she had come from – Gaia's first and only true daughter - and here she was

now a tree, vast and strong, massive and unshakeable in the centre of the plain, each branch full of fruit.
Amidst it all there was, amongst all others, one branch that stole the eye and was the feature of this new tree.

A like a wooden carving of a hand held out in elegant repose, held out in its grasp a single red apple. Perfect and succulent and alive with power untold.

It shone like a beacon of hope and curiosity and potency from the tree.
No one, but no one, could ever have resisted its charms.

And this is what God could see.
His great love, his finest creation, had become his undoing.
He had learned his true fate and meaning, and he had born his own end.
The tree was knowledge; the apple was curiosity. The once barren and lifeless plain was now fruitful and alive with the blood of nature.

The flowers and the grass that had been grown from Lilith's blood, sweat and tears, now taking root, fertilizing the plain from desolate nothing to blooming and beautiful glade. Where once there had been naught but dust and sand, now was rooting trees and bush and thicket, vines crawling and climbing and growing on the walls of small Eden, crushing it with ease, pulling them down and squeezing them to insignificant dust. The border between plain and garden now impossibly removed, the two intimately now bonded and linked, one and the very same.

Yahweh stood with his hands by his side, shocked and stupefied, his mouth agape, the plain was now a field of brilliant emerald, full of water, forest and berry.
Flowers and trees; bushes thick with fruit, seed and nut.
The land was massive and beautifully lush.

Lilith in losing herself to the nothingness had given the world

everything.
So it was written, and so it was done…

And so it was done.

* * *

- 8 -

Michael saw them coming, the kids of the estate, enjoying the summer holidays and dressed in shorts and shirts, sandal and trainer. Backpacks full of treats and lunches, each with a glint of adventure in their eyes, ten or so children, each beckoned by the code in Michael's window.
All of them here.
All but James.

Michael tried not to show it, but his face was flushed with perturbed anger.
James had to be here, to show his strength, to highlight his dominance and position; he had to do this in front of the other kids.
He waved his hand above his head, and the eyes all came to him.
"Where is James?"
No one knew, or so it seemed.
Shakes of the head, blank looks of vague eyed wonder, no one seemed to have a clue or care, then Poppy, a smaller girl with pigtails and a thin wire-framed pair of glasses raised a hand.
"I saw him in the top conker field. He was reading up by the Buddha."
"On his own?" Michael enquired. The girl nodded curtly and pushed her glasses back up the bridge of her nose.
He huffed, a baffled and angry expulsion of air.
"Who wants to get ready for conker picking?" He asked the rest of the gang, and everyone raised a hand, regardless it being late August, there were the earliest signs of a good harvest of conkers this Autumn, the biggest ones not usually available until mid-October, but some monsters sprouted early in late September, and the kids of the estate were spoiled for choice with two fields filled with about a

124

dozen and a half chestnut trees, full of the early signs of the bloom to come.

Behind this was the peace garden, which contained a giant mock golden Buddha, and a gravel Zen garden, full of weeping willows and eucalyptus bushes, herbs and flowers grew around the edges of the gravel, and benches were laid out in a semi-circle. Why there was a peace garden here the kids never knew, but they did know it was a quiet and serene place, often they would go and lazily read or collapse on the benches and watch the show the sun made through the willow branches as the clouds came and went before it. Projecting shapes and colours, light and shadow in mesmerising fashions.

Michael strode off, from the top of the field, past the height marker and the angry beehives, hopping the fence toward the conker field.

The kids, robotically, without breaking to think for themselves jumped the fence and followed, some with balls bouncing and kicked against the wall of the garages that were side on to the field, and some with stones being thrown at drains and trees, lazily chucking what they had at whatever they could.

As is the way with children with idle hands.

The conker field was less than four minutes from the gate of the field, running along the top row of houses, Michael soon was at the turnstile fashioned into the hedge by some engineering and enterprising elder brother of one of the kids, he bounded over effortlessly and landed sharply with a crunch on the small patch of early dead leaves. A minority of red and browns in a field full of green.

He was followed hastily by two or three of the elder gang, and then the squabbling younglings. As the final few jumped over, Michael had already found James – who looked genuinely unhappy and displeased to have been found.

Michael was already over to the bench and poking at James' book.

Poppy looked upset that she had tattled, she had betrayed the knowledge of James' whereabouts naively, and unawares that it was to be such an issue with their fearless leader. The look on Michael's

face was both upsetting with its angry red hue as it was his sudden
motion toward James when the boy had done nothing wrong.

Poppy had liked James, she thought his awkward shuffle was cute,
his glasses that always seemed to be losing themselves down his face
- he always having to poke them back up his nose much like she did
with her own - his chuckle was warm and full of life.

He was a good guy, and suddenly, it dawned that maybe Michael was
not.

Michael stood in front of James, his hands planted on his hips, James
looked up from his book once only and carried on sitting quietly.
Michael stared down on him, blocking a shard of light that lit him
from behind, a silhouetted aura around him.

"James." Is all he said. A single foot tapped out at James' foot, James
shuffled his foot backwards, and adjusted in his seat, still reading.
'THE SILVER CHAIR' by C S Lewis in his hands, a hardback
edition he had bought at the book fair last spring at school.

"Why are you not at the den when I asked you to be?"

James looked up and saw the indignant rage brewing behind
Michael's eyes.

"Because you didn't ask me, you put a number in your window, and I
chose not to pay attention to it, because I am enjoying my book and
wanted a quiet afternoon. No other reason. Truth be told, I don't
really want to have to be around people today, especially children."

Michael did not break his gaze; James looked at him in return, lazy
eyed and with a look of nonchalant ambivalence.

"What do you mean 'children', James?"

James put his book down in his knapsack, marking the page
fastidiously, and stood up slowly gathering his bag and his water
bottle.

"I mean, Michael, you. I did not want to be around *you* if I can help
it; I don't really want anything to do with you. I think you are cruel,
obnoxious and frankly, a bit of a pleb."

James walked off, his face neutral, no happiness nor sadness on his
lips – just a neutrality that spoke wonders and volumes about his
sincerity.

Michael did not react at first his limited mind digesting the words, and then, from somewhere inside him deep and dark, his hands spoke more than his mouth could ever articulate.

Everyone who was there remembered what happened next.

* * *

- 9 -

In my window I can see everything on our street, the scurrying of the kids to and from whatever game or den they had been hiding in, the mothers slowly weeding out in their gardens, fathers cutting grass with various machines and gadgets – from petrol engines that broke the early summer afternoon's silence with whirling, revving violence, to the manual rota blade machines that make the sound of cogs turning and leave the grass cut like an old man's beard.

Michael's stupid sign is still in the window, two sides of the blu-tac have come away, and the paper folds back from the glass, dog-eared and flapping. I want to run across the street kicking in his door and rip the stupid thing to shreds and throw the remains around his room. Instead, I close the curtains and return to my bed where the bedside lamp is bright and perfect to read by. Devouring Lewis's description of Narnia and the magic it holds.

I'd love to say I am calm and comfortable, but, I am not.

Even when I crave my solitude I know when it needs to be inside or out, and the weather is tapping at my window and asking me to come out to play and I know it knows I want to go, and who am I to argue with it? So, I pack my bag up with a water bottle, the book and my hat, and I shout out for my mum.

"Mum!"

Silence greets me. Obviously outside in the garden, enjoying this lazy sunshine and enjoying a glass of wine and orange juice, she secretly thinks no one knows she enjoys, but which is the worst kept secret in the house, and probably on the estate.

I lean out of her and my Dad's bedroom window, see she is hiding behind sunglasses and a book as well.

"Mum."

She turns and arches her neck, one hand above her eyes, a visor from the sunshine almost directly overhead, sunglasses or not, the light is a beam covering her and washing over her.

She smiles up at me.

"What you doing up there, Jamie?" Her pet name for me.

"I called, but you didn't hear me. I'm going out to read in the Buddha garden. Is that ok?" Even as I say the words "*I'm going out...*" she is smiling.

"Of course sweetheart, take some of the cake your Dad got from the club on Sunday. Be back by the times the lights are on. Ok?"

I nod and close the window, even as I am I can hear the muffled "I love you," from the other side.

Left unreciprocated and unanswered.

But she knows I love her too.

I throw the cake in the bag, and I make my way out the front door, toward the Buddha garden, it's hard to be evasive on this estate, so small and so open, everyone seeing everyone else's business.

Gossip traded like currency.

And as I go up the road and turn right to cross over and climb the cattle gate, to have a brisk walk through the hilly field where the Cornish cows wander freely, mingling with the two curmudgeonly goats, I see Poppy, beautiful dress, cute smile, and thin glasses escaping her face, caught and captured and imprisoned back on her nose with a swift push and a sniff.

She smiles at me and raises a gentle tiny hand to say hi, and then just as quick she darts off round the corner. I already know she is still watching before I turn around and catch her frozen in a moment of horrified embarrassment before she is gone fully, Heaven knows where.

She knows very well where I am going as well, she having seen me here twice before while she was adventuring in and around the conker fields.

After the fields, negotiating the goats and the cowpats the Buddha garden is a beautiful haven in the little paddock behind the conker trees.

The weeping willow gives a low roof to protect from the majority of bad weather, and the fences keep you away from wandering animals. The Buddha is brilliant company, silent, contemplative and peaceful. My favourite person on the whole estate by far.

I sip my water, I eat the cake in nearly two whole mouthfuls, and the chapter of my book is exciting and wondrous, allowing me to disappear into a world of fantasy and brilliant escape,

The sunshine was warm, the breeze was cool and gentle under the canopy of the willow, and the Buddha was the perfect company. I am slightly distracted by the image of Poppy at the bottom of the street, stood half peeping from behind the wall, and the speed with which she ran off. I imagine it was a girlish impulse, but still... Girls, in general, scare the life out of me and to think Poppy may have some form of crush, or something makes me sweat in terror.

I don't get girls at all, they don't make a tiny bit of sense and seem to be more complicated than any Mechano set.

And I LOVE Mechano.

It's a lovely afternoon, or at least, it feels like it could be. Right up until the sound of the gaggle of kids at the bottom of the field by the fabricated turnstile, made by Dennis, the brother of Harry, one of the Park Road kids. Dennis who moved away with his mum when his and Harry's parents divorced, Harry staying with his dad, eleven years between him and his brother.

I can see through the trees the shadow of someone approaching, and already know instinctively it is Michael. His lumbering footsteps nowhere near as swift and delicate as his archery, he stomps like an a angry bull, his massive shoes, gargantuan feet and ridiculously stocky legs stamping on earth and twig like it was Tokyo and he was Godzilla.

His stupid face and frame bare down on me before I know what to do, but the book is brilliant, and thankfully, it is not hard to concentrate on something else other than the stupid child in front of me, one I would just as soon never have to see again.

"James." His foot kicks out at mine as if I did not know my own name.
"Michael." I barely whisper
"Why are you not at the den when I asked you to be?"
"Because you didn't ask me, you put a number in your window, and I chose not to pay attention to it, because I am enjoying my book and wanted a quiet afternoon. No other reason. Truth be told, I don't really want to have to be around people today, especially children."
"What do you mean 'children', James?" He sounds hurt, angry. Brilliant...

I can feel where this is going, and before I can control my brain or temper, my mouth is spitting out the words in such a dauntless fashion I am at a loss as to what to do next.
I realise the bag is already packed, the book is already away – my hands moving independent from my mind – much like my mouth, and I say what I have wanted to say for weeks, if not the entire summer.

"I mean, Michael, you. I did not want to be around *you* if I can help it, I don't really want anything to do with you. I think you are cruel, obnoxious and frankly, a bit of a pleb."
'Pleb' was spat with such disdain it was a cutting and awful insult, tempered by a half laugh as I said it, I cannot move down the hill any cooler or calmer than I am, at the bottom I catch Poppy staring at me and then staring at her feet, clearly guilt-ridden, the person who told Michael where I was.
I don't blame her, she had no idea how much he hates me, so I smile at her and wink, she catches the look with a sudden brief glimpse, a half smile, no sooner there than stolen away by shock and awe, her eyes darting to the side and up, stolen attention by something else happening behind me.

I hear Michael spit out my name.
I hear how furious he is...

I can feel the air beside my ear move and the whistling air spin past me at a stunning speed.

I then hear the impact of the rock that has been thrown at me as it smashes into Poppy's face, pulverising her skull.

The wicked and wet snap of her nose, the tinny break of her thin spectacle frame, the glass lens cracking and splintering, a shard in her eyelid, jagged and thin like a needle.

I can hear the forced, frantic bubbling of her breathing through her blood-filled mouth, and I see the teeth scattered around the feet where she fell.

I count five before I am forced to stop by the rising bile toward my throat.

And amongst it all, the size of a cooking apple, the half smooth and rounded and half jagged and pointed rock that was thrown at me by the psycho Michael.

Missing me entirely – though how, I could not tell you, his aim never being anything short of perfect – and which impacted with a wet, sodden sound against the small, fragile, delicate porcelain skull of poor Poppy.

Who dies right there in front of me, one eye fixed on me, a hand reaching out to me, and then just as suddenly limp and lifeless and gone.

The light in her eye distant and dull.

A final wheezing gasp of blood contaminated airways trying and desperate for oxygen and her body shaking with a rictus and then it too lay limp and done.

All the kids stopping silently, shock running through them like a contagion.

Airborne and immediate.

Hands rising to mouths, eyes splintering in tears – a dozen or so confused, angry, upset, terrified kids all staring up the hill at Michael, whose arms dropped to his side and face looks blankly, calmly back at them, one at a time, before he slumped to a cross-legged collapse on the dirty ground, his hands in his lap.

His eyes now affixed only to the hands upturned and cupped on his knees, trying to figure out where the rock came from, what Devil possessed him to throw it, why the sudden rage that took over his frame and controlled him as if by remote.

Not that it matters.

Michael was the least of my worries, the last thing I can spare attention on, as I fall to the floor and cradle Poppy's head, gently stroking her hair away from her face, wiping the dirt from her china white cheek.

Poor, sweet, innocent Poppy.

I look at Robin, one of the kids from Edgcott, the neighbouring village, and I summon the words with fragile force, my mouth dry and croaky, but immediate.

"Call a fucking ambulance! Somebody get some help… Quickly!"

Not that it mattered.
Poor, sweet, innocent Poppy.
Dead at 13.

* * *

CHAPTER FOUR
The Pitch

"He's a man way out there in the blue
Riding on a smile and a shoeshine.
And when they start not smiling back
- That's an earthquake…
A Salesman has got to dream, Boy.

It comes with the territory."

- Arthur Miller – Death of A Salesman.

"If lightning is the anger of the gods, then the gods are concerned mostly about trees."

— Lao Tzu

Michael sat at the table silent and surly. His hands passed the golden cup from palm to palm. His eyes fixed solely on the man in green opposite him. His dark blonde hair tussled and tumbled into his eyes, loose ringlets, they seemed to shine from whatever source of light hit them. The man opposite in green had long, lustrous golden hair, almost white in places. His eyes were fixed stoic and solidly on Michael.

The cup moved in a rhythmic pace between palms, a metronome of sound and motion, fluid and calm. The gesture at odds with the fierce, concentrated disdain behind the eyes. Both a sharp grey-blue, staring forebodingly into the amber brown eyes of the man opposite, the man whose eyes seemed aflame with intention and invention.

"I cannot imagine that you have come here for pleasantries, brother." The man in green touched his fingers on both hands together. Sat back into the chair, and gave a wide, genuine smile.
The blue eyes were fixed on him, no blinking, no movement, just solid concentration and a growing sense of brewing intensity, some way toward anger.
"Come on, brother. Do something. Say something. Your silence bores me. It is like we are children again…"
The eyes still fixed and charmless, the mouth a sliced sneer of revulsion and ambivalence. The cup still passing from one hand to the other, the methodical beat steady and unbreakable. No movement of any other part of his body.
No Blink, no sign of breath being drawn, just the cup from one palm to another.

PAK PUK PAK PUK – the rhythms steady beat, unwavering, unchanging.

Lucifer could take it no more, and his temper, like a rope between two horses pulled in opposite directions, at first frayed and

134

then snapped.

He lunged over the table and snatched the cup, and in a single movement the golden beaker smashed and shattered against the far wall.

Michael in an effortless gesture had left his chair, lightning fast reflexes had seen him clear eight feet of the room in a second his hand now around the throat of Lucifer, who was lifted off the floor by the momentum and thrust heavy, with a thud that sounded like wet meat on the butcher's slab.

The air left his body from every pore, and he hung limp and vulnerable, his hands clutching at those of Michael, that were suspending him a foot from the marble floor with no sign of exertion or strain.

Michael had strength enough in reserve to have raised him four or five inches more and still not break a sweat.

As beautiful and elegant as Lucifer was, Michael matched it in brute strength and brutal efficiency.

Lucifer tapped Michael's hand to show sign of submission and surrender, Michael ignored this and instead squeezed a fraction harder. Lucifer tapped again, and his eyes, beautiful and full of fire wrought, dulled a second, and then a twist of panic washed over them as the eyelids opened wider in a single gesture of slow-burning anxiety, Michael squeezed a fraction harder still.

His mouth did not betray his feelings, the sneer of effortless strength fixed tight and secure. But, Lucifer could feel that Michael's hands were smiling where his mouth refused.

The grip was something tangible, strength seemed to jolt like electricity from the fingertips pushed deep into his jugular like a pulse of fire, the warm, calloused palms were fragrant, despite the ravages of battle and folly, Lucifer tapped more ferociously than before. His throat made little whimpers. Gurgling sounds of panic escaped his lungs despite his best efforts to stop them. His mouth now a gritted grimace of sheer madness and fear, he tapped and tapped.

Finally Michael released him with a silent smile.

Lucifer hit the ground gasping. His mouth wide, saliva and froth flecked in the corner of his mouth, each gagged and hacked breath saw spittle and blood drip from his jaw. He rubbed his throat and chest, promoting a healthier breath that did not come, from bended knee he looked up at Michael now standing over him and looking down with emotionless candour.

"So what, if not to kill me, is your mission, Michael?"

He barely recognised his own voice, a rasped bark, broken like china on a granite floor.

Michael's eyes gave the briefest flicker of a smug arrogance; Lucifer realised he had maybe bitten off more than he could chew with this latest stunt.

The Morningstar born he may be, but this creation was suddenly so full of emotion and energy beyond his comprehension, his brothers each so full of hubris and attitude, it made his grand self-esteem suddenly seem to pale insignificant in comparison.

Michael, the Figurehead of the Host - He who was like God - stared down at The Morningstar and he said a single word, asked a single question.

Lucifer knew that this world was just starting to crumble around him, his golden radiance amongst the heavens was no good when it came to his siblings, who still considered him the runt, regardless of him being the eldest, Raphael was a mountain – regardless of his part within the tapestry of this world and the work he was tasked to do, Raguel was built from steel, his wings had seen more flight than any other of the original Host – travelling to and from land and mountain, sea and ocean had given his body pure strength, Michael had always had strength untold.

In comparison, Lucifer was merely a beautiful robin amongst these ravens.

There he lay, amongst the golden shards of the cup that he had smashed, blood seeping slowly from his mouth and throat into the tapestry of the carpet.

The shadow of his brother imposing and gigantic above him.

Michael, who spoke to the Father exclusively and held his counsel.

Michael who was beyond reproach.

Lucifer began to fear that his grand plan, born of a plot a millennia in the making, may not be as watertight and perfect as he had planned, he feared this may well be his undoing.

Michael bore down on him, and spat the word - the question - with utter contempt.

"Temptation?"

And his hand, solid and rock-like, connected hard with Lucifer's jaw in a backhanded slap and the Morningstar's lights went out.
A sudden, unexpected wash of darkness over the light.
Lucifer was undone.

* * *

- 2 -

There was a frost when she woke up, just a light one, a silver sheen on the grass like someone had sprayed the green with a light, translucent spray of diamond dust. The trees had a shimmer to the bark which, even now, was slowly warming and an otherworldly mist evaporated from between the creases of the wood, the cracks and crevasses that made the skin and texture of the bark released the cold like a kettle boiling and steaming up a kitchen.

The sky was an almost perfect azure blue, and the sun was a blurry yellow dot hidden behind the cold atmosphere, almost impossibly thin clouds still alive enough to gauze the colour into a fuzzy warm smudge in the air above the houses on Hawthorne Grove.

Kay looked out of her bedroom window, her extra large Red Wings jersey was falling from her shoulder at an angle that her shoulder and collar bone were almost perfectly framed, the first tantalising curve of breast peeping from the collar, a fine shade of areola peeking from the material of the shirt.

In her hand a quickly cooling cup of tea, like a thick milky soup, the

137

colour a golden treacle she grasped the cup between two hands, fingers interlocking as she peered out the window in her room to look at the garden and investigate the morning's weather. She smiled widely, her eyes big and hungry for adventure, the thin, beautiful line of her lips a stunning pink cerise that gave way to brilliant white teeth and a smile that was at the same time intoxicatingly perfect and full of wanton danger.
She was a paradox in motion, delicate and beautiful, jagged and deadly, a nymph in real life.

She sipped greedily from her tea, slurped at the brew with giddy charm, and collapsed into the sofa, a slumping, soft huff of the cotton and polyester sighed from the cushions as she nestled in legs curled under herself, and she enjoyed the warm line of sunshine slowly crawl across the wall to her face, bathing in the glorious ochre shower of life.

Today was going to be a good day.
Kay could tell.
The sun never felt this good unless there were amazing things afoot and the good times were going to roll.
She took another noisy slurp of her tea, a splash of the liquid dribbled in the corner of her mouth, slowly trickling down her chin.
A pink, cherry tongue darted out and licked it clean, Kay gave a girlish giggle, so fancy-free and innocent.
She stretched out and smiled wider as the bones and muscles gave their hearty creak and crack and groan. She let the sunshine wash her clean and awake.

The perfect start to the day.

Adam sat on the fallen wall of Eden, where the fresh field had been suddenly borne from he had no idea, He wished he could share this with Lilith, but, felt that his wife would not appreciate the lush colours and creation that had suddenly sprung into their life. She was always so distracted by the lagoon and by their father, always so busy with worship to notice the sunshine and the green grass and livery that roamed amongst them.

Adam loved the new world that had become so prominent and immediate into his life. Eden was bigger now, wider, more expansive. It had a thousand new smells and a billion new contours, shades and shadows.

His mind was racing with impossible excitement at all of the new things he would have to name, catalogue and tend. His gardener's fingers already stained green from plant, seed and soil, tree, leaf and pond.

Adam.

The Gardener of Eden.

He sat naked upon the wall, a hand full of seeds and berries, lazily popping them one at a time into his mouth, a solitary leg idly kicking and swinging from the boundary barrier that had fallen into the place known so recently as the plain, now a few thousand acres of green, lush fields, trees and forests bursting and jutting from the horizon, flowers crawling and winding around the stone and granite of the wall, and animals and insects fluttering and roaming in and around the new world free and untended. His mouth was an awkward, stunned, dozy picture of joy.

He was not a stupid man, was Adam. Far from it, but his simple needs and wants were always easy to mistake as a lazy minded trudge, his sleepy, vacant smile was almost permanently on his face, belying a sense of doltishness, giving the impression of a man with no faculties in order, lost in his own world and thoughts, blind and ignorant to the greater importance of things.

Yet, Adam was far from stupid.

He had tended the green and pleasant land of First Eden. Every species of flower, animal, mammal, reptile and insect had been given name and identity by his hand, his happy service toward the world he was born into was charming to behold. Yes, he could seem unburdened by the idea of things, his mind would wander on flights of fancy and his eyes would sometimes be a sleepy, dull blue stare. Regardless, Adam was the Lord of the Manor of Eden and his job in caretaking this land made him tired and weary beyond the pale and his goofy sense of half-witted impudence was easy to be mistaken. Even if God had created all of this, if the plethora of gods beyond the hills and valleys and sitting in creations in the stars and clouds and wide cosmic expanse above Adam's head – had of had a hand in Eden, even in the early days, as Lilith had attested too, Adam was easily working twice as hard as God was now with his dutiful and daily cycle of work and loving routine around the flowers, the plants and the flora and fauna of Eden.

The new plain that had burst from goodness knows where to infringe on the wall of Old Eden, well, it presented him with new duty, new challenge and a renewed sense of need and purpose. Adam sorely wished Lilith were here to see it.
As much as it may seem he was more interested in the beast who lumbered and lay in these plush green fields, Adam always desired the woman.
His heart burned in the way only a man's heart could for the touch of her flesh.
Something that, recently, was sorely lacking and not given.

God watched him from the edges of the hill that fell down in an emerald slope of foliage and flower toward where the wall had stood, dividing the Old Eden from the expansive and lifeless plain. He watched as Adam popped seeds, one by one into his mouth and swallowed, how he would absently swing his leg from the knee as he straddled the wall and allowed the insects to nestle and wander his naked, sun-baked and mud-caked skin. God watched, a sadness collapsing over him like a cloud full of rain slowly building and bulging over a city. Ready to pour and pour.

Adam did not give any indication that he had heard Yahweh approach.

Slow, silent steps, that barely allowed sound to exist around him, Yahweh was resplendent in an aura of gold and silver, a halo above his head burned like the white-hot ore at the heart of the biggest and brightest star in the night sky.

Adam still carried on swinging his leg, but he raised a hand gently in a hello gesture and waved to God when he was fifteen feet or so from him.

"Good morning, Father."

God froze, he tried but was unable to avoid the smile of pride that escaped his lips, always forgetting how intelligent and strong and perfect his children were, always under-estimating them and their constant evolution from silent husks to thinking, creative souls – imbibed with wonder and life by the environment and world he had created for them.

"Hello, Adam, son."

"Father. Where is Lilith, my wife? I wish to show her this wondrous new world I have discovered."

Yahweh placed his arms behind his back, one palm resting in the other hand, he walked casually and sartorially over to the wall, where he took a seat next to Adam, and gently lay a hand on the man's chest.

'Man.' – God thought. Really little more than a child, this creation no more than fifty or so year's old – but young, time was slower then, Yahweh did not control the flow – it was a living entity even beyond the touch of Death. God often thought if Death had been telling the truth then the last two things in the universe remaining once everything else was dust and memory would be Lord Mort himself and Master Time – stood wondering who would go first into the bleak ether.

Now, as it was, time was starting to coagulate and form into a lineal thing, harder and harder to manipulate, more structure, thicker, oozing like sap from the tree down the bark, rather than flowing fast and wanton like the river.

He could see days and evenings began to separate and the two aspects beginning to lay negotiation terms down for how they would co-exist.

Still, fifty, sixty or seventy years old – Adam was nothing but a man barely out of his adolescence – relatively speaking. And the look of sad, hungry need was tangible. God sighed, lay a hand on Adam's chest and hand and looked him directly in the eye.

"Adam, son. Lilith has gone away. You will not see her again. She is no longer of this Eden; her life is out there in the vast plain beyond the wall."

Adam stopped swinging his leg, his head dropped momentarily to his chest, his chin gently brushing the skin of his breastbone.

He opened his mouth once or twice to speak, and then stopped, swallowed hard before continuing and saying that which he had on his mind.

"She has gone?"

Yahweh nodded, the look in his eyes was a piercing golden glow, it dulled slightly as he swallowed back on something close to emotion. "This saddens me." Adam let go of God's hand and stared hard out onto the plain.

"I shall miss her, she was loved. Though I doubt she knew nor cared. Regardless, she was loved."

Yahweh swallowed down a bitter lump in his throat and pushed hard on to Adam's breast. Adam looked at him in a quick flick of shock and tried to back away, Yahweh persisted.

"She was indeed loved, but, she is gone."

Adam looked down at God's hand, as God persisted in pushing hard against his breast. "She made her decision to leave. She chose the world beyond these walls, and she will not return again."

His hand now stood like a spider on the breastbone of Adam, who began to try and move away backward from God, but God's other hand grabbed his arm at the shoulder and held him tight.

"Worry not about Lilith, my son, she will be fine. As for you... I have a gift that will make all better. Allow me..."

He pushed harder, Adam winced, God's palm flat now against Adam's chest and his fingers squeezing out pushing into the flesh. Adam opened his mouth in silent anguish, as the red hot fingers probed into him deeper, the skin opening around them, the hand disappearing into his flesh, the skin and muscle of his breast giving way like a viscous mud to God's incandescent, scorching hand. Yahweh yanked hard and fast, Adam arched in agony at his spine, his chest pushed out, his arms grabbing onto God's, flesh burning at the touch of the Deity.

God gave a fluid tug, and with the motion from Adam's body he pulled a rib free. Adam clutched at his chest, pawing at the tender area of God's violation.

He looked at God in stunned, open-mouthed exasperation.

God waved his rib at him, gently, highlighting the bone, turning it between his fingers, rolling it between index and thumb.

He held it out in two hands, pinched between the same digits, smiled and let a little-relieved sigh of laughter escape from his mouth.

"Adam. I love you. Dearly. My first creation upon this Earth…"

Adam smiled weakly at this sentiment, his hands still rubbing and checking ribcage and chest, no wound, no burn, no damage – but still tender and shocked.

"Thank you, father. What have you done?"

God looked at the rib, then to Adam.

He allowed himself a wide, happy smile. This was control; this was his full control.

"I have allowed you a gift, a very special gift."

And he pulled the rib like it was made of clay and started to reshape and reform it. The calcified relic bending oblivious and easy to his will.

"I made you from the hair atop my head and the breath within my lungs. Lilith was made from the dust of the earth and the breeze on the ocean. These things I borrowed from other realms. It was a mistake I will never repeat. So, from your flesh, formed and born, I give you Eve. Your new wife."

And though he could not yet see the betrayal that would haunt yet him again, Yahweh breathed life into the new form and shape he had built. A visionary beauty.

Bright auburn hair flowing down perfectly round, swollen breasts. Legs that were long and curved, a back that arched in magnificent and magical ways intoxicating the eye and heart. Eve was perfect and beautiful and naked.

Adam stared at her with his mouth agape, a smile of lust and love growing fast and steady on his mouth.

Today really was his lucky day.

A new garden and a new wife.

And even as he stared at her, the memory of Lilith began to burn like sulphur from his mind.

"Thank you, father."

He allowed a tear to roll down his cheek.

"She is perfect."

And God smiled, for at that moment, she was.

She was the most perfect thing in creation.

Neither Adam nor God, Nor Eve in her empty-minded infancy, felt the wind change. The sudden shift in the air. They did not hear the sound of branches bowing and grass bending to the sudden chill that blew over the new fields bordering the garden. A cold wind enveloped the plain, it insidiously tingled and crawled across the land, like a carpet of locusts crawling across crops acres deep, imperceptible and stealthy but bitter, angry and lingering.

Lilith was dead, but her spirit infused this land in every way.

Deep tendrils of the first woman in creation bore down into this Earth's core, wrapping around the soil, the sand, the bedrock.

A soul infused upon the land, a spirit crafted into the seed.

Lilith's spirit lingered.

And Lilith's spirit wanted retribution.

It wanted revenge.

* * *
- 4 -

Rocks had been carved into the mountain face that were wide, tall and beautiful. Each step would have required rope and muscle, time and effort to climb for a normal man or woman, but, the God's strode them twenty or thirty feet tall, stepping them easily and effortlessly, the steps proving pebbles in the way of their haste to reach the mountaintop.

The mountain was bleak and grey against the warm and vacant summer air. Eden was far off to the East, where the first humans - Adam – and Eve now, sitting in Lilith's absent spot beside the first man - were unaware of these gods and this place, to the west. Their curious natures limited to the garden and its contents, never beyond the bounds of the tree that now stood centre of the plain. Earth had been a planet crafted and built by many hands; already gods were forming their own cultures to allow colours to be pinned to masts by early citizens to this land created by their own hands. Humans curiously distorting and building history and legend in the name of beliefs yet to be fully formed or cohesive in their primal and primitive minds. But legends that were already the fires, axes, tools and stones that inevitably would be crafted to strike down their fellow man, sooner or later, the consequence of which always leading back to the gods themselves.

Zeus was sat at the head of the table, beside him was Odin – his one eye alight with icy fire, staring around the plateau at the assembling gods from every walk and slice of life, every caste and religion. Ganesha sat down on the huge stone chair next to Zeus opposite Odin and exchanged nods with the two great old Deities. They curtly returned the glance and gesture; Zeus stood earnestly, the chair next to him was empty, the God, who sat here conspicuous with his absence. Zeus raised his arms to quieten down the assembled Lords – he spoke clearly, his voice a bellow of authoritative power and control, when he spoke, everyone listened.

145

"Brothers and sister, I have requested the presence of you all here today – at the Pantheon, the table of the gods for a grave and most worrying reason."

The Goddess Gaia took two steps forward and rolled a perfect red apple across the table toward Zeus, it had a single bite out of it, Odin grabbed the apple to look at it, the significance obvious and fully aware to him. He touched it, and the apple crumbled to a fine white dust like sand upon a beach.

Zeus smiled wryly.

Gaia did not smile back.

"Yahweh." She said.

"You have gathered us here because of Yahweh and his sudden exclusion of this committee. Because of his sudden isolation and the pushing he is constantly undertaking of the rules we set upon the beach. The incursions he has made into other territories and kingdoms and his hungry activity at our borders."

Zeus looked at Gaia with keen eyes; the glare was passive, his eyes belied a sense of exhausted truth that gave the game away and confirmed what the Goddess was saying.

"Is this not true?" was all Gaia said to finish.

Zeus looked at Odin, at Ganesh.

The two brothers nodded sagely at Zeus, the eldest of the gods here assembled, with Yahweh, the first two who awoke upon the beach – he was Head of the Pantheon, Leader of the council of gods – Zeus stood up and walked toward Gaia, his hands open and palms out toward his sister.

"You are exactly right, Gaia, my love." She took his hands, and the two leant in and embraced.

Odin poked at the dust that once was the apple, he pinched the powder and examined it. The significance was already well known around the gods. Each blessed with the eye of the future and the past, and could see the fine threads that governed and made up the universe they now inhabited. Each could watch the lines of destiny playing out, the pulse amongst the threads, the cosmic chess game unfolding, and pieces falling in places pre-destined and pre-written. The only parts of their futures which were murky and unknown were those threads that lead to their own deaths and rebirths. The consequences blurred, the knots of destined intangible, tangled and knotted, too many frays and lines to be able to loosen and learn.

Each God aware that any day could well be their last.

The feast to come of worship and tribute was slowly trickling and building to vast flowing rivers for some gods, whilst others were already starved and parched as civilizations fell in deluge and in fire, in battle and in disease.
When the last of the worshippers fell – the old gods knew the face and cold hard hand of Lord Mort would be upon them, as Death led them to the Ether or the holding cells.
Neither one place better or worse than the other.
Either an eternity in cold, dark, absent oblivion – or a room in which to wither like grapes on the vine in a frost, sipping meagerly at the thimble of love from the few starving remnants of your choir.
Zeus beckoned Gaia to sit in her chair, carved and hewn from a granite boulder; it was bristled with flower and with green moss, and it had a lush green life to it.
Zeus walked around the table and lay hand, ran finger across, brushed the hair and shoulders of each God who sat. He looked around and shared a rich gaze with each member of the table.
He finally came to his own chair, and he choose to stand instead of sit, as his speech was to be one of jagged and rich importance, he felt standing would lend gravitas and authority that it much needed.

"I have called you all here because already, a mere millennia or three after the beach, waking as we did in naked confusion, sand in our mouths and hair, eyes adjusting to the light of the water and the sunshine – even as Lord Mort stood amongst us with his sword and scythe – even now, so soon after our birth, we are facing the demise we were warned and have lived our lives in fear of.
Already some of our brethren have fallen and are gone and never to return. The feasts of the past have been taken and are destroyed, the

morsels that remain are spread thin and weak and are barely enough to make our strength to oversee our flocks.

Yet... Of us all, one God still feasts in abundance, stealing from our tables, eating our bread. Taking from each of us and burgeoning his already bursting fields of sheep.

Our cattle, our animals... These humans who throw their belief into our goblets and flacons and let us so greedily drink down their tithes and tributes – each one of them, ready to have their heads turned to join the larger flock that Yahweh is building. His monopolizing of the faith and his trickster ways in giving himself many names to have the humans scatter and fight amongst themselves – it is not how we agreed this would be...

Is it?"

The throng grumbled agreement with his statement.

They turned and looked at each other, this multitude of gods, all sat or stood around the table, Demigods, Master gods, sons and daughters of gods – The highest and lowest of their orders, the chief and lieutenants of their caste, they each grumbled loudly in agreement.

Zeus, his silver beard and his silver white hair perfect around his chiseled and angled face cast a frown, and his lip quivered with an unhappy grimace.

"I said, is it?"

The whole table shouted as one.

"NO!"

"We said, under oath to the raven-winged figure of Death himself that God would not kill God. Even as we sit here not a single one has cast a stone against the other. Yes, we are not fully unified as one council – we have disagreements, we argue, we fight. But we have never killed another of our kin. And yet..."

Odin stood angrily – his hand squashed and crumbled the goblet of clay he drank from to a pile of fragmented shards, and he swept the remnants angrily to the floor.

"And yet... our people begin to burgeon, when they multiply, they learn to pillage the houses of each other God's land. They have learned to burn, tear down and destroy our house of worship, these

148

people we create may damn us in the process to the Ether of the next world.

We knew this may happen, were prepared for this organic surge of independence and wrath from these humans we create – but not one of us prepared for…"

He looked around at the mass of faces now staring back eagerly.

"… For a God taking many names and building abhorrent monsters who trickle doubt and infamy into the world, poisoning our flocks and setting these self same people against each other, taking aliases that feed and sustain you even at the bleeding of people who may say they love you. Our brother watches this terror he supplants and sits back and lets their murderous natures grow- hoping that they will feed him to the point of gluttony."

The Pantheon table roared in approval at his anger.

They hit the stone of the table and clapped loudly, the land below shook with the sound of thunder, clouds building into a grey and angry soup in the brow of the mountain, and slowly descending into the valley and around the villages and settlements.

"Yahweh has abandoned this table, he has abandoned his brothers and sisters, and he has set out on a path that makes him a danger to each and every one of us… We have not seen the dawn of murder yet, but this is growing and stirring, our tiny colony of humans, our breeding ground for this world we have created, already, there is a poison amongst it spread by Yahweh sown by his winged sons… They say they are mapping the world, and we allow them into our lands as envoys for his kingdom, yet, they litter our land with infamy and doubt. No more I say! No more!"

The table all stood and clapped and the primal city at the bottom of the mountain all stood in shock as the storm broke free and began in earnest. Rain pelting down on the land, skies as black as smoke, and thunder as loud as the God's clapping and stomping shook the mountain and the valley.

Zeus called order amongst the Parthenon. He beckoned for Odin to sit. Repeating the gesture with his other brothers and sisters.

"When we awoke, Lord Mort stood over us, he gave each of us a
secret and a name. One name... One."
He sat himself. And still, patting down for the gods to quiet down, he
raised a single finger to the heavens.
"Even as we sit on our thrones and we oversee our flocks, and we
play and we toy and we meddle, we have always allowed the great
game to survive unsoiled. We live, we fall. We are no different at the
end than our people are. People who are built on the guide our
brother created, his Adam and Lilith the template of our own people.
One world, one human.
Yet, Yahweh lives under many names, plants seeds of doubt and fear
amongst our world with these Angel sons at his command, plants
idea and curiosity amongst our lands and goes by many names, many
faces and many guises - killing his own flock and devastating the
common order by allowing this monstrous plain to rise in green
chaos – and all the while turns his nose up at this council of brothers,
sisters, of God one and all... Yahweh has drawn lines of battle
against us and declared his sovereignty even now above that of Time
and Death themselves. He has thrown order into chaos; he has burned
the bridges to light his way into the unknown darkness."
Zeus looked around at the stern, solemn, indiscriminate eyes of his
kin.
"I have a guest who would like to speak. I have invited him here
today. You could say he is a new member of the Pantheon of Gods.
His place earned from action rather than birth, his place amongst us
guaranteed from the actions of his own father... He is my guest, and
therefore, should be considered yours as well.
Do not act discourteously, for I believe we have a solution of sorts. A
way to our errant brother that may yet save us all."

The table began to fidget and animatedly talk amongst themselves.
Zeus looked at Odin and Ganesha, the Elephant God stood and
roared primal scream at the table, he slammed his hands down, larger
than tree trunks, strength untold rippled through his enormous arms.
"WILL YOU HAVE OUR BROTHER'S GUEST?!"
He bellowed. Stared angrily amongst those gathered, they sagely and

150

quietly nodded, or voiced an approval, looking at the Elephant God and then Zeus next to him, Odin to his opposite.

Zeus nodded happily he beckoned to the stairs, as the glow emanated brighter with each and every step up the massive steps.

Lucifer made his entrance and smiled widely.

His halo of golden fire was where the light had come from, his golden blonde hair long and elegant around his shoulders.

Green robes rippled with silver, that seemed black at first glance and silver bangles on each of his arms.

"Good evening, uncles, aunts, cousins one and all. So happy to be here amongst you all, at last. So good to meet the family we have heard so much of. It really has been far too long coming… I am so happy and honoured to be here."

He bowed serenely, and upon rising, he caught the gaze of Gaia, he smiled again, his teeth were perfectly white, his fine, thin pink lips were beautiful and welcoming.

His bright brown eyes shone with that corona of fire,

He saw that her eyes were the same colour, her lips were a mirror of his own, her hair shone a blonde shimmer matching his own.

A flicker of understanding shivered through him.

"Well met, grandmother." He held his bow to her longer than was normal for a greeting, the reverence genuine, the courtesy and love true.

"How I loved your daughter fiercely. Her name is carved with grace deep into my heart. I live and bleed my life in honour of her. Dearest Lilith, most beautiful of the garden."

Gaia raised a hand to her mouth in sadness and happiness together, the creature in front of her was so beautiful and so perfect, such a reflection of its own mother, Lilith, Gaia's own daughter – born from the clay of the earth and the wind of the seas, elements that she had birthed into the infant universe. He was so much like the Lilith she had been denied and watched die from distance that her heart broke into a thousand tiny pieces.

His eyes were the same colour as her own, connective tissue between two entities.

"Lucifer. The Morningstar bright. Well met, Grandson..." she whispered with her voice breaking slightly like frost on a lakes surface at dawn.

"Welcome to our Parthenon."

Lucifer looked around and smiled widely and sincerely at each of the gods here.

He looked at Zeus, his Uncle.

Lucifer bowed once more, a shudder of pain ran down his spine where his wings once flexed in beautiful plumes, now a scarred mess of muscle and memory - he tried in vain to ignore it - and a single thought ran through his mind.

Three words.

"For. My. Mother."

And he realized this was as close to home as he had felt in a very long time.

The feeling burned his heart and mind, for he knew that it would not last, and he ached for what was about to happen. With his own plans and machinations growing inside him, for revenge and for respect, they had to be kept at bay whilst he laid out his plan and idea for these long unknown relatives to help him strike back at what he had lost.

"For my Mother." He thought.

The vision of the tree in the garden, and the single red apple dangling from its most beautiful branch, like an extended arm holding it in beautiful lithe fingers.

Lucifer Morningstar sat down at the foot of the table, and with Zeus - his uncle of sorts - at the head, the two of them laid out the plan and the next actions that would make or break the world.

Lucifer sat back in his chair. He stared at James' nervous, exhausted face, and he smiled. A wide, toothy, welcoming smile. Even as he was out of place in the man's lounge, in his suit of onyx black, rippled throughout with emerald green, shimmering whenever the light hit it.

His tie was the same shade of green with a perfect silver tie-pin. The pin was a fine slither of silver with what appeared to be the shape of an apple held in a hand, carved and shaped from the metal delicate and beautifully.

James stared at the pin; the sunshine glinted off it like a slice of a razor's edge cutting through the dust of the room.

James's fingers continued the circle round and round on his temples. His breathing was laboured and deep. His chest rose and fell in huffed chugs. Lucifer looked at him, this mess of a man, this shaggy, shuffling heap of human and his smile waned somewhat, weakened. It broke the charade of charm and instead took an altogether much more somber, real shape.

"James. Are you ok?"

James huffed and puffed and continued rubbing his head in distracted and angry fashion.

"… Because, I appreciate this is probably a massive life-changing event for you, I have smashed your fragile perception of reality. I appreciate how awe inspiring this must be… But, regardless, James, I need you to calm down and listen to me as I have an awful lot to explain to you."

James breathed in deeply, and slowly raised a hand from his head, and toward the air above Lucifer.

The Fallen Angel followed the finger, his eyes moving to where the index digit was aimed and realized what the fuss was.

A storm of flies circled like a cyclone around Lucifer's head.

A tumultuous tornado of buzzing, a crescendo of sly static screeching.

A whirlpool of vicious black movement.

Lucifer looked up and snapped to realization, his hand clapped on his mouth in mock horror.

He looked back at James, who was shrugging heavily at the shoulders, unable to deal with the mass of movement, the inky black dots that were now haloing Lucifer's head, like a scrap of shredded rubber, circling round and around heavily and forcefully.

"Oh! Do you want me to make them stop? Is that it?"
James nodded, his chest now rising and falling in heavier ways, hyperventilating.
"OK. Then can we talk like real men?"
James nodded again but his hand waved apoplectically toward the flies, swatting the air violently.
"Done." Lucifer clicked his fingers and as if someone had flipped a switched the halo of flies fell dead in a heap around his armchair, a perfect circle of black.
The flies individually popped and fizzed like kernels of corn, and the heap of dead insects first transformed into a pool of tar that stained and seeped into James' carpet – causing him to sit up in baulked fury – then it ran and oozed toward the shoes of Lucifer, before joining with the leather, pulsing up his leg and absorbing into his suit, and disappeared like a quickly drying stain, upon the black material.
A shimmer of the emerald flickered throughout again.
"I apologise, since the fall I have had to make do with halos of any variety I can get my hands on. Sadly, the grace of God does not last long in idiot brother's hands... but, this is a story for another time perhaps."
Lucifer shivered as the wetness of the tar dried off, and clicking his neck, and circling his head, he opened and closed his mouth, and as he returned to James, a fine, almost imperceptible shake of palsy ran from his head to his toe, his eyes rolled back into his head, black and marbled, then slowly losing the darkness and returning to white, as his iris shone with a corona of fire around perfect deep and beautiful brown eyes – he colour slipping as he relaxed to a stunning lagoon green.
The mirror of his mothers.

A single fly still circled around him frantically, then slowed and then fizzed out of existence in a tiny waft of smoke.

James slumped forward and nearly hit the floor as he passed out.
Nearly.
Had it not been for Lucifer's keen reflexes, a fluid movement
between armchair and floor, his arm cradled under the falling head of
the human.
Catching him. He picked him up so he could lay James down on the
sofa.
He rolled him into the recovery position, and took a long hard look at
his stubbly, awkward head, his glasses that were too small for his
face, his eyes that were small and catlike, his beard that looked at
once like it was grown out in hours and had been on his face forever.
A ragged mess of hair and colour, auburn, ginger and brown, spread
messily across his wide round chin.
"Oh, James. Must you really pass out now?"
        Lucifer had obviously been watching James for some time
before today. He had to. The importance James held for him meant
that a daily window had been open for the past 32 years of James
life, even as he was in the cell, sipping noisily at rationed sunlight,
rationed grace.
Even as he wandered in the fields of Nephilim and saw the
bloodletting that Michael and his other brothers had unleashed in the
war before and after The Fall. Even as he had carved Hell into the
mountainside at the very edge of the plain, staring down at the tree of
knowledge, Lucifer had expected more of this man.
Yet, here he was. Simple, inelegant, rough around the edges and
passed out with a line of spittle and drool dripping fragrantly from
the corner of his mouth.
Lucifer allowed himself to smile a weak, exasperated smile. Looking
around the room, he took stock of who James Edmunds was while he
lay here sleeping in terror and shock.
The ornaments. The armchair. The books on his shelves and the
knick-knacks on his dresser tops.

The Box that rested in the centre of the broken table.
Hard, unopened and mysterious.

The ingredients of the man laid out and bare for the whole world to see. Ready to be divined by clever minds.

Lucifer breathed it all in, and devoured the idle memories James had psychically inflected on the items, his eyes closing and flickering as he touched the Silver Frog that his mother had given him when he had moved into his first home away from her and his father.
The photo of the Charles Bridge in Prague that had the sun setting down the water, and people busily going about their business, even as James and Kay had stopped to pose for the Czech man who charged next to nothing to have the photos taken.
The warm paperweight James had seen and bought without thinking from the car-boot sale when he and Kay had visited the market in Finmere.

And then the photo of Kay next to the sandy coloured art card upon which was printed a tiny footprint. The two pictures in a hinged double photo-frame.
Kay and Footprint facing each other.
Written underneath the footprint were two words only – "MY BOY."
Lucifer picked this up, stared at it longingly, drank in the resonant memories attached, making sure to drink only enough to understand the pain, the loss, the memories. The deep meaning it held for James. It was a heady draught, warm and autumnal, smells of leaves falling from trees and bonfires, the sound of a gurgle and a giggle, he could taste the sterile hospital and the morgue – a bitter tang, but not unpleasant. Finally, he could see and taste the colour blue and the colour green – Kay's favourite and those that were draped on her coffin, and on the coffin of their boy, Callum.
Lucifer held it gently in his hand, and his smile was a precious, appreciative one.

A single tear formed in his eye, and as it ran down his cheek, it sizzled and dissipated leaving a fizz of steam.

"Please put that down," James said. Standing up unsteadily.
He looked at Lucifer.
The Morningstar had no smile now; his face was blank and
expressionless. But his eyes were warm and understanding.
"Of course." He gave a gentle, half smile – James returned it briefly
– "I did not mean to be rude."
James nodded, and walked toward Lucifer and took the frame from
his hands, without thinking he touched the face of his late wife and
ran a finger down the print of the foot as one would do when tickling
someone, the movement of finger on glass made him half cough a
smile and laugh.
"Not rude. I'd just rather you didn't touch please. It's not for
touching. I hope you understand."

Lucifer nodded. He understood perfectly.
He unconsciously ran two fingers cross his tiepin, and his index
finger circled the edge of the apple carving and he smiled again,
broad and wide.
"May I bend your ear, James? I do have something of the utmost
importance to discuss with you."
James looked the angel up and down.
Lucifer stood elegant and tall, his hair fell about his ears and
shoulders, his arms were long and lithe, but clearly muscular and full
of unknown strength, his suit was black in one light a burst of
emerald and green, in other light rich and dizzily black.
He was beyond words beautiful.

"Lucifer, eh?"
The angel nodded.
"Hmm. If I had of known, I was to have visitors I would have tidied
up a bit."
They both shared a smile and smirk, a half laugh. James held out his
hand and looked at Lucifer squarely, stoically, no fear, no horror, just
a man offering another man a hand.
"James Edmunds. Nice to make your acquaintance."

And Lucifer took his hand and shook heartily.
"And yours, James. And yours."

* * *
- 6 -

"Mum!" Kay shouted from the bedroom, the door slightly ajar. Through the gap you could see the devastation that was usual for a twenty-something single girl's bedroom.
Clothes everywhere. Ornaments and trinkets upon the dresser, makeup and perfumes bottles scattered wildly – yet in some incomprehensible design of filing – perfectly able to be divinized by the room's occupant.
"Mum!" she called again. Louder, half peering around the door.
"Yes, Katherine?" Kay's mother called back. "Are you ok darling?"
"Mum, please don't call me Katherine... I hate it."
"But that's your name dear. Katherine Genevieve Woodman."
"Ok... But I prefer Kay, ok?"
"Whatever is going to make you happy, sweetheart."

Kay's mother had a gentle, softly spoken Welsh brogue. It was painted on every word she said in delicate brushstrokes, lending every sentence a warm poetry.
To listen to her speak could have put wild tempestuous babies to sleep in minutes, so warm and welcoming it was, so safe and pretty.
"Mum, have you seen my overcoat? The thin one I got last Christmas. I want to go for a walk, but it says that there may be clear skies, but to expect a chill in the wind later. Last thing I need is another bloody cold!"
Kay continued to throw and discard clothing with no discrimination around the room, not a single inch of carpet was not covered by the clothing and fabric of vest tops, oversized t-shirts or cardigans two sizes too big for her slender and busty frame.

Kay was a beautiful girl. Her body was athletic, without being muscular, her limbs long without being gangly. Her eyes were two perfect almonds in a face that would have made romantic era poets cry. Her hair fell in light curls around a long elegant neck, over shoulders that drew two lines in the collarbone toward the chest, where two perfectly perky and shapely breasts perched. Not too big, not too small, but just beautiful and complimenting of her frame. Her hips were wider than what you would expect of a girl her size especially sat as they were below that waspish waist. And her legs were long with only one minor flaw being a slightly knobbly knee on her right leg, from a horse-riding fall when she was twelve.

She had long fingers, with nails that were cut short and painted with clear acrylic and French tips. And she wore very little makeup. Instead, her dress sense was used to paint colour to her eyes and cheeks, allowing herself only a fine line of lipstick or lip-liner to accentuate her gorgeous mouth.

She was – without a doubt – a natural and phenomenal beauty.

"It's in the spare room, love. I took it out of the car two or three weeks ago and forgot to hang it in your room. Hardly surprising too, considering you can barely get in there with all that junk on the carpet!" Her mother called from the bottom of the stairs, taking two or three steps up to see if she could catch a glimpse of her daughter.

Kay gave an appreciative "AHA!" and bounded out of the room. She perched precariously on the top steps handrail and leaned over blowing a kiss to her mother.

"Thank you, Mam." And blew several more over-exaggerated kisses down the stairs.

Gwyneth, Kay's mother, caught each one and acted out putting them in her pocket.

"I'll keep these for later, never know when I will need a kiss from a Princess."

Kay smiled, wide and proud.

"Thank you, Mam." She said again, this time more gently and personally.

Gwyneth returned her smiled and walked down the stairs toward the kitchen.

"Think nothing of it, my darling."

The jacket was hanging loosely from the collar on a coat hook that was in the spare room. The room itself was a mauve monstrosity that had a three-quarter sized bed, two bedside tables and floral sheets and curtains held open with purple and lilac tie-backs. A room now reserved for miserable aunties and grandmothers who regularly visited when chronic illness or loneliness set in. Maudlin, unhappy woman who draped sadness around their shoulders like scarves and shawls and tainted the world with insecurities and pessimism.
Kay and her Mother tolerated these visits as much they could. Sisters and aunties and grandmothers, each bringing a weight of their own world along as baggage.
Whenever they came Kay's father Trevor would disappear into his shed to tootle and mess about with his models and painting. Escaping the house of nagging, Welsh women and immersing himself in word of miniature World War Two aircraft and battleships.
Kay loved him dearly and often wished she could join him on every occasion.
Sadly – it was a no girl's club, no matter how much she coveted, she could not take away his only refuge in these times.

She threw on the jacket, picked up her light autumn scarf, a pattern of reds and oranges and yellows. And skipped down the stairs two or three at a time.
Into the arms of her father who was coming out of the dining room, glasses half perched on his nose.
"Afternoon Katherine. Don't you look a picture of autumnal brilliance today?" He lay a solitary kiss on her forehead and carried on toward the kitchen, newspaper in hand and glasses precariously perched defying gravity. His accent was a booming, but lyrical, Swansea one. He sounded like Richard Burton. The charm of an actor behind a miner's exterior.
"Are you coming with us to the Churchyard today?" he called back as he went from the one room to the other.
"No Dad, I'm popping down the park now for an hour or so, I'd

160

rather have a bit of time on my own if that's ok?"
Trevor Woodman stopped in the doorway of the kitchen, and
dropped his newspaper to his side, pushed his glasses higher up to
the bridge of his nose and smiled a small, loving grin.
"That is absolutely fine, my love, I understand." He hesitated, and
looking down at the floor, then back to his daughter he added:
"I miss her terribly too." And he smiled again, and the newspaper
was back up and his head was back into it and he left the doorway.

Gwyneth came out of the kitchen and handed Kay her handbag, a
small leather satchel imitation, the colour of oxblood.
"Thank you. I'll be back soon, ok?"
Her mother nodded, and gave her cheek a big kiss, and wiped the
remnant away with her thumb lovingly.
"Of course, my love, I'll see you soon."
And Kay exited the house, warm sunlight in her face and cloudless
skies over head.

* * *

On her way to the park, only a short stroll of fifteen or so
minutes, Kay saw many things. Some that stole her attention and
played on her imagination, like the three-legged Alsatian puppy that
skipped through the leaves under the walkway by the river, where the
treetops bent in like a canopy and shielded from rain and wind.
She saw the workmen bantering and goading each other as they
worked on the traffic lights by Gulliver's Crescent, works that had
disrupted and caused chaos on the roads for three or four weeks now,
seemingly no closer to ending than when they first went up.
She saw two people she assumed were lovers sat on a bench by the
Whale's Jawbone, on the Hotel side of the Park, arguing quietly
between each other, the girl crying as she laid out some story to the
man, whose anger visibly rose with each second of her story, and
which culminated in him screaming some accusatory insult at her
before motioning to hit her – something that made Kay stop in her
tracks and stare intently, this in turn was picked up by the man, who

threw a final insult and gestured conspicuously with his hands, before making some threat to some unknown third party.

Clearly the other invisible character in their tale.

The man demonstrated his unhappiness even as he was making his exit, leaving the woman in tears on the bench. Kay had two minds of whether to see if the girl was ok but chose to not get further involved. Instead, she made her way up through the trees and the winding stairs that lead to the Working Men's bridge, and over toward the town centre and the Park side of the river.

She took the side exit out of the shop and wandered down toward the War Memorial, crossing paths with a young man shuffling his way up toward the top of the hill and the Abbey entrance to the shops.

The two caught each other's eyes, he staring at her in the way a man would any beautiful woman way beyond his league and ability to woo. Hungry eyes, alive with lust, but, softened by a genuine appreciation. Not a danger, not a threat, an admirer of fine and beautiful things.

Kay smiled back, bashfully, understanding his need and want, his silent desire – and liking this attention. He was an ok looking guy, his walk was kind of like a penguin in a hurry, his hair shaggier than she liked, but not without its charm, and his glasses – though thick – highlighted two beautiful cat like eyes. His smile was warm and friendly and the gentle way he cast his glance down and up again, trying to break eye contact and failing, causing him to smile wider, more embarrassed, endeared him to her.

She gave a gentle giggle and carried on down the path toward the copper soldier stood sentinel over the park.

And there, she sat and she thought about her great-grandmother, resting a single Lilly she had bought from Kendall's Florists, at the foot of the statue.

Her great-grandmother's favourite place.

* * *

162

"What do you mean you are pregnant?" Leon's voice was barking now, the edge of anger had arrived. That sound that was reminiscent of grinding razorblades in a pestle and mortar. A crazy, uncontrollable danger to it.

Leon threw Nessa's hands off of his own and sprung up from the bench.

She sat holding her stomach, the oversize hooded sweater now coming into focus on her round frame.

Her hair was in a tight plait, pulling back her hair tight to her scalp, and she wore too much eye makeup, she looked cheap, Leon thought, cheap like a tart, a dirty, cheap, prick-teasing tart.

He was angry that she shared blood with him, that this painted little bitch was his sister.

"Pregnant how?" he demanded.

"I told you, I have been seeing someone, it's not his fault, he used protection, it must have split or broke, it's an accident. But I love him. I want to keep it."

"This is Tyrone ain't it? This is that fucking Tyrone who done this? I know it is..."

Nessa sat up and held a hand out toward Leon.

"No. it's not him, I haven't seen or spoken to him since we broke up, I promise. This has nothing to do with Tyrone."

Leon hit her hand away; he spat on the ground.

"Shut up!" He looked Nessa, his sister up and down and tutted loudly.

"Look at you. No better than Mum, like a painted whore throwing it about town... Tryna tell me it ain't nothin' to do with Tyrone. Shut up if I believe you. I can smell that wanker all over you. You lying bitch."

Nessa reached out to grab his sleeve and calm him down, and Leon raised his arm up as if to administer a slap. Nessa retreated back raising an arm herself to defend his blow, and as he was about to unleash, he caught the woman staring at him from the other side of the street next to the Southwick hotel.

He looked at his sister, eyes narrowed, teeth clenched, then back at the woman reaching into her coat for a phone no doubt. Common sense flushed over him again.

"I'm gonna find him, and I'm gonna kill him. You see if I don't, Ness. You see if I fucking well don't."
And Leon left the canopy of trees, overlooking the Whale's Jawbone, and his sister crying on the bench.

* * *

He'd been up since 4.45am, but for some reason Tyrone was still not sleepy. Work finished twenty minutes before, and all he wanted now was a cigarette and a beer.

Tyrone worked for a cleaning company, and he had done his usual routine of three buildings in the town, one after the other, hoovering, emptying bins, cleaning desks and disposing of waste water from coffee machines and tea urns. Headphones in and some R'n'B or Jazz classic bursting away in his ears, massaging his eardrums and kicking his brain into a hypnotic state of mind as his hands and body worked independently on the routine and jobs like a metronome. One bin following the other following the other until all that was left was black bags chucked down waste pipes into dumpsters below.

Tyrone did this six days a week, Monday to Saturday. The Saturday was overtime and purely for his own need to find somewhere else to live, somewhere better than the small box room at his parents, which he had found himself trapped in after the break up from Nessa and the subsequent loss of the flat they had rented together.

He rested up by the back exit of the Shopping Centre, perched against a wall; he lit a Marlboro Light and sucked back on his first and only cigarette of the day.

This pack of ten had lasted him seven days now. He still had four left. He was giving up in stages, and had reduced his need from twenty or thirty a week to less than ten. By the end of next month he hoped to be on two or three a week max, the month after he hoped to be off altogether. He had always been good at reducing his need for something by denying himself the pleasure.

164

He had done it with alcohol, something he drank rarely, but craved daily. And he had done it with weed and pills as well – when he lived with Nessa, these were something he had taken in abundance, no thought for himself or others – his ridiculous sense of immortality driving, and his self-esteem, his reputation and his bank balance had dwindled to nothing.

It had cost him his friends and almost his family to see the things out of his life.

It had certainly cost him his girlfriend and best friend – Leon had not spoken to him since the day he packed his clothes in two bin liners and jumped in the taxi to his folk's house, apologetic beyond words, tears in his eyes accepting he had blown his life into a spiral of bad decisions and stupid mistakes.

His parents – two well-regarded members of the local church, community spirited and neighbourhood watch committee to boot – had accepted him back without question when they saw how he had crawled back on scabbed knee over hot coals of his own shame. They felt bad he had put himself into this position, but they loved him all the same and wanted him to find his own path again.

He had done so, more or less, worked hard and without complaint and slowly but surely the pieces were being put together in the rightful places again.

His life was starting to resemble something akin to reasonable and respectful again, even by his low standards.

He took the final few drags of his cancer stick, flicked the stub at the nearby hedges and exhaled a rich cloud of blue smoke from his lungs, followed the cigarette up immediately with two pieces of gum.

The taste was awful, with the tobacco and mint mixing into a heady blend of smokehouse peppermint in his mouth, but it was better than the taste of acrid tar and formaldehyde, which he swore he could always taste.

Tyrone flipped the hood up on his sweater, and took out his phone, he looked down the way toward the Bangladeshi restaurant and looked at his mobile, his father had agreed to meet him here, Tyrone had agreed to drive him to the Garden Centre from work

165

before going home and taking a break and catching some shut eye... If sleep would come today.

But, unlike him, his father was late.

Tyrone clicked through the messages to see if he had gotten the time or maybe the rendezvous wrong, but they both confirmed this was where and when he should be, so he leant back and waited.

At the top of the narrow walkway from the restaurant and Nightclub "Marianne's" – The screeching of a car was heard, it stopped just shy of the bollards outside the nightclubs entrance, having driven up the hill into oncoming foot traffic.

Tyrone looked at the car dazed and confused, before realizing that it was Leon in the driver's seat. His face full of rage and his mouth spewing indistinguishable bile, every other word some Fuck or other. In his hand, before Tyrone could even think, he saw Leon had a pocket knife.

And as he looked at the knife, he completely missed the left hook that clocked him under the cheek and smashed him back into the wall, gashing his face and drawing quick, red blood.

The blows came in hard and fast and all Tyrone could do was defend from the right hand and that blade jabbing and swiping at him.

What this attack was for he did not know, he caught maybe three or four words, spat vengefully at him by Leon, something about a baby, something about his sister, the word *whore*. Leon kicked and punched and jabbed out with the knife.

Tyrone had hold of his right hand and leant into the jab and twisted his body round, making Leon lose his foot and fall into his own flailing arm.

The whole of his body seized for a second, Tyrone moved his body backward, still holding the right arm, as he stepped back the knife twisted, and both Leon's arms went limp and loose.

Tyrone let go of his arm and stood back, as Leon fell down to his knees and then slumped to the floor. He saw the knife sticking out of Leon's abdomen, the red of his blood seeping and saturating round the wound, he leant down and tried to apply pressure and stem the bleeding.

"What did you do, man?" Leon gasped in bursts of breath.
Already a small crowd of people had gathered, some were casting accusatory fingers in his direction, blame was being attributed to him, and then one women, thirty-five or so, took out her phone and snapped several photos as Tyrone leant over Leon, his hand on the blade, for all intents and purposes looking like he was driving the knife home.
The flash on her phone going off each time and with it, something primal and uncontrollable in Tyrone's mind became alive with fire and confusion and took over.

Tyrone grabbed the blade.
He would never be able to tell you why.
Except he knew the knife was his, and he thought he had lost it, did not want to lose it again. Memories of that camping trip were all he could remember.
Being seventeen and sitting around an open fire he had helped build, sipping from a bottle of beer he had stolen from his friend's dad's garage, and smiling and joking and laughing with friends.

This was all he could think of as he ran, hard, fast, half-dazed and detached from his own mind. Bursting briskly through the park, past the war memorial and down toward the ponds.
His mind flying the vehicle that was his body.
Allowing him one single look behind to make sure he was safe and away from the terrible scene...

And as he turned to look, this was when the girl stepped back and straight into his path.
Two more strands of fate's masterplan tying themselves inextricably together.
Two less frayed and loose ends.
One more rope to dangle from...

* * *

167

James had been waiting in town now for two or three hours, he had drank all the coffee he could handle, his skin felt electric and jittery. His eyes ached and his head pounded. So he had taken the walk down toward the bandstand, and sat on the bench next to it, even as kids danced and sang and ran around the stand itself.

Down to his left the Pagoda sun house was full of people enjoying this Indian summer in late September. He had his phone open and stared at it ponderously as he waited for the call from his office's American office.

Three candidates had been put forward for the job in the Seattle office. Two years of secondment to the headquarters, working on special projects, overseeing some of the development of the company's new web-technologies, and being part of the development team for the company-wide data flux update.

He had worked for the best part of ten years in his UK office from the ground floor to systems manager, building the security net, supervising the new platform for the call centre staff, and had watched as the company had developed from an up-itself garage enterprise into a multi-million pound corporation, had been present for two buy-outs and a merger and now had the chance to finally take the step to the next level.

Three candidates and only one telephone interview each. He had been waiting for a week for the call. Delayed by storms and a black out beyond anyone but God's control, he had been told that it would be today. Before five o'clock.

So here he sat, in the Abbey Park, watching the giant Abbey clock tick down each minute.

It was now 3.30pm, and he had already screamed at four people to get off his line and not call back till at least Thursday.

One call centre selling insurance had gotten an earful of inventive and obscene anatomical instructions on where they could put the call. His own mother, calling from New Zealand had been told to "hang up the fucking phone, woman!"

James had sat with his bottled water, a bag of cherries and the laughter of kids and families in his ear. Then, he had seen the woman from earlier again, wandering down past the memorial and toward the pedalo pond.

168

He watched her, while sat on the bench, his elbows on his knees, staring at the phone and the woman intermittently, realizing the woman was getting far more attention. He smiled and laid the phone down next to his leg, the ringer was on loud, and he would not miss it.

He very well knew that this was his one and only chance, and miss this call he could kiss Seattle goodbye.

He looked down the hill toward the pond and smiled as the girl threw some bread into the pond at the fat, miserable ducks. He laughed as they surrounded her feet all at once, and she let out a gasp of surprise and a giggle that made this September day feel like the warmest day of summer and he laughed too.

She took a step back from the ducks, even as she did she threw another handful of breadcrumbs into the water, and the ducks turned tail and went after it.

The woman took one more step back, without looking and the hooded boy clattered straight into her, his head turned behind, looking over his shoulder. Two or three other people scattered by his barged run.

The woman took an elbow directly onto the back of the head as their two individual worlds collided in a sickening fashion. She arched back as if in sublime pain, then flopped forward like someone had turned her off at the mains, her head struck the pole of the hand rail by the pond, and even as she fell forward, limp and loose-limbed, James was already flying down the path toward her hand clenched around the phone.

The dial tone a piercing triple ring - going off in his hand.

Seattle on the line.

Clenched in a fist now purple and red at the knuckles, and then suddenly drenched as it and James submerged into the pond. He relinquished his grip; the phone tried ringing again, but gave nothing but a watery warble and then floated down toward the shallow end of the pond, before submerging and sinking to the bottom.

James had forgotten all about it but for a single fleeting second of regret soon drowned with the rush of adrenaline and the cold September water, the memory of his call, his phone or why he was in the park was soon altogether erased from his mind the minute he had turned the woman round and administered the first breath of life into her lungs.

She smelled incredible, even considering the algae-filled pond water she had collapsed into. She was utterly beautiful, and he was stood watching and applauding himself as a disembodied spirit as the whole spectacle unfolded.
He couldn't help but laugh at himself from his incorporeal self as he shouted the immortal line.
"SOMEBODY CALL A FUCKING AMBULANCE!"

As the girl sputtered back to life and blinked her eyes, foggy, confused and half awake – James snapped back into one single entity, and realized that no matter how hard he tried, no matter what situation would ever present itself and no matter what woman he may ever meet in his life...
He would never be so cool again.
And he would never love anyone like he loved this girl here and now.

Unlike when he had been in this position with Poppy, who had died in his arms, turning his introverted nature even more deadly upon itself. Her poor, lovely face smashed with the rock.
He realized that here, he could help this girl, he could save her.
Indeed, his rescue breaths and chest compressions had saved her, even now she looked up at him, her hand clenching hard at his own, her beautiful eyes staring deeply back into his own.
She asking where she was, and he introducing himself and telling her she would be fine, he would make sure that she was fine.

He smiled at her as she squeezed his hand gently, in that way that one knows someone is letting you know that they trust you. He gently squeezed back, and she half smiled at him, tears in her eyes, and her head banging with the concussion.

Even so, she looked at the man who had helped her, and she knew even then, this was the man she would spend the rest of her life with.

James, for his efforts, felt the exact same.
More so...
He felt he had achieved something beyond anything he thought himself capable of.
He felt amazing...

He felt like a Goddamn hero.

* * *

James sat guardian by her side as she went to hospital; he waited in the foyer to meet her parents having called them from her phone, explaining the situation and how he had made sure she was ok. What had happened and how it had happened... A garbled account, peppered by his own perception, he told of the boy in the hood and the knife and the unlucky collision that was no one's real fault – just "One of those things" – Kay's parents thanked him, and traded numbers and kept him in the loop. Kay was in hospital for a fortnight, the impact with the pole had caused her a minor fracture, she had broken her wrist when hitting the water, and the concussion was a particularly bad one.
The whole time she was in the hospital all she thought about was the man who had revived her.
For his sins, James could think of nothing more either, even losing Seattle meant nothing to him when he thought of her lush hair, her lips and her almond shaped eyes.

As for the hooded boy and his story, the local press picked up the rest and shared this with the world, Kay's parents learned all they needed from the paper.
The hooded young man having given himself up to the police, arrested for the manslaughter, it was not until video surveillance was released that showed the knifing was not his fault; more or less a

stupid accident caused and brought on by the attacker himself. His explanation was understood to be a consequence of panic and shock; he was released of charges within three months.

The ex-girlfriend blamed herself for everything that happened, she nearly lost the baby, but pulled through. Eventually moving in with the father. Leon's best friend.

When Kay was finally released from hospital, on a cold, damp Tuesday, she had wandered outside to meet her parents who had said they would be parking up and ready. Instead, waiting with flowers was James. Smiling awkwardly and shuffling in that unique, loveable way he did.

Kay had never been so happy.

They had a whirlwind romance this is true, but, it worked. It was right, it felt right for them both and Kay's parents could not love James anymore if they tried.

James, on his part, barely spoke to his brother and sister, his father had passed away five years previously of a heart attack and his mother was enjoying her retirement in New Zealand. Living off the insurance and pension payout from his father's death.

He had no children; he had no wife or girlfriend. The day he saved Kay's life, he had two fish and a flat and a job that had soon hit dead end – not that it mattered.

All he cared about was the woman on his arm, and the fact her parents liked him, LOVED him in fact, this was nothing but a bonus.

The two of them referred to the day they met as "the day Kay took a swim." Both of them agreed that love at first site was a thing made up by greeting card companies and idiots, but it was difficult to argue with fate. So, the day the swim had taken place was forever sown in their minds as the anniversary of their relationship.

"And fuck what anyone else thinks" Kay had so elegantly put it. James laughed and agreed, something he had grown accustomed to around Kay, the woman was invariably right about everything, and this was something he fell into with no argument.

Usually, at work or play, this kind of Know-It-All attitude would

make him angrier than anything he could name, but with Kay – well – it was true, she did know best, and he was happy to concede the point and drink in that smile she always transmitted.
He loved that smile.
He loved Kay. Mind, body and soul.

When the day came for him to ask her to marry him, it was the day that they were looking for houses. And it happened, as luck would have it, right in the back garden of the house that James now sat in with Lucifer.
Right in front of the awful estate agent Estrella.
It damn well nearly ruined her mental holiday.

And as these things usually were with James, it was unplanned, unrehearsed and incredibly charismatic beyond his own belief.

* * *

The house had been so beautiful. Small enough to fit their life together snuggly and warm, in awe and drunk on the soul of the other. Yet, big enough to fit their individual worlds as well.
This was one of the reasons Kay loved it so much. This and the willow in the garden, The tree that seemed to slump in sadness and shake as if crying, that made Kay smile with its elegant bow, its shaggy curtsy.
Kay had held James' hand all the way round except when it came to the willow.
She had walked outside on her own, and stared at it, pulled her coat up around herself as the shiver of memory ran through her.

It looked exactly like the tree in her great-grandmother's garden.
It had the same silvery branches, the same thin and lean trunk. The green of the leaves and the foliage was like a lush, fertile field. Brimming with a gentle blossom, pink and white and beautiful.

The trunk was twisted like a staircase, leading to some exotic attic, full of mystery and adventure and secrets. Kay stood holding her arms around herself and let loose a giggle that James heard from the kitchen as he nodded vacantly and verbally grunted affirmatives to things Estrella was winding off about details of the foundation and the architecture of the surrounding schools and a million other boring things he had managed to block out as he stared at the women he loved through the open side door at the rear of the house.

James raised a finger to the agent and asked for a moment. The agreement to buy had already been made. They had seen the house from top to bottom, Estrella was already fastened the bikini up for her date with the hot Cuban/Mexican/Colombian bartender boyfriend that she was going to seduce later that evening in her mental cave – where the holiday she was buying with this commission was already playing on loop ad infinitum inside her own mind.

Kay had asked to see the garden one last time before they leave, and James had said he would talk details with Estrella while she did. This was a bad idea, but he loved Kay unquestionably and understood that when she had asked to see something again, it clearly held meaning for her.

"Are you ok, Boo?" He had asked, as she startled slightly and turned to him, a tear in her eye which she thought she had caught and a warm, wisp of a smile on her lips.

"I am fine," she coughed once, it was a weak, broken sound, welled with further tears barely concealed. She coughed again, stouter, stronger, inflicting a tone of manliness in it.

"I am brilliant in fact." She smiled at him genuinely and it damn near broke his heart it was so beautiful.

"Yeh, you are," he said, it was said in a way you could hear his smile in the words.

"Smooth, Eddie, smooth." Kay had goaded. Eddie was her name for him, this or Jim. Never James. She never ever called him James – it was too formal, it rolled off her tongue like she was speaking to her father or boss. So Eddie or Jim it was.

"My grandmother had a tree like this in her garden when I was younger. It was damaged in a storm and we had to dig it up. I remember sitting under it when I was a kid, reading Famous Five books and other Enid Blyton stories. Just makes me smile when I think of it. It was one of my favourite places in the world. Even now when I read on a bus or a train or something, I imagine the bark against my back and the shadows from the canopy and the wind gently blowing my skirt and hair. It's a sad memory but also my happiest."

"Happiest, eh?" James said, looking coy and crestfallen.

"Well, it's in my top two. The other is a fat-faced idiot staring down at me with the taste of cherries on his lips telling me I will be ok."

James smiled. "Fat-faced idiot is it?"

Kay laughed, she covered her face with her hand, coy and playfully.

"Yeah. The fattest." She smiled widely.

"Who I fell in love with straight away and will never stop loving even past the day I die."

James shuffled on the spot, nervously. His hands went into his pockets, and he looked down at the floor then back up to Kay, shyly smiling.

"Well…" Now he coughed. "Crikey."

And she laughed. It was as radiant as the peak of the hottest summer's day and washed over him like he had collapsed into the coming tide. He loved it.

Kay grabbed his hand and tried to drag him to the house, and he resisted.

"Come on stupid, we have to go, I think the estate agent is getting tired of our company, I have seen her yawn three or four times now while we have stood out here."

James held her hand nodded, Kay turned away and started walking, she got about four steps dragging James behind her when she stonewalled to a stop as he held her arm and hand and made her unable to move.

She turned around to look what he was doing and as she did he had taken his other hand out of his pocket and was holding it out to her. The look on her face was one of confusion and surprise.

Was what she saw real?

She struggled for her bearings, to regain composure. The game between the two of them was one of constant one-upmanship, it had gotten serious and out of hand in the last few weeks, but now – NOW – Kay had to agree to herself that this was as much as it could go before she had to concede he had won, something she was loathe to do, but, was willing she thought after today's little coup.

"Katherine Genevieve Woodman." He held in his hand a simple silver band, indented in the metal three small stones - an emerald, a ruby and a yellow hued diamond.
He held it pinched between index finger and thumb and he smiled so wide when he said her name, knowing full well how much she hated the full title her parents gave her, but unable to help himself.
"Will you be my wife?"

Estrella almost threw up in the kitchen.
She had to pretend to take a call for fear of laughing at the awkwardness of his question, and she wandered off coughing to hide her giggles.
Kay, to her credit, stood with her mouth just gently open, her head tilted to one side, and a tear running down her cheek.
"That ring is beautiful." Was what came out of her mouth before anything else.
James had to laugh, he had expected that it would be something other than "YES" but knew he could never predict his loves next move, her wit was sharper than Zorro's sword.
"Thanks. It was my grandmother's…" he shuffled in his inimitable way again.
"Soooo…" He looked at her and offered the ring once more.
"My arm is getting pretty tired holding all this bling. What do you say we put it on that finger, and you give me an answer?"
Kay snapped back to reality, looked at the man she loved smiling awkward and gawkishly at her and threw her arms around him.
"Yes. Yes… I'm sorry… A million times yes, of course it's yes you idiot!"
And she kissed him hard and lovingly on the mouth as his hand went to the nape of her neck and into her hair.

"I promise I will keep you safe and love you and make you happy."

Kay backed away, took James' hand, and looked him directly in the eye.

"You have never done anything but, Eddie." And she smiled wider than she thought she had ever smiled before, slipped the ring on her finger, held it up to the sky and giggled, jumping up and down on the spot.

James had never been happier.
He had never been more in love.

* * *

- 7 -

The intricacies of the multitude of myths and histories of most of the world's religions were long since lost to rumour, happenstance and legend. Realistically, no one has ever really structured a concise or genuine history of any of the world's major religions - living or dead - that resembles the actual truth of where it came from and how it sprung into being.
Suffice to say. The accepted histories we have today were designed by committees and signed off to add romance and flair to third, fourth and sometimes fifth-hand accounts.
Chinese whispers layered upon Chinese whispers, where truth somewhere along the line became blended into fiction and what we are left with are stories of magic, mayhem and chaos, dressed in finery and delivered with ceremony and a forced, moribund set of traditions.
Almost entirely man-made.

This is not to say that religions are false or wrong. Merely to agree that most of what we take for granted, the complex stories, the doctrines, the beliefs carved through thousands of years of word of mouth and collected in books we then deem and elevate to "Holy

Status" – well – a lot of it is incorrect and contradictory and, in some cases, downright insulting to the majority of right thinking, free-minded individuals who do not need or want that belief.
More is the pity.
Because... and this is said from a position of some understanding... Half of what is actually true is a million, million times more interesting and amazing than the fictions that are being passed off.

Zeus, for instance, was the great-grandson of Gaia in religious texts and histories in the Greek Pantheon. Zeus the son of Cronos, the Titan, who in turn was Son of Uranus – the Primordial God, Gaia's Son and Husband.
Born from a virgin birth from Gaia's womb, she took him as her husband, and together they birthed and bore the six Titans. Cronos castrated his own father and imprisoned him and in turn was overthrown and imprisoned by Zeus, King and greatest of the Olympians.

It is a visceral and enjoyable story.
But a story it is all the same.
Elements are true, parts are from fact. But, be that as it may, at the end of the day there will always be the beach, the sand, the waters cold lapping tide and the single truth I lay upon them all.

Nought but name and secret whispered to their ear.
Before I shared the cosmic law down upon them.

My name is Death. I was there on the first day of these gods you have now, and those who have long since fallen into silence and oblivion. You will all meet me one day.

I will not talk about the world before this one. Too many bad memories, too many mistakes and bad decisions to dredge and drag up.
Instead, let me tell you of the day I met Yahweh and Gaia, Vishnu and Odin, Ganesha and the pantheon of gods who woke upon my little sandy corner of the world and the things that followed soon

after.

The universe was a bleak, lonely black. Obsidian ultima. A scorched canvas of nothing. Made real from wiping the board clean of that which came before. The OLD gods, the vicious, hateful beings who made the layers of eternity their soiled and ugly plaything.

Burned out and broken, their world and time ended as yours began, with a big bang.

The essence of what was inverting, folding in on itself and then popping back out the other way, and with it, as always, the beach. Each grain of sand upon it the remains of the world before. And before that, and before that, and before that...

This is not your first attempt at "Life" – these gods you have now nowhere near the beginning of the queue. Cast into a vast line of previous realities, where there is only Me and the Darkness, and Sister Time.

I do not talk to my sister, she does not, in all honesty, talk with anyone. She merely is, happy to be, nothing more. Her presence felt more readily than even mine in every room, every mind, heart and body across the globe and beyond.

She was there on the beach as well, but hiding way back, behind the rocks, watching, and just... *well*... being.

As she does, as she is known for doing.

I paced up and down the waters, as each new body washed upon the shore, and soon there were a thousand deep. I went to each body, and I leaned in close, gave them name and form, life and being, a name from my own tongue to their ear and waited whilst they woke, one by one.

Soon, there were a thousand faces staring at me, naked and lost, confused and cold and scared. So I introduced myself, as I have done countless times before.

"I am Death," I said because, I am.

I stood amongst them all, sword on hip and scythe in hand. My robes cut and stitched from the countless universes I have removed and returned to oblivion, a slither of fabric from each to remember and to mourn.

I looked around them all and I said:

"You are gods and you are born, each a creator and destroyer all. Remember – whatever you do from this point forward - there was once darkness and nothingness from which you came, and in that I was King.

I was here before you came, and I will be here long after you leave. One day, we will meet face to face again, and we will not have quite such a pleasant chat as we did this day. I am death. And you are all my children."

Or words to that effect.

I said to them how I would walk with them to the ether of oblivion when their day had come, hand in hand to their final departure and I would be the last thing they saw, much as I was the first.

Countless thousands of gods have I slain. Whisked to the door at the end of this world, once opened and walked through, never to return. One day I too will see that door myself, no doubt, because when all is said and done. When my sister is laying dying at my feet, time slowing down to nothing, I will carry her in my arms, as the last few grains of sand drop to the bottom of her timer, and we will walk through, finally to discover what is on the other side.

It is my only payment for the work I have done.

To finally see the world beyond my wall.

"Remember," I said, "I was here before you woke, and I will be here long after you leave this place." It was true the first thousand times I said it, and it will be true the next thousand more.

But I digress.

I wanted to tell you about the God Zeus.

Yahweh's brother, and the first woken amongst the gods of the Greeks.

You see, Zeus watched Yahweh – your God – very closely. As any younger sibling watches and learns from the elder. Zeus was second only to Yahweh in age – being the second to receive his name, a quirk of fate and time; my sister again playing with her threads.

He watched closely to everything that went on in the garden in the early days.

Dressed as an eagle. Cloaked in the skin of an oak tree. From behind a swan's black, curious eyes.

Zeus walked in the skins of many creatures, and from these vantages experienced every form of carnality and awakening he could. But, it was seeing his brother create Lilith, from elements made by their sister Gaia that made Zeus want to experiment with his own part of creation.

He watched as Lilith offered herself to God in the waterfall. Silently, he witnessed the sexual awakening of woman in this new world. And he wanted a woman, a daughter of his own. He wanted to see and taste and hold these emotions that were being brought to stark life by his older brother.

Zeus found a patch of the ground, and he and his sister set about building. From the clay, as he had seen Yahweh do, he molded the body of Pandora. Gaia breathed life into her frame, and she was the first of his people. Each of the Olympian gods, who had gathered around Zeus and sought his leadership, his guidance, presented Pandora with a gift.

Music, clothing, beauty and speech.

Like Lilith, who would have been her half-sister, she was incandescently beautiful. Like Lilith, she was imbibed with a natural curiosity of how the world worked. And in her garden, she looked and clambered for all the hidden secrets and mysteries, trying in vain to solve them one after the other.

Zeus gave her a gift as well.

He called to her, to meet him at the centre of his garden. A copy of Eden, circled by mountains that blocked the eyes of others, gods not of Zeus's table, of Yahweh most of all, from watching or witnessing Zeus's game.

Yahweh unaware that this land bordered his own Eden across the vast barren plain.

"Pandora, my daughter, my love. I too have a gift for you."
Pandora sat eagerly. Her clothes were really no more than webs and silks, thin and fragile, barely hiding her nakedness. Zeus resisted the same sensations that had bewitched his brother; Gaia was always watching – he could feel her eyes on him always.
"Father. What have you there for me?"
And Zeus revealed a Pithos. A beautiful clay urn, decorated and laced with gold and bronze, and sealed with a wax bond around a decorative clay cap.
"This is the most incredible gift. I give you the gift of trust. Within this urn are secrets and lies, evils and dangers, monsters and sprites. I give this to you, daughter, as a sign of my trust in you, my trust that you will do as you know you should. Keeping this world safe and free from harm by forever guarding this seal."
Pandora stared at the wax seal greedily, seductively, intoxicated already by its allure and deadly charm.
"You must never open this urn. Lest you free the evils that gods have created upon this world and suffer the consequences of such a betrayal."

Pandora took the urn, promised never to open the seal.
And then promptly did.

By this time, Prometheus had already stolen fire and unleashed it upon the world. His twin, Epimetheus had been employed as Pandora's husband within this paradise.
But he was lazy, errant, dunderheaded.
Pandora had no interest in this absent God. So, one evening, she

opened the urn for no other reason than it was there and the temptation to see what was inside was too great for her to resist.

Before the Apple, before the serpent Zeus had pre-empted and foreseen temptation.
Presented it, and allowed it to be taken advantageously.
He sat back and curiously watched as the evils of the world seeped into the soil and the seas and permeated the world.

And he smiled.

Pandora was stricken to dust, much like Lilith was confined to the plain. He erased the garden from existence. Sent Epimetheus to the mountains, and gathered the urn and buried it deep beneath the earth of his broken, failed and wasted garden.
This being the one place in existence he knew he could trust to keep it safe.

Zeus had known from the start the errors and mistakes that would come. He resisted the urges inside himself to lay with his first created daughter and allowed the play to roll out in front of him. The urn was real, the evils too, these were free and dancing over the back of the world now, something alive and loose since the earliest days of creation.
Gifts from the daughter of the *other* Eden to the people yet to come.

The urn was the only thing that could imprison them again. A natural cell for that which was broken, twisted, tortured and frail.
Evil being all of these things and more.

* * *

The urn sat untouched for untold millennia. Buried under earth so sacred and holy that it was scorched and parched and arid. The colour of deep rust.

The garden of Zeus cast to nothing and returned to the plain. It bristled with a crawling movement, blown by the winds and stretched, pulled and spread wildly out into the plain beyond the scattered remains of Zeus's failed, broken garden.

The sands became legion. Its deep colour scorched into all parts of the world it touched, soon, a desert – vast and angry - had formed.

It was lifeless and void of anything with breath.

Baked heavy under an undulating yellow sun, burning down in a concentrated push of heat and exhaustion. Within the desert, you were nothing, a speck, another grain of sand amongst trillions.

Somewhere under all this was the urn. Only it was no longer an urn. It too was dust.

The wax seal broken, the cap removed. The pressure of a million, million evils bursting free like water from an immeasurable underground geyser, like volcanoes exploding magma and pyroclastic clouds over the world. The release of everything inside had cracked the great, decorative Pithos, leaving it smashed and fragmented.

Zeus had collected the parts and reformed it into a crude jigsaw of a cube, placing inside it a box made of the thinnest silver, inscribed with nothing more than an X in fine, engraved bronze. The pieces of the Pithos urn had been turned into lining for this silver jewel box, which in turn was placed inside another box formed of the bark of willow trees and then inside an oak tomb. A puzzle of boxes laced in curses and godly promises, hexed by the thunder god, the swan, the eagle and the oak's seed. And buried so deep in the earth, shifting and moving even as the tectonic plates split apart, and the world became the patchwork quilt we know today.

Soon not even Zeus knew where the box was kept.

It was a relic that was spoken of in legend, never seen by prying eyes, and only ever handled or touched by Zeus and Pandora herself.

The cursed box of all evils. The only thing that could be used to box evil again.

The most powerful relic of the forgotten world of gods.
Unknown to all.
Oblivious to its power except through the tales of Hesiod and Homer,
fairytale and myth.

Soon, the desert was turned again into green and lush fields;
soil sprouted amongst the dust of the sand, and the lifeless plain gave
way instead to the will of the First amongst the garden. To Lilith's
plague of root and tree, flower and plant.
The ghost of the torn and abandoned daughter of Yahweh had seeded
the ground of the world and had birthed the oceans deep with her
waters from the violent and ragged birth of the host. Her blood had
provided the nourishment for the seed of her footsteps, and her final
birthing crack had sprayed her essence into the clouds, causing the
rain to fall fast, and deep, and righteous across all of creation.
The creation of Yahweh and the plethora of others gods together.

The first steps of Earth had begun amongst the garden. And
even as Adam and Eve had laid together and given the world Cain
and Abel and the infant Seth, the world was forming into that which
we now know.
Other gods making their own template of man, stealing wholesale
from Yahweh's blueprint, the world became populated with people
of all castes and colours, creed and shape.
The first birthing pool of humanity formed, beginning to take the first
steps into the wide world of history and destiny.

Lilith saw all; every flower was her eye, every blade of grass
her fingers, the wind her tongue and the waters her rage. She was
everywhere, infecting the Earth. Giving humanity an abundance of
everything they would need.

In the centre of it all a tree imbibed with holy knowledge, born from
the bones of the woman herself. A thin, beautiful branch twisting
from the trunk; like an arm, its hand holding a solitary apple.

185

Red and inviting.
Unknown to all, the roots spread for thousands of miles, deep and deadly through the ground, connecting every continent and one solitary root wrapped tight around a box, made of oak, holding a willow bark box inside, which in turn held a silver box inscribed with a solitary bronze X which held lining made of a Pithos urn.

Pandora's Box, now safe in the coils of a tree that once was a woman.

Lilith's revenge and retribution safe within this indestructible idea and root of life.
A gift for her eldest son.

Soon to be delivered.

* * *
- 8 -

The garden had been growing at a wild pace. Adam was starting to show signs of weary bags under his eyes that shadowed the deep piercing hazel hue. The dark circles were there as a result of his tireless, unquestioning guardianship of the grounds of Eden. He would tend and tidy flowers, clear path and forest floor. Walk amongst animals ferocious and tame; all of the animals loved him and let him be as he wandered naked and harmless through their midst.

His unwavering love of this luscious and bountiful garden matched only by his love of the woman who lay with him every night, fed him food to fill his belly and gave herself unto him every evening.
Their lovemaking was wanton, rabid, vicious and full of animalistic intent.
But, it was also loving. The two were deeply in love.

Eve would come to him as he sat in the shade of the oaks and baobabs, sipping water from leaves that had captured honeydew and

186

frost that thawed and tasted like perfect mountaintops in winter.
She came from the clearing by the wall, where they had made home.
Her naked body was a renaissance painting of brilliant contours, long
legs topped with hips that were thin but shapely, a heaving breast
with two perfectly round nipples, the same pink as her lips.
Her eyes a blue he had never seen before, her hair an auburn brown
that fell in curls that came to a fine blonde tip. She padded like a
panther on a hunt through the grasslands, into the dense forest and
would pounce on him as if taking down her prey. Her teeth sinking
into the flesh of his neck, biting and sucking his muscle hard, always
marking him. Her nails like claws digging into the soft skin of his
buttocks and chest, drawing lines of deep red and bloody lust into his
body, leaving her signature on his flesh, stating he was hers alone.

Adam would lift her up and carry her to the nearest tree trunk,
where there he would enter her. Thrusting hard, each movement and
gesture enough to draw deep, heaving breaths from his bride that she
followed every time with a shorter, softer breath, her legs wrapped
around his body, pulling him into her deeper, the two of them
climaxing in unison. Hot, salty sweat falling from their backs,
running down the nape of their backsides, down legs that quivered
now and shook with the release of their love from one to the other.

Their lovemaking always witnessed by a bitter, envious God.
Once bitten by this same passion, twice shy by its sudden betrayal
and mockery.

Yahweh would sit on his throne, made of twisted and
malformed branches, laced in silver and gold, high and wide and
beautiful in its ugliness.
Around him the sons of his union with Lilith, now grown to a hungry
adolescence of sorts.
Wings of pure white, akin to those of a swan or heron. Halos of
silver, sparkling and fizzing with pure celestial power, each formed
from a sliver of a star, no wider or thicker than a hair, but each more
powerful than any volcano, than any waterfall, than any inferno.
Michael stood to his father's right, decked in a silver chest
plate that was lined with a fiery gold ingot. By his side he had a

sword that was formed from the flame of the Earth's core and had a hilt that was made of the branch of the first tree in Eden.

It burned slowly, its blade red hot and resembling oozing lava, a ballet of reds and oranges and yellows, slipping between a dull, warm red and a rich, incredible orange, its edge a line of pure, blue fire. His blonde hair a dirty, sandy colour that fell in clumps of ringed curls tight to his scalp, and tussled down past his ears.

Michael's eyes were a harsh, deadly and serious blue. His brow fixed in a permanent scowl like he was perplexed or puzzled by something all the time. His lips were clenched in a grimace of disdain. No emotion passed his features, except the impassive boredom and ambivalence that came with knowing you were second only to the Morningstar, and if not for him, would be the eldest and rightful heir to the throne.

Regardless of him being his father's protégé and favourite of the eight babes of the host, the golden Archangels assembled, Michael always felt second best when put on a pedestal to the carefree, curiosity of the dawn-bringer.

The other lords of the host, the Archangels Raguel, Gabriel, Raphael, Uriel, Remiel and Saraquiel each held a dominion of the burgeoning Earth. Remiel had been tasked with watching over the dead; he was a hunched, stocky creature, his hair naturally short to the scalp, his eyes a colourless brown of mud, his hands small but wide. He was the quietest of the host, aware that his dominion was yet to build. And he would merely be called upon to watch and guide the spirits when they came to the gates.

Raguel was lean and emaciated; his skin sat tight on his bones and flesh. His eyes were deep amber and his wings were often preened and softly feathered.

He wore them tight to his back as if they were part of some grand cloak. His dominion was over the Earth, watching as the land formed, crafting with his father and liaising with the other gods of creation to map and cartographise the vast planet that was being born below, outside of the garden paradise. The Earth was still so young and he had seen the coming of many new creatures and the first concise pangs of birth from other deities, he had witnessed so much of the land breaking and reshaping that his mind became bursting and bristling with baffled love for the place. He often sat on mountaintops sketching the landscapes in a vast tome that sat in the library of Heaven, and so, he also became the keeper of the records of Eden.

Uriel was tasked with standing guard at the gateway of Eden; Yahweh gave unto him a sword of pure flame, a twin of the sword worn at Michael's side. He stood sentinel at the gates of the garden with no waver or argument, guarding his father's other children and the paradise beyond. Yahweh would come to him and lay a hand lovingly on his shoulder, and tell him of the pride he had for his duty, his love of his son for the unwavering strength and poise he displayed every day. Uriel would show no sign of the pride that swelled inside of himself, he simply stood and watched, and nodded. Yahweh could feel the pride, he drank it in, its heady intoxicating aroma was all he could taste when around Uriel, but he liked its tang and spark, so never let it be known it was evident.
In the latter days, as our story grew on and the last days of paradise dawned in, Uriel was moved from the Gate of Paradise, but to the ring of fire that was put around the tree in the plain, the tree of knowledge, singled out by the God as forbidden to Adam and his bride.

Raphael had been tasked as holding dominion over medicine and healing. His hair was a dazzling copper, he had a short stubble that bristled out from his chin, it too a deep copper, his lean face was really quite beautiful, eyes of a deep green, and a smile almost permanently fixed to his mouth. He would tend with Adam in the garden, healing animals that had fallen sick, touching trees that were hit with blight or malady, a single touch enough to heal and fix any illness. He would sit with Adam for hours and hours and discuss the plants and their properties, teaching the first man how to survive in the forest and beyond the walls if ever that day did come.

189

Saraquiel was the angel of the host that Yahweh employed to stand watch and dominion over the fellow angels. His kingdom was in Heaven itself, standing as judge and guard over his brothers, drawing them to the throne and judgment if necessary. Working directly for the good of the kingdom to keep peace amongst the dominations of the host.

His face was always covered with a hood, his gaze was always down, he rarely spoke to his brothers, and rarely was seen at the great table of the host, if so, he was almost always silent and aloof. His position meant that when he did remove his hood to lay his gaze upon someone, it would almost always precipitate violence and action. The fear from the other host soon gave way to a sense of foreboding resentment, if he recognized it, Saraquiel never showed it bothered him, and instead, he would smirk under his hood in silence and ignorance.

Then, there was Gabriel. Gabriel sat at the left-hand side of the throne.

His kingdom and dominion were legion. Where Michael had been tasked as God's proxy upon the Earth, to undertake the tasks fit for a God with Yahweh's blessing, Gabriel had been given the burden of being his messenger. Where Michael held a sword of fire, Gabriel was given a coronet of gold. A horn that heralded the arrival of God, visiting the other deities in their lands and parts of creation, he would herald his arrival with a long blast of his coronet, and land amongst them, six wings upon his back, each a beautiful, pristine white.

Gabriel was sent to Earth many times in the early days of mankind, and his importance was universally recognized amongst the men of the Earth,

Michael would sneer at his brother for his duties, tapping his hand on the sword's hilt, whilst mocking the coronet Gabriel had over his shoulder on a length of silver rope.

Deriding his position and duty, mocking the deliverer of messages and warnings – something that drew Gabriel closer to Lucifer, who, for his own efforts would always be there for any brother of the host who would need his love or attention.

Lucifer did not sit on either side of the throne; he relinquished his seat to the left for Gabriel, who he deemed more deserving of it. He cared not for the right hand where Michael perched – his disdain for the idea of power when powerless was a joke to him.
Lucifer, it had become clear very early, was more curious with the land below, the earth, mountains, seas and oceans - and, more importantly - the power of man.

So, with his glorious wings, that were thick with white feather - much like a swan's, large, muscular and beautiful – he would glide through the heavens, soaking in his sunshine, dawning each morning and setting each night with his command, Lucifer would watch and witness the movements of Adam and his bride Eve, floating down and observing the routine and rituals of the man and his woman. Curiously wandering and convening at the forbidden tree and looking at the branches that would hold out fruit, the one beautifully elegant branch that resembled an arm with an outstretched hand holding an apple.
A vague recollection coming to him as he glared at the tree, something about it he recognized from deep within.

Every day he came and stood outside the circle of fire, and spoke to Uriel, who would ignore his request for entry and stand fast, his sword of fire drawn.

"Oh come now, Uriel, brother. It is not as if I am the man himself; I am an angel. I wish to see the tree, I wish to taste its fruit." He would charmingly approach the guarding archangel at his post, and his sibling would every time denounce and reject his admission.
"Lucifer, our father has forbidden it, this tree is knowledge, and he who eats of it is cursed for the rest of their days, whether it be man or angel alike. I have sworn an oath that I would never leave this post, and I swear now I will never allow you in. Now be gone from my sight and stop your pleading."

And every day Lucifer would leave, disheartened but with more resolve to try again. He wandered the fiery wall and would test the gates and defense, only when he could find no chink in its perimeter,

191

then, he would sit and stare at Uriel at his post, his sword drawn and in hand, blade as fiery and bright as the wall it guarded. Something about the wall and the tree was out of place, why have this forbidden thing so prominent and in the centre of all of the rest of paradise. Lucifer's pre-occupation became one of nagging need, illicit yearning for answers, and he toiled and troubled his mind with the puzzle of the tree for many days and nights before finally demanding to know the answers for the questions of which he obsessed.

Lucifer had visions, often, of a green-eyed woman, crying, her hands reaching for him before being thrown back into a wall of nothing, evaporating before his eyes. He wondered why and who this could be. Eve visited his dreams too; her skin like a serpents and her tongue forked whispering secrets of the earth to him as he slept. But her eyes were a rich hazel, a slither of blue on the edge of a light brown. The green of the woman who reached for him were a sparkling, ethereal emerald hue, like fresh grass capturing dew in the chill morning. He wondered if this was his mother, who Yahweh was unshakably silent about, who the other host, his brothers, did not care about nor ever deem worthy of mention.

Yahweh had always spoken of how the archangel were the first true sons of God. The eight brothers were his first-born host.

God would talk of his deep love for the boys, their power, and their devotion unquestioning.

The love that he drank from them, and their dauntless worship was clear enough for anyone to see – however – he always knew Lucifer was different, was not of the same fabric as his brothers. A spark of something else lived inside him, burning embers of another's will.

Yahweh watched Lucifer, his curiosity, his tactical and analytical mind always pushing and probing, tapping away at things to understand the deeper reason for their being, the way they worked. He would watch as Lucifer tried to pull the world apart and examine every tiny facet and detail, learning about the universe on the minutest of levels.

Often Lucifer would sit in the garden in silence watching Adam toil on the land, never raising a hand to help, and often going days without saying a word, just witnessing the man. Adam did not mind, he preferred to work in peace. The constant chatter of angels like Raphael, who would twitter and chirp for hours without stopping, drowned Adam's every waking moment with chatter and interruption. Lucifer, on the other hand, would sit, watch and stay out of the way. Adam would take breaks, sweating and huffing, chest heavy and worn from the exertion of the day, Lucifer would always have some food or water for him, sharing any bounty or treat he could find.

Often the two of them sitting in silence, splitting bread or fruit smiling. Occasionally sharing a laugh, never exchanging a word to the other.

From the outside looking in it seemed strange, the two men – human and angel – however, they knew what it was and why it was humorous, and they carried on regardless.

Lucifer passing a two-fingered salute to the man at the end of the day as he flew high into the sky, to beckon the sun to sleep.

Lucifer, the bringer of light, would also extinguish the sun each day to preserve its flame.

Well aware it would be needed again soon enough.

When Eve was around, Lucifer would watch her from the shadows. Something about this woman shook his trust. His skin crawled around her like she was something toxic and poison. His flesh would pock as if like a goose, the hair on his neck and the feathers on his wings would raise in heckles; he would be washed over with a sense of anger and resentment.

He could not explain.

Eve had done nothing to prompt this, but, this garden seemed to retreat from her when she walked, imperceptible to anyone but angelic, the trees would shudder, the grass would wilt, and the flowers wane a fraction in her presence.

Lucifer noticed it almost immediately, and soon, he had the same reaction.

He would not understand, could not comprehend.

Eve was a beautiful specimen, even for a human. Lucifer would appreciate her curves, her ample breast, her wide hips, and the gait of her legs when she walked, and the slight heave and rise of her chest with each breath. But, beauty alone could not sway his mind off the way she brought a wave of nausea and mistrust when she was around.

He would bite his tongue and swallow his feelings down, and still speak to her.

He had too.

Eve was unlike Adam. Adam had a deep understanding of things, mainly from tending to them hands on, where Eve, was born of a curious nature like Lucifer's own, but it was clipped, limited. She was curious to a single point then stopped and never followed the threads through, stopping way short of the true fulfillment that Lucifer always hungered for.

Yet, this was how he knew he could get more understanding of the tree and find all the answers he had coveted.

Yahweh, of course, saw his fraternizing. Saw his firstborn speaking and sitting with the humans, it worried him. God's mind was not built to worry, it was not built to handle the distraction of emotion. God's minds were complex and vast, but they relied on simple needs and wants, appetites and distractions. So when they obsessed and worried, it was amplified beyond reason. They wished for simplicity and satisfaction. To have everything as they demanded and no deviation. They created and expected the world to follow to plan. The dawning of humans brought new challenges, where gods were gods – they expected Humans to follow suit like angel had, Yahweh expected the god's example to come apocryphal, standard and law.

Yet, his own fraternization with Lilith, who he had built and loved and lay with, who he had taken in the waterfall and filled with his godly seed, creating his host, Lilith was still his guilty secret, his one guilty mistake.

Yahweh thought that he had dealt with the matter, yet, even when he looked upon Lucifer, Lilith's eyes would stare back at him. Lucifer's eyes a passive, green emerald when he was calm and serene and contemplative, bursting to life and fervor turning into brown eyes with coronas around the iris like orange embers and flame when passion arose inside him.

The colours burning deep and heavy, fire behind his eyes.
Then just as quickly, the fire would wane, and the hypnotic green of
Lilith would return, melting Yahweh's mind in intoxicating and
confusing ways.
Lucifer's hair was blonde and deeply radiant, drawing the light to it
and throughout its heavy fall around his shoulders.

Even his frame was a male composite of his mother's – lascivious
angles, deep strength hidden behind lithe limbs, his face an
androgynous beauty that recalled his mother's perfectly.

In Lucifer, Lilith had created a constant remembrance of Yahweh's
lapse in godliness.
Yahweh would look upon him and see Lilith smiling and smirking
back, the first slice and step in her revenge.
So… He was absent from Lucifer, distant, unobserving. Lucifer did
not much care for his father's pious and holier-than-thou presence; he
did not bask in the warmth of his glory, nor in the heat of his love.
Lucifer found warmth in the sun, and the stars and the curiosity that
permeated his spirit and being.
His father was dull warmth in comparison.
        Even as his brothers doted and fawned over the attention the
God would give and attend to them, Lucifer shirked it and struck out
to find his own slither of creation away from the host and his
"duties".
But – Yahweh, ever the creature driven by the one vice he could
never shake off, pride, always came beckoning Lucifer to the circle
and table of the host again, demanding the union of his first born
sons, believing to have them together would negate his need to lie
and create more falsehoods to hide his misdemeanor. Instead,
keeping them close meant he could exert control, patterns of
repetition and guide the host to his bidding entirely.
Lucifer was always a dissenting voice, always a fringe opinion,
unifying his brothers – even Gabriel, caught in the riptide and wake
of Yahweh's demand – against Lucifer and his ideas.

So it was that the day Lucifer came to God and demanded answers to questions he had thought long since forgotten and dead, Yahweh banished Lucifer the first time from paradise.

Setting in motion the seeds of civil war.

* * *

Yahweh had started to build his heaven above even as his creatures of Earth were building their Eden below. Adam and Eve were with child, seen hand in hand in the garden, lay beneath boughs of tropical trees, hiding in the shadows of the exotic flora and fauna Adam had brought to bright and bold life in his time on the Earth.

In the west, beyond the mountain range at the far end of what was once the plain, Zeus had begun his creation, and was building land and garden, and reshaping the plain beyond the mountain into a new vista of the earth.

His brother and sister gods were slowly crafting their own gardens and landscapes too, from mountainous peaks laced with snow and with haggard, sharp rock, to lush forests dense with trees and mist, so very tall and full of new and wonderful life that had never before been seen. Insects and reptiles not thought of in Adam's menagerie. There were icy lands of deep, blue, crystal cold, that were placed north and south of this infant Earth, and the oceans were slowly filled from cups and goblets that poured continuous streams of life forth into the deep canyons of the plain, filling them and connecting them to the lonely sea at the eastern edge of the garden. An edge that every morning birthed the heralding light of the Sun, born from the ocean of the garden, and spinning its warm cycle overhead, before crashing behind the mountains in the west every day.

Zeus had begun to mimic and copy every animal he could, contorting his mind and body round every shape they held, whether it be the massive bulk of a buffalo, or the lean, slither of a boa constrictor. He mimicked until he could copy every animal he had met and observed.

196

Yahweh was fully isolated now, speaking not to any other god or goddess. He preferred the solitary confinement of his garden, his masterplan even now building momentum, as Yahweh would map the Earth and build strategic parts of his own blueprint for the larger world, he would always have one eye turned inward to Eden – his Eden – and the children of Earth, now bearing the first of his new race and breed of animal, he had called man.

Zeus had often turned an eye to the east and wondered what was happening in his elder brother's creation, and then, Lucifer provided him answers and more questions.

Access and a conduit to the future.

Lucifer had long since been visiting the world beyond the plain. He had accompanied Raguel on cartographer runs, observing his younger brother drawing the land and documenting the world that was being borne outside of the walls of Yahweh's creation, sharing the lay of the land between gods, even as worlds began knitting themselves into a solidified land.

North, south and west had slowly drawn together to form a conglomerated Earth, the mountains ranges had divided eastern Eden and the larger world for as long as the world was a barren and dusty plain, but, still, Eden stopped just short of joining the rest of the Earth.

Yahweh had forbidden it and refused. Keeping his world to himself.

Raguel and Lucifer had landed in the mountains, met by Epimetheus, the demigod and brother of Prometheus.

"Well met, cousins. Welcome to the Parthenon."

Lucifer stood silently behind Raguel, letting his brother fulfill his duty.

"Well met, cousin. These lands be fruitful." Raguel delivered a graceful bow to the young god. He saw it returned to him, and the two stood and clasped hands at the wrist in a strong, fraternal handshake.

"It is good to have you return, Raguel. Zeus's land grows fast and thick; you have much to document with your work. And you, Morningstar – Lightbringer…" He turned to Lucifer.

"My lord Zeus would speak with you. He has requested the pleasure of your company if you would do him the courtesy?"

Lucifer smiled warmly at the god, and bowed, gently, without giving an inch of his brightness or majesty. Epimetheus smiled and nodded, not returning the bow, realizing the game that was afoot.
"I would gladly speak to The Lord Zeus. Long have I heard stories and whispers of his greatness from my brothers, I yearn to drink his glory in myself."
Epimetheus nodded, he beckoned Raguel to continue his duty, the younger angel passing a final gaze his elder sibling's way.
"To your duties, Raguel. I will meet you for our departure henceforth."
Raguel left the mountaintop by the spiral of carved stairs, making his way down toward the land below.

Lucifer and Epimetheus took flight, Lucifer on his perfect wings of white, Epimetheus on invisible wings that were betrayed only by a shimmer in the wind, looking to the world as if he were floating in midair or traveling down from the mountain toward the parched land below them on a cloud of warm air, the shimmer like the sunshine hitting warm desert and giving the illusion of waves and flickers.
It was a graceful and perfect descent, with the two beings silently hitting the dirt and landing with naked, padded feet.
Epimetheus walked with his hands in front of him, folded hand in fist, his head was raised high, his chin strutting. The lean musculature of his body made him look like a teacher striding the halls of some great academy of learning. Lucifer had his hands behind him, he folded his wings in over them, like a cloak draped on his shoulders, the tips of his feathers dragging on the floor, a sweeping, brushing noise followed his every step.

"I hear great things of the gardens being tended in the west, how some of our cousins are crafting hanging and cascading paradise's full of animals that Adam would never be able to even dream of. I hear of vast oceans full of water dwelling creatures of magnificent

size and design that are changing and morphing of their own will into new shapes and forms even as gods watch them breathe.
Have you seen anything of this?"
Epimetheus cast a curious look to his younger guest's question, as they reached a wide and monstrous oak door. Its hinges were of bronze craftsmanship that defied logic. Twisting, perfectly shaped patterns of elegant and beautiful design that looked impossible to the eye, but which ran the width of the wood.
Epimetheus opened the door with two hard, heavy arms, pushing in as the door gave way in the centre with a groan and creak – before a sharp dagger of light poured out and illuminated the demi-god and his angel ward.
"I know nothing of the west, I know only the mountains and the stone."
He beckoned in Lucifer to the room beyond the wooden door, bowed regally and subserviently all at once, and closed the door as Lucifer strode in.
Lucifer looked back as the door groaned with the pull of Epimetheus's strength.
The angel had a look of curious panic on his face, the demi-god smiled and let out a little laugh.

From inside the room, a voice welcomed the archangel.
"Welcome, Morningstar. Nephew"

Zeus was sat in the room, alone, upon a throne of twisted and crafted oak that looked like vines running in and around each other, like wicker, built into layers, shaped into a chair for royalty.
Above the head of the chair was carved from a single piece of oak a beautiful and perfect eagle, wings spread and head bowing down as if to strike on some unseen prey.
It was as deadly looking as it was beautiful.
Zeus was sat on the chair, leant forward, his arms on the rest of the throne, and his legs wide and planted to the floor that was a rich and spotless marble.
The room otherwise was completely empty, and it's blank, milky whiteness was an assault on the eyes. Lucifer stood in the room, the

199

doorway now invisible behind the shroud of endless white. In front of the powerful, stunning and handsome God.

"Your Majesty."
It was all Lucifer could manage to say, for the first time in his life he had found himself genuinely lost for words, this creature before him oozed charisma, power and charm. But you could feel – beyond anything else – his glory, emanating from his every pore, a thousand fold more than Lucifer's own father, whose glory was sticky, sickly like an over-indulgent tar, that cloyed and soon, like too much food consumed at a feast, filled you and made you queasy.

His own father's power was an ugly, tarnished glory in comparison to this wondrous, incomprehensible God before him.

Zeus was a shard of white light piercing the darkness and drowning the night in sun.
Yahweh was nothing but a candle in the vast cosmos of space when placed next to this God before him.

Lucifer bowed, and spread his wings to their full span, his halo was a white-hot circle of silver and fizzed and glowed with impenetrable light.
Zeus stood, slowly, deliberately, and walked toward the bowing angel, he looked at the halo, the wings, the shape of his guest's flesh, the strength inherent deep within the skin and bone, the mane of golden and perfect hair that tussled in long lines down his neck and back.
Zeus looked at this child of God, and he smiled.

"You look very much like your mother."
Lucifer wavered, his gaze span from the floor to the God before him.
Zeus saw the green eyes ignite at once into the tempest of mahogany and fire.
Zeus felt the prickle of curiosity, the sudden rush of rage that pulsed through the angel's muscle.
"Oh… she was beautiful and full of pride and curiosity just like you.

200

An uncontrollable, tempestuous beauty. Full of question, full of wonder, full of love."

Lucifer tried to not let the anger overtake him. His mother was a taboo he had long since learned was not to be discussed, but which he panged and yearned for more knowledge of.
His father never spoke of the woman who birthed and bore them…
Instead, there were stories of comets and stars being the womb from where the angelic host was born. Shaped from dust and stars.
This was all Yahweh muttered and lied to them.
Lucifer knew differently. His blood spoke to him of a woman with green eyes.
He knew that the host was eight bastards under the thrall of a father who held back his love.

"Your mother was the most beautiful woman I have ever seen…
And what she did, what happened to her…" Zeus took a moment to breathe and reflect, his eyes wandered to the left, as the memory washed over him.
"What happened to her is an affront to everything we agreed when we – us elder gods – were woken and brought to life upon that beach, staring at the sun in confusion and longing. Nothing that you and your brothers cannot relate to, eh?"
Zeus smiled then, wide and genuine. He stared down at the archangel, who, in comparison, looked like a boy in the presence of the god.
"Come now boy, one bastard to another, tell me it is not so?"

Lucifer held his bow a fraction longer; he then slowly let his arms fall elegantly to his side.
His wings began to fold into his back, tucking into themselves to form the feathered cloak. His head rose in small movements, until his neck, back and legs stretched to their full size, straight and perfectly elegant.
A picture of pride and strength.

"I do not know who my mother was, my Lord Zeus. I know of lies

201

and stars, comets and dishonesty. But of my mother, I know nothing."
Lucifer swallowed hard on his emotions; his face was a blank stare of humble need.
"But I would dearly like to learn."

Zeus smiled. He looked at how the angel before him had lost all his fear and curiosity, and instead shone now with nothing but dented, false pride and longing. It was a heavy, succulent flame of pride that echoed in Zeus's mouth as the taste of red apples.
He nodded graciously, and held out his arm to the throne, beckoning Lucifer to sit.
The angel looked at the seat and then the God again, who waved toward the chair to sit once more, with more definite haste. The fire behind his eyes waned, the emerald returned, a perfect colour of the shallow midnight sea.
"Be my guest."
Lucifer walked toward the chair; his hand ran across the smooth, indescribable wood that was so brilliantly and impeccably worked and manipulated. He ran his fingers along the surface that gave him a prickle of energy, a natural electricity that ran cold through his skin.
He took his rest on the hard, oak seat, and leant back.
His mind flushed with imagery and sudden knowledge.
The eagle burst to animate life and screeched to the east, its wings stretched as if to take flight, it shifted and transformed into the shape of a cockerel, crowing at the morning sun.

Zeus sat cross-legged on the floor before him.
His godly essence not dented by such peasant-like seating. He looked at the Morningstar, sat comfy on his throne, he held his hands out palms open, matched Lucifer's gaze with one of soothing warmth.
"Let me tell you of the beach. Of your mother and of the plain that once stood to the east - barren and dead and scorched of life. Now alive and bursting with power."

Lucifer leant back and drank in the remnants of the God's power that lingered in this incredible chair. He stared hard at the God before

him; the roles reversed but the power very much the same.
Zeus clapped his hands together. Snapping Lucifer into bright, alert life again.
"Let me tell you of the man you call father... My bastard brother."

The chair had awoken dormant memories Lucifer realized only he, amongst the host, must have had. Staring into the silver-blue eyes of the god known as Yahweh. Who held him in his arms, watching as a golden, muscular and forceful hand, held in its tight fist a woman by the throat, how the woman struggled for breath, her face discoloured and ugly from his brute strength. Staring into the beautiful eyes that quickly darkened into red, bloodshot pools.
Lucifer nodded, his mind still drinking in the power of the chair, he saw his mother for the first time since that morning he was born. The throne opening up pathways and portals in his mind that had long since been closed and locked tight by Yahweh, now gaping and allowing in light and memory and dark knowledge sparking behind the bright fiery eyes of the archangel.

"Let me tell you of the where's and whys and how's and who's of the Heavens, every secret of Eden. And let us be friends you and I. My blood, my kin, my nephew..."

And with this, Zeus told the Angel of the Morning Light everything. Every little detail.

Every. Little. One.

* * *

The garden was quiet and still. No wind blew, the air was warm and arid and sweet smelling as the honeysuckle and the roses lent a scent to the air that hung happy and homely for everyone to imbibe.
The shadows cast by the tallest of the trees drew lines into the green forest land and grasses that gave cool respite from the heat, if

only for a short while, the shadows ticking down as time moved with the flow of the sun.

Adam and Eve were laying together under the bow of a willow whose lowest branches had become heavy with the weight of jilted blossom, tilting down as if to brush the ground in a mope, the tree was large and beautifully coloured, and it smelled like warm sap. The blossom pink and white, like no other tree in the garden.

Adam stirred as he heard the flap of wings overhead. He had no expectation of an angel today, no lessons were needed nor planned, he kissed his wife on the forehead, gently and lovingly, and patted her hair to beckon her to lay back and return to sleep.

He pulled himself up using the thicker of the lower branches, and emerged from the willow's curtain of blossom and leaves to be faced with Lucifer, hovering just overhead, above the tree, naked but for his wings and halo, the archangel joined the man on the ground and his wings at first stretched to their widest width, flexing sinew and muscle, before folding back in on themselves and bending like a cape to his back, covering his shoulders and draping around him. An awesome, white cloak of feather.

"Adam." The archangel said to the man.

"Lord Lucifer." The man retorted, offering a curt, short bow of his head, and a flick of his hand, welcoming the angel to his home. "How may I help thee, sire?"

Lucifer allowed his lips to curl into a welcoming grin, his teeth were just visible behind the pink lips, his eyes were a cool glow, the orange a thin line around the chestnut brown.

"Lilith." The angel replied.

Of a sudden, the man's face dropped to a look of surprise, worry and loss.

But, mostly, of fear.

"How do you know…? Her… Her name… How?"

Lucifer unfolded his wings; he was no longer an angel, but a cloud of smoke and of dust, of furious nature and of formless, shapeless essence.

204

He contorted and pushed, and a whirlwind of grass and smoke enveloped the man, corkscrewing around the tree and the branches. It began as a waft of movement before a bellow of smoke and then a hand was clasped around the man's throat, as the arm, shoulder and then full form of Lucifer reconstituted in front of him, his strength and righteous anger lifting the frame of Adam, who held on to Lucifer's arms and hand as he was picked up by the throat, was throttled, and pinned high to the tree.

Adam gasped and spat, foamy saliva dribbled from his lips, and rested on his hand, as he grabbed tightly to Lucifer's hand, which squeezed and constricted his windpipe harder.
"My mother. Your first wife."
Lucifer's grip tightened and tightened, the hand had changed now, no longer was it fingers and flesh, but the constriction of a python, a multitude of snakes now existed where each finger previously had, his hand and arm was now the taut, reptilian flesh of a boa, and the eyes were yellow and thin, a black slither of obsidian hatred placed perfectly in the centre of the yellow pool.

Adam gasped, choked and his windpipe snapped and his eyes burst into bloodshot red balls and the purple and gagging flesh on his face let out a final silent huff of air, before he convulsed, and his eyes burst within his head...

The bursting is what woke the man from his sleep.
Sweat was pouring down his back, his brow a wet mop of perspiration and panic, hair stuck to his face. His stubbled beard - dragged and cut short using a blade given to him by the angel Raphael, to cut crops and wheat, berry and bush - was sprinkled with a draft of wetness from his disturbed sleep, as drool and spit, gagged and vomited up in his nightmare, rested on his cheek and lips.
Adam bolted to a sitting position, his hands reaching for his throat, to see if the mark of the angel's hands still rested there, to see if the capillaries and arteries had broken and burst like a damn. He raised the blade that he kept by his side, resting against the tree trunk and looked at his reflection in the spotless metal, his eyes were white and

fine, no blood vessels broken or torn here.

The man sat with his head in his hands, drank in the warmth and the dryness. There was a stillness on the air as the wind lay dormant, sleeping.
A blanket of summer and sunshine had been dawned on them.
He left the bow of the tree and went to where he had stored the water from the evening's frost, a fold of leaves and reed that formed a gutter to collect dew and the evening's fresh, cold air crystallized and thawed by morning.
He threw a double handful of the precious water into his face, rubbed his eyes and then drank a handful scooped and drawn to mouth.
His beautiful wife, even now in her pregnant state, still striking and shapely, came from the curtain of leaves and blossom, stretching. She smiled toward her husband, who smiled tiredly back.
"My love... did you not sleep well?" she asked, draping herself to his arm, running a finger in circles on his chest.
Adam looked down at her small, fragile face, its awe was obvious for all to see, attractive and pure, the face was one of innocent and beguiling beauty.
"No, my love. Nightmares. Do not worry yourself... I believe I may have worked my mind into a stupor, and it ran away with visions and images beyond my sway."
Eve reach up to his lips, he stooped his head, and they shared a kiss, his head cupped and held between two dainty hands.
"It was only sleep, my husband." She kissed him again.
"Tonight you will sleep the slumber you are owed." Adam smiled down at her, his mouth wide and his grin toothy and happy.
"Thank you, Lilith."
His eyes opened suddenly, wide and scared.
Eve looked at him, curiously.
"Lilith?" she asked – her face was blank – there was nothing behind the question tempered with emotion of any kind. She was curious but not accusing.
"I said lily. Like the flower. Beautiful, white and fragrant. It is delicate and yet grows in such extraordinary surroundings, in such wonderful conditions. You are like the lily, my love."

His eyes were scared and sparkled with surprise and quick-witted energy. Even as his mouth told the lie, his heart fell heavy and cold in his chest and a prickle of sweat formed and pooled in his armpits and his back.

"*You* are the lily, my love," Eve replied. "For you are the strongest willed and most striking of the whole garden."

She placed a final kiss on his cheek and wandered into the shadows.

Adam collapsed in tears upon the ground, shaken by the nightmare and his slip of the tongue and mind. Of the ghost of his wife long lost.

Sobbing heavily into the soil of the garden, by the tree he called his home.

* * *

Eve walked down to the waterfall, she was naked as ever, her skin a sun-baked golden-brown, her hair falling long, almost to her hip, and she cradled her belly, full of child, in her small, pristine hands.

The water had a fine mist rising from it, as the sun overhead gave it energy and warmth. The water tried, with no luck, to keep its chill. The steam rose all around, and Eve walked tender-footed into the water, steam rose from her body too, as cool water met the warmth of her skin.

The water was falling heavy from the height of the cliff face into the lagoon. The deep blue of the water from above met the gentle green of the still water below and made a soup of aquamarine, which appeared the colour of sapphires.

From above, the angel watched.

Lucifer kept his eyes on the woman, as she strode into the water deeper and deeper, and then submerged herself completely.

Her head rose again, arched at the neck, so her face first broke the water, a deep breath and a sigh, and the water formed an arch with her hair and neck and spine into a fin of pure rainbow as the sun reflected through the wetness. Moisture capturing the rays and refracting on the cliff itself.

Her shoulders rose and then bobbed, and she was under the water again.

Lucifer waited until she was fully submerged to dive in. He penetrated the water naked and like an arrow, his wings were already being pulled into himself before he cut the water apart using his hands, and as soon as he had hit the lagoon below, Lucifer had lost his form, no longer angel, but reptile.

Long, slithy and limbless. He was a snake. A grass green adder, with a fine orange line running from his forehead to his tail tip, his eyes a deep yellow, circled by a thin, almost imperceptible orange halo.

His tongue darting in and out of his mouth that housed delicate, needle sharp teeth.

His girth was a couple of inches wide. Reaching at full stretch five or so feet in length.

One long, muscular serpent.

He slid and spiraled through the water, until he reached the woman, wrapped himself around her leg and writhed and rose around her body to the surface.

Eve gave a little cry of fear, taken by surprise, she tried to pull back before realizing what was happening. She reached down for the creature that had wrapped itself around her, but had slipped in a tight coil around her waist, the head had slid up her torso, over the naked belly, between her ample bosom and had wrapped around her neck loosely before pulling away to look her direct in the face.

She moved her head one way then the other, and the serpent mimicked and mirrored.

Her eyes closed so did the snakes, she closed one eye, the snake would return the gesture, and she pulled her head back then pushed forward the reptile did the same.

As she realized that the animal was doing this, she let out a weak, sigh of laughter.

The snake had coiled around one leg, and had invited its tail tip to the crevice between her legs, the tight mound of her pubis, and it flicked and shook, barely touching the sensitive part of her pubic muscle, tantalizing close the fold of skin around her sex.

Eve sighed a different sigh now.
Her chest heaved and fell in heavy gasps of air, as the snake shook and flickered by the most sensitive part of her body.

"Wife of man." The snake said.
And Eve's eyes shot open and looked at the snake, there was confusion, and shock, no other animals spoke to her – she frequently spoke at the goat and the horse, the birds and the rabbits and geese. But the talk was always one sided, the dumb creatures bleating, growling, neighing and snorting at her – true – some birds copying with warbled mimicked cries – but never conversing, certainly never calling her by name.
She sighed heavily again as the tail of the beast ran and flicked between her legs.
"And what do I call you?" she said, in trembling whisper.
"Merely serpent. That's all I am. I come with a gift for you." And the creature unwound from the woman, the tail whipping from between her thighs, and running up between breasts, over a shoulder and then coiling down her arm.
Swimming to shore and winding around itself, into a tight coil, its tail whipping to and fro and its tongue licking at the air, blinking gently and slowly, watching the naked woman walk from the water, mist rising from her every inch of skin.

Eve sat cross-legged in front of the serpent, which rose slightly from his coil and wavered back to front, side to side, watching hungrily.
"Let me tell you a story of the garden in its earliest days – Wife of man. Of the plain before the wall fell and of the tree in the circle of fire."

Eve smiled at the creature.
"Tell me true, serpent. I am amused by your speech… I will listen."
She beckoned, pray the serpent should continue.

"… Long before the birth of Adam. Before he was born from the nothingness brought forth to life by the father, your Lord God, this garden was nothing but a dry, arid, empty space of chaos. Naught but a beach, and a tide… Collapsing into a vast oblivion, eternally black and empty. Upon this…

Yahweh and the gods woke.

One minute there was nothing, the next, the beach was as full as your belly."

Eve smiled, and her hand absently, unconsciously, rubbed the tender, full stretch of her womb and stomach.

"…The cosmos was born in the blink of an eye, and Death walked vanguard amongst the bodies of the gods. Of Yahweh your father and lord, of Zeus of the western mountains, of Ganesha, Vishnu and of the Gods of Fire and Wind, Earth and of Air.

A beach, full of mighty beings, appearing from nowhere.

Lord Death gave unto them a name and a secret, each held in their minds and tongues, one day to share back with the black-cloaked master of the other realms – and each was a God born…"

Eve stared in hypnotized thrall at every word spoken, absorbing them deep within herself.

"…Yahweh looked at the Earth, and the plain, and the sea. He took the burden for the wasteland upon himself, and forged from the dust and the sand a garden of pure green, flowered with every kind of colour and shape, with his sister Gaia, he built the trees and the dirt we call soil, and he made a wall of stone crafted from sand and dirt, and he had built a circle of purity and wonderful creation.

From this other gods took heed and went off to find their own circle of land, and new paradises were born way beyond the plain, past the mountains and into the furthest western lands. Beyond your walks and comprehension, so happy are you and the man with your tiny part of the Earth."

He flicked his tongue out and tilted his head at the woman; she sat in silent wonder soaking in his story. Lucifer, deep within the serpent's frame and shape, smiled heavily and drunkenly.

The serpent uncoiled and slithered to the woman, crawled into a spiral along her arm, and looked her in the eyes, deep and close.

"… Adam was born. The first man of the Earth. And he tended the garden, named the beasts and the animals – giving me my name as well – and he managed the flowers and the trees, bathed in these waters and slept in the shadows of these trees.
Yahweh had made secrets as well; he had built, and he had destroyed.
From one of these secrets the angels came. And… You."

Eve smiled.
Her eyes were now drunken, intoxicated by the gentle sway of the serpent's head, which she followed, the voice that was barely a whisper was all she could hear seemingly pounding in her head.
The serpent continued.

"… The wall of the western garden fell as the plain had sprung to vivid and sudden life. The angels you speak to, who watch and tend your needs, which love and protect you… They were just babes at this time. Growing fast, life ran through them at a faster rate than humans, so, they developed into men in short blinks of the world's eye.
And the once empty, wasted plain crept and broke the wall and merged with Yahweh's garden. He could not scourge or burn it; he could not erase and destroy it. It flowed and grew with power way beyond his understanding – so instead, he allowed the grounds to flow together, but, circled a tree at the centre of this new Eden with a burning fire, which, at the edge of the flame stands an archangel now. With flaming sword and immovable honour.
Stopping you - man and woman, you humans - from having that which was always intended for you… and you alone."

Eve snapped back to sudden wakefulness.
The last comment the serpent had said had done this.
A spark of something inside her came to vivid and animated life.
Curiosity, whose seed lived inside every living being – far from the

grasp of any god - took plant and shoots began to grow and crawl inside her skin and toward her pure, impeccable heart.

"What is the tree? Why must it be isolated and kept from us so?" She looked at the serpent longingly, one hand pulling its head gently back to meet her eyes, the serpent acted coy, but, inside Lucifer had snared and hooked his bait inside the gullet of his prey. "That is the question. Is it not?" Eve nodded.

The serpent uncoiled from the woman, and dragged itself away, toward the water's edge. The woman rose to standing and watched as the reptile left. The snake turned one last time and caught the woman's gaze. "Perhaps you should speak to your husband. Maybe he knows of the tree I speak, of the fruit that hangs from its branches, succulent and red and ripe for picking. Full of what is kept from you..." Eve looked toward the serpent, then the forest from where she had came, to the serpent again as it slithered into the water. "Wait!" The serpent stopped, half submerged, its head coiled back, and its tongue probing the air in front of it. "What is the fruit? Why must we not taste it? Is it poison?" "No," the serpent said, the faintest lines of a smile formed in its reptile mouth, sharp teeth showed and its tongue flickered eagerly and hungrily toward the woman. "Not poison." The serpent, turned slightly, looked at the water, then glanced finally at the woman, saying matter of factly. "It is knowledge."

And away into the water the creature went, fully submerged again. Under the aquamarine sheet of liquid. Eve watched for a second, maybe two then ran smiling, giddy and excited back to her husband... Knowledge.

The mere sound of the word was sweet and rich and trickled down her throat like a sordid, incredible honey.

"Knowledge."

* * *

Eve had run to Adam, bare feet pounding the forest floor. Holding her belly and gasping for breath from the exertion, she had bounded into the forest clearing by the weeping willow where her husband sat, sharpening a length of bamboo to use for fishing, making a sharpened end to poach and spike the salmon and the trout that swam in the streams that ran through the forest, like veins and arteries in a body.

He took to his feet immediately upon seeing his wife and her outward demeanor. Worried something had happened. Since his dream, the man had been on edge, had been jittery and easily rattled today. Seeing Eve's mood made him no better.

"Husband!" she cried, "Husband! You must follow me! There is something beyond the wall that you must see."
Adam was confused and perplexed, for he had seen all he had wanted beyond the wall, into the plain. At first so happy he would have more life and garden to tend, the garden soon became sinister and strange, trees bearing fruit that he could not understand. Weird, sharp flavoured fruit that looked like fruit he had seen in the confines of littlest Eden – but now, had strange twists and mutations. Oranges the colour and taste of blood, fruit that was no more than the seeds of a larger plant, full of bitter seed and little essence. He had seen trees that were withered and broken, but which bore the most beautiful blossom and fruit, that were both poisonous and inedible. Apples that were tiny and tasteless except for a deep, sour tang, yellow fruits that were small and angry in their flesh. He had witnessed thorns and roses, insects landing on plants that then ate them whole, opening and snapping shut with sharp, needle-like teeth.

This was not the garden he had expected and been excited about.

And there, in the centre of this weird, ugly new world, amongst the trees and fruit and grasses of multiple shades and bush which bore poisoned berries and violent sharp thorn and prickly spindle, there was a tree that was twisted and warped and had a branch that looked like an arm elegantly outstretched, with one hand, with long fingers, holding a solitary bright red apple.
He had touched the trees bark, and his hand was instantly thick with sticky, raw sap, the smell of which was putrid and amber.
The scent like warm flesh, parched and in the sun too long.
A tang in the air around it of sweat and of blood.
But the apple was a brighter, heartier and more delicious shade of red than he had ever seen.
The skin shiny and plump, there was a solitary green leaf that stood in deep, rich contrast to the colour of the apple's skin, and the branch really did hold a stunning resemblance to a human arm, craved or grown, impossibly from the wood itself.

Adam had been about to eat of the apple, to pluck it from the branch and bite into its welcoming, alluring and wanton flesh when a voice behind him stopped him. His fingers mere inches from the fruit, curious and hungry and demanding, his fingers waved in the air frozen mid-lunge, by the voice of a thing he had never before seen or met.

Uriel, naked but for a leather belt that fixed a scabbard to his hip, a scabbard that held and sheathed a sword of pure flame. The creature drew the weapon and held it out to the human, the blade instantly lighting up into a green and yellow flame, with a deep orange heart.
"This tree is not for you. My father has decreed it."
Adam's arm slowly dropped from its reach, the fingers still longing of their own mind for the fruit. He turned to look at the man before him, the arm with the sword still outstretched.
Grey feathered wings sprouted from root on his shoulder blades and back - grand, majestic things, large and imperial.
Uriel slowly lowered the blade, and a shoot of fire and green-hued,

heat-haze sparked off the blade and rooted to the ground ten or so feet from the tree.

The winged man started to walk slowly in a circle around the tree, and a fence of fire sprung to radiant and rabid life wherever the blade and root touched.

A circle of flame had been drawn into the earth, forcing Adam to retreat back from the tree before Uriel, the archangel of the host of Heaven, son of Yahweh and brother of sorts to the man of Eden took his place in the small gap in the fire, directly in front of the tree as you saw it through the clearing. He sheathed his sword once more, the flames shrinking to a permeating, pulsing blue fire that rested by his hip, leaving no trace or mark on his flesh, and he crossed his arms and stared up and down at the man who stood before him.

"What is your name, creature?" Adam demanded.

"He is Uriel, of the Host Incarnate. One of my children in the land above this land."

Yahweh was now sat behind Adam, resting upon a boulder, his elbows resting on his knees, as he leant forward, looking around at the flower and the plant and trees around him.

"He is here at my request to stop you from eating of this tree and its fruit."

Adam turned suddenly and started at his father's voice.

"Father…" He bowed his head and touched his chest above his heart.

"I was just exploring this new land… The new fruit and vegetation, the trees and such… It is a strange land, is it not?"

Yahweh stood, and looked around, more closely at the leaves and roots, the plants and shrubs. He stared at the tree and felt sure that it had eyes and stared right back at him from behind its fiery curtain.

"Strange indeed, Adam, strange indeed."

"This creature… is he of my blood?"

Yahweh shook his head.

"This is an angel, one of my firstborn sons. I have eight, of the Host Incarnate.

Several hundred more were born from the hair atop their heads and the feathers of their wing. A vast army I have of servants in my kingdom, but only eight do I call my son. They guard and toil in my paradise above that you will one day see. His name is Uriel, you should never after this day need see him again."

Adam went to Yahweh, who beckoned him over. He felt a surge of love and comfort as Yahweh put his hand around the shoulders of the man.

"Adam. I have given you all that you see. You can eat of any bush or plant, you may climb and use any of these trees and roots, you may eat of the flesh of any of these animals and insects – however – the one thing you may not do is talk of, ask questions about, nor eat from the fruit of the tree right there."

A long, tautly muscled arm reached out, with a hand rolled into fist, one solitary digit extended pointing at the tree, as the curtain of fire subsided some and then sprung back into violent and vicious life. Yahweh's finger seemed to be copied by the hand-like branch holding the apple, pointing right back at him.

"That is my tree. Forbidden to the whole of mankind, and guarded night and day by my son whose sole purpose on this Earth and in this life is to protect and stand sentinel over that fruit.

To eat of that tree would mean your banishment from this life and the light of my grace, do you understand?"

Adam looked at the tree, his heart yearned for the red apple that hung solitary and demanding from the branch.

His eyes gave an intense glow, tears welled in the corner of them, partly from the intensity of the fire, and partly from his need and desire to taste of the fruit.

But, steadfast, he nodded and agreed.

"I understand." He said, then, after a deep breath and another hungry glance at the tree and the red apple – he added.

"I think I understand."

Yahweh squeezed the man's shoulder tighter. "I am glad. For I love you and do not want to see you banished or alone in the world to the west, never again to return to this garden paradise you have helped me to create."

He stopped walking with the man, freezing him in his tracks with a sudden pause, the God came round to Adam's front and bowed slightly to lay a kiss upon the man's forehead, and then he was gone, as he took a step into a fold in the world he created, spiriting him some other corner of existence in the blink of an eye, Adam stood alone, now many steps away from the tree, so all he could see was the dull glow of fire behind the green and fruitful wall of branches and bush that beckoned you out of the tree line before the clearing.

The whole time, the smell of the sweet flesh pervaded his nostrils. The phantom taste of blood and love upon his tongue. From his imagination and thoughts of the red apple he wanted so badly to bite.

The apple he knew he would, even now, one day take as his own.

* * *

From the cliff face, overlooking the lagoon, Michael stood watching.
Lucifer had been neglecting meetings of the host, he had been running around, hiding and fulfilling his own personal agenda in the green of the garden, secrets hidden from his brothers' table and his father's ears and eyes. Michael did not appreciate these petty dalliances and disobediences.
The silver tips of his wings curled as he swooped down to land on the rock, he strode to the edge just as Lucifer pierced the water, and then the lithe, thin frame of the serpent slid effortlessly toward the wife of the man.
Michael stared in revulsion as the wings of his brother folded and shrunk in on themselves into the skin and flesh of the archangel, even as his bones and limbs shriveled to nothing transmuting into the shape of the serpent.
It was not the fact that the angel had transformed, though this was repellent enough in itself, but Michael could not fathom how he had managed this trick, nor – more pertinently – why an angel, especially one of the Host Incarnate, an archangel of the higher Heaven, would

choose to become such a creature as a snake.

He watched silently and out of sight, turning to beckon toward the sky, and cloud burst from on high and the faint shadow of Saraquiel descended. His hood still over his eyes, a shadow cast on his face to his mouth, only lips that were thick and red peered from behind his mask.
His wings were like those of a magpie, black and white, thin and slender, and he carried with him the mace his father had created, a hammer-like staff of pure silver.

Of all the host, of the eight brothers of the archangel order, Yahweh's sons and blood, no one spoke to Saraquiel except Michael. Lucifer had open disdain for both brothers. Michael for his folly and arrogance, his uppity sense of importance and his aloof and judgmental nature, acting like the eldest when Lucifer was honoured with this title. While Saraquiel was hated because Lucifer had no time for silent smirking idiots. He would not attend meetings and gatherings of the archangel precisely because he was considered a runt by his younger siblings, his opinion was universally ignored and mocked, and his independence threatened.
Lucifer had given his left side of the throne to his brother Gabriel – for good reason, he was not worthy nor interested in the honour. Lucifer had no pride about his position, he simply had curiosity and a burning core of needing to know more, a hunger for information, knowledge and adventure.
Michael would have walked into the white-hot, intense fire of a newborn star had his father commanded it. He was nobility and sanctity and civility through and through, his fidelity was unquestionable, this unwavering loyalty was one of the reasons he was held with such contempt by Lucifer and – even - Gabriel – it made him unbearable, his devotion made him boring, and Lucifer could not comprehend a life of blind servitude to anyone but himself and the ever expanding mind he had begun to fill with wonderful and dazzling information.
Michael in turn hated that this yelp, this ungrateful brat, could not open and accept the true love and adoration that was given when

218

one followed the oath that Yahweh had been building. He hated and feared Lucifer's need for freedom, they were of one blood. He was scared that this seed on curiosity would one day ignite in himself, so, he rebelled against the thought and stayed pure to Yahweh's teaching and light.

Michael had taken Raguel to one side upon their return from the mountain in the far west. Michael disliked these other elder gods, did not trust them. Upon the return days after they had left, Lucifer had seemed more distracted than usual. Where usually he was smiling and laughing, jibing and playing wantonly upon the surface of the Earth, hiding in Eden and watching the man and the woman – he now stared at Eve from the shadows on the Heavens above. He watched the man go hither and thither and waited for the woman to be separate, and he made his leave and descended to Earth, to follow and stalk in the shadows, never talking or fraternizing. Just observing from distance, always following the woman, always ignoring the man, or, on the odd occasion he saw them together he was seen gritting his teeth and spitting at the sight of him.

Michael saw this all.

He took Raguel into the throne room, where Yahweh's seat, a simple silver chair, was sat. Either side of it a brass and wooden chair sat. Michael's and Gabriel's, the right and left hand of God.
"Tell me about the sojourn to the West, brother." Michael had said to the standing Raguel, who held his loose graphs and maps in a bag that hung over his shoulder and to his hip.
Michael sat upright, authoritatively in his wooden chair.
"What do you wish me to say, Michael?" he pondered.
"Tell me of Lucifer. What part did he play in this mission?"
Raguel stopped smiling and stepped forward, Michael raised a hand and flicked a finger backward to command he step back.
"I do not understand, brother."
Michael stood up, and his wings flexed out, two perfect and massive wings, strong and cream white but for silver tips. He walked down toward Raguel and his hand rested on his scabbard of the fire sword.

219

The blade of which was forged in the heart of a dying galaxy. "What did Lucifer do on this mission, brother? It is a simple question. While you were mapping the lands being born into existence from the gods of the western mountains, what did our brother do, how did he help, what were his movements?"

Raguel smiled then and tried again to move forward to speak to Michael personably, once again, Michael's hand raised to stop the archangel. This time, the gesture was met with a wall of air that barred Raguel from moving at all.

Raguel frowned, and then a wave of fear washed over him. The grand doors of the throne room slammed shut, and he spun on his heel as the draped curtains each shut out the grand windows of the room. Stained glass of scenic moments of the recent and distant past, each one inspiring and beautiful. The vast pool of crystal clear water that acted as a divining portal, with which the archangel and Yahweh could observe the garden began to turn a darker and darker hue, before it was black, viscous and solid, like tar frozen in a lake far below zero.

And the room began to plummet in temperature, and the breath from their lungs hung dry and apprehensively in the air.

Raguel spoke freely now, passive and emotionless. He spoke everything Michael wished to hear.

"I did not see him, my Lord. We arrived at the mountaintop greeted by the lesser god Epimetheus. I was beckoned to the valleys and the hanging gardens being birthed and crafted in the south, and Lucifer – his Lord Lucifer – was summoned by Zeus, the God of The Western Pantheon. He left on wing with Epimetheus, and I did not see him again for a number of days. For all I know, he was with Zeus the whole time.

When we returned to the garden and the halls of Heaven, Lucifer had said nothing to me the whole journey. He was silent and brooding and has been ever since.

I did not dare ask him the trouble, because, Lord – I knew he would not share, and thought nothing more than it was Lucifer being Lucifer."

Michael stood now in front of the other angel.

His brow was furrowed and bent, his eyes serious and perplexed.

He stared at the angel for several long and silent minutes.

Raguel held his gaze, and showed no response, passively taking the stare and the scrutiny of the creature in front of him.

Finally... Michael broke into a beaming smile. The draped curtains flung open, the tar in the viewing pool uncloyed and loosened becoming clear and dazzling again, and the fire in the torches surrounding the walls of the throne room ignited once more into bright life.

"Very well... thank you, Raguel, you have done well to tell me. I ask you speak to no one else of this, do I have your word?"

Raguel stood and stared at his brother. He slowly nodded, and took a step back and bowed.

"Of course, my Lord."

"Good. You may leave." And the door flung open, Raguel did not wait to exit back the way he came, stepping backwards to the giant doorway closing the huge portals as he did.

Michael strode to the viewing pool and looked down, he could see the whole of Eden, the entirety of the paradise and the plain, he concentrated on the man and woman and saw the startled Adam jump to life from his bad dream, of the hanging boughs of the willow at the south of the lagoon, he saw the movement from the bush as the archangel Lucifer bound from brush to rock, rock to cliff overlooking the lagoon. Michael watched as the woman slowly made her way toward the waters to have her daily morning bathe.

Michael ran to the window that stood directly behind the throne, in its stained glass montage today was the depiction of the stars and the moons, formations of planets and the massive shooting star that the archangel were told was crushed in Yahweh's own hand and shaped into the eight sons he loved today, born from the cosmos on high that cushioned and surrounded the heavens. A story all the archangels believed and had no reason to see as lie or otherwise.

Except Lucifer. Who startled nightly in his sleep, who dreamt and chattered in his slumber of green-eyed woman and the fact she was choking...
Of the pain in this woman's heart.
Michel had at first tried to sooth these terrors, then Raphael had tried with his medicine, then Yahweh had explained Lucifer had the third eye and was seeing what was to come for humanity, the future was his gift, and he could divine the path to come, hiding behind lies and falsities to keep his secret safe.

Michael believed Lucifer thought there was another reason, that his curiosity was a prideful and selfish journey, that his wings were unworthy of archangel or host, and he had determined that Lucifer, his eldest brother, the eternal firebrand, the independent, the adventurer, was really no better than a usurper and a liar and was up to something.
In his mind Michael was sure his suspicion was noble, his task was righteous. Michael, who is like God, Yahweh's pure right hand – would stop this petty insurrection before it had even started.

He dived for the window, the glass became at once a transparent shimmer, then a translucent wave, and then was nothing but a waft of memory on the air, as he burst through and spread his wings past the glass boundary to descend to Eden, the window returned to perfect clear clarity and shape as soon as he was through, a seamless clean and colourful portal again standing strong and bold, overlooking the chairs of God and his council and lighting the trail of a shooting star in blues and silvers across the throne room as the sun moved from east to west.

* * *

On top of the cliff, Michael watched Lucifer, or, more truthfully, this creature that Lucifer was wearing as his skin now. He watched as the reptile slid between the woman's legs, how the tantalizing touch of its tail had spurred the woman into shivers of pleasure and near ecstasy, even while carrying the man's child. Michael watched as Lucifer whispered into her ear, and he heard every word the serpent said, as clearly as if the tongue were speaking into his own.

Saraquiel stood cross-armed and still listening as well. He did not move His motionlessness was that of a golem or statue. Indifferent and ambiguous.

Michael did not pay attention. He had beckoned the judge of the archangels and the lesser host because he wanted to air his suspicions and not lose his temper against his brother should he have witnessed or seen something.

Michael regretted having called Saraquiel down now, as what he was witnessing was disgusting him on a base level. He scowled at the sight below, and he turned to Saraquiel.

The hooded archangel raised a hand to stop the Right Hand of God from speaking. His hood simply nodded silently in gentle acknowledgement.

He had heard; he knew what had made his brother Michael angry. These were firebrand truths – were they truths at all.

These were revelations that the woman did not need to be hearing, and Lucifer's forked tongue spread a dissent, a seed of something clearly meant to bloom into a larger and more devastating flower.

"Temptation." Michael spat. "He is breeding temptation where it never before existed in these human's minds. Why? What end does this have?"

He looked anguished and angrily at Saraquiel. The hood was still over his eyes, and his lips remained impressed in an ambivalent, impassive silence.

"Temptation…" Michael said once more, it was snarled, flecks of foam and spit was on his lip and spun off in angry splashes.

He saw the woman run from the lagoon in the direction she had come, and then the serpent, thick and long, slid back into the water, and under the ripples something shook and vibrated before the archangel Lucifer shot from the water's depths, a cascaded of droplets around him, his wings wide and beautifully displayed, he span from the water into a pirouette in the sky, and then, just as quickly as he had penetrated the water, his throat was in the hands of the warrior Michael. Who had dived off the cliff and smashed straight into Lucifer upon straightening from the mid-air dynamics. Michael slammed him hard against the far tree trunk of some vast elm, and the tree shook and groaned. Saraquiel had swooped down on silent wing and just as Michael was about to lay fist heavy and furious against Lucifer's jaw, the silent, hooded, archangel of the court evaporated into a wisp of smoke, it flicked and flitted and reformed in between the two – Lucifer suspended high in the air from his throat and Michael, red-faced and visibly furious and frenzied. Saraquiel caught Michael's fist in his hand with a crack like thunder that shook the surrounding trees, a tremor of aftershock exploding in a circle all around them.

Saraquiel raised his head, his eyes were absent, all there was beneath the hood was darkness and shadow, but his mouth now smiled, a small, twisted smile, as Saraquiel's other hand raised to Michael and the index finger wagged side to side.

"No. No." It said where his mouth remained silent.

He grabbed hold of Lucifer's shoulder, and letting go of Michael's fist he instead took his brother's arm at the elbow, looking up, nodding to the sky, the hooded Saraquiel, Michael of the right chair, and Lucifer – the Morningstar, all disappeared in another thunderous crack.

The three angels turned to dust, vapours of smoke and then nothing as the world folded in on them and they were transported, on the sonic wings of the judge angel, into the throne of Yahweh himself.

There, to ask questions of each other and hide answers in riddles and lies.

"How do you have your tea?" James asked from inside the kitchen, his eternal hiding place when times were weird or hard, up to his elbows in cups and kettles and milk and tea bags. He came out and popped his head around the frame of the hallway door into his lounge, finding Lucifer sat cross-legged in front of the parcel.
He had not touched it but was unusually drawn and smitten with it.
"I will have it exactly as you have it, as was customary in the days of old."
James came the whole way into the lounge.
"I have it subdued and tepid, with far too much milk."
"Then so be it. Sounds charming…" Lucifer replied, waving affirmation at the man over his shoulder, while still staring at the box.
He turned to James and pointed at the parcel, enthusiastically.
"I really think you should open this."
James looked to the box, then to his guest, then to the box and his guest again.
"Did *you* send it…?"
Lucifer stood up and backed away from the parcel, waving his hands in denial.
"Oh no… this…" he pointed to the box, "is not *my* doing."
James smiled weakly at his protestations.
"But you think you know who has sent it?" he said, rolling his sleeves up over his elbows.
Lucifer smiled widely, then crossed his arms behind his back.
"Oh." He said, charmingly, full of good humour. "I KNOW that I know who sent it."

James walked to the box. A rush of dizziness was shuddering up him as he approached it. The sickly feeling of electricity flickering up his skin and over his spine. He looked at the box, and even this made him want to be sick.
There was nothing good about this delivery, nothing good at all, and he was not happy that it remained in his house goading and mocking

him. Ignorance for a while was bliss, but now, with the archangel –
as if that too was happening – harping on about it, James could not in
any way, shape or form ignore the bloody thing now.
"I don't like it…" he said to the angel.
"It has made me feel sick to my stomach since it turned up on the
bloody doorstep. I threw it away, once, and it bloody came back an
hour later."
Lucifer smiled and sat back into his comfy armchair.
"Yes. I'll tell you now… things like this have a want to do that; I am
afraid."
James looked at him, in his hand was a spoon, and on his shoulder a
tea towel. He was absently hitting his thumb with the spoon, making
a popping noise with the round back of the metal utensil rapping off
his knuckles.
Quite by accident, distractedly, he hit his knuckle once jaggedly on
the edge and let out a little sigh of pain, looked at Lucifer once more,
then the box, and said…

"…With a fucking bow on it."

James went to the window, where he had put the bow earlier, and he
threw it at Lucifer.
Lucifer caught the bow in the air and examining it with great interest.
"Now… tea." Said James, making his way back into the kitchen to
continue his mildly annoyed, banging and clambering.

Lucifer left his chair, made his way toward the kitchen to
where James was making so much noise and commotion. Lucifer
leant against the doorway, inside the arch, and cocked his head to one
side as he regarded the man. Drawing a measure of this creature,
whose life he had so rudely gatecrashed.
The man was slightly overweight, yet, he wore it well. He
was a stocky man who had clearly gone a bit to seed, had allowed
muscle to sag and loosen and you could see defeat in his shoulders
and his spine, as he stooped and trudged, like his hip was struggling
with the idea of bipedal movement, allowing the shuffle to take over.
His hair was short, dark blonde, teetering on brunette, and he wore

glasses that perched just too low on his nose so that he had to push them up his bridge constantly.

Despite this, however, he was a good-looking man – for a human. Lucifer could not stop staring at his eyes, which had a flick of the feline quality about them, and were made massive by his spectacles, when in reality, when the glass was removed, they were relatively small for his head.

The fallen angel witnessed how his smallish hands busily fidgeted and tapped on every surface, clicked and drummed while moving things around from one place to another. As if they were lost without a pen to push, or a page to turn, or keyboard to tap under tip. He watched as the man flung open pantry doors and cupboards and threw teaspoons at the sink; bouncing them from one rim of the bowl to the other, before drowning under the warm suds in a satisfying gulp.

He simply watched the man, fascinated that this was who had waited so long to find.

James, for his part, caught the shadow of Lucifer in the doorway and carried on regardless, unmoved, and unwavering in his ritual of tea creation. Like a wizard concocting some potion, he zoomed and flashed and sashayed around the kitchen cutting Jamaican ginger cake, squeezing teabags on rims of ill-matching coffee mugs, tapping spoons before flinging them away, throwing teabags into open binbags, and smashing every cupboard shut with little regard for manners or noise complaints.

He turned toward the angel and offered a plate with cake on and a coffee mug full of milky tea that had a colour as pale as Lucifer's hair.

"For you."

Lucifer accepted graciously. Looked at the cup, then the cake, before meeting James sigh with a smile after making a "Mmmm!" noise as though this was some rich, baroque, tea party offering.

James looked at the angel earnestly, his hand, under its own control now there was tea in it, surely conspiring with James' taste buds and stomach, automatically raised the cup to his lips and took a big, noisy, gulp of the milky brew.

Lucifer mirrored him.
James slowly lowered the cup, his face devoid of a smile.
"What do you fucking want from me?"

Lucifer lowered his cup. Slowly. Looking James in the eye - the man
pushing his glasses up his nose to full height - the angel smiled
weakly and truthfully for the first time in millennia.
The bravado and the charm slipping from his face as he did, and the
lines of the prison rippled through and showed themselves in his
skin, he was without doubt the most beautiful thing James had seen
that was not his wife or son. But it was an otherworldly beauty, one
which had been ravaged and marked with experiences, trials and
turmoils. Victories sweet and defeats as bitter as anything on Earth.
Lucifer sipped again from his tea, closed his eyes and savoured the
flavour.
He took a small, tentative bite from his ginger cake, and smiled
again, warmly, offering a salute to the man – his host.
James nodded, almost unnoticeably. He blinked slowly and with
great caution.
Lucifer swallowed back his cake with a final mouthful of his tea,
placed the cup on the plate and put it down on the sideboard.

"James. My friend." He said, holding out his hands to the human,
openly, almost as if begging.
"I am here to offer you the keys to Heaven."
Lucifer looked worn out, exhausted and sad, as his façade all but
disappeared.
"The final days of this Earth are coming, and the great chess game
we play in the vast cosmos above is winding down to its final few
moves.
I am promised my two thousand years of darkness; it is a war I
cannot lose.
But, I must have my champion, my one King above all others who
will rise and command my multitudes."
James nodded.
"The Antichrist?" He asked
"Yes. That's right." He smiled a relieved grin that the man knew

228

what he was talking about.

"I'm here to crown you my Antichrist."

And James nodded. Once.

Drank down his tea, in one greedy and gluttonous gulp, and smiled.

"Of course." He said.

This and nothing more.

He gestured to get by the angel, Lucifer stood up straight and shuffled awkwardly out of James's way. The two exchanged pleasantries as James thanked him, smiled and wandered into his lounge.

Lucifer watched him go. He was suddenly confused by the reaction to the conversation and offer and followed James's shuffle.

James was sitting down on the sofa, and staring at the box.

Lucifer followed him through the door, sat at the other end of the sofa, looking at the man staring at it.

Silence permeated the house.

Deafening silence that screamed in a void of sound.

Then James looked at the angel and gestured toward the parcel.

"You really think I should open it?"

Lucifer nodded.

"I do. I really do. For your own sake, if nothing more."

James stared at the box. Then back at Lucifer.

"Antichrist, eh?"

Lucifer nodded. Still somewhat confused by the nonchalant and throwaway manner of James's reaction.

"Excellent," James said, holding two thumbs up.

Lucifer did not really understand the gesture, but he mimicked it regardless.

James stared harder at the box.

At the nondescript, brown paper wrapping. At the string, the postmark, the chicken-scratch capitals of his address. He was curious he had to admit... But it was a scared, child-afraid-of-the-dark curiosity that precedes monsters and ghouls jumping out at you from shadows, or falls from great heights and the elation you feel before a moment of pain.

He was scared to death of this box, and he was only now admitting it.

"Bollocks to it."

He turned to Lucifer.

"I'm fucking opening it."

Lucifer smiled wide and brilliantly.

James climbed down off the sofa, and put two hands tantalizing close to the box, his skin immediately prickling up in goosebumps, the wave of nausea rising inside of him.

He had not felt like this since the day in the park, watching Kay's head bounce off the pole, before that, when he heard the rock impact on poor Poppie's skull, the sickening gurgling noises she made as she died drowning on her own blood and bone in his lap.

His eyes rolled deep into his head the closer his hands got to the box...

And just as he was about to touch the string, rip the paper off – with Lucifer leaning forward in excitement and peaked curiosity, clinging tightly his hands clenching the cushions, willing James to rip the wrapping in chunks and reveal the booty underneath...

The door shook with a rap, rap, rapping.

And James snapped back to life and normalcy again, his hands falling to his sides.

He looked to Lucifer, who stared back, and raised his arms in a shrug to deny any association with the noise.

James stood up and went to look out of the window to see who was at the doorstep, and as he went to shift the net curtain, he was face to face with a black, sleek, muscular horse.

And two more of varying degrees of ugliness and horror were chewing his flowers and eating his hedge.

230

Lucifer stood up. He knew exactly what this was, and he was unhappy.

James cursed loudly at the horse in his window, staring and snorting a fog on the glass.

"The giddy fuck is this?" he barked in surprise.

He went to the front door, flung it open.

There were just horses, three of them... Nothing more.

He looked around and took a step out of the door, the fresh air making his insides hurt, before realizing there was no one there and turning around back into the house, shooing an inquisitive nag from following him inside.

"There's no fucker there." He said, obviously half to himself in exasperation and half to Lucifer, as he walked into the lounge.

As he did, there, stood by the box was War.

Sniffing around the plate where once there had been Jamaican ginger cake, prodding at the crumbs and busily sucking the morsels from her fingertips was Famine.

Lord Death sat on James's armchair, scythe resting against the arm.

He stared back at James.

"What. The. Absolute. Fuck?" James said.

Lord Death looked to the man and pointed to an envelope that was resting on the dining table in the corner of the room. It was a sepia parchment folded neatly with a black seal and a red ribbon on.

"We are the Riders of the Approaching Storm, The Horsemen of the Apocalypse. Heralds to the end of days. We are here James Edmund's with an invitation and an offer."

"Oh really..." James said.

"I suppose you want me to be the fourth Horseman, yeah?"

Death had a look of slight confusion on his brow.

He looked questioningly at James from the armchair.

"How did you know?" he said matter of factly.

James looked at Lucifer, who was silent and still, and stood with a confused glow of panic about him.

"1...2...3" James counted the horsemen, prodding an accusatory finger in each direction.

"Unless the other one is off out parking his pony, I'd say you were a member down."

Death smiled wide and ugly then, his teeth pure white, there were too many of them inside his head, and it was as if James was staring at a greedy wolf grinning greedily upon his supper.

"Why, yes. That is exactly it. We have need of a rider for our council, and I have watched you for a long time... You have everything we need, everything we desire and everything we are missing."

"Well, isn't it my lucky fucking day, eh?" he said, looking not to Death, but to Lucifer.

"First I'm the Antichrist; then I am the fourth Horseman... Whatever next... Queen of England?" James said, melodramatically, throwing his arms in the air.

At this War laughed heavily and loud, it shook the room, it startled James back into life and he looked at the man's rich copper hair that so complimented his red tie and a smart, baggy, deep burgundy suit. War laughed again and pointed to the parcel still laying on the floor.

"What's in the box?" War bellowed.

James looked at him in incredulous anger. His hands balled into tight, white, fury-filled fists.

He stared at the huge man in red, at the thin, sickly woman now licking his plate and prodding at the carpet for more crumbs and , then, finally at the elegant near albino in the almost black, deep rich, navy blue suit sat comfy and long-limbed in his favourite armchair.

He looked at Lucifer, who saw what was happening, and tried to wave and gesture for him to not do what he knew he was going to do...

But to no avail.

James turned back to the man in red and screamed.

"I don't care who or what the fuck you are, I could just about deal

232

with the Devil here..."
Lucifer tried to interject – "James..."
"No, I'm sorry... Your horses are eating my Rhododendrons, so get them off my lawn, and piss off..."
"James... Don't..."
"No, shut up, Lucifer... I don't give a flying bastard monkey who they think they are..."
War let out a belly laugh at the expletive-spewing human stood in front of him. His laugh was a cacophonous chortle that sounded as patronizing as it was loud.
James span to meet the gaze of the massive, red-headed, copper-bearded man dead on. Unafraid.
"I'm sorry, Brian Blessed. Is there something fucking funny? Is this a comedy to you? Invading another person's home, just gallivanting around uninvited dressed like an extra from Flash fucking Gordon you ginger-headed twat?"

War looked at Lucifer, his laugh stopped silent and short as though a radio was turned off at the mains.
The smile on his face lingered for a moment as he looked at Lucifer, who was now uncomfortably nervous and having a hard time hiding it.
"Master War, please... don't..." Lucifer raised a hand slowly and passively to beckon the Horseman to not follow through on his next action. For a glimmer of a fraction of a millisecond he had thought it had worked.
"Twat?" War said to James.
"Ginger-headed twat. That's right." James said his face now rising to a warm beetroot in anger; he had taken a step toward the man in red as he said it.
War looked at Famine, who was on the floor and picking the morsels still that she had found snagged in the carpet fibers.
"Twat?" War said questioningly to the atrociously thin woman.
"It means pregnant goldfish... I believe." Famine responded absently; she raised the sofa with one hand effortlessly, finding a tasty crumb of biscuit.

"Twat," War said quietly again, letting the word roll around his tongue and mouth as if trying it on for size. A half sneer smile on his face to James.

"Twat." James said, another step closer to the man – Lucifer was now sweating.

"T. W. A. T… Now get the fucking fuck out of my house you absolute basta…"

Before he could finish the sentence James was on his back, in the hallway, fifteen feet from where he started.

Lucifer had lunged forward to try and stop the strike, but to no avail, he watched as James contorted and flew, as if in slow motion, through the air and into the hall with an almighty crash. Sending chips of wood and plaster flying with him.

As for James, he did not feel the backhanded slap that blasted him off his feet and through the doorway, nor did he feel the moment his face planted solidly against the ceiling. His nose was obliterated, an odd, misshapen mass of blood and sinew, his cheekbone too, his right eye had popped and smashed in his head from some fragment of bone slicing upwards. His arm was contorted in weird angles, and his leg was jagged from a deep compound fracture that stuck out of his thigh and squirted blood across the floor and onto his white magnolia walls.

He tried to speak but all that came was a grunting, gurgling, whimper, and he spat four teeth into his lap. A bungee of saliva, blood and snot dangled helplessly from his open mouth.

He gave a slight hiccup and a giggle as if the sight was incomprehensibly silly… then his eyes rolled back again, and he flopped to the floor dramatically.

Lucifer ran into the hall as James passed out sniveling. He turned to the doorway he had just come from that lead from the hallway to the front door and through to the lounge. What he saw was a chunk of plaster and wood smashed and broken from where the man had hurtled back and through, impacting heavily with the light in the hall

– which smashed and fragmented into a thousand slithers of glass and fiber - before bouncing off the ceiling face first and crashing with a slide on his backside to a sitting position under the coat rack.

As Lucifer looked at James, then the lounge, where War stood with his fists raised, ready to fight again, then back to James, unconscious and slumped and broken on the floor, several coats all fell off the rack and landed on his body.
Lucifer huffed a resigned and flabbergasted sigh hard.
"For Heaven's sake!"
War laughed heavily and with great mirth from the lounge, his fists loosened and fell to his belly, he began pointing to the other Horsemen and then to the coats and the hallway where the man lay.
Lucifer spun on his heel and stared at the horseman –
"Don't you dare." He said, cold as ice and with chilling layers of menace. His eyes were burning with that harsh corona of fire around the iris.
War shut up immediately, his smiled disappeared, somehow when the Morningstar said be quiet, or shut up, those eyes made you do exactly that.
Whether you were Horseman or not.

Lucifer took the coats off the man and picked him up, gently and delicately in his arms, he carried him into the lounge, noticing the silver double frame, lay on the floor, broken and mangled as James had hit the wall, taking out half of the Welsh dresser and chest of drawers where the frame stood.
The picture of Kay had been ripped asunder by a snag of wood that smashed and shattered the silver frame. The half with Callum, James's late son, was untouched but dusty from the plaster.
Lucifer looked at it on the floor, in pieces, and gestured to War.

"Pick that up."

War was no longer smiling, he looked at Death who was sat impassive, unimpressed on the armchair. He had found James's journal and was flipping the pages with boredom and a gesture

235

bordering on contempt, he did not even look up at his brother.
Instead, he just said.
"Do as the angel tells you. And fix what you have broken."
War looked at the room, the wall, the plaster, the wooden doorframe.
He looked at his sister, still cross-legged and hunched over flicking
through carpet fibers and down the sofa sides looking for crumbs.
He looked at Lucifer holding James in his arms, flopped unconscious
and breathing with a snorted labour from his various facial injuries.
He looked at Death. He was indignant, defiant and angry…
"He called me a twat…"
"And up until three minutes ago you had no idea what that word was
or meant. You had never heard it before, and it had never existed in
your vocabulary for you to have ever grown any emotional reaction
to one way or another. Yet…" Death said, rising from his chair in
effortless, ominous stride, standing almost nose to nose with War.
"When your sister suggested a meaning, even before ascertaining if it
was even true, you… Lord War, second Horseman of the
Apocalypse, master of the hound and canon… YOU… Threw the
one man in the known cosmos who we were not supposed to hurt,
damage or touch in any way…" He gestured to James, then the wall,
and hallway.
"THROUGH A FUCKING WALL."

Death now had War by his hair, and was lifting him from the ground
and elevating him high.
War clenched at Death's hands and tried to pull free, his legs kicking
and swinging like a man on a rope doing the gallows' jig.
His teeth clenched hard, and he grunted in pain.
"So get out there now, and fix immediately what you have broken…
you, utter, utter twat."
Death threw the red-suited horseman through the door, he slid,
smooth yet heavily into the far wall, and the coat rack collapsed and
landed on him.
His eyes burned a scarlet, glowing red, and he growled at the blue
and black-clad Death, heaving himself to his feet.
Famine slowly, as if watching a tennis match, stared between her two
brothers and licked subconsciously at her fingers, thick with sticky

dust.

Lucifer shooed Famine out of the way with his foot and lay the man down on the sofa.

He was covered in blood. A bloody bubble of snot and mucous inflated in the space where his broken jaw and smashed nose met.

"Oh, James" Lucifer muttered fearfully under his breath.

He tried to wipe the bubble cleaned, but the man was clearly dying, choking on his own blood and bone.

"Lord Death…" he said to the Horseman.

But Death and War were staring at each other in a Mexican standoff, snarled lips and growls from the Rider in Red, and a blue steel stare from the Black Rider, who had shown the silver and fiery sword on his hip to his brother.

"LORD DEATH…" Lucifer screamed.

"Edmunds is dying."

Death slowly folded his jacket over his hip, as he did so, the broad silver blade faded into transparency. War slowly calmed down and was shrugging the coats off of himself.

Famine had made her way over to the man, she gently held his hand. She looked at Death, gravely, and shook her head fearfully.

"He is not dying, I have not allowed it." Death said, with an air of arrogant ambivalence.

Lucifer did not care the consequences, he grabbed the Black Rider's arm harshly and with a deep swell of strength dragging him to the body and pointed at the man who was broken and beaten and smashed laying in a coagulating pool of blood on his own sofa.

A sofa he had dearly loved.

"Then why… Lord Mort… Is he dying?"

Death leant in, looked at the man, listened to his breathing and a thin, but immaculate arm, which pulsed with an imbued silvery flash of magic, reached to the carotid artery of his neck and touched for a pulse.

There was silence for a few lingering seconds.

Then Death pulled his hand away...

"Well..." He said. There was a pause.
"Fuck me." He followed. And he went to the armchair and slumped into it with a huge huff from the aged and worn fabric cushions.

Death had no idea what to do.
"Lord Mort...?" Said Lucifer, his face clammy and nervous.
He had the look of a man who has lost everything and was only just learning of it.
Death, the master and lord of the world beyond, the creature that was like the gods and who walked gods to the place beyond this place.
The head of the Riders Four, Lord of The Apocalypse, Shepherd to the other side.

Lord Death was all out of words.

James Edmunds, the man who would be Antichrist. Death's candidate for the Fourth Horseman in Pestilences seat. The isolated, tragic, widowed husband and bereaved father.
James.

Was dead.

* * *

CHAPTER FIVE
Wiping the Slate Clean

*"When I buy a new book, I always read the last page first,
that way in case I die before I finish, I know how it ends.
That, my friend, is a dark side."*

- Nora Ephron, When Harry Met Sally

When the ambulance arrived, there was a frenzy of activity. People were coming out of their houses to see what was happening. Mothers and fathers stood holding their children in loose hugs around the neck, holding them close, watching and witnessing the body being taken into the back of the vehicle, paramedics looking shocked at what they had seen. Faces clearly shocked by the devastated face and skull they had just had to bear witness too.

Cars were re-routed around the ambulance, which blocked all of one side of the road, and the hedgerows and front gardens were bristling with people trying to get a look at what was happening. One policeman, who had arrived in tandem with another car from the nearby constabulary, was directing traffic while his colleague was taking witness statements. Another officer was talking to people at the top of the road, asking about what commotion they had heard and what they understood to be the story here.
Another was stood by a plainclothes officer called from duty in the neighbouring town to come and manage this scene. When he saw James, his face was white, and his knees were weak. He had never seen anything like this before, his stomach was churning, he had so wished he had not eaten as big a lunch as he had before seeing what he had seen.

James was sat in the back of a police car; a junior officer from child services was knelt down beside him, holding his hand. James' mother Margaret stood being consoled by another mother, deep in a tearful embracing hug, as James just stared down at the road, and took in the scene. The gurney lifting into the back of the ambulance, which bore upon it poor dead Poppy. He looked at the blue and white police tape that cordoned off and blocked access to the Conker field, of the forensic officers who now were placing upside down "V" shaped place tabs on things of interest in the field where Poppy had been hit with the stone. One took James' bag, full of the flask of cold, milky tea, his "The Silver Chair" book and his other belongings. He watched as one police car left, with Michael in the back, sat next to his mother, his head down and crying. He stared at James through the window as they drove past, his eyes closing a fraction smaller, a hateful glare at the boy who he had meant to hit.

James watched this all in silence.
His mind not working at a speed fit for the situation. Everything seemingly moving at a fraction the pace of normal time, slow-motion blurs from everything as he stared down the dynamics of fluid motion, each tiny shift sending ripples flickering through the air behind everyone.
James stared on, seeing auras and patterns being painted in the airwaves by every person in attendance.
His mind clung onto the colours as a way of distraction from the gore he had all over his hands and clothes from where he had held Poppy until the Ambulance arrived.
The stain of blood on his mouth and cheek from where he had attempted CPR, even as Michael had attempted to stop him, snapping awake from his stupor, refusing to believe he could have done what he did, shaking his head and wondering how the rock had found its way into his hand - and furthermore - why he had thrown it?
All Michael could think about was the burning desire he had, the overwhelming urge and need to throw something, *anything,* at James. But no recollection of where the stone had come from, desire or no desire - he knew damn well it was an awful and outrageous thing to do.
But – still – throw it he did.

Michael looked at his hands and down at the flattened, smashed face of the 13-year-old girl… Then felt a sudden and unreal flush of rage unknown even for Michael, a boy who had his own issues and anger problems, when he saw the target of his sudden ire laying the girl down, tilting her head and administering the kiss of life.
As fruitless and as futile a gesture as it was.
Every breath he gave was echoed back with a gargling, choking glottal from the girl's nose and throat.
James tried to give heart massage as well, having been shown at

school in an after class, first aid lesson.
But nothing helped.

Who knows? It may have, had he been given time and opportunity to continue, but, Michael came running down and grabbed him off the girl and threw him tumbling into the barbed wire at the bottom of the field. The one that circled the Conker trees and stopped the lamb and cattle from breaking into the side orchard by the main road.

James tumbled into the wire and covered his eyes for fear of serious injury. His shirt snagged, and he tore a hole in the sleeve. He brought himself to standing straight away and stared at the slender, enraged Michael, who blocked his way to the body of Poppy and also his exit from the field.
"What the hell are you doing, Michael?" he snapped, his voice a broken rasp of upset and of anger.
"What is *wrong* with you?" he added, throwing his arms in wild gesticulation.
"You've killed her... You... You have KILLED her." Pointing at Poppy's body, lay prone and vulnerable on the leaf-strewn soil.
Michael looked behind him, at Poppy's body. He saw the collective faces of the kids from the gang, some in tears, some hugging others, some holding their mouths in shock and awe, silence and terror.
All of them, without question, terrified of this new Michael they were seeing in full light of day for the first time. The shroud of leadership removed and the cold, harsh, stone-like bully that had dictated and demanded so much of them all summer suddenly clear as the sky above them, for all to see.

Cruel, ruthless, driven and utterly unhinged.

Michael looked at them, and his mouth went to speak, but idly opened and closed with no sound, he looked at Poppy's body, at James, and he gave a half-sigh, a half-laugh of reservation as he realized how he looked to others and how he was now regarded.
His childhood over.
He looked down the hill and saw the first of the cars coming up on their way to the next shift at the factory at the top of the estate.

Staff in hatchbacks and coupés driving up the hill. Accelerating past the turnoffs to the different cul-de-sacs on the steep gradient of the hill.

Michael saw the car coming, the kids moving to the other side of the road, and he bolted, jumping over the fence, he ran straight for the road and the car.

He went to jump into the oncoming traffic, without even thinking, and just as he was about to throw himself into the path of the oncoming car there was a screeching snarl of brakes and a thump and thud as Jake Eddery, who had lived at the top of Park Way, slammed into Michael and took him out of harm's way.

The kids all screamed and screeched in excited and frightened bleats and sighs, and James collapsed down on the spot, crawling to Poppy's body, before cradling her close and holding her cooling, dead body until the hands of the ambulance paramedics removed him.

The passage of time for James becoming fluid and disjointed at this point.

Jake Eddery had seen the commotion, one of the kids had come running and slammed on his front door as he prepared his dinner before a shift. From the netted curtains of his kitchen he had seen Michael storm across the green hillock and toward the horse chestnut field, he had watched as the dozen or more kids followed in varying degrees of excitement and fervor.

Jake pulled his nets back and looked up the field and watched for a few seconds and saw Michael make his way to the top on his own, with Poppy climbing after him but staying at the bottom of the field.

He watched for a few seconds more. Not able to see what was happening at the top of the field, but seeing James walk down, spin on his heel and the rock smash into Poppy's face – though he could not hear the impact himself, his mind filled the gap with a flash of a sound in the form of a sickening crack and a wet pop.

He saw the prone and defenseless girl hit the deck like a puppet whose strings were sliced and James's sudden reaction of falling and kneeling by her side

By this point, his hands were off the net and he was flying out the door to see for himself whether this was an elaborate joke. The closer he got, the clearer it became that this was no joke. Seeing the blood on James, face, the anger in Michael's sudden surge at the other boy. The shouting and argument between them as James removed himself from the barbed wire, then Michael's sudden bolt for the fence.

Jake was already on the street, could read the situation enough to see what Michael had seen and planned. He ran, hard and fast, tackling the boy within inches of being hit himself by the Ford Cortina that screeched and slammed to a stalled stop on the street.

Michael was screaming and crying, weeping and struggling. Jake could barely hold him down. He restrained the boy as delicately but as sternly as he could and commanded one of the girls in the group to run and get Michael's parents. Screaming at another young boy he demanded that he run into his house and dial the police to say there had been an accident, and they needed an ambulance and fast response immediately.
To Michael he calmly told the boy to stay still and stop struggling, his knees harshly placed holding down the thirteen-year-old's arms, even as he struggled and kicked out from underneath him.
To James, holding Poppy in his arms and sobbing silently, the tears straining from his eyes, Jake simply shared a look. A quiet, fleeting meeting of eyes. He nodded, letting James know that he saw it all, that he was going to be OK.

James nodded back. Weakly, almost unnoticeably.

He appreciated the gesture and the act of stopping Michael from harming himself.
But as for everything being OK…
This was when it dawned on him that nothing, ever, would be same or normal again.

Not one little bit.

* * *

"What do you mean he is dead?"

War looked down at the body laying on the sofa. One eye stared back, its pupil tiny and the light gone from it. The face was obliterated. The eye that had popped bled out in a rivulet down James' cheek. A sticky, horrendous smelling clear fluid congealed with the blood, setting hard on his skin.

The cheek bone was a jagged protrusion that stuck out in a weird and horrible angle from the flesh of his face, and his glasses were tangled in the curl of his hair, caught from the nose rests in a knot of sticky, blood matted hair and thin metal frame.

War poked the man, not once or twice, but repeatedly. His hand getting harder each time, leaving dented purple welted bruises on the body.

"Wake up!" he shouted at the body.

"Wake up weak, fleshy thing!" He flicked at James' smashed nose. Took a step back ready for a reaction. Nothing happened.

War looked at Famine, who held the man's hand, and was staring at the fingers, clearly enthralled by the residue of the Jamaican ginger cake that sat somewhere in the gullies of his fingerprints. Famine caught his gaze and looked up at him and said two words.

"He's dead." And returned to her examination of his fingers.

The copper-haired horseman looked at Death. Collapsed in the armchair and murmuring to himself, looking paler than usual.

"But how can he be dead?"

Death was ignorant to the question, continuing his whispered monologue to himself.

War looked at Lucifer, who had been chewing his fingernails staring at the body and the other characters in this farce in the lounge. He and War shared a brief moment of confused eye contact; War shrugged a *"HOW?"* and Lucifer responded with his hand on his mouth, and his left arm holding the elbow of his right, nervously padding his feet side to side with a shrug-shouldered *"Don't look at me!"*

245

War took it, and it was enough of a gesture to break his already waning patience.

The Red Rider stomped to Death and grabbed him by the dark navy lapels and raised him high in the air off the armchair, pulling him close to his face.

Death had no chance to react, so lost in his own little world, he did not snap out of it until it was far too late.

War had him a foot or so off the ground, and he was mere inches from War's face, his deep ginger beard with the two white flecks from the corner of his mouth down was matched by a deep red and angry face, his eyebrows, a mess of ginger and grey, were slanted into a ferocious, creviced and pimpled browed frown.

He shook the Lord of Death effortlessly. It was as if any strength the Reaper had - had all but fallen from his bones, and he was a flap of dirty, lifeless cloth on the breeze.

War's breath was a red-hot, spicy tang of heat and fury He spat flecks of saliva when he spoke, and he quietly muttered in an irritated fashion at Death.

"Why. Is. He. Dead?" Death snapped to bright and vigorous life, and his clear, steel blue eyes sparked to their usual veracity. He placed his hands, a pallid, waxen white on War's rough hands and tapped submission gently and intently.

War loosened his grip and put his elder brother down and pointed at James, whose one eye stared back still, accusingly. War did not like it and changed his point to a flat hand, covering up the gaze.

"You are Death. You are! He should not be dead if you do not command it... So why? Tell me!" War demanded.

Lucifer stood still and quiet, both hands covering his mouth now; his hangdog expression was a mixture of flabbergasted confusion and outright horror. His grand entrance into James' life was descending into chaotic ruin in minutes, beyond any control of his own.

All he could think was why the hell had these Horsemen turned up. After all, had he and Death not struck an accord, was there not a deal in place?

A two thousand year wait for retribution and vindication scorched

and set asunder in mere moments, in front of his own beautiful and fiery eyes.
He could cry, he really could.

"I do not know." Death said, simply and elegantly.
He waved a hand at the body of the man. It was a heavy, yet vacant gesture that bore a lot of questions yet asked none.
"It is like he is not there. I cannot touch him, I cannot feel him, his presence is before me, but his soul is not, it is... lacking..."
War looked at the Black Rider. His brow went from anger to confusion, and back to anger again.
He then resorted, finally, to ferociously annoyed confusion. The stern eyebrows bent outward and raised as he collapsed on the armchair himself. Death watched him, looked at Lucifer, who removed his hands from his mouth and openly and wildly shrugged once again.
"I have no fucking clue," he said to Death.
The pale man looked at Famine.
"He is dead, Sire." She said.
"I KNOW HE'S FUCKING DEAD!" Death screamed at her and stormed out of the lounge, through the devastated doorframe, through the wrecked hallway and into the kitchen.
Everyone watched him leave, dramatically in a bellow of his dark clothing and silver-white mane.
War gave Lucifer another of his angry eyebrowed stares.
"What is he doing?"

There was a lot of noise from the kitchen, the cupboards opening and closing and banging and slamming.
Lucifer went to shrug again, and realized this was a stupid repetition of ineffective gestures, and stormed out too, following Death.
He stood in the doorway, wiping his face with his hands, rubbing his chin and fixing his hair, and then asked quietly and coolly of the Reaper.
"What are you doing?"

Death spun around with a look of complete frustration, fear and confusion on his beautiful face, it was mixed with a look of determined passion and a mission statement drawn in the serious brow.

"I AM MAKING A CUP OF FUCKING TEA." He shouted slamming a cupboard shut. A teacup boisterously fell over and clattered with the plate below. Death and Lucifer held each other's gaze, trying to ignore the smashing thud from the cupboard. Several more cracking and tinkling noises came, then, silence.

"Do you fucking want one?" he finished, the question now a forlorn plea for help.

Lucifer lost all composure and his fake, postured solemnity and earnestness drained from him. His shoulders slumped in conquered sag again. He nodded halfheartedly and with no enthusiasm.

"Yes please... Tepid and subdued and with far too much milk."

Death looked at him seriously, nodding in defeat.

"Sounds delightful."

And they both watched the kettle as it boiled, steaming up the kitchen with its heat.

* * *

After Poppy's funeral James' parents decided that it was maybe time for James' father to take that promotion offer and the requisite move that came with it. They could uproot from the estate that was full of memories, mostly now bad, slowly taking over the few good ones and fogging and clouding up the Edmund's family world.

The family were looking for places to go, away from the estate and the focus they had unduly gained, somewhere James would be able to live in peace.

James had not gone to the funeral. Poppy's aunt, who had brought the young girl up since the death of her mother when she was nine from leukemia, had invited James; indeed, she had insisted, to no avail. The kids of the estate had said how the boy had attempted to help her, how the quick reaction to try and bring her back with heart massages and the kiss of life was all he had thought about, even when Michael had thrown him to the barb wire fence.

248

Poppy's aunt, Cressida Clarence, had been touched that so many of the kids came to his defense, confirming that he had tried to do the right thing in such a wrong situation. She was very aware that also – the stone – it was meant for James, not her niece.

Cressida had shown up at James' parent's house, and there had been no words shared when the door was opened, James' mother simply opened her arms and welcomed the woman with a hug. There were silent tears, a few hushed nods and quiet words not able to be overheard, and then they retired to the lounge where they had a scotch and held hands.

Clearly tea in this instance was not enough of a tipple for the situation.

James could scarcely understand a scenario where tea was NOT the answer.

He wondered this as he sat down with a book, curled into the nook of the airing cupboard, huddled in amongst the blankets and the sleeping bags reading in the dark by torchlight.

His new favourite hiding place, cramped and close and his.

All his own.

Margaret explained to Cressida why James had not wanted to go. How he had said that by going the focus would not be on the little girl, who deserved to have people remember her for being as loving and brilliant as she was – and not have someone turn up who would make heads turn, and whispers form. James did not want to be responsible for muddying her memory as he had been for her death.

Inadvertently or not.

He truly believed that he had caused the family enough harm and pain, and simply wanted to stay away. Saying, as was typical of the young man, that he would pay his respects in private on his own, in his own way.

Cressida sat and listened, and nodded.

She understood.

She thanked Margaret, sipped down her scotch, gave her excuses and made her way to the door to leave.

Upon getting there, for James' benefit alone, she raised her voice to one that was little less than a shout, the tempo and timbre perfectly calm, and said,
"James should know at least that no one, least of all Poppy, would ever blame him for this. No one blames him at all. I would like it to be known that this is the solemn truth."

James had heard; the words were clear to him.
It softened his mood somewhat; the torch went off, and in darkness, pure and immovable, James cried

Two or three weeks after the funeral and James had built a new routine and ritual. Having heard what Poppy's aunt had said, he would pack a backpack with: his CS Lewis book - now THE LAST BATTLE - his flask of weak looking, white tea, a sandwich, a banana and some chocolate biscuits wrapped in cling-film, and he would walk to the church in South Atherton village two miles from his house, over the fields and brooks and up by the sewage treatment plant. He would go over the troll bridge by the tiny off-shoot of the canal, and then over the kissing gate by the Fox Pub, to trudge the short distance between there and the doors of St. Leonard's Church – where lay Poppy's grave.

He sat cross-legged by the gravestone and placed the chocolate digestive biscuits on the top in a line, five in total. The birds from the trees quickly joined him, curious as to what treat was brought today by the boy. This boy who came to the graveyard most Sundays and sat in the yard reading and sipping from his flask cup.
James took out his book and opened at the page marker and began reading out loud. Now and then he would take a bite from a sandwich, swallow it down with a cup of cold tea, and continue. There was a magpie, a blackbird and a robin on the top of the gravestone today as his audience, as well as Poppy, tucked up and warm under six feet of earth.
The birds ate slowly, ignoring each other except for an occasional squawk or peck at the feathers around the neck of their neighbour, on the whole, an attentive and appreciative audience. James loved their

250

fearlessness and the peaceful and gentle way they tapped and devoured the biscuits, especially the robin - dwarfed by his compatriots, but the most bolshie and forward of the three.

He enjoyed the solitude of the graveyard and how the people he knew to be in here, buried and rested, were much more than just forgotten shadows, but were real life heroes and villains, bona fide history lessons everyone. Each grave its own story.

His kind of people.
Story people.

On this day, just after the bells chimed for 3 pm, and the rest of the congregation had gone, James entered in with his backpack, and waited for the final few cars to leave after service, the Vicar waving him welcome and locking up, to retire to his warm house and his Sunday lunch. James saw a man stood over the grave of Poppy. He slowly, carefully wandered up and took a seat on the bench just by the big stained-glass window, protected from outside by a thin crisscross of mesh, stopping birds entering the awning and breaking the coloured glass that caught the sun so well and beautifully.
The man caught James' eye as he walked past, a glance James had kicked himself for allowing, before he strode to the bench to wait.
"Was she a friend of yours?" The man had asked.
James looked around to see if there could be anyone else that may be the man's intended target for the question. But, they were alone just he and the man.
"I'm sorry. Are you talking to me?" he answered quietly, his voice little more than a whisper.
The man turned around.
His dark suit was an incredible shade of green, a deep green the shade of the waters of Mediterranean seas.
He wore a big greatcoat: black, with a fine woolen blend. Round his neck, he had a scarf that was green tartan, a rich pattern.
His neat, short, golden-blonde hair was tucked underneath a black fedora, with a band the same colour as the suit.

His shoes were muddy and old; they were a sudden contrast to his impeccable tailoring. Worn in, scuffed and muddy.

"She was a friend. Still is I suppose. I was there when she died." He said. Standing. He slowly walked to the man leaving his backpack on the bench.

The two of them overlooked the gravestone.

There were peck marks from sharp beaks on the top of the granite, and a fine yellow and white moss had already started to settle in, even so soon into Poppy's tenure in the yard.

"Shame. So young, so beautiful..." he looked down at James.

"I am a friend of the family, paying my respects on a flying visit." He added nonchalantly.

"My name is Littlehorn. Her mother and I are cousins. By marriage, long story, convoluted, *messy*. But cousins nonetheless." He offered James his hand, removing his fine leather gloves.

James looked at it, momentarily, and then took it with a tight grip – as his father had always told him – *"you are no kind of man if you don't have a handshake befitting a pope or pauper, strong and dignified... Grip, grip, grip, son, that's all you need."*

"James Edmunds."

"Lovely to make your acquaintance, Mr. Edmunds," Littlehorn said, his smile an intoxicatingly wide expanse of teeth and thin, pink lips.

"Tell me, James, do you know this churchyard... St. Leonard. Are you aware what he is the patron saint of?

James did not, but, as ever when posed with a question he had no answer for, his mind and heart burned for it deeply.

"I don't, sir."

"Sir! Is it?" Littlehorn laughed, taken aback by the child's manners. "My father is 'Sir'. Okay, James? I am just Littlehorn, please. Shall we sit?" He motioned to the bench.

The bench was easily visible from the main road, a T-junction that went left for Rokerton Town, or right toward the estate, and every car that approached from the village could see straight into the churchyard and see them even with the green bush that ran the edge of the fence. James was not afraid of the man and agreed to sit.

"Would you excuse me one second?" he said, motioning to the

gravestone and seeing the hungry birds in the birch tree that was bordering the graveyard and Atherton's farm next door.

James took out his biscuits and ran them over to the gravestone laying five out in a row. Malted Milks this week.

The bird swooped down and began their feast.

James nodded a salute to the magpie, who cawed back shrilly and carried on eating.

He then said something Littlehorn could not hear to the gravestone and saluted this too, with a touch of his forelock. James returned to the bench.

"Sorry… they'll only interrupt us otherwise." He said.

Littlehorn smiled.

"Well, it would be rude of me to gatecrash your routine so completely… so no apologies necessary." James offered him a cup of tea; Littlehorn took it curiously, smelling, he drank it down in one. "Delightful…" he said and meant it.

"So. St Leonard, young man, is the patron saint of prisoners and those who have been incarcerated. He is the carer of those lost to time and punishment. And, as the stories go – he visits every prisoner once, usually upon their first night in chokey… giving them three secrets that they can trade or barter with in the prison. Every prisoner holding three key pieces of information that could – at any time – be just what is needed to get them that extra inch of security or comfort. Only three mind! And once gone – they are gone…. Done and dusted, your connection to the saint evaporates and is sand on the wind."

James looked at him enthralled. He smiled and nodded.

"How do you know?" He said.

"Well. Don't be scared, young man… but, for a time, I was a prisoner also. And I met him."

James offered him more tea in a trance-like manner.

"You?" He said, wondrously. "A prisoner?" Littlehorn nodded. "What did you do?" James asked – without thinking – the words escaping his lips before he could stop them.

"Sorry… that is rude to ask. Apologies." He blurted. Littlehorn took the flask from him and smiled deeply.

"No apologies. It is an obvious question, and you would be the first not to ask..." he laughed.

"I was a political prisoner. I was locked away for a long time in a deep, white cell, with only one window, and no door that I could get to because I dared to believe a different way existed for my people than my king believed."

He went silent... his eyes, a curious mix of green and brown and a thin line of orange shone in the muted daylight of the afternoon. James stared at them as Littlehorn sipped his tea some more.

"Anyway... I met him once. I was unfortunate that when I met him it was many years into my sentence, but still, he told me three secrets, and he shook my hand, planted a kiss upon my forehead and... he was gone."

James nodded, sagely, the story being one of the best he had heard he was keen to share it with his dad who loved facts and general knowledge.

"Did you barter with the secrets?" James asked.

"No. I was isolated, I had no jailer, I had no cellmates - was all alone, so my secrets slowly made me mad... for a time... And still I have them now. All three..." He gave a mischievous smile to the boy.

James took a sip from his flask, and just before he hit the metal to lips, he mouthed "WOW!" in amazement.

Littlehorn smiled, and he sipped from his cup, gulping back the milky, cold tea, sweet and weak, and yet so refreshing in its simplicity.

"James. Thank you for sharing your tea and for allowing me to humour you with my story. Also, my apologies for interrupting your time with your friend. I can tell that she meant an awful lot to you – if the peck marks on the headstone are any indication... and the size of that robin..." He pointed to the headstone as a fat, chirpy robin bravely pecked away at the Malted Milks. The boy and the man laughed, the robin stared at them buffing out his red chest in prideful ignorance.

"Let me give you something for your kindness."

James shook his head, immediately he felt bad. "I can't, sir... Honestly, it would be rude."

Littlehorn shook his head and waved James' protestations away.

"James... I learnt long ago that these secrets were not for me. They

were for me to give. So, as a way of saying thank you for your
company, your tea and your ear, let me give you them, and hopefully
they will be useful to you where they were not for me."
He smiled at the boy. James looked at the floor, then up toward the
man, and then he stood. Looking directly at the man stoutly he
offered his hand again.
"Okay, I will accept your gift if you tell me one last thing."
Littlehorn regarded the hand on offer, removed his glove and took it
in his own hand.
"Go on…"
James looked very seriously and hard at Littlehorn, his eyes glazing,
holding back tears.
"Tell me, and mean it… I am responsible for her dying?"
Littlehorn looked at James, and something stirred within him. Some
wave of his past pushing at the walls, trying to come forward shaken
and woken by this statement…. He held it back, barely, with all his
might. But, how often had he asked the same question… How often
had he wondered the same thing of the one he had met so briefly?
James was crying now, weak tears straining down his cheek,
Littlehorn could smell the salt; he could almost taste its acrid
bitterness on his tongue.
He held the boy's hand tighter, it was warm, and it felt safe to James,
he took the hand in his other, cupping James' hand now in both of his
own and leant down.
"James. My friend. You are absolutely not to blame. And never again
– NEVER AGAIN – ever think you were."
James' eyes burned a fierce orange for a second, then returned to the
rich hazel, he shook unsteadily on his feet, and then came back to full
Cognizance.
He looked at Littlehorn, who shook his hand curtly twice, smiling.
James smiled back, shook his head somewhat, and nodded.
"That settles that then."
Littlehorn nodded agreement. "Yes. It really rather does."

The two of them released the other's hand; Littlehorn
returned his gloves, the biting winter air was coming in, and the
breath drew memories of its presence on the air.

James tidied his flask away, stroked Poppy's headstone and watched as the birds flew away back to perches and treetops and bushes where they came from, and as he was packing away to leave the graveyard, Littlehorn gave a little cough, to get the boy's attention.

"So… your gift as way of thanks."

He pulled from inside his coat a small brown envelope, and upon it was a black seal.

It was not addressed, had no mark or date. It looked ancient.

"These are the secrets St. Leonard shared with me, by thank you for your company. You will know when it is the time to open it, and hopefully when you do the secrets will have meaning for you in your time of need."

James took the envelope and put it in his pocket with a brief second glance.

"Thank you, Sir."

"Sir, eh… I do like your manners, boy. It's rare in this day and age… Keep hold of them, you'll be unique amongst the world one day." He laughed. James did too.

"And, thank you. It has been a pleasure, young man. Take care, and keep an eye on our Poppy here – ok?"

James saluted the man, and without a second look, Littlehorn exited the churchyard, whistling to himself, an unusually bright spring in his step as he got to the gate. A crow sat perched on the post, Littlehorn stroked its head once, and the crow jumped to his shoulder, and the two of them left.

James watched him go, amazed, and then pulled the envelope from his pocket. He rubbed the warm and worn paper, smelled its rich aroma, and smiled as he returned it to his trousers and then backpack on he ran hard and fast home.

It had been an incredible, weird, wonderful and unique day…

* * *

When he was out of sight, Littlehorn ducked into a thin alleyway between the houses of Hathaway Lane and Dupont Avenue – towards the playing fields.

He held his stomach; the crow jumping onto the fence in front of

him, turning its head this way and that to watch and witness the
happening before it.

The man opened his jacket, and the coat melted around him, pulling
high onto his back and forming two jet-black wings.

His faced grimaced and popped as the hair on his head grew and
flowed free down his shoulders, and his face morphed into a
younger, more beautiful shape.

Lucifer.

The pang of the memories of his mother. Worried, frightened eyes
staring back and then being pulled away, disappearing into nothing
and empty space. The cruel, angry laugh of his father as he pushed
her, flying, into the plain.

The thought shaking around in his infant mind.

"Am I responsible for her dying?"

The first thought in his white dwarf of a mind, incandescent and
scorched upon his soul forever.

Lucifer looked at the crow, who cawed gently and satisfyingly at the
angel.

The angel mimicked his head movements and his glare. He laughed
quietly.

"My friend…" he said to the crow.

"You have no idea how easy you have it."

The crow caw-cawed in agreement, and Lucifer, on his beautiful,
vast black wings, took to the sky…

Today had been a good day.

* * *

Lucifer had made his way into the garden. He stood, now
with his jacket removed and his sleeves rolled up, the tie loosened
and clipped to his shirt by the silver pendant.

He was staring at the shed and, next to it, the weeping willow.
Something about that willow was eerily familiar.

He held in his hand a steaming hot cup of tea. Milky, it was as pale as the skin on Death's bones. Death came outside and joined him. His deep, dark, navy blue suit in contrast with Lucifer's rich, dark emerald suit made them look like Asian businessmen in a casino.

Death, also holding a cup of tea, walked to stand next to the angel.

"What steals your attention so, Lightbringer?"

Lucifer sipped his tea as he stared hard at the willow.

"That tree is staring at me." He said, sipping again, not breaking his eye contact with the bowed and mournful branches of the tree.

"It is looking at me funny." He added.

Death turned his head slightly to the left, looking at the tree like a curious puppy. He took a step toward the tree and raised his hand, the open palm divining something Lucifer could not begin to bring himself to figure out.

Suddenly Death clicked his fingers and pointed at the ground and turned to Lucifer.

"Here." He pointed judgmentally to the ground at a shallow dip in the green grass around the root of the tree, the grass a slight, yellow hue here.

Lucifer looked at it, bent down, plucked a blade of the grass and sniffed, he recoiled immediately, as if the smell was a rotten slice of chicken breast left in the sun on a warm, humid summer day. He tentatively tasted the grass, and popped his teeth and lips together, and spat.

"Ah…" he nodded to Death, who smiled that razor slash of a smile, so unnaturally made, the sound of his smiling was the sound of sutures popping, of a wound opening. A sticky and sick sounding peeling of flesh and muscle.

"Shall I?" he said to the angel.

"Please do, I have questions." He gestured with his free hand, the one not cuddling a cup closely, to allow Death to do his thing.

Death waved his hand in a floating motion over the yellowed earth and grass and then pushed down with his palm – as one would a French press, pushing the water down and filtering the coffee. He pushed hard, meeting some resistance, before turning his hand, and pulling his clawed fist upwards, as if he had cupped and was yanking something free from the grass. The resistance gave him some trouble, then passing his cup to Lucifer, with two hands, he repeated the gesture, and the earth gave a pop and a shrug, and the patch of yellow suddenly folded outwards, as ash rose to the surface, and then slowly reconstituted speck by speck into a half smoke, half flesh creature, horrific and incomplete and somewhere human.

A woman – around 35 or so – stood naked, swaying and wafting on the gentle breeze.

A zombie made from ash and from the earth, built from the human remains of a woman whose cremated leftovers were spread and poured by the foot of the willow.

The creature looked at the two beings in front of her. One side of her face was broken and cracked, not fully formed, the eye was a blank grey marble, with a fine line throughout the centre toward the scalp. She looked at Lucifer and nodded weakly, but to Death she gasped a breath that coughed out dust and specks of ash in a fine cloud, and she theatrically bowed to him, and said:

"My Lord Death. So good to see you again."

Death nodded a bow and swished out his hand in a gesture of acceptance of her greeting.

"I apologize creature, but your name evades me. Cremation. It does this, you appreciate?"

It was not really a question, but Death dressed it as one.

"I understand, of course, my Lord." The ash woman said.

"My name matters not, sire. It matters not. Lately, anyhow…" she laughed, then coughed up two or three thick plumes of smoke and ash again, the crack on her face widened, her eye folded inward.

"And this is my darling child…" The ash woman turned, shaggy and heavy footed, to show the baby who had been cremated and poured at the foot of the willows root and trunk as well, Death having brought them both back inadvertently together.

Lucifer looked like he was going to actually vomit, the flush of red on his face from the air in the garden suddenly bleached to a pale white.

The baby on the woman's back had one arm that clutched out at the air, its mottled, grey face was gasping for breath, and it wailed a

hushed cry as it bellowed out ash, smoke and dust with each snivel. The woman turned again, and smiled widely. Half the mouth had subsided, shifting the features down on one-third of the face, the ash losing substance and animation. A fine line ran from temple to chin; the face was slowly losing its verve, crumbling and falling away from the other half.
Death noticed and clicked his fingers to get her attention.

"Woman, this tree, tell me its story and be quick about it..." Death commanded.
The woman frowned forlornly, her voice shook and resonated with an inflected echo as the mouth spoke in a disjointed fashion.

"This willow was grown from a splinter of wood snapped and stolen from the spear of destiny. Or so my grandfather tells me. This tree was brought here as a sapling by my family from the homeland in Lanciano, many, many generations ago. Grown from saplings dating back hundreds of years, to the time of my ancestor, the Roman guard Longinus.
The man who ki..."
Both Death and Lucifer finished the sentence in unison.

Death, because he had met the Roman. Lucifer because the man he had killed was his own brother.
"The man who killed the Lord Jesus Christ."

The woman smiled and nodded.
"Yes." She gave a choked cough. "Or so my grandfather tells me."

Death frowned; the layers of coincidence were defying his understanding of order and chaos. He looked at Lucifer, who had gained some colour back in his cheeks, but looked forlornly at the tree and the ash woman.
"Tell me... creature. Why are you resting here? What happened to you and your child?"

The ash woman sagged somewhat under the weight of the question, looked down at the ground, and then back to Lucifer, her other eye now cracking, and the crevices in the ashen feature becoming more prominent and horrific.

"My husband was a loving man. All he had wanted was a child. I shared this desire, deeply. We loved one another unquestionably. And he was so happy when I told him I was pregnant."

She stared at the house and pointed.

"We made this into our home, and he proposed to me right where you are standing now, and he told me he loved me, and I told him I was pregnant, and we laughed and smiled and cried and – of course – I said yes."

Lucifer weakly smiled.

"I can see how happy the memory made you."

"Yes." She said, turning her head toward the tree. "But the happiness did not last."

Death shook his head; the dust was falling off of her in clumps now, and arms dissipated on the breeze and her legs were waning and fading as the solidity of her frame was breaking.

"We married, and we laughed and loved and lived here, and then when it was time for me to have the baby – my beautiful darling baby – something happened in labour, something broke… and…. I… I died."

She coughed the last two words.

"And your child?" Lucifer said.

Death answered, not the woman.

"Died also." His head bowed, "26 minutes later. I remember her now."

The woman nodded. She smiled, and the jagged, broken mouth subsided more, and it was a grotesque face of harsh lines and ugliness.

"My husband took our ashes, and he scattered them here, under the place I asked him too.

The place of my greatest memory. The tree where he proposed to me."

"Your husband's name, woman… Was it James?" Lucifer asked, his voice panicky, he too had grasped hold of the turbulent lines of coincidence, and was riding them toward a frightful and fraught conclusion.

"James? Your Highness…" The ash woman said, she laughed, and her voice cracked and echoed more, a reverberating strain on the accent, electrical and haunting.

"No, your Highness. His name was John. John Inverness. My Name is Delor…"

But she broke and fell in clumps of ash and soot, and faded deep into the ground, back from whence she had came.

Death gestured the grass to once again swallow her and the baby up.

"Delores Chapman. Married to John Inverness. He died from his own hand. Five years after the death of his wife on a hospital bed in Swindon. Complications from childbirth taking her life. Her daughter, Katrina died 26 minutes later."

Death looked at the tree. His steel blue eyes shone in memorial and reminiscence.

"John Inverness sold this house. He took the money, and he gave it away to the local hospital's child wing fundraiser. Every penny. Then he walked out to the train tracks wearing the suit he wore on his wedding day. Waited for the 15.57pm train to Reading and took a walk in front of it as it reached the station platform.

He was killed instantly."

Lucifer nodded, he looked back at the house.

"James bought the house from him, didn't he?"

Death nodded.

"I rather imagine he did, yes." He said, gloomily, resigned and tired.

"And then Kay and Callum both died in childbirth as well, didn't they?"

Death nodded again.

"Do you know what's more, Master Morningstar?"

He shook his head at Death's question.

"Longinus, the spear carrier, the guard of the mount. He lost his wife in childbirth. And his son died soon after."

Lucifer nodded slowly, understanding the curse that had been dragged here from the holy land, by way of a small town in Italy, dipped and draped in miracle, and planted slap bang in the garden of the house of the man who was chosen to be Lucifer's envoy to the final days, bearer of his flag and honour.

Chosen also by Death as his ward and brother, to take the mount of Pestilence's horse, and claim his right to be of the Table of Four.

One man, in the centre of a cosmic dogfight.

Lucifer walked slowly back to the house. Death called for him to stop, looking worried. He started to follow and lay a hand softly on Lucifer's shoulder.
"What are you doing?" he asked, sincere and quietly.
Lucifer looked the man fiercely in the eyes.
"I am going to move James' body to the shed. We need to have it out of the house, and that is as good a place as any for him. I am then going to have a sit down and think what next to do… Probably with more tea, because, God help me, it's all I can of doing right now."

Death nodded. He dropped his hand to his side, and shrugged, he felt as lost and bewildered as Lucifer looked.
"May I join you?"
Lucifer nodded and threw his arms up in a dejected wave.
"Why fucking not."

And, they walked side by side into the house.
Shoulders slumped, and spirits bent.
The weight of history pushing them down, down, down.

* * *

The money that had been thrown into the house was negligible. They could easily afford it with the inheritance that had been left to Kay from her grandmother and with James' savings, having lived in one bedroom bedsits for a few years he had saved enough to be able to place the bulk of the deposit, and then a fair portion towards fixing the house up.
The real issue was the long list of repairs that presented to them when they moved in that demanded their attention.
One thing after another.

The house was a lovely three bedroom semi-detached, in a quiet little area, the nearest neighbour an elderly lady who had dachshunds. She had a hearing aid the size of a small remote control in her ear and was still almost permanently asking for people to repeat themselves. She almost never bothered the couple, except for the occasional bark of her tiny legged hounds. The other side there was a five or six-foot walkway that lead into the garden from the front gateway, a short walk around the front garden by way of perfectly spaced paving slabs. The front garden surrounded by a little hedge that stood five or so feet tall, thin, and lush green. The lawn a perfect shade of summer; the corners cut out and bricked off ornamentally, where roses and rhododendrons grew and flourished, Kay loved them both, so tended them regularly.
The walkway led round to the back gate and into the big rear garden that had the weeping willow that Kay had so dearly loved upon viewing the house, as well as a little fenced off area where a shed was clearly intended to be put before the previous owner sold up and shipped out.

The two young lovers were aware that he was a widower and that his wife and child had sadly passed away suddenly, though they never met the man, they could feel the way the house had been left to fall into a dusty mess with his bereavement. They knew no other details, no other minutiae of his past, just the basic facts and the evidence of his despair. The struggle they had was to bring out the colour and the life that had once thrived here. It was a good amount of work, taken on with candor and glee by James and Kay. Truth be told, it was one of the main reasons they loved the house so much, you could see the treasure beneath the dust and gloom, the bones were showing, and once meat was put upon them, the house would be awesome and brilliant and – well – their home.

This was all they wanted. A home they could call their own.

James was stood in the garden looking quizzically at the weeping willow, and the bald area that had been cordoned off with planks. He smiled over at Kay, who was weeding out a corner of the garden to plant more flower seeds and brighten her garden up.
"I might finish this corner and get myself a shed. I could potter around in it, get some slacks and a cardigan and pootle about in there, making models or writing stern letters to the editor… It could be my old man cave! What do you reckon?"
Kay laughed. She stabbed her garden fork in the soil and dragged herself to her feet, dusting herself off and brought herself to standing. There was a certain effort to her movement that went unnoticed by James, but Kay had recently felt it, sluggishness and a tiring malaise. She made to her feet a little unsteadily and made her way to her husband. Throwing her arms around his waist, she planted a kiss on his cheek and smiled.
"I fully support your raging decline into middle age… Go for it, Eddie. Maybe we can then put a bed and a little pair of curtains up and use it as a summerhouse when your brother comes round."
James cackled, and gave his wife a tickle, she laughed back and baulked at this sudden surprise attack.
"Stop it!" She cried, stifling a filthy laugh, her arms tight around her man.
"You know I am only kidding…" She lay a kiss on his lips, and he pulled her in tight toward him kissing back hungrily. She kissed his lips one tender last time, her signature.
"You know I am only joking…" She smiled widely. "Your brother is never staying here…" She laughed and kissed his nose and then ran off toward the kitchen, her giggles still dangling temptingly and teasingly on the wind.

James watched her leave. He looked back as she waved at him and blew a kiss from the kitchen through the window.
He blew one back after catching hers and pocketing it.
He turned to the planked areas of the garden, adjacent to the willow, and he smiled.

He was going to build a shed.

* * *

They had been in the house for three months and had conquered the majority of the little battles they had to face to bring the building up to their high standard. Room by room and bit by bit they had transformed the shell of a house into the home they had always wanted, the colour and life was flooding the place with a joy and a brilliance that was a reflection of the husband and his wife entirely.
The gardens were taking shape and life with each hour that Kay dedicated to them. The kitchen was a wonderful and vivacious sanctuary of smells; spices and sweet dough, fruits and flowers – fresh everyday – trimmed from a single bush and put in the kitchen, one single flower resembling a giant daisy that added the perfect finish to the room and unlocked its life completely. The bedroom had been finished and made into a beautiful hideaway for the couple that worked perfectly as an escape at the end of the day, as well as a place they could while away in comfort and decadence on lazy lay-ins and duvet days.
They had made love on every single surface and corner of the room. Deep and passionate, frivolous and free, loving and intense.
The room was their one true isolated paradise. The door remained closed and shut to visitors, no one allowed to enter beyond the portal, to taint or desecrate their own slice of the world. It was theirs and theirs alone.

The house was coming together and the marriage was a strong one, full of giddy child-like laughter and so much love. The two of them were deliriously happy.

James had started to work on his section of the garden in earnest. He had drilled a hole through the dining room wall that pulled out to the garden, had taken apart a plug socket to route power out on a large extension lead to the garden. He had dug a trench in the garden two or three inches wide and four inches deep, insulated this with plastic and rubber guttering, and drawn the power to the shed's outline. He had covered it and isolated it, and was working now on digging into the ground and building the foundations.
He worked hard and relentlessly, wanting to get this finished as soon as possible, to have a place he could work in freedom and solitude, taking up the encouragement of his wife to go self employed and start his own IT and web-design business. He had never told her about Seattle, she had never known how she had been instrumental in his career coming to a sudden and abrupt full stop – neither did he want to tell her, or – more poignantly – did he care. He had taken a job that had become his life and discovered a woman who had replaced this lonely, isolated existence and brought him joy and happiness and back into the all too harsh light of day to realize how isolated and alone he had really been for so long.

As far as he was concerned, the woman was an angel bringing him back to his path.

He dug into the earth; shovel hitting the dirt, his foot pushing down, and then scooping earth into a wheelbarrow, which in turn was being shifted to a skip out the front of the house.
His muscles were becoming defined, his lungs had never been more awake or enthusiastic, and he was enjoying this hard graft.
Digging away and making a future one shovel at a time, much the same as the room-by-room rebuild in the home was working toward a bright new life.
As he slammed the shovel into the ground, there was a dink and a resistance as the edge of the metal hit something hard and immovable.
He tried again, and the reverberating shiver ran up his hands and elbow as the force once again was encountered.
He got closer and started to dig using the hand trowel, uncovering a

267

deep root that was not connected to any specific tree that he could see in the area. Certainly not the willow, it was a deep brown, and it was thick, thicker than the willow's biggest branch and a quarter the size of the willow's trunk. James wiped his brow the sweat pouring off him.

He poured some water from the watering can on the earth and washed away some of the sediment and loose soil. He saw the root had once belonged to what must have been an apple tree or something similar. The name of the street was Orchard Gardens, so, it had not surprised him that there were some fragments or remains here.

This one, however, was something else.

Big and thick and it had a colour, unlike anything he had seen. A deep, rich brown that was like a rich coffee, it also had scorched marks, as if the wood had been burnt by some intense inferno.

He poured more water on the wood and soil, and dug a little deeper and then with his hand trowel he hit something else that gave a distinct and echoed metallic clang.

He tapped again two or three times and the noise rang out again. There was something buried under here, wrapped in the root.

With watering can and trowel, James toiled in the soil for a good twenty minutes, uncovering the corner of a box. A silver shine that had become oxidized and yellowed with age and element was clear in the earth. It was entwined within the roots tendrils and was clung to tightly by the wrap of root in a Boa Constrictor-like grip. The only way he could free the item was to uncover the trees foundation and then saw the tight roots, which could damage the box. But, this was a mystery he wanted to solve, so he dug deep and uncovered the root as much as possible, yanking it free from the compacted earth, and its dirty, mud and clay prison, and was so close to pulling it free when Kay came out and called him.

"Eddie. Sweetheart... I think I need you..."

James turned and saw the woman was pale white, her face surprised and lacking in any colour. She held something in her hand, and she looked... not concerned... but...

"Are you okay, Doll?" He said, dropping the root and walking to her. She had begun to start crying, and tears streamed down her face, as he got closer, his heart pounding in his chest, worry fogging his mind and his eyes becoming misty with concern, he could see she was happy, that her tears were from a happiness, not a pain, her colour was pale due to surprise, not shock. His mind raced with question. "Are you okay?"

She put a finger on his lips to shush him, pulled his head in and kissed him hard, her lips warm and welcoming, each new motion from them making him feel at home and safe.

She kissed him hard, her tongue touching his; he returned the gesture, and she pushed him gently away, breaking the kiss, leaving one tiny touch on his lips as an afterthought.

She still held his head and leaned into him and he hugged her, one hand on the base of her back, the cleft of her buttock just on his pinky, the other hand on her shoulder blades, gently circling with an open palm and a finger tracing lines on her skin.

He could smell her sweet breath in his neck, as she kissed his neck once and whispered calmly, with a husky chill running down his spine as she did.

"You are going to be a daddy."

And she kissed his neck deeply then, gently, she playfully bit his ear.

* * *

Water splashed on his face, and he came too – he was in a dark room, no windows, no light, all there was illuminating the place was the light from the halos of seven archangels.

He spluttered, and he spat, and he stood up and realised his arms were bound by silver rope at the wrists, similar ropes also bound his legs.

He was naked, barely able to move, kneeling down.

He had been unconscious. His head on his chest, his face hurt, a dull roaring throb in the eye from where Michael's fist had smashed against his skull.

Had he have been a human the blow would have obliterated the face, skull and the eye – no doubt.

He would most definitely have been dead.

"Lucifer. My son. Stand up."
The voice was Yahweh, it shook the room with a deep grumble, echoing off each and every surface and taking a deep resonance that each echo that followed.
"You stand accused of bringing the garden into disrepute, and sowing seeds that were not yours to sow."
Lucifer looked around to see where the silver and electric blue halo was that signified his father, but it was nowhere he could see.
"How do you plead?"
Lucifer looked around, there were three haloes to his left, three to his right, and he could sense one behind him, but could not see it.
He had no doubt this was Michael.

"How do I plead?" he asked.
"How do I plead." This time it was not a question, instead a statement to himself.
"I would answer your question, father, but I would ask one of you first."

The room fell silent, Lucifer, bound and bruised, illuminated by nothing but a weak circle of light on himself from above and the glow of his own golden halo, smiled. He could feel Michael's anger rising, the need for blood and battle coursing through his veins.
He heard the shrug and heave of his brother's white wings flex and ruffle.
"Come on, father. One question… and I will answer all of yours."

Silence.
Then a roar, as Michael slammed into his side with the hilt of his fiery sword, knocking Lucifer into a spin that was stopped only by a sudden flex of the rope on his limbs from left and right.
The Lightbringer gagged and spluttered a harsh laugh, spitting a wad of bloody saliva onto the floor in front of him.

Michael was now somewhere to his left, hidden in shadow, his halo was dim and weak, and he could not see nor feel its grace.

"HA! Setting your hound upon me father? Is that how it will be? Scared to face me yourself as you have always been… Scared to look me in the eye.

I wondered long why this might be, why I was such a disappointment to you, such a shame you had to carry… But…. It's not me who is the shame to you is it?

It's not about me at all; it is just about who I remind you of…"

There was silence again.

It became broken by Michael's roar and a sudden smash in the ribs again, but from the right, catching Lucifer unawares. Knocking the air out of him, leaving him dangling on the sudden taut, tight ropes heaving a croaky laugh.

"Do I really remind you of her so completely? Is your shame so much that you cannot bear to stare upon the memory she left of herself, taunting you every day? Is that it, father?"

The roar again punched deadly from the silence.

And Michael and his fiery blade were now directly in front of Lucifer, the blade swung heavy directly at his skull from above in a downward, swooping swing.

"ENOUGH!" Yahweh cried.

Michael's sword rested a mere inch from Lucifer's face. Lucifer had raised his head to take the blow full on, easily to cleave him in two. The flames now licked and spat on his flesh, leaving a faint line of blister and scorch on his skin. It healed quickly, and burnt again and repeated this cycle as long as the blade remained where it was.

Lucifer smiled at the blade, he looked down his nose, seeing his brother, murky in the shadows, outside of his light circle, he winked, mischievous and dangerously.

"Maybe next time, brother mine." And he licked the blade, it sliced his tongue in two, and the individual sides hissed and flicked at Michael forked like the snake, before healing back into one tongue again.

271

Michael's face was a repulsed, furious grimace, sneering as he held the sword idle and heavy, but steady an inch from his brother's face. "Where are you, father? Come now… Let's not stand on ceremony, let's talk like proper people. Like the apes, eh?" He waited, and the electric blue halo of his father erupted into bright, animated life behind Michael. A hand came to rest on Michael's shoulder, and the sword's blade dulled and the flames cascaded and eased. Michael relaxed, and he dropped the sword to his side, placing it safely in his scabbard.

He took a sidestep and allowed Yahweh forward.

"I am here, Lucifer."

Lucifer smiled, a sneer of utter revulsion and contempt.

"Ah, father. Dealing with your problems yourself at last. How quaint."

Yahweh smiled. It was a deadly viper smile, taut and emotionless, dripping in barely concealed venom, ready to strike and attack at any moment.

"How do you plead, Lucifer? To the accusation of Temptation, of Sedition within the council of Archangel, with fraternizing with gods, not your blood – how do you answer to the accusation of assault on the woman, Eve. How do you plead?"

Lucifer looked at the God in front of him, twisting his head to one side; he had a sad look of dismay and despair.

"Assault? What assault do you speak of? I have not laid a hand on the woman, not a finger… Unlike you, father, dearest – I have heard all about your indiscretion in the lagoon, of the shame you have hidden from the brothers before you. Sons, one and all to you."

Yahweh stepped forward, closer, took Lucifer's head in one cupped hand, its thumb circled and stroked Lucifer's bruised and swollen face.

Gabriel could be heard from the left, his face became illuminated by the light.

"What does he speak of father?"

Yahweh waved Gabriel back, not looking at him. Instead he concentrated fully on Lucifer and whispered quiet and calmly into his ear, loud enough the witnessed assembled could hear.

"How do you plead?"

Lucifer said back, just as calm, but with a hint of frustrated boredom. "Born of a star, that fell from the heavens and which you cut and divided and shaped into eight perfect sons, brought to bright life by your own breath. The archangels, council and host incarnate. From us, you created the rest of the host – your servants in heaven, watching down upon the paradise and doing the bidding of their one lord and master. Their loving and doting father. One lie after another, after another.

Like everything else you have created, a terrible, shameful, pitiful lie."

Yahweh asked one more time, now holding Lucifer's head in two hands and gave him a shake, just once, as if to shake the answer he wanted free.

"How. Do. You. Plead?"

Lucifer interrupted the question cutting Yahweh off on the last word. "You took the woman into the waterfall, you cavorted with her, unable to help yourself and you filled her belly full of your seed. And we were born, the eight sons that you used, abused and lied too. You banished her to the plain, murdering our mother… you killed her with no second thought. It may not have been murder by your hand, but, you killed her all the same.

As well as if you had have ripped us from her womb, and thrown her to the dogs.

You murdered her."

Gabriel stood forward again and pointedly questioned the God - "Father?"

Yahweh's hand swung out and slapped Gabriel in the cheek, for his pertinence, he then grabbed Lucifer's head hard, squeezing in both hands and screamed in his face, spit flecking and landing on Lucifer's eyelid and lip.

"HOW DO YOU PLEAD?"

Lucifer was waiting for this moment – had been hoping for it - and when Yahweh leaned in, his stupid pride once again taking over and the words Lucifer used poking and prodding at his shameful open wound, the moment he thrust his face into Lucifer's screaming, the angel pulled his head back and then unleashed a violent and fearsome head-butt that connected with Yahweh's nose and caused instant damage.

A sickening, clap of bone on bone shook the room. The entire host audibly gasped. Michael was visibly shaken, did not now what to do, lost for words and action. The silver, illuminated blood that was inside Yahweh's veins splattered across his face, the God staggered back his hands leaving Lucifer's face and immediately going to his own. A pool of silver, luminescent fluid poured from his face. His flesh immediately swelling. Tears forming in his eyes.

He looked to his hands and then to his son, who smiled and spat at Yahweh's feet, and the God screamed a horrendous roar of pure rage at the bound angel, one hand, strewn and stained with Godly blood pointed at Michael, and then at Lucifer and Yahweh gave his order. "Kill Him."

Michael pulled his sword with no second thought, Lucifer had been waiting for this moment and twisted into the rope binding him, his wrist cracked and broke, the rope went limp on his skin, and he slipped the hand out, with a shake - an effortless gesture – the bone clicked back into place, and he immediately set to releasing his other hand.

Michael's sword sliced the air and connected hard with Lucifer's right wing, it cut a fine, perfect, gore-flecked gash through at an angle across the top of the bone and down, Lucifer let out a guttural yelp of agony. With both his released hands, he swung in a double-clenched, fist-clubbing motion into the neck of Michael, who fell immediately to one knee, choking back on the blow.

Lucifer reached down and released the binding on his feet and once free he kicked out harshly at his brother, his foot connecting hard with the chin of Michael, who sprawled out onto his back, his sword spinning out of his grip.

Lucifer was bleeding heavily, with gritted teeth he flexed the two perfect white wings the feathers stretched in as full a spread as he could tolerate, the right wing was limp and shattered.

With little hesitation Lucifer reached behind his neck, grabbed the wings from the shoulder and with a forceful and violent yank, ripped

274

the two wings right off his own back, an arterial spray of blood slashed the air to left and right.

His eyes rolled into his head, and his legs wavered under him, he had screamed an incredible howl of pain, shock had taken his colour. He looked across the room, suddenly alive with light and saw that not only had the host incarnate, his seven brothers of the archangel been present, but also the lesser host - the secondary angels, those born and birthed from the archangel's hair and God's breath. The caretakers of heaven, God's worker ants in his new heaven, high above paradise, where he sat and watched the humans and the Earth in mad-eyed isolation. One God cut off from his own sibling gods as he selfishly planned his empire without them.

The room was full of confused and scared angels; the host incarnate were each making way to either Yahweh or Michael. Gabriel alone of his brothers, holding his cheek – swollen and bruised heavily - looked at Lucifer and mouthed one word. "GO!" and pointed at the end of the vast hall, which had one door in and out.

Lucifer held his wings, ripped and torn from his body, and threw them to the ground, he ran to the door and bound in a giant leap, whilst in the air his body contorted and shifted and transmuted and he was no longer angel but a blood-soaked lion, swiping and slashing at any angels who got in his way.

Angels of the lesser host now were being ordered by Uriel and Saraquiel to attack. Some, lost in the events that had just been witnessed, looked confused and conflicted, the entire host of heaven's higher and lower order – archangels, dominions, cherubim, seraphim and watchers all had seen Lucifer cast accusation toward their God, Yahweh, and had seen the God's petulant and violent reaction – unable to defend the words thrown at him, unable to cast innocence upon himself – The host seemed split, some ran toward Lucifer in a wave of arms snarling faces and violent and righteous intention, whilst some stood stout and strong between Lucifer and the advancing horde, defending the Morningstar's escape.

These confused, divided few looked at the firstborn of all angels,

Lucifer, who had always spared time for every creature of Earth and heaven alike, and they stood together – each and every one of the same thought that this was the right thing to do, this was righteous action - and created a wall between the Lightbringer and the attacking wave.

Lucifer, inside the lion, could not believe what he was seeing; a roar escaped his throat toward Yahweh, being tended to by Raphael. It was a snarled and victorious scream to the God and the God alone it was simply:

"LILITH!"

Yahweh turned toward the lion and ordered the entire host to attack. "Kill that whelp! Kill that creature now!"

Two hundred brave angels stood in Lucifer's way as he charged down the door, his form shifting from lion to charging elephant midstride. With no effort, he smashed the door hard, sending splintered fragments of wall and wood every which direction.

He collapsed through the door and hit the other side with a hard thump, already the elephant was gone, and what hit the floor wet and half unconscious was just Lucifer. Already the defenders of his escape had been scattered and swiped aside by the army of advancing and dedicated angels, those who had blocked the way to Lucifer who had not been taken and battered poured through the wall behind the wingless archangel. Three angels grabbed him and dragged him to his feet and ran for the nearest exit, a broad and stunning stained-glass window that shone at the far end of the corridor.

The others fought and held off the attackers after the Morningstar's blood.

Michael had found his way through the throng, blazing sword madly scattering angels into fragments of cleaved meat, blood and wing, halo and head fell around in gruesome carnage.

There were more who had made it to the window and they bore the unconscious and injured Lucifer high on shoulders as nearly one hundred and twenty angels smashed through the window and took to wing to the west, to the mountains and the edge of the plain.

Behind them in the windows obliterated remains stood Michael, screaming Lucifer's name as he made his escape.

Lucifer, who was carried upon the back of one lone angel, massive of frame, white-haired and silver winged, briefly woke and looked back to see his brother screaming an anguished and terrible cry after the escaping angels, for Lucifer in particular. He looked down and saw the tree, circled in fire, one solitary apple hanging from the branch shaped like an arm and hand.

He swore he saw the woman and man looking up to him, confused and scared.

He saw the mountains and the sunset, and he smiled weakly at its beautiful and perfect light, and then he lost consciousness once again. The sound of wings soaring and swooping, flapping and fluttering all around him.

The host was torn in two.

And now. Lucifer, it seemed…

Had found himself an army.

* * *

- 3 -

open the door, you're free. it's time.

It was not the words that surprised me, nor the fact that it was left
without me sensing or hearing or being aware of a messenger. No.
This all made perfect sense when you saw the signature.
Indeed, it was the signature with which I am taken aback.
We did not always get on – and though he owed me a favour, I never
once thought he would return it so…
The signature simply read.

ego sum mortis

"I am of death."

The crease in the wall burst and fell, and the portal then
allowed an unknowable, unquenchable thirst inside me to feast
finally somewhere near its fill.
Bathed in perfect light, my skin became alive with the sunshine and
the mornings rays as daylight – pure daylight – drenched the room
and covered me in its healing beautiful power. My muscles felt taut
and fluid all at once, and I could move without the ache and pain of
the previous aeons weighing me down.
For a moment, I simply allow the seconds to pass and sip
heady from the goblet of this feast, and then, I make my way to the
door with no second thought.

Would that I had some idea of where I was, but, I am lost and alone.
Or so I thought.
A voice suddenly booms out, and a shadow covers the light as before
me a vast cloaked creature lands on raven wing, and bows to me.
Death, from above.
"Well met, Lord Mort."
I give the entity a curt and honourable bow. He deserves no less.

Argument rages to his origin and his true purpose. To his power and to his influence.
I have respect enough for the creature – respect I know he feels, and I have been imprisoned for a long time, by his hand but not his command.
I knew one day I would see release in his gaze and the doorway to the world beyond, or, taste one's freedom.
Today is that day.

"Angel." Is his reply. Never one for ceremony.
"Your father makes his move. A new Lord rises to power of sorts in the east. They are calling him the messiah. Word spreads of his influence and his life. He is young, merely a baby – but whole nations are shifting, and, the end of days are slowly forming."

I am dazzled by his immediacy, his sudden sharing of this information.
Death is usually the most succinct of creatures of creation.
He speaks only when beneficial to himself and usually his silence is stonewall.
"Am I to be taken to the ether, Lord Death… has my time come?"
Death shakes his head silently.
He points to the star in the sky, bright and incendiary.
"That is your worship that is your tribute. You are free, Lord Angel. Your time has come to take your place upon the board, and the end game can commence."
"This child. What is his name?"
Death removes his hood and offers out his hand in which is held a letter. The letter has a fine script upon it and a seal of blue. I recognise the hand of Gabriel.
My dear brother.
I take the letter and slip it within my robes.

"His name is Jesus. The people call him Christ. Born of peasants in Bethlehem. Already hunted by a King, already revered by the powerless. He is to be your father's proxy."

I nod and offer Death my thanks.
He raises a hand to stop my thanks.
"He is your father's son, Master Angel. Born a virgin's birth – your father's seed in the belly of a woman named Mary. This man is your brother, by blood and by flesh."

I admit, this takes me aback.
Zeus was famous for his dalliance with the humans; his appetite is legend and myth.
But Yahweh had already made this mistake once before – from where my brothers and I were a pride-stinging reminder daily.
To take the dangerous step of bringing another angel to the world, so boldly, so brazenly then – truly – this was his end game.

"Lord Mort. I thank you for my safe release and passage from this land. And, for this news. My gratitude as always."
I offer him my hand, to which he gives me nothing back.
But smiles – a thin, sickly smile that makes my insides hurt and ache – but he offers no hand.
"My duty commands I walk the gods to their next life beyond, or to the cells to sip the meagre worship that still exists. Your goblet overflows, my Lord Angel. You are as a god now; your time is here, and your sentence is served.
These lands are your kingdom now, this cell your palace. I merely give you the keys.
Your thanks are received, but unnecessary."

Death then looked at me, deep and silently, as if weighing up a decision and whether it was of merit to himself. Before he nodded, sagely, to himself and span his scythe behind himself, and lopped off both his raven-feathered wings in one effortless and fluid slice. No pain, no grimace, instead, a mild smile from his ugly and hateful lips. The wings slumped to the floor, and then, using his scythe, he scooped them and raised them, and offered them to me to take, ceremoniously and with no hesitation.
"You are a god now, angel. Unique, individual – a god made by the actions of rebellion and of folly – your own father does not see that

by allowing you dominion and kingdom, throwing you into hell, you are legitimised. By demonising you in scripture and in fable, he adds weight to your legend and table. Your feast grows daily with people now worshipping your name, multitudes of lost, ravaged peoples – all straining for some light in the darkness – all using you as their candle to safe passage home – the worship and tribute feeding you even now. Just as your uncle, the god Zeus had said… You made yourself a god with action and have now gained the followers to sustain you. As long as Yahweh exists, I doubt your flame will go out soon, it burns brightly, as befitting of your name."

I took the wings, beautiful and perfect, strong and sleek.

"A god angel cannot be without wings to bear him home. My gift to you, Lord Angel. May they convey you safely."

He bows, no smile, no hint of needing anything in return. A genuine moment of sincerity between the spectre and the pretender god.
I am honoured.

"Thank you, Lord Mort – for your gift is too much, I know not what to say…"
"Then, Devil, say nothing at all. And know that I understand all the same."

From his back erupted two new, massive, obsidian wings and with an easy and simple gesture, the spread and stretch of the wings blocked out the light.
Death flapped them once hard, and then took to a dark, thick-feathered wing rising higher and higher.
He looks down at me and casually throws me a silver key.
Rising higher still, he smiles that slice of flesh on his face again,
"Until we again meet, angel."
And he is gone.

I cannot resist, and call after him.

"I am angel no more! I am Devil and demon and adversary born... I AM LUCIFER MORNINGSTAR. Yahweh's firstborn son!"

His wings flap and swoop a single strong gesture, and he is gone.
"Jesus that they call Christ." is all I can say.
My brother, born into the east. Nothing but a babe now.
Already having kings and kingdoms quaking with his name, already having the people rise and come together.
My father's paradise slowly but surely spreading to every corner and plain upon the Earth.

His grand finale unfolding with me yet to take the stage.
I take the wings, and they come alive in my hands, levitating and holding themselves in the air of their own power, I turn into them presenting my back and shoulders and a white-hot moment of pure agony scorches onto my soul as the flesh of my body bonds with the flesh of the wings, and – at last – with a shrug and a tender grimace, the wings are one with me, and I am again whole.

I spread and stretch the sinew and feather out. The muscle is heavy and feels good upon my back, and the power that courses through me imbues me with a confidence and an arrogance I have not felt in some stretch of time.
There is planning to be done; there is planning, and there is retribution to be sought.
But first, to see this brother of mine, this blood and this enemy.

Every devil will have his day and mine has finally, at last, been found.
Freedom, morning light and purpose again all mine...

* * *
- 4 -

    "The tree is his greatest weakness. He will guard and defend that with his every angel he has. And, all it will take to make Eden

282

crumble will be one taste of that apple on the lips and tongue of the man or woman. And believe me… They both want it."

The wounds that Lucifer had received had been tended and cleaned and he had sipped of elixir and of potion to calm his fever and his illness, infection spread from his wing stems to his flesh, a gangrene had set into his golden, angelic flesh, and he had very nearly faced death on two occasions as his illness spiked and the sickness set in. Indeed, the raven-winged entity had been seen circling the mountain, his vast black wings shaking storm clouds into fluttered and obliterated wafts of mist and bringing a morbid shadow onto the pantheon.
Lucifer, however, was made of staunch stock, strong and insistent, he had recovered. Delirium and fever subsiding, and with it, Death departed the land once again.
The noise of his wings sounded like distant thunder rolling away.

It had been days until he was well enough to move from his rest to walk the lands of Zeus and his gathered God siblings. When he finally felt well enough to do so, he found one hundred and twenty angels of the various orders had followed him to these mountains. Loyal, humble and loving. Each one had followed Lucifer because of his fearlessness and his guile when facing a mad, egotistical, arrogant God master – who had agenda beyond their ken, but of sinister intention and misguided intent.
Each one stood loyal and proud of the Morningstar, each willing to lay their lives on sword tip and pyre for him.

He was met by the angel who had borne him aloft his back to these mountains, massive of body and grey winged and white-haired. The angel named Nithael.
"My Lord. I am glad to see you are recovered and well. Your men have stood vigil for you while you rested."
Lucifer smiled at the angel, he had seen him in heaven, busily commanding the horde of worker angels of the lesser orders, his perfect salute returned every time by Lucifer, remembering seeing no such courtesy returned by Michael or Raphael.

"Forgive me, sir, but I do not believe I have ever been introduced to you by name – though I recall you from the halls of heaven."
Nithael gave a brief flicker of a smile, and went to salute again as it had been instilled in him from creation to do, Lucifer grabbed out and held his arm firmly.
"I do not want salutes." He said, his voice solid and forceful.
"I want your name, so I can thank you. You were the angel who took me on your back and carried me the entire distance from the halls to the mountain – were you not?"
Nithael nodded. His arm loosened in Lucifer's grip, and the archangel relaxed his hold.
"I am the angel Nithael, sire. Formerly of the Principalities, then of the Order of Angels.
Your brother – Gabriel, he ordered me to be your bodyguard, and it is a duty I will undertake to my grave."
Lucifer fixed his grip again on the wrist of the angel, but this time, he held his forearm as you would a friend, a hearty embrace that was full of respect and of brotherhood.
Nithael looked down, and then followed the gesture and held Lucifer's forearm tight.
The archangel brought the grey-winged angel close, and lay a hand on his shoulder, and patted heavily.
"Thank you, Nithael. Your bravery and your loyalty will not be easily forgotten."
Lucifer threw his arm around the angel's shoulder and drew him close to a hugging embrace.
Nithael's hands dropped to his side, the worker bee mentality still fogging up his mind, such individualistic gestures were alien and unknown to him, but, still he took pride in the generous act, and when Lucifer pulled back and held the angel by his shoulders, the archangel smiling wide and thankful, Nithael smiled back and nodded.

"For you, sir, anything. I am here to serve."

Lucifer nodded. "I am not your master, Nithael. I am your brother. Do well to remember this; I will not have hierarchy in my company.

All are equal be they angel, man or god."
Nithael nodded.
"Come… we have work to do."

There had been many days since the archangel arrived, and only when he was healed, and his strength returned, did he take the invitation to the Pantheon to talk amongst the elder gods. His father's siblings from the beach.
In this time he had spoken to Zeus many times, indeed, the God had been at his side upon arrival demanding the caregivers of his flock to deal and clean his wounds – he sent in his healer gods to tend and suture his wounds, he had himself sat by Lucifer's bedside and spoken at length about his memories of the beach, of his and the elder gods first days – how they had separated and cut the fabric of creation amongst them, how the universe was stitched and stuck together like a giant patchwork quilt. And, how… There were always gaps in the void, sometimes slacks of cloth were left out, and these were where the coming gods would build and create when their time came.
He smiled and laughed, and he drank heavy and heady aromatic wine, and he would sit vigil and sentinel at Lucifer's side.

It was Zeus who had taught Lucifer the art of transmogrification. The skill Lucifer had employed in becoming the serpent, the lion and the elephant.
Taught upon his visit with Raguel and his meeting alone in Zeus's throne-room.
It was Zeus who taught Lucifer of his mother…

One night drunk on this wine Zeus had leant into Lucifer's ear and said, matter-of-factly:
"Were that I was your father. To you and the archangels all. A caring, loving, generous father I would have been."
Before he slept, sat next to the bed.
So different from Yahweh; so free with his emotions. So thirsty in his appetite. So open with his mood and praise. Lucifer had wished the secret to be true as well.

Rather a loving and giving father than the despot that he had left
behind.

* * *

"The tree is his greatest weakness. He will guard and defend that
with his every angel.
All it will take to make Eden crumble will be one taste of that apple
on the lips and tongue of the man or woman. And believe me… They
both want it."
Lucifer had shown the assembled gods the layout of the garden.

He showed the placement of the collapsed wall, the tree within the
circle of fire and how the plain had been transformed. The green and
lush vegetation now spread to the lands just before the mountains. An
entire continent of grasslands, marsh, tree and lake.

"Yahweh can only sense his own angels, I have 120 loyal guards
who will come with me to the garden, for my retreat to my father,
but, if you provide me ten strong, loyal hand – god or demi-god,
disguised, hidden within the form of animal or creature, then you will
be undetected – and as long as we can get to that tree, to the fruit, and
give man and woman the chance to taste and see what their paradise
really is, then we will have succeeded.

"What is this tree?" Odin had asked. His giant head hidden behind
gold and bronze refined armour, his one remaining eye a shard of ice
blue, his jowls serious and meaty.
"It is knowledge, my Lord. The entire knowledge of the world – the
betrayals and the disappointments, the reality of the world – rather
than the fragments of truth that Yahweh allows these humans. It is
everything Good, everything Bad, every pleasure and every pain…
The combined experience and truth as learned by the one human who
has tasted and experienced the true nature of my father."
Lucifer stared directly at the Norse god. His eyes did not flicker a
movement, but the green had subsided and the fire had returned.

286

"Who is this you speak of? Whose experiences could so taint and impregnate this tree with such power?"
Gaia answered – she held a hand out to quieten Lucifer's rising animated response.
Instead, the goddess took the lead and left her chair, moving around to her grandson's side.
"It is my daughter, his mother. The first human of Creation. Lilith."
The table looked in silence at each other; Ganesha gestured to the head of the table for confirmation and Zeus nodded.
"It is true." He said.
"Yahweh lay with her, he fraternized and shared his love with her, they shared themselves completely – and he left his seed in her belly, and she gave the archangels life.
Yahweh banished her, and she died in the plain, fertilizing the barren soil with her tears and blood and her life and she turned that lifeless void into the continent of life that now borders this mountain, which touches each and every one of your lands.
Her water mingling and conjoining with your own, her grass and yours one and the same. From her blood, Lilith seeded and gave life to this world we have made.
The tree is her final resting place. The apple her mind reborn – full of wonder and of knowledge, of fear and of truth and of freedom.
One taste at the lies upon which Eden, if built, will crack and pour and drown the damned place."

Lucifer smiled at the table.
His Halo was a burning white-hot circle above his head.
He slightly bowed his head and took in a deep breath.
"Believe me when I say this Lords and Ladies – Yahweh does not care about you, any of you. He would not shed a single tear for any of your passing; he would kill you all if he could.
Eden is his playground, his ant farm. He watches down upon it in idle amusement and regards his sons with much the same engagement. He does not care… it is all idle games, all he cares about is feeding, of filling his belly with the love that is poured out to him, and if this is from Eden, or from any of your burgeoning lands and people, so be it. He would crawl over each and every one of your

desecrated, starving bodies to have the love of one of your flock.
He will not stop until everyone – EVERYONE – in this world, is
pouring tributes to his table for him to feast.
There is no soul; there is no love. There is only appetite."
The table stared at him, and a murmur of agreement and fear spread
amongst them.

"He would rip your hearts from your chests to feed upon the power
inside, but he knows he cannot, so instead, he has a race of creatures
bred for spreading fear amongst the people, and with these creatures
he will steal your flock one by one, and he will build houses and
temples and places of worship, and he will turn man against man, in
his name, to fill his belly.
Each death will be a morsel more to his feast.
You will die, one by one as your people abandon you and follow his
way – or die trying.
And when it comes to the final days, he will set his people against
each other – each fight for a different one of his names. He will be so
satiated that he will swell and bloat and suckle on their power for an
unknowable age.
And you... All of you... Will be in the land beyond, facing the
shadow of Death as he escorts you out this life."

From the shadows a great gust of wind, as wings unwrapped, and
Death stepped forward.
The table as one stood in his presence, except Lucifer, he had paid
tribute to this creature already upon his bed – dreaming of the cloak
and scythe – promising great riches should he spare his life, Lucifer
sat, and toyed with a knife that lay upon the table. He nodded
greeting with respect to the black-winged creature, in his mind it was
enough.
Zeus took a step forward, courage blocking his fear.
"Lord Mort." He nodded.
"Zeus." Death nodded.
"The boy tells you the truth. The woman who fertilized your plain,
who birthed this new world you look upon – is somewhere between
worlds.

Dead – but alive – in flux and trapped beyond the grasp of even me.
Her life forfeit to this madman.
There must be balance, there must be equilibrium. Life and death and
here and thereafter."
Zeus nodded his understanding.

"But rest assured, Zeus. I will not allow God to violate the pact. Not
one of you… regardless the cost…"

Zeus understood, his desire to usurp the god to the east was heavy,
but he knew the pain of consequences would be heavier still.
He looked across the table.

"I need ten volunteers if you are with me, we leave at the next new
moon."

* * *

- 5 -

War had carried James' still, lifeless body to the shed two
days previously. The effortless, bored way he carried the body was as
if it was made of paper. The door to the shed had been left open two
days earlier by James' encounter with the flies and his need for
sudden escape. When they had reached the shed, the insides had
stunned even the Riders of the Apocalypse. Pestilence may have
enjoyed the state, as filthy as it was, full of dead insects and rusty
danger, but War – prideful and clean, even when up to his knees in
gore - did not.
Famine followed him and with her tiny, waifish hands she had
opened the door and they had been dazzled by the sheer amount of
junk in the place.
Not to mention the carpet of dead flies, bluebottles and other
creatures.
Courtesy of Lucifer and his grand entrance.
There were boxes upon boxes of unfinished models, half-
assembled toys and unfinished books. There was one box that had the

word "Callum" on it, whether it was items they had bought for him themselves – James and Kay – or whether it was unused items from family and friends, The Riders would have no idea, but they had known now that Callum was this human's son, dead soon after birth. Indeed, thanks to this Callum – in part – Death had seen James as the perfect candidate to turn the tide in their favour. Just as humanity had always created War, created Death, created Famine – they drank heavily and deep from the fountain of loss as well. Pestilence was dead, forever taken beyond the veil to the new world beyond the shadows. Escorted by their brother Death. But James would have filled his seat in the best way – bridging myth with humanity, joining the world of the ether with the world of the flesh.

The apocalypse complete with the new rider – *Sorrow*.

But, this was now no longer the way.

Instead, the key to their rise from servants to masters was now dead by the vast red hand of War. Not even the creature who controls the afterlife, who deals with the concept of death could stop his demise.

The Riders were at a loss. And the apocalypse was fast approaching, after a two thousand year build up. The end game was now in sight; the last few moves left on the game board beckoning.

Famine picked up a broom and brushed out the final few flies, with her weak, feeble frame she conjured some intense strength to shift the boxes to the back of the shed, heaving her entire weight to move them. She then wafted out some blankets and placed them down on the floor, where War rested James clumsily on top. The two entities gave a final look at the man, whose errant, single, uninjured eye still stared at War from the floor. Tired of his accusatory glare now, he reached into the shed and firmly turned the man's head to the side, averting James' glare to stare at the underneath of a chest of drawers that had been turned into a worktop. The man could stare at the dust and the spiders that dwelt under there.

Anything but keep staring at War, who had grown a complex over the man's accusing glance.

"I did not mean to murder you." He said to the body. It was a strange apology.
"I merely meant to teach you a lesson in impudence. For what it is worth, I apologise."
He patted the man's chest in a "There, There" fashion – as though this was enough to make amends. He looked at Famine, beckoned that she say something herself.
The thin, distressed looking woman looked at War, looked at the body and then back to War.
"You died. We are sorry."
War shook his head in a dismissive and curt way and slammed the shed door.
The padlock that hung on the hinge was replaced, the clasp locked and the two Riders of the Apocalypse returned to the house. One in a crimson suit, with a deep vermillion waistcoat, which held on a bronze chain a fine vintage pocket watch, full copper curls and a beard of pure rust. His magnificent sword jangling at his hip. The woman in a fine cream trouser suit, with a veil and a scarf of off-white, a fine silver belt. A locket hung around her neck, in the shape of a set of scales.

The day had become colder.
The clouds were drawing in, and the sky had lost its earlier blue brilliance and instead had become a darkened grey canvas full of the imminent threat of rain and thunder.
War had looked at the clouds before he entered back into the house, he gave a mirthless chuckle.
"Storm is coming." And he entered the house and shut the door behind him.

Lucifer and Death were sat at the table drinking more tea, meditating over a game of chess. The man in red and the thin woman in white entered and stared at the two of them, they in turn stared back, silence hung in the air.
It was broken by War, suddenly animatedly glowering in impatient anger.
"SO?" Was all he said.

Death shifted in his seat, sitting up right and with hands on his knees, he looked at the red rider and mimicked his question.

"So." His mimic altered only in as much as he made a statement rather than pose a question.

War pulled up a chair and sat heavily.

"What do we do?"

Death looked at Lucifer, and the two gave a gentle, exasperated laugh.

"Well, unless you have a replacement lined up – which I am guessing you don't – because I sure as hell didn't think to do that either, I'd say we are undone. We may as well sit tight and wait for Yahweh to come out and wipe the slate clean, with us all stood idle on it."

War looked at the two – as they shifted back into the game with which they were playing.

"Is that it? Is that your plan?" He asked, looking at Famine for backup, the woman feebly gestured to the two for an answer.

Death answered. Not looking at his brother.

"That is our plan."

"It is not much of a plan," War said, leaning in menacingly to Death.

"You are right, master War. It is not much of a plan. We did have a better plan, albeit one that was doomed to failure – but at least it had legs.

I planned to recruit Mr. Edmunds to my cause as the Antichrist that will meet Yahweh's avatar on the battlefield and negotiate my victory and two thousand years of Godhood.

However... This plan was ruined when some obnoxious, angry, ginger-headed twat went and KILLED MY FUCKING GUY!"

Lucifer threw the chess-board at the wall and pushed the table out of the way angrily – rising to meet War eye to eye.

His wings burst into a full, beautiful, raven-coloured flare.

He was as big as he could make himself, and staring unblinking into War's red, straining, furious face.

War was choking back a righteous, incandescent fury, his fists balled into tight and violent hammers, the two men faced and stared down the other in silent and tense stalemate, before the silence was ruptured by a sigh from Death, who had stood, and started making his way to the lounge from the dining room where the chess game had been undertaken.

"He was our guy too, master angel... Do not forget that. But... He is now dead. He is dead and he is gone, and even I cannot bring him back or stop it from being so. Therefore..." he put a hand on the door, his legs faltered, his voice was heavy and words defeated. "What does it matter?"

Death went into the lounge, collapsed heavy into the armchair, and sobbed.

War and Lucifer looked at each other still, but the posturing was falling apart, Lucifer's wings had sagged and folded in, War's hands had softened, and his fists had opened and fallen loose to his side. The two men both raised an inquisitive eyebrow to the sound of the creature Death and his tears and cries.

Lucifer was the first to retreat, slowly, and cautiously.

War followed suit, and the two found a calm and slow decline from their hostility to a more moribund curiosity at what was happening in the lounge.

Lucifer looked at War and pointed to the door. He wagged his finger in awkward contemplation. Trying to find the words.

"Have you seen this before?"

War shook his head.

"You?" he looked at Famine, who was rooting through the cupboards trying to find something to eat, finding some custard creams at the back, opened and half-eaten.

She froze as if caught in some forbidden act.

"He doesn't cry. He is Death."

"So no then?" Said Lucifer, he rubbed his face with his beautiful hands, and sighed a deep huff of air, halfway between a yawn and a groan.

"This is a fucking disaster."

And Lucifer walked into the lounge too, collapsed onto the sofa, followed by War, who took the other end, and Famine, shuffling in munching on custard creams.

The four of them sat in silence, briefly and occasionally ruptured by the crinkle of the packet of biscuits and Famine greedily crunching another down.

To which, Death sobbed some more.

* * *

James' head was turned in sideways; his devastated eye was now solidly covered in a dried and congealed blood and scar tissue. The wounds on his face were just as heavy with sticky, firm fluid, but his uninjured eye was an unblemished patchwork square of white and pink that still held some odd beauty.

The eyeball had been emptied of life, it was vacant and drained of the sparkle, but it still maintained a curious intensity regardless.

The light blue of his iris was still a sharply concentrated tone, but the pupil was a pinprick of lifeless dearth.

However, having been put into this pose by War, James having had his gaze averted from the accusing stare at his killer to the focused glower under the make shift work top, he had now had his sight fixed on a tangle of root. Cleaned and polished, and tucked under the unit. A thick, alien spiral and shoot of oak, which had been salvaged and kept and cleaned to a brilliant, vivid colour.

And next to it, under the unit, the corner peeking out from a newspaper wrapping, was a fine silver box, beautiful, elegant and intricate.

The box gave off a delicate hum, a slight vibration, and there was a radiance emanating from the bottom of the worktop that shone out and gently, carefully caressed and illuminated James' face.

Giving the shed a pulse and a heartbeat.
The dead man the only witness.

* * *

Lucifer had watched from afar to begin with. Observing this child grow into a boy, and then a young virile, questioning adolescent, then a young man. Jesus was good. Lucifer found himself hating his own nature of thinking of this man as an enemy. He was no enemy; this boy was just as much a tool of his father as Lucifer and his archangel brothers had been.

This boy was an innocent who had been born into a role beyond his understanding and brainwashed into a purpose he may never have wanted.

Indeed, rather than fearing or hating the boy – Lucifer found parallels with himself and his own brothers; a wave of pity, common links being shared and regret being felt for Jesus. Loving the man rather than hating him, knowing full well that on Earth now full and brimming with peoples of all the gods, so many opinions and ideas, so many thoughts and points of view – this was a land that did not deal with difference in the way that made sense, it was a mad, chaotic planet, made of many hands, fast setting about and tearing the garden they were given to shreds. Destroying and stealing rather than sharing and building.

Lucifer watched as this young boy questioned his elders with thoughts and ponderings that that they simply could not answer. Though he was born unto the "Jews" – as they had taken to calling themselves, Jesus did not prescribe to any set principle of living, any one dogma or doctrine. He was beginning the early steps of crafting his own belief system, a very singular idea and vision, based on questions and answers, and designed to make the boy understand better this world he lived in, and the reasons why man had so spectacularly become so flawed.

Lucifer admired this, he watched for hours as this unknown brother poured over and thoughts and philosophies and worked out every edge and facet of a statement, its true meaning, its hidden meaning and the meaning displayed on the surface so often taken for granted. He watched as the boy began to build his own church of thought that was so different and so at odds with his father… Yet was fearful… Because any clash of heads with the God Yahweh would invariably be won with catastrophic consequence by the God. Yahweh did not do losing well.

After years of watching the boy, Lucifer began to make himself known to this brother. The first time was upon Jesus himself talking and asking a question of a teacher in the temple about the part that Satan had in the fall of Eden.

Lucifer watched silently from the shadows, wrapped in a comfort of the veil between the world where Jesus lived and the supernatural plane that bordered our reality, much like heaven bordered above. He heard the deeds he had undertaken be twisted and mentioned in context alien and insulting, and - when Jesus was alone – he unfolded himself from the shadow world and confronted the boy.

One lazy leg dangling over the side of a layered stone wall, and the other resting up, bent at the knee. Lucifer lay back, his hands behind his head, and he whistled to himself as the boy walked back toward his home from lessons.

Lucifer was on the wall that lead into the fields that pushed between the temple and the row of homes made from clay and stone where Mary called home, housing Jesus and Joseph, cozy and small, but full of love and trust.

As Jesus walked past Lucifer had stopped whistling, and called to the boy.

"Are you the one they call Christ?"

Jesus looked at the man with a cock of his head.

"Christ, sir?" he shook his head, and Lucifer opened his lazy slumbering eyes and sat up. His legs now straddled on the wall, his hands loose on his knees.

"Not I. I am sorry. I don't know a Christ, sir."

Lucifer smiled. And swung one leg over the wall and jumped off in a smooth, fluid motion, his booted feet hit the ground with a slight bow in his knees.

He smiled at the boy.

"Sir? Am I?" He walked slowly from the wall toward the child Jesus.

"My father is "Sir," boy. My name is Lucifer." He bowed

dramatically and theatrically.

"You could call me Brother I suppose. We share a father after all."
And he looked at the boy, his lips parting in a wide toothy grin.
Jesus stared back, a confused flex in his brow.
"Brother? Sir… I think you must be confused. I am the son of Joseph
of Aramathea; Mary is my mother – you sir could not be my brother,
you and my father do not look a day older than the other." He bowed
gently and gave a small, edgy, nervous smile that was gone as soon
as it arrived.
"I apologise for the confusion, sir. I suppose you must have me
mistaken for someone else. Please forgive me wasting your time."
And he ran off at a wide paced jog toward the houses.

Lucifer watched him go. His smile wider now.
"He doesn't know." He said to himself.
He looked up at the sky heavenward and smiled shaking his finger at
the clouds, and laughing.
"He has no idea what you have planned for him… He has no clue! "
He laughed louder, and did a small dance, shuffling in his own circle,
to his own entertainment.
"You have not changed a single bit… you miserable old fool!"

And Lucifer closed the world around himself – retreating to his
marble palace in Hell as he danced off whistling.

* * *

As Jesus slowly learned of his own place in the world, during
the next fifteen years he had fleeting glimpses of the whistling man,
always on the edge, in the peripheral. It was as though the man had
become his shadow, his own personal cloud, that wandered not far
behind and occasional cast shadow down on him.
There had only been two occasions before the days leading up to the
forty days in the desert, however, that he had reason or opportunity to
speak with the man, both times about the meaning of brotherhood.

Jesus had grown into a strong young man; his muscles were sculpted from his helping Joseph, the man he had called father, in the joinery. The carpentry had lent him a strength that imparted itself upon his sine. His muscles were drawn and built upon hard and long hours of graft.

His eyes were intense orbs that were full of focus, when fixed upon you, they felt they were boring into your soul and dismantling you bit by bit, piece by piece, until you were laid out in individual slithers for the man to divine holy and unearthly meaning from.

He scrutinized you with deep, rich blue eyes, which were at once as cool as ice and as intense as star-fire.

Jesus had become his own man over the fifteen years since Lucifer had disarmed him on the wall, with his whistling and his asking if he was "Christ" – at the time it was a word Jesus had not heard or understood, but slowly, a word that had crept into his ear from others around him, rumours and legends abound. And slowly but surely he realized that, yes, maybe he was this Christ that was being mentioned. It felt more and more like there was a purpose for him each and every day, a fire inside his belly had ignited and refused to abate, the feeling something like a yearning hunger for something more, no matter what he did nothing could quench its powerful pang.

Jesus began to look for the blonde haired whistling man everywhere. To talk, to learn, to understand.

Lucifer, for his part, had grown fond of this boy, now a young man. He had watched from afar and seen him grow stronger and older. Maturing into a wise, attentive, strong-minded young adult. He had unlimited potential for love – helping everyone who asked, often with no prompt. He was quiet, he kept to himself, he loved his mother, and he gave Joseph – to his death – a loving, dignified respect. If the man knew he was not Jesus' father, he never showed it. Loving the boy as much as he loved any of his other children of blood.

Jesus was there for his family and his kin and his neighbour, and he worked tirelessly in the joinery even after Joseph's passing, to provide the work needed for his village to keep moving and operating in such savage and difficult times.

In this whole time, the boy visited the temple and lived a mostly pious and pure existence. There were girls, his head turned on occasion, he had red blood in his veins and acted like any hotheaded male. But in the years before the desert, Jesus was just a normal boy. Yahweh never visited him, never bothered him and certainly did not seem interested in blanketing him in swaddling, keeping him pure and safe away from eyes that may be prying.

In his way, Lucifer had come to love the boy more like a father than a brother.
This child, who would be his enemy. This brother his father had pitted against him.
This Demi-Angel.
This Arch-Nephilim.
He watched him grow, obsessively, knew more about him than maybe his own mother. He had learned of secret and story that no one else would be privy too. He watched the boy succeed and fail in every facet of his life, always on the edge of his attention, watching and hoping, supporting and nurturing with whispered words of encouragement at every activity, every moment, that he – Lucifer – often wondered if this was not all part and parcel of Yahweh's plan to make Lucifer hate himself more for having to unwind eventually this love into a battle to the end.

The Morningstar had laughed at his folly of loving the boy, even as he knew that they would one day face off against the other across the battlefield.
Lucifer was waiting nervously for the day when the catalyst came that turned this mild-mannered boy into the warrior that would eventually have to die by Lucifer's hand.

But…
It never came.
And instead Lucifer watched and loved and learned, as the boy did,

all about this world now full of men and greed.

* * *

It had been three days now since James had died by War's
hand.
The archangel who had fallen and his Rider compatriots had sat and
watched the hands of the clock fade and tick and fade and tick, the
day taking an eternity to move on.

The entity of Time was as elusive and as shy as ever, but still –
Death's sister - the only real independent entity in the whole of the
universe, did her duty and kept feeding the world more minutes with
which to eat.
Lucifer had sat motionless in front of the parcel, in the brown
paper wrapping, the simple string around the box tied into an
inelegant knot at the top.
He absentmindedly fumbled and toyed with the bow that James had
thrown at him before answering the door. Shifting it errantly between
fingers and thumbs, before finally he put the bow back on top of the
box, using extreme caution and patience, gently laying the bow down
as if it were a cherry on top of a particularly delicate and unhappy
bomb.

"What is in the box?" War had said to him, as Lucifer sat cross-
legged staring at it.
"I could not tell you for sure. It is not mine to open and tell; it is
James'. I could speculate forever, but this is another person's
mystery.
War huffed disapprovingly.
"I don't like mysteries. I like absolutes. Love – Hate. Life – Death.
Black – White.
This is what War deals in, not half answers and riddles."
He left his seat and stomped over; pushing Lucifer aside he went for
the box.
Lucifer held his arm gently and looked at the giant man pleadingly.

"Please do not touch it. It is not for us to toy with, it is James' alone."
War looked at the hand upon his arm, then at Lucifer.
"I would remove the hand, boy. Or lose the arm." Lucifer looked
perplexed, against his own nature, he relinquished his grip.
"Please do not open it all the same."
War looked at Lucifer and pushing his head closer in toward the
archangel, with a forceful shove, he pushed Lucifer two or three feet
away in a slide.
"Fuck off will you."
He grabbed for the box.

Despite his size, his strength and his anger, no matter how hard he
tried and no matter how valiant or forceful his efforts, the box – as it
had been known to do – simply would not move.
It sat dormant, unshaken, unchanged.
War looked at it again, and tried once more, pulling with rigid
backed, gritted teeth and a red face as every muscle on his body
popped and came to live with candor.
The box remained unmolested.

War looked at Lucifer and then circled around the box, before trying
again from the other side, same direction and routine. Again, no
response, no luck, no movement.

He had sweat pouring from his forehead, and his teeth hurt from how
tense he had clenched them.
Eventually, he gave up and sat down.
"Fucking box." He spat at the thing.
"Heavy?" Famine asked, poking dejectedly at the wrapper of the
biscuits, the last few remaining crumbs
"Shut up." War replied.

Death witnessed this all in silence, his hood high on his head,
and his cold, tepid tea in his hands, as his scythe rested uselessly to
his side.
"Lucifer. Did you send this package?"
Lucifer shook his head.

"Not I, Lord Mort, I thought I knew who did, I almost learned myself the answer to the mystery, but then you knocked at the door."

Death sipped quietly from his cup, holding his saucer.

There was a sweet slurped sip, and then the tinkle of the cup being placed back down, as Death stared at the box, uneasily.

"I do not like it. It fills me with sadness and a sick dizziness. I am Death, I should feel neither of these things."

Lucifer nodded agreement.

"Shall I cover it with something? A blanket or a cloth?"

Death nodded, he smiled weakly. War agreed, Famine shucked back the biscuits wrapper to catch the final crumbs in her mouth, a single thumb raised in oblivious agreement.

"Fine..."

Lucifer wandered into the kitchen, remembering seeing the cupboard under the sink, and a variety of materials under there.

He grabbed an old bed sheet; it was a spruce colour green, and he threw it out and lay it on the box. It hit with a hard flap, and then the room fell silent, as if someone had turned off an electrical item and the itinerant buzz that you forgot existed was cut short, now apparent with its absence.

There was a moment or two of quiet, and calm, they all looked a trifle happier.

Then...

The bed sheet burst into fire and scattered ashes and dust everywhere around the parcel.

A flash and burst of flame, then a puff of smoke, and all that remained was dust, ash and the shallow, almost imperceptible buzz again.

All four of the creatures in the room froze upon the ignition; Death had found his jaw hanging idly open, his eyes wide and bulged.

War had actually started his body flinching, to which he felt great shame and a nagging sense of self-loathing. Famine had dropped the biscuit wrapper on the floor, her hands still frozen in the pose she had before, casually hanging in front of her mouth, as if still holding it pouring the crumbs into her open gullet,

Lucifer had felt the glow of fire, and enjoyed the burst immeasurably.
But he too had been startled.

"Well… Blow me." Was all he could garner by way of a reaction.
As he said it, the front door gave a heavy bang and knocked and all three heads swung to the sound.

Lucifer stood, looked at Death, who also stood now, he looked at War, who stared heavily at Famine, who was now awake from her stunned silence and stared back at Lucifer.
"There is someone at the door." She said emotionlessly to the archangel.

He shook his head in stupefied disbelief.
"Fine… don't all rush, I will get it."
He made his way to the door, straightening his tie, unrolling his sleeves and doing the links back up, and grandly throwing on his jacket and buttoning up.
He stroked his hair, golden blonde and beautiful, and he fixed a bright smile on his lips.
As he reached and undid the deadbolt, and the sliding bolt, and yanked down the door handle and opened it, his smile at once disappeared and he was left with a look of angry, unshakeable hate.
"What the fuck are you doing here?" This was all that came from his mouth without once thinking. His arms fell to his side; fists balled, and his head found a pride and strength, stoutly staring forward, his chest puffed.

The thing on the other side of the door made no noise, no fuss; it was silent.
Lucifer stared intently forward, his wings now half-spread, and the feathers ready to stretch the full extent of their span, but coiled like a spring for battle.

"Good to see you too, son." Said Yahweh. As he stood on the doorstep in his three-piece, gold ochre suit.
A thick, sickly, ill-looking smile upon his golden skin, the colour of caramel and sunshine.
His eyes a deep, cavernous glare.
"I see the party is all here…"

Lucifer's wings fell limp, as Yahweh took a step forward.
"So…" He said.
"Let's all have a little chat, eh?"

* * *

- 6 -

The elation of learning he was to be a father was unlike any emotion he had ever known. It was still early days, three months in or so, but he had told everyone that mattered, and – thanks to his new start-up business – he had left work and was rolling with new business pouring into his inbox daily.

James had been working tirelessly in between his projects and client's jobs with decorating the final few rooms in the house.
Painting his and Kay's personality upon wall and surface, making their mark in each room from top to bottom, bottom to top.
The final room being the small box room that was now ready and waiting for their bump to bloom and be born.

With each brush stroke upon the wall, each drip and drop of paint, James had developed a rich and wholesome love for the baby that was yet to come. He had smiled through three coats; a rainbow mural and a picture of a windmill atop a hill overlooking a rich, green meadow below. His son or daughter's room was to be a perfect little haven and would provide him or her sanctuary, safety and happiness.

He already knew he would be an amazing father.
And so did Kay.

When he had finished his painting James would lay a final kiss on his fingers and touch the wall, as if signing his work with love, then kiss his wife on her forehead, tell her he loved her, and then he kissed her bump, where his child was percolating and baking away, in its perfect round, beautiful oven.

He traipsed down the stairs, shuffled into his garden and would escape into his shed for an hour's downtime – where – he had been busy at work stripping back the root, sanding and finishing it into a beautiful work of art; the silver box that had been trapped in the tangle of root was empty but quite beautiful. The metal was not quite silver, the antique dealer friend had told him it was some strange silver alloy, but not worth a lot at auction due to the rough etchings and engraving, and the fact its insides were broken and shattered clay, held together by some shallow bonding of some form.

James did not care. He kept the box for knick-knacks and personal treasures – worthless to anyone else – but priceless to this complex and strange man.

The first thing he had put in the box was a small, square, vintage papyrus envelope, sealed with a black seal, which he had been given as a child. He remembered the day he was given it in the churchyard by the man called Littlehorn, who he never did see again – and who Poppy's mother had said must have been a cousin from marriage, though she did recall seeing him at the funeral.

The envelope had been kept with James for years, usually carried inside a wallet or close to his heart in a shirt breast pocket, never opened, some random lucky charm he carried due to some weird routine or superstition. James never knew what it said inside, but knew that the envelope was symbolic more than anything. Maybe he would open one day.

Curiosity had only nearly gotten the better of him on one occasion, and the seal was partially picked and chipped, but he had demonstrated some amazing reserves and stopped himself before anything had been ruined too much.

Now, the box sat on his shelf, collecting a dusty sheen and full of odd little remembrances. An acorn from the oak tree that he and Kay had had a picnic under on their third date, or the cinema stub of his first date when they saw *The Notebook*, which Kay had told him was her favourite film. He had taken her to a matinee performance on some cold midwinter evening, surprising her with a drive to a cinema out of town that showed classics on Tuesdays, the act of doing so had made her mind set that this was the best man she had met beside her own father.

The silver box had been cleaned and tidied and he had shown it to Kay, who was not keen for it and asked he not bring it in to the house, thinking it was an ugly and unclean thing, friendly laughter at his excitement toward finding it, hoping it could be some ancient fortune, when it was described as being a "novelty" or an "ugly botch job" by experts.
James had loved it, it reminded him of books he read as a child, finding something that had no purpose and filling it with treasure to make it live again.
Found under the earth. Abandoned and lost for years.
Yes, he would have loved the thing to be full of worth, but thanks to its smashed and broken innards, the clay pot lining that had been broken and now reassembled a mosaic inside. It was really nothing much more than a curious keepsake that reminded him of the day he found out he would be a father. The same day he had found the root and the box, under the very shed he later built and in which he know kept safe all his most personal and ridiculous toys and projects.

The box was now a locker for all the most important and obscure things in his life, the little things that tied his experience with physical artifact.
The prison for his most personal objects.
The imperfect silver box that was now home to his three secrets and his kitty of trinkets and junk that linked him to his wife and his unborn baby.

An ark of secrets and truths and love and memory.
For James' eyes only.

* * *

- 7 -

The ten gods had walked onto the Plain taking on various forms, some birds – taking to wings and fluttering from branch to branch, tree to tree in silent flurry, some mammal – crawling and sneaking on four legs using bush and grass as cover as they slunk quietly toward the garden, some had changed to snake and reptile, using the low grasses as hiding places as the vanguard of one hundred and twenty angels - all now free of mind and will, all following the course of action they each deemed worthy and right – into the plain, and there, into the sight of the god they had left behind.

Lucifer was in the centre of the procession, no longer naked, he wore green robes, as beautiful and perfect as the emerald, and as dark and as sinister as the tall grass at midnight. It quivered around him, as he walked into the plain, around him the spread wing of his legion of fallen followers.
Yahweh saw the approach, and smiled a weak, sickly grin as he realized his son was braver than he had seemed, was bolder than he could have thought possible, was as brazen as he had hoped.

Michael had a garrison of angels, each holding horrendous looking weapons ready and waiting at the jetee of Heaven that overlooked the garden. Each and every one fell to the earth, ready and willing and waiting for the order to shed blood and murder their shamed, runaway kin.
Michael watched Lucifer with angry, red, feeble-minded eyes. A cascade of ill feeling and hatred coursing through his body, unsure when he had found this grand loathing for the Morningstar, but knowing that the bitter acrid taste of his hate upon his tongue made him feel alive and righteous. He hoped that today would be when his flaming broadsword would cleave the angel asunder and rid the world of his ugly, egocentric, arrogant presence.
Rid his life of the angel who stood above him always in the hierarchy.

His elder brother.

The angels walked to the tree, where they found the archangel Uriel, he drew his sword and stood stoic prepared for the attack he thought would be imminent. His ground marked with malicious and violent intent, his blue flamed sword ready and thirsty for the advancing party.

No attack came.
Instead, Lucifer walked forward and offered two open hands to his brother – a serious intent upon his face – he stood three or four metres from the archangel guarding the tree.
His band of fallen stopping ten metres further back, circling around the flames.

"Brother. I have come to surrender to discuss terms of peace with the host and our father."
Uriel smirked at him, looking at the assembled angels, all who stood palms out, showing no intention of attack or malice.

"What game is this Lucifer? You abandon paradise and the heaven above to fall in line with gods of the West, washing your bloodline away with unworthy half-gods? You should be ashamed... Father will have your head on a pike at the gates of the Eden."
Lucifer did not show any sign of emotion. Instead, he thrust his hands gently toward the archangel.
"When last I checked, there were no gates at Eden's wall. This was a garden that connected all others, but was the first. Why should such gates exist if not to isolate and insulate ego and dull pride? I have no time for such trivialities. I want to expand my wings, not tuck them into a belt forever more... The other gods can show us so much more than just our father's mad playpen. Why can you not see this?"
Uriel spat at the Morningstar. It hit him below his eye, a thick, sticky wad of mucus.
An unworthy, despicable act for an angel of the host incarnate.
"Do not call me brother, you whelp. You lost my bond when you spilled our father's blood. You are a traitor and a pretender to our

host and nothing more. Would that I could strike you down right where you stand."

Lucifer reacted now, subtle and pointedly, he gave a soft laugh. "Better than you have tried and failed, Uriel. What makes you think you are any better than Michael? Fourth from the womb, you are nothing but first amongst the weakest. Back to guarding your petty circle of flame and lies."

Uriel took the words as though he was slapped in the face; his brow creased deep and ugly, and a rage was flickering and twitching upon his lip.

He turned a deep red and a bellowed snarl formed as he thrust forward with a deep swing of his sword.

Lucifer stood sharp and still watching the sword approach him at a terrific, forceful velocity and he barely winked when the arm of Uriel fell dead and detached, silent and severed from his body with a pop of grisly, wet horror.

From behind the fallen angels who circled the tree, the animals crept and slithered, stalked and flew. From tree to tree, brush to thicket, and grass to ditch they came. Ten animals, each with a silent thought upon their mind, to get in and to free the tree of knowledge from its fiery prison fence.

As the angels circled and surrounded the tree, one silent serpent snuck quietly to the far side to where Uriel had stood.

As he had raised the sword in violent fury, the serpent had sprung and changed shape mid-strike into a terrifying orange and black tiger. The swipe of its claw had taken Uriel's arm clean off at the elbow, and the flaming sword fell extinguished and smoldering to the ground.

The archangel had looked stunned and open-mouthed at the wound, down to the arm that grasped the hilt of the sword weakly, and to the protruding bone and spraying blood from his stump.

Uriel turned to face his attacker, and there before him was Gaia. Naked and perspiring a fine gleam of sweat, her eyes a deep green, her lips a perfect pink, thin and beautiful. She looked at the archangel, and she nodded a salute of apology.

"I am sorry. But I cannot stand by for this tyranny any longer. Even from my own grandchildren…"

She swiped her arm across Uriel once more, as he raised his stump to protect himself another chunk of blood and muscle was torn and slapped the ground wet and dead from Gaia's tiger clawed hand.

He spun with the force and was met with a clean flash of the flaming sword, now held by Lucifer, and his torso tore clean and slippery from the shoulder to the hip, as Lucifer split him in two with one single slash.

His face looked at Lucifer with confused and pained eyes, as he mouthed his final words

"But… Why, brother?"

And his body fell in two to the floor, his insides sprawling in a sickly and sticky mess upon the grass of the plain.

Dead, quite dead.

The fire around the tree died too, a circle of scorched grass lay around in perfect shape around the tree, and from the ground, the roots rippled and stretched, the first time in an age it could stretch the sleep from its shape and form, the roots bursting from beneath the ground and with moss covered tendrils it wrapped around Uriel's body and pulled it deep and hard below the ground. The body of the archangel returned to the bosom of its mother. His new form now one with her new form.

The branches burst anew with a green and terrific life and leaf.

Lucifer looked at the sword and with his eyes now alight, fire burning deep inside and behind, he screamed a howl of anger, anguish and glory at the heaven.

Waking Yahweh from his gawking, mocking slumber. An act of brutal intent that made the God realize that Lucifer was no longer a boy, but a man returned to set his father to rights.

For only the second time in his life, Yahweh felt something close to fear.

Michael saw the flicker of trepidation and screamed the order for the army of the lesser host to attack. Hundreds of wings took flight and the one hundred and twenty fearless fallen sprung to life and wing to meet the angels that were so recently brother and kin in midair. Savage weapons meeting in sparks of metal, fury and death.

* * *

Zeus had led on, his body that of an eagle, the shape allowed him a high wind with which to float effortless and quiet into the lagoon. He dived into the waterfall taking his true shape upon hitting the water, under the cloak of the water, deep and white and heavy, he saw the corner in which he had hidden those countless years before, watching his sibling make love to the woman Lilith, the ministrations of their sex, the heave of her breast, the thrust of his manhood into her, the wild abandon that took him over, turning him drunk and brooding, hungry and lustful for her flesh and her soft beauty.

The act that started this insurrection.
He sat placid and quiet, on the thin ledge, remembering how jealous he had been to see his brother take the action. With no thought of consequence or reproach.
He had loved the woman, he truly had, and the thought made Zeus mad with lust and jealousy. His mind on fire with thoughts and desires and ideas for revenge.
He glowered in the waterfall.
Waiting for the new lady of Eden, Eve, to take her daily bath in the cool lagoons waters, waiting and watching, trying to shake the lingering memories that seeped and stuck to these walls and permeated the skin and mind like thin needles digging and burrowing deeply into the soul.

Zeus waited.
His skin falling and shrinking and his body turning from man of an imperial silver glow to a snake of white and silver scale, and eyes of deep impenetrable blue, two thin slithers of black running down them

vertically. A thin and tactile tongue slipping out and tasting the air as it waited.

* * *

Michael dove into the arena that was Eden, his sword out and pointed sharp and aflame toward the ground below like a javelin, piercing the air in a sonic whistle that rippled around his naked body as he hurtled downward.

Lucifer had him before Michael could realise what was happening, and as he landed on his feet in a sudden yank of his wings, pulling his strong, supple body up to land with a thud and a crack of the air, forming a crater around him, Lucifer was already in and on him with the second flaming sword that had fallen as Uriel had.

There was an almighty shatter of thunder as the blades collided and sang a song of brotherly rivalry and pride.

The naked, muscular tone of Michael crashed heavily with Lucifer's thinner, more lithe body, the swords singing and screaming as they clashed blow after blow.

From everywhere in the sky the Legion of the lesser host fell and impacted with bodies of the one hundred and twenty fallen angels who followed the Morningstar tumbling and thudding the ground, mortal wounds jagged and bloody on both sides as bodies died in agony and ecstasy around the two archangel.

Lucifer parried and thrust, his handling of the sword more balletic, more refined, he wielded the weapon as would a fencer, light and deft of touch, his footwork agile and light, his blows and strikes like cobras, calculated and timed with minimum exertion and maximum impact. Michael, in opposition, was a violent madman, no character, just butcher's swipes and swings, his handling of the blade primal, clumsy almost, but deadly.

Two fallen came close, having dispatched three host with ease and surprising horror, they swung into Michael and with a fluid parry and a sidestep he swung the broadsword upwards slicing one fallen from crotch to forehead, the body falling in two pieces, split asunder spilling intestines and offal like rain upon the ground, a sudden burst of sweet, sickly meat smells filling the air.

With his other hand he had caught the arm of the other fallen, carrying a mace, and snapped it at the elbow, he then thrust his sword downward through the collarbone, and pierced the heart in the angel's chest.

Gasping for breath and with a mad panic in his eye the angel thrashed wild and wantonly. Michael twisted his arms in, and with a yank of the sword, he carved the angel straight down the centre into the thorax, so the body fell awkwardly in half, but still alive, the shuddering mass of flesh from shoulder blade on his right side to the hip of his left side, he flapped horrifically trying to hold himself together, before he coughed his insides out and twisted on the spot, all three parts of him falling in a spiral of gore and death.

Michael swung again wildly with no time between breaths toward Lucifer, who caught the blow on his blade and raising a kick smashed Michael hard in the gut.

Michael leaned in and caught Lucifer with a blow to the jaw with his sword hilt, and smashed a gash into the Morningstar's cheek and lip, leaving a ragged tear that flapped and bled instantly.

Lucifer followed his scream of sudden pain with a reverse sweep of his blade that crashed hard against Michael's torso, leaving a deep inch and a half gash that ran from hip to collarbone. Michael took to wing, clutching his stomach and chest and retreated crying in pain.

Lucifer collapsed hard to the floor, only narrowly missing being caught unawares by an angel with a spear when Nithael dived into the weapon's way and took the blow straight through the throat. The giant fallen angel snapped the weapon at the blades edge, and then drove the spear shaft through the eye of the attacking angel, the whole while the blade of the spear struck and penetrated through his throat and vocal chord, blood gushed and spat from the wound in angry torrents. His hand went to his throat, and it squeezed, he turned and looked at Lucifer and nodded a weary and battle torn salute, before falling to one knee, with his gauntleted hands, he fended off two more attacks from host angels, swords bouncing with sparks off his forearms, as he drove the small, short sword he had into the angel's chest and twisted.

A second angel pierced Nithael deep through the back, the pike tip of his spear appearing just next to his heart through the front of his chest.

He span and threw his sword hard and sharp, hitting the host angel in the side of the face shearing off half the skull, the angel and his face both fell hard and dead to the ground.

Nithael coughed up a lungful of frothy blood and seeing a final host angel approaching, he spread his wings wide to protect Lucifer, who was now dispatching two host with his flaming sword, before a giant burst of thunder signalled the appearance of the archangel Raguel. Lucifer's brother looked around at the devastation, the blood and the terror that had invaded the garden, and he screamed a bloody roar at the fallen angel Nithael.

Running at the grey-winged giant, Nithael threw the spear shaft at the archangel the aim had a deadly precision, but Raguel was more than prepare, and effortlessly he caught it and snapped the weapon in mid air.

Raguel leaped onto the fallen angel and grabbed his widespread wings and screamed revenge once more. A terrible, sickening, tearing noise burst through the air. Nithael tried to scream, but the spear tip in his throat had seen to it sound was impossible; instead, all there was, was a weird gurgle and a wheeze of air.

Raguel tore the wings down; the pressure pushed Nithael's chest out, and his shoulder down, and a creak and a groan of skin suddenly gave up as the fallen's chest exploded and his shoulders gave way. All there was left was a split ribcage, with a slowly fading heartbeat apparent, and two dead arms dangling lifeless and useless behind, as the archangel had literally burst the fallen like an overripe fruit, the grey wings lost strength and rigidity, his head fell back, and a final spray of the spear tip in his throat sprayed high as the angel coughed and gasped a final breath, before Raguel pushed hard on the neck and head and tore it off at the shoulder, leaving it dangling behind the compressed, split-apart body in a ragged pantomime.

Brave, fearless, giant Nithael.

Lucifer tried to articulate his rage in sound, but nothing came from him as his breath had become a metronome tick of fluidity and motion, his body was now working independently from his mind, and the flaming sword had made a dance in the air before Raguel before the archangel had any idea what was happening.

A valley of cuts and crevasse of wounds opened on the body of Raguel, his arms and his legs gave up contact with the rest of his body, his head slid awkward from his neck, and his hands hit the floor all while Raguel tried to move.
Each body part falling away from the body before a final spinning swipe cut Raguel's head clean in half horizontally from ear to ear. The archangel dismembered with a ballet of swordplay before he could even feel the first blow.

Lucifer fell to the floor, as he watched the roots of the tree of knowledge gush upwards from the ground and pulled the individual parts of Raguel deep into the earth, taking the boy home to his mother's breast.
The tree grew lush and green, more foliage on the highest branches burst to life.
The hand shaped branch was still holding the only fruit.

Lucifer began to weep, his bones and muscles a sore, blood mess of pain and sadness.
He looked around and saw the terrible wrath unleashed upon the world, and all he wanted to do was take a step toward the tree, wrap his arms wide around it and eat that apple that taunted him so.

He saw, far away from the battle, the bodies of the gods slip off silently toward the willow and the lagoon. Only nine though.
He looked to the tree, and something was wrong, the new leaves and

greenery on top of the tree was now fading, the branches were tired and barely contained their own weight. He turned and saw the shape of his grandmother skipping into the forest.

He called out. And his grandmother span and looked directly at him. "I am sorry…"

Gaia mouthed the words silently; she looked down sad and forlorn - the Morningstar glanced backwards – he thought he had seen her holding something in her hands, and he was right. The apple was no longer on the tree. Instead, the goddess had taken it.

And the tree, his mother, was now greying, drying up and wilting.

The branches were weeping and thinning, the trunk losing its pride and width and magnificence and instead, fell and bowed to the ground.

Then, before his eyes, the tree burst into fire as smouldering, violent balls of inferno fell from the sky, the second wave of host invading the garden.

Michael now calling manoeuvres from the safety of on high.

The tree was dying and withering before Lucifer's eyes.

The plain around him greying and yellowing as the earth itself scorched and died, as though a great drought had been washed over the land. Arid and dry and sapping life from every plant and flower, all dying in the same way as the tree of knowledge did.

Lucifer torn between his ailing, dying, vanquished mother and the gods who he had brought to Eden to help his cause, now abandoning him and his kind to get bitter retribution against their arrogant sibling.

His own grandmother sacrificing her daughter's ghost and her grandson for the revenge she had long craved against the God, Yahweh.

* * *

Death walked amongst the battle, invisible and calm. He strode amongst the bodies of angels who had fallen speared or struck dead from the skies, sparing a moment to touch and tend to each one as a black-clad nurse amongst the soldiers.

Each dead entity he touched rose in a vapour and mist above the body and with a flash of blue, yellow or red, they burst into a fine dust as they were escorted to the world beyond.

He strode through and gave each soldier their moment, a hand or a gesture of faith and respect as the mist and vapour disappeared and vanished upon the cool morning air, now torn and violated so by the battle and the slaughter.

Of the one hundred and twenty fallen angels that followed Lucifer east, now only thirty or so remained, the rest were butchered by blade or spear, violence and mutilation met upon their angelic flesh and no quarter or mercy given.

Heaven's host had also seen a massive loss. Three hundred wing tore and killed by the unrelenting attack and rampage of the fallen. Wings and limbs torn and scattered, the dead and dying face down in the churned, quick, dying mud of the plain garden. The earth now cracked and parched and the tree of knowledge in the centre on fire from the weapons and hell unleashed from the sky by heaven.

Death walked to the tree. To Lilith's new shell, the indignant honour of dying a second time made only better by the fact that this time, Death had been present and allowed her murder to be painless and free of the horror that was so rich in her first half-death.

He beckoned her spirit from the wood, the ghost of Lilith seeped and poured - a tar-like substance that quickly congealed into a beautiful figure of a deep, charred, black-skinned, dark-shaped woman.

Soot and nature had damaged the spirit beyond normalcy. Leaving this ghost to be a version of the woman, still beautiful, but with a demonic and deadly veneer.

Her hair fell in dark locks about her shoulders, her breasts heaved up and down as she gulped back the air of this ghost world, she bowed

317

beautifully and with grace to the entity of Death.

"Well met, sir. I am happy to be able to make your acquaintance at last."

Death smiled to her, charmingly, his lips still a terrible shard of skin gashed by a razor so fine it could cut the very moonlight, but this smile was genuine, and it was warm.

"Well met, Lady Lilith, first of the humans." He bowed gracefully to the woman.

"Your son fights for your honour like nothing I have seen in my many lives upon this world. You should be proud." He gestured to Lucifer, on his knees and lamenting the burning tree, hands full of parched and dusty soil, fast declining back into the lifeless plain. The tree now a withered and forlorn looking shrub.

"He strikes at Yahweh's heart in your name... Who knows, he may even find victory."

Lilith reached for Lucifer, stood in front of him, her in the ghost ether, a whisper of a memory lingering on air that was merely electricity between breaths, and he on the soil of the fading, dying garden beyond the wall, crying at the devastation and loss he had to witness.

Her hands touched his cheek delicately and electricity like a static shot from her fingers to his face, with his hands quickly following to touch the sensation his skin suddenly felt.

Lilith took to her knees and stared directly at her son.

Both hands grabbed his cheeks, and the electricity moved between ghost and flesh again. She held as tight as the whisp of her body would allow in this strange halfway world, and she said to Lucifer as he looked up in shock, staring her dead in her eyes, the fire in them dead and embers now, a rich aquamarine meeting the same hue of his mother's, two beings together but separate, his hands touching his cheeks, over her fingers, as she said, fiercely.

"I love you, son."

And Lucifer smiled, something inside him touched an resonated, he felt something was happening and allowed it, his instinct taking over, and he said back.

"I love you, mother. This is all for you."

Lilith smiled widely, looked at Death who nodded, Lucifer repeated himself
"All for you."
Lilith broke into a billion tiny dots of ash and disappeared on the wind.

The last thing to go her fingertips and her smile.
Death bowed his head in respect and loss.

Finally, he had gained the one who cheated him.
Finally, balance was restored.

* * *

Eve saw the smoke as she approached the lagoon. Adam had followed her into the brush and down toward the water. There, waiting were nine gods, each wrapped in the body and shape of a different animal.
Now around the water's edge was a raven, a tiger, a hyena, a cat, a crane, a snake, a monkey perched on a low-swung branch of a tree that overhung the lagoon's water, and a deer watching on from the thicket, a tangle of antlers heavy on its brow majestic and threatening. Stood amongst them, draped in a thin, wisp of clothe that was a misty blue, and see-through, quite lithe, incredibly beautiful and with deadly, lethal looking eyes was Gaia.
She smiled at the man and woman, and she pointed at the woman and her heavily pregnant belly.
"I see you are with child."
Eve nodded. She then gave a gentle shake of her head correcting herself.
"Twins." And she smiled.
"Are you an angel, my lady?" she asked of Gaia.
The goddess shook her head serenely.
"No. I am not. My name is Gaia; I am goddess of the Earth, all you see was built upon design of my hand. Corrupted and made unclean by your God."

Eve looked at her husband. Adam looked angry and shaken by these usurpers in his garden.

"This garden was built with my hand, our lord and master may have planted seeds, but I tended, I fed and watered, and I built the colour and bounty that surrounds us. I do not recall seeing you here when I slept by its root and spoke to its shoot daily when I cut back its leaf and saw to its feeding.

Unless you were hiding and admiring my work…"

Gaia smiled. She held her hand out in which she held the red apple, which Eve and Adam recognised immediately from the tree.

Forbidden and barred from their touch.

Adam looked west and saw the smoke now for what it was.

"What have you done to the garden beyond the wall?"

A voice came from the cliff face. Yahweh stood looking down.

"They have torn it apart and set it to the torch. Your garden burns Adam, son. Your garden is dying, the tree of knowledge is ash and these gods amongst you are responsible. Their petty charges and vacant lies bring them to paradise to lay accusation and terror at my feet… To destroy all the good that I have made here."

He strained a moment and two incredible, golden wings, the colour of rich syrup burst from his back. Eagle-like wings, they spread in a glorious show, and he dove off the cliff, the wings catching the air and gliding him toward the ground.

Behind him stood Michael, now wearing a silver chest plate, holding his wounds together, his sword now a spear of incredible weight and blue with flame.

Saraquiel stood beside him, his hood pulled high, and a mace of wicked black in his hand, shaped like a hammer, its onyx colour rippled with veins of white – like a dark marble. They both glided to the lagoon, and Gaia looked the angels up and down.

"More children. You bring more children to the grinder?"

Yahweh dismissed Gaia with a gesture of a thrown open hand, silencing her.

"Not children. You have met Lucifer… you know well that these are no longer children, Gaia. These are my guard and my clenched fist, the host incarnate, my proudest achievement. My boys."

From the lagoon's waterfall, a voice rang out echoing.
"Proudest achievements are they? One would think how you hid their birth, how you lied to them for an age of their true origins that it is a strange way to treat something you are so proud of... or... Maybe you have forgotten what happened in this cave, hidden behind falling water, with the woman you gave to Eden before this fat, bloated pretender."

Zeus exited from the waterfall, the falling liquid shimmering and transforming into a fine mist in an aura two feet around him, not a drop touching his skin.
"I saw it all, Yahweh, I watched it all from the shadow. I saw you tear the world apart with one greedy, lustful blunder, your passion aroused and your mind lost, and the panic that followed.
I saw it all."

Eve looked at the silver-haired god, who stood bold and beautiful, a silver halo around him a look of pure malice and sick envy on his face.
Gaia looked at the woman, smiled and grabbed her arm.
Michael jumped forward and struck out with his spear, Gaia barely avoided the impossibly sharp edge of its tempered blade, felt the lick of the flame on her skin, a scorch of blister drawing a line on her skin. She pirouetted and smashed the archangel with a backhand slap that sent him sprawling.
She grabbed Eve, and threw the apple at Adam, and pushed Eve into his arms.
"Go. To your tree. To your hole in the ground beneath the willow's branches. And there, you and her, awake with a single bite – and see how the world you know is nothing but lies and lust."
Adam looked at the apple, its red, shiny skin a hypnotic fever dream, its warm fruit flesh throbbing in his hand.
Eve took a hand to his and covered the fruit with her palm, and immediately, she too felt the power in the fruit.
She looked at the man and he to her, and they ran.

Yahweh screamed after them.

"Where are you going…?"

They ignored him and ran, Zeus laughed and sprung at the golden-skinned brother, and a rain of blows landed on Yahweh.

Yahweh's golden halo, a single, blistering band above his head, shone and blazed in furious power, Zeus grabbed at it, his hands baking and melting to the hollow ring, and he smashed Yahweh's head off the lagoon rock and into the waterfall.

He grabbed the golden god's throat and picked him high off the ground and pinned against the wall. Saraquiel made his move for the waterfall to stop the assault, but three gods – the tiger, the monkey and the hyena were upon him. The monkey beat with rock in hand, the tiger swiped and slashed at the angel's naked flesh as he parried and beat the attack away with his hammer, and the hyena snapped and bit at his legs and hips. Saraquiel slashed and swung his hammer madly, connecting with the monkey, he sent it flying with a sickening crack, its neck shattered and broken, a shard of bones stuck jagged from its throat and silvery blood spraying thick from the wound, the monkey staggered and gagged and fell, crawling in a spastic circle in panic and pain, before slumping down and laying still.

The tiger took a smashing club to the muzzle, the sound was like a boulder being split in two by lightning, a sick, wet, groaning burst of sound, the beast retreated into the forest whimpering and bleeding heavily.

Saraquiel swung at the Hyena, and it clamped its teeth upon his thigh, the angel fell to his knee, and the hyena chomped and snapped at his throat, clenching flesh between teeth, and chuckling as it bit down with the warm blood of the angel running into its mouth, Saraquiel clutched at his throat to stem the bleeding and prise the Hyenas mouth open, as he did the God Animal went limp and gave a high screech of agony, as the head became severed from the body. Michaels spear sliced down fluid and deadly. Saraquiel fell down, gurgled and spat a bloody huff of air, he spread wing and took off toward the heaven and Raphael, who could heal him.

Michael was immediately attacking the remaining gods and had set sight on Gaia, who smiled a deadly sneer, and parried and hid behind tree and brush.

The deer who had been hiding behind the thicket charged at the Angel, its thorny antler low and charging, Michael removed them with one gesture of his spear, and with a second h removed the head with ease and little resistance.

Gaia took the opportunity to make her move. In her hand were two rocks, one she threw at Michael and he span narrowly avoiding its crushing weight, as he span, Gaia screamed Saraquiel's name, as he turned to face the origin of the scream the rock smashed him hard and deadly in the face and his wings went limp and dead, and he fell hard and fatal to the water below.

His face obliterated by the hefty sharp stone, his hood pulled back to reveal an Eyeless face, the top half of the head almost torn off by the rocks force.

Michael screamed vengeance and with an almighty heave of his spear, he took Gaia's head with one mighty swoop of his blade.

For a moment, all was quiet. The garden and the lagoon went silent and still, and the Goddess looked at her Grandchild, sneered one final time, and then her body toppled hard, the head falling in the opposite direction. Landing stiff upon the floor and with a sick, final thud.

The blood that poured out of her body was a thick green ooze, it ran slow and awful, and as it did, it burned into the ground of the garden and seared a line amongst the rock and the soil.

The garden shook.

Mother Earth was dead.

* * *

From the fire and the battle in the sky, the ether opened, and a being came forward to greet Death. The alabaster-skinned entity removed his hood and looked at the mist move in twirls and spirals as the creature came toward him.

Clad all in red, holding a sword that was made of primordial, rough, unfinished bronze, the giant man beamed in glorious and dizzy elation.

He held his hands out wide, and he looked at the devastation, the clash of steel on steel, the pang and smash of sword on flesh and the wet sound of bodies clashing and connecting in furious battle.

The red-clad man laughed loudly as he stabbed his sword into the ground.

A fracture of cracks and thin veins of chaos spread out from his blade.

Time looked on, hidden by the tree line, watching from some high branch.

She was a silent, impartial observer.

Never a rider of the coming storm, but certainly a key figure in its countdown – some would argue the most important figure – counting as she did the very grains of sand that counted down the end of days, started just as soon as this world had begun.

She watched as her mad brother escaped the bleak, empty vastness of the ether world – that bordered this new creation – and he strode heavy upon the world he would soon carve his name across in deep crimson letters.

"Brother!" he exclaimed loudly and threw his arms around Death, who patted his back gently and sagely, as one would a sibling that you respected but did not necessarily like.

"Finally, the game is started…" he followed.

"Indeed it is." Death acknowledged.

"It starts."

"Ha!" the man in red barked loudly.

"War."

The smoke filled Eden, and the apple tree withered in a darkened angry charnel plume. Lucifer picked up his sword, and he headed toward the lagoon.

"War." He said again, his arms wide and his face a huge, demented

grin.
And the man in red laughed louder still.
War had come to Earth. And he was hungry for his fill.

* * *

Zeus's hands grasped at Yahweh's throat, his thumbs pushed into his oesophagus – and Yahweh slowly choked with the throttle. Zeus pushed harder and shook his elder sibling like a rag doll.

"I saw it all, as I sat in the shadows and I watched you take the woman and fill her with your love, you entered her right here, where you choke now, and you pinned her to the wall and you picked her up and you thrust deep inside her and filled her with your seed and loin. I saw it all from that corner, as I saw many things… I watched her every day. I would come into the garden as a crawling creature or a bird, I would sneak into this paradise you built, and I would watch her.
I was so in love… I craved her flesh upon my lips, to taste her in my mouth, to feel her wet upon my lap as I speared her with my meat. But… alas… It was you, brother… always you."

Zeus squeezed Yahweh's neck and the golden skinned God clutched hard at Zeus's hands and tried in vain to get him off. His eyes were going a silver, bloodshot glaze, and his lips were turning blue.

"I wonder what would happen if I saw this through. If I choked the life out of you right now? I do not feel any different, it does not burn me to choke you, it does not hurt or harm me, in fact, I am enjoying it. I am beginning to wonder – was this rulebook we have lived by a lie as well? – if I killed you now, would I be treated as a pariah or a hero for slaying the despot of Heaven?
Shall we find out?"

Zeus squeezed tighter still, he pulled Yahweh closer to him and whispered into his ear.

"You did not deserve her. You did not deserve to be the one to take her.
I wish so much I had the guts to have taken her the countless opportunities I had presented me, I would rather I had split her in two with my love, than stand by and watch helplessly as the plain did the job you could not.
You weak, pathetic, fool."

Yahweh kicked out hard, but the kick did nothing, his arms began to go limp and loose and his eyes rolled into his head.

"I loved her, Yahweh. I would have taken good care of those boys and I would have remembered her for the sweet slice of quim that she was, I would have built a thousand, million copies of her, and I would have taken and forced myself on each and every one in her honour, and they would know what it is to be loved by a God."

Even as he said it, the water was split in two by a thunderous shake, and the cave shook and groaned.
Zeus lost his footing, and he dropped Yahweh, who slumped to the floor heavily.
Zeus spun round and saw through the jagged curtain of water the body of Gaia hit the floor in two pieces, as her head rolled and rested in the lagoon waters, her eyes just above the water line, blinked once as she looked at Zeus, then they rolled into her head, and the garden shook again.

Her death raising forth an earthquake that shook the whole of Earth. Cracks fractured the febrile land, and the planet shook everywhere at once.

The ground splitting and separating from surface to core, as the plain and the surrounding connected gardens of the many other gods suddenly became continents and ruptured and split from each other, the oceans and seas suddenly flowing deep and rich and cold into gullies and valleys and cascading rich and torrential into the canyons to fill the earth with liquid and land.

Gaia's death bringing the great separation of the Earth.

Michael looked at Zeus, now peering out from the waterfall, and pointed his spear at him.
"You," Michael said. His eyes a fixed pinpoint of steel blue fury.
"Him," Zeus said.
A single finger pointed at Lucifer, who had burst viciously with sword raised, flames leaving a trail of vengeance behind him like a whips tail, as he strode and marched down in anger at his brother.

Zeus smiled.
Giddy excitement at this turn of events. He reached into the waterfall and pulled out Yahweh, and held him ragged in a choke, on his knees before him, one hand grasping Yahweh's halo, he yanked his head back, and the other arm suspended Yahweh still forearm tightly on his windpipe.
"Watch as your two perfect boys murder each other. And know this is all your fault you spoilt, malicious fool. Know this is because you took her from me, and you did not share your prize, you killed her and took her from me."

Yahweh gasped a choked breath and stared at his two eldest children as blue-flamed sword crashed heavily on the green and orange flame of the spear.
The silver and white halo of Lucifer glowing ferociously in opposition to Michael's golden and blazing ring of grace.

The smash of the blades created a spark of white light that illuminated the whole garden and the valley beyond and was impenetrable and blinding.
The fire and the sonic boom that followed scorched and tore the lagoon apart, and everything good and green died in righteous, fiery fury.

This was War.

Lucifer stabbed out angrily at his brother, and his sword glanced off the silver chest piece Michael wore now to protect and hold together his open wound. Michael span the spear around in a vicious circle, and angled it down in a slash that sparked off the broadsword, a shard of metal jagged and broken flashed off and took a line of Lucifer's bicep, leaving a deep gash, Lucifer retaliated and kicked Michael hard in the thigh, whooshing the sword around he shattered the back of Michael's calf, sending him reeling, down onto one knee, Michael spiked his spear high and hard, and it tore into Lucifer's shoulder, piercing through to the other side, both men gave a ferocious and angry, pain riddled scream.
Both fell to the ground.

Lucifer held the spear and pulled hard, the weapon dropping to the ground, his shoulder cauterised by the green fire. Michael tried in vain to rise to his feet, but his left leg was broken and shattered with a deep crimson gash across the whole muscle.
He and Lucifer stared in mutual hatred at each other.
Michael lunged at his brother and a heavy punch landed Lucifer in the mouth, Michael fell on top, throttling his elder brother, first of the host.
Lucifer tried desperately to free himself, he kicked and slapped out, one hand high in Michael's throat, the bigger, younger angel managing to shake his grabs and protestations off.
Lucifer's eyes began to turn bloodshot, they rolled heavy in his head, his face now was bright red, and he felt the heaviness in his eyelids, and his mind was screaming at him that he had to do something, or he was surely dead.
Zeus kept his choke on Yahweh, hard, the god of the host held Zeus's arm and barely managed to keep his wits and life about him.
Zeus shook his brother, and laughed, a mad and dangerous laugh, but one tempered with the sound of a man who knows when enough is enough.

"Tell your general to release his hold. I will give you Lucifer. I will surrender him to you. But you are not to kill him, not to harm him further, he will be your prisoner, but I will return and finish the actions of this day if he kills him or touches him any further. Do you understand me, brother?"

Yahweh dribbled heavily; spit flecked from his mouth as he tried to articulate his agreement.

Zeus squeeze his choke hold harder.

"Are. We. Agreed?"

Yahweh nodded limply, and Zeus let him go, he dropped into the water, just as Michael raised Lucifer up to smash his head down on a blunt, ugly rock beside him, and kill the whelp bastard son of heaven.

Yahweh threw his hands out and screamed.

"STOPPP! Michael! Stop!"

Michael turned, startled and his hands loosened slightly on Lucifer's throat.

He looked at his Father, blood stained and gasping, choked near to death by the silver god Zeus.

He dropped Lucifer down to the sandy beach; he missed the rock by centimetres.

Lucifer threw his hands to his throat and rolled over, gasping and gagging.

Michael stood with the aid of his spear, his left leg a ruined mess of muscle and sinew and blood.

"What would you have me do, father?"

Yahweh shook a hand in begged patience.

"Do we surrender Eden to these savage from the west, this apostate half-gods? And their bastard lord and master?"

Zeus walked toward Michael, as he did, his skin burst alive with fire and hatred.

Michael backed off and painfully brought the spear into a defensive stance.

"Do you think your toys and trinkets can harm me, angel? Do you think sticks and stones can kill me? I am a God. Side by side with Yahweh I was right beside him on the beach when we woke and I know secrets of this Earth that you could never hope to learn. So threatening me is useless, you speck."

He slashed out and knocked the spear away.

He grabbed Michael by the chest plate and pulled him close and hard. Raised him off the ground and turned to face Lucifer.

"This brother of yours is infinitely more important than you or any of your kind, and you will not touch him again. He is your prisoner, and he will be given up to you to secure peace, but you will not harm him, do you understand?"

Michael looked at Yahweh, gasping and rubbing his throat in the water; he looked at Lucifer rolled on his side and holding his shoulder and throat.

He looked at Gaia, her head just bobbing in the water, decapitated and dead. And Michael smiled.

"I understand. But I see also gods can die, your sister here is evidence of this. So return to Eden once again after today, Lord Zeus, and I will take your head as I did your sister's." He smiled warmly and fearlessly at Zeus.

The god looked at Gaia's body, at the head, at Michael.

"I appreciate your passion, angel. But words are words."

He dropped Michael heavily, and his left leg gave and the archangel collapsed hard to the ground, he let out a yelp of pain and started over to his father.

Zeus picked up Lucifer and stood him up the flames around him evaporating.

He helped the archangel and Morningstar to his feet and held him by the shoulders.

"I am sorry, son. But I must relinquish you to your lord and master. You are too important to allow to die. And, they will kill you if you are not their prisoner. There is a game now afoot, and I have pieces moving even as we speak, you will be invaluable in seeing the end game through. So know I am sorry and that I love you. But this is exactly as it should be."

Lucifer looked at the man, his eyes blazing with crimson, tears rolling heavy from them. He looked pained, but, trusted Zeus as he trusted no other.

Without this man he would not have known his mother, he would not have seen her release from the tree, and he would not have gained closure or revenge for her imprisonment.

Even now, the fractures and cracks that sprung from her roots, withered and dead, were breaking the ground and Earth into new structures and shapes, and Lucifer could feel a shift in the balance of the world.

No longer was this a garden, but a ravaged island amongst a sea of tears and death.

Salty and braying and vast.

He nodded at Zeus. And Zeus lay a hand on his shoulder, the wound healed with a single touch, he could feel the muscle stitching together and the flesh reconnecting from the spear, all that remained a deep and throbbing line in the skin, slightly bolder than his golden flesh. He also knew that this was the pleasure before one final act of pain. He nodded once more to Zeus.

"See that the woman and man eat that apple. Save me a bite. But do what you need to do to end this and start the next chapter... I am ready."

Zeus looked at Michael and at Yahweh, he looked at Lucifer and kissed him atop his forehead.

"I loved your mother deeply, and more than anyone could begin to know. I will never forgive your father for taking her from me or this world, and I promise, that one day I will deliver something that will give you the path to start again. Do you understand me? It may be given in strange and unexpected ways – but I will deliver the things needed to repair this failed world."

Lucifer nodded, he did not understand, but he remembered the words and burned them into his mind.

"I am sorry that this will hurt."

And Zeus tore the halo from Lucifer's head, a sickening, horrifying sound of flesh being torn in two by hand came from the halo, as Zeus yanked the glowing grace from above Lucifer's figure.

Lucifer screamed and held tighter onto Zeus' hips, and the ground and Zeus gave him a kick with one foot as he pulled harder with both hands, and with one final terrible effort tore the grace and halo from

Lucifer's form.

Wingless, Graceless.
Lucifer was now the god he deserved to be, born anew.

Lucifer hit the ground with a final roar of pain and shock, and he was soon unconscious with the lagoon lapping at his face - gentle and warm.
Zeus, looked at the now dead silver ring in his hand, no fire, no fury, no power and he threw it hard to Yahweh, it smashed against the rocks beside him, obliterated into a fine sparkling dust, no fragment survived.

"I deliver your son back to you. Bounty for this battle. Paradise is torn, and the world is now shaped as it has decided it wishes to be. We are all reset to square one, and the game begins anew.
Learn from this, Yahweh, learn that your actions have consequences and that we – your siblings and gods all – will not tolerate your impudence and arrogance again."

Zeus walked away to the willow, leaving Lucifer, Michael, Yahweh and the remains of Saraquiel and Gaia dead in the water.
He stomped on, to the humans and the apple, and the final act that would rebuild this Earth how it deserved to be.

Yahweh clung to Michael and pushed himself to his feet, he staggered toward Lucifer, stood over the man. No longer an angel, barely recognisable as his own son. He nudged the figure over with his foot and grabbed the man by his lapels and threw him over his shoulder.
Holding Michael around the waist, he opened the land before him up, and walked through, the world and heaven merging for one second, then the seem closing and leaving the lagoon empty but for the blood of the fallen and the rumble of the earthquake now battering the whole of creation and reshaping it to continents and islands, new lands and new topography.

The great shift taking place that would start the second age, and the start of the new chapter of man.

* * *

Adam and Eve were sat inside the willow's leaves, huddled close together.
Adam laid gentle kisses on his wife's head, his hand rubbed her belly that was so big now from the babies inside.
He told her the love he has for her, she repeating the same sentiment back, both sure that this is the last of their world before darkness and the collapse of the tree and the heavy fall of the world around them.
Both terrified by these new gods and this horror they had seen unleashed from land's unexplored west.

From the clearing by the lagoon strode Zeus.
He pushed through the curtain made by the willow's leaves, and grandly entered their home. Both humans – man and woman – threw themselves back from his presence in fear, deeper into the shadows as if the darkness would give them escape, as Zeus sat down, quiet and idle on a nearby root.

"Adam." He said to the man.
"Eve?" He asked of the woman. She nodded.
"Ah. So good to finally meet you." Zeus said.
"I am Zeus. I suppose you could call me an uncle - of sorts – blood of your father and master God. I am master of the lands to the west. I have watched you often, especially you, Adam, learning from you, seeing what it is to be human in this infant world - the hunger, the ambition, the love."
Adam stared hard and intently at the god before him, shielding his pregnant wife.
"I must thank you. From you I have learned many things. My version of man did not work out so well – Pandora – I named her. She was too curious, too happy to play with that which was forbidden and not

333

hers. But you…"

He pointed at Adam with one finger.

"You have always been happy just to move around and live one day at a time, tending to the garden, tending to the animals, your honour and your pride in your work so apparent – never asking for anything from your God except his smile and grace and presence, however big or small that may be."

Zeus smiled.

"Do you have the apple?"

Eve shifted forward, moved from under her husband's arms, she looked at the god before her.

"I do. Your Lord."

Zeus smiled widely; he slapped his knees in humour.

"Your Lord! Hah! Such manners from you, such good manners… Would that you knew the extent of which you have been lied too, my love."

Eve looked at Adam, who shook his head gently, and looked downcast to the ground.

"Oh come now, Adam, tell her. It will be no secret once you taste this fruit. Everything will be known."

Eve looked at Zeus, and in her hand was the apple.

"I need you to make a decision, Adam. Do you tell her the truth, and keep some grace in this situation, with all these lies you have been party to? Tell her of the first day and the first queen of Eden, or do I let her bite and find out in the worst possible way.

Your God having abandoned you to this choice. You and her alone to decide what will be your next action from this day on…

I know you love Yahweh, your God, and I do not begrudge that. He created you, and you are welcome to love him.

But, I need to know that you can honour her memory as I do, and I need to see you loved her, or, that you did not – and I will leave you and your new bride alone."

Adam did not look at Eve he raised his eyes sadly to Zeus.

"I did love her, your grace. However, she never loved me, and Eve – my bride, the woman who will be the mother to my children and who

I love with all my heart above even Yahweh himself – she is all I care for now."

Zeus nodded.
He looked at Eve and the apple.
He looked at Adam and his sadness.

"I understand, child. She was a wild temptress; she was different from you or this garden – different from Yahweh and any of the gods. She was unique, and she was powerful. I do not hold against you that you went to love another. So thank you for your honesty."

He looked at Eve.
"What are you talking about, husband? Who is this other?"
Adam looked at Eve sadly, slowly, he held her hand in his and his other hand to her belly.
"Before you there was another woman in Eden. Her name was Lilith. She was my bride. But she did not love me, and she left. God – our Father – created you from my rib and gave you unto the garden and my life as a gift and said I was to love you always, and I do, beyond words, beyond action – you are all that matters."
Eve looked at Zeus, forlornly.
"Is this true? Does my husband speak truthfully – of the woman and of his love for me? Where is she now?"

Zeus pointed at the apple.

"He tells the truth. He loves you like nothing I have ever seen, more so than his love for this garden or the God above, his love for you and those boys in your belly is incandescent and above reproach. But, this woman existed, she lived, and you hold all that remains of her in your hand.
The only way for you to know for sure, to become aware of what has happened, and how it came to be is to bite and swallow the flesh of the one who came before you."

Eve looked at Adam, and at the fruit.

Adam took the apple and looked at his wife.

"I will eat from this if you wish, then you can eat from it, and we can start the day with eyes wide open."

Eve nodded.

"The serpent said the tree is knowledge, that the apple is life. Bite and then tell me you love me, once I bite, I will know if it is true."

Adam nodded, closed his eyes and took a deep bite of the delicious red fruit.

His teeth penetrated the skin, and the flesh below was sour and sweet, and his bite left a trail of fine blood in the fruit.

He chewed, and the flesh of the apple mingled in his mouth with the salty taste of meat, and his mind burst into wildfire.

Eve took the bleeding fruit and bit hard from the flesh as well, and more blood came, flicked on her bright, red lips.

As she chewed her eyes came to wild alertness, and she looked at her husband, who stared back, and the whole knowledge and history of the garden and the beach, and the gods, and Lilith's hard, awful death unfolded in their minds.

Adam cried, Eve covered her mouth in shock, and the two of them looked at the other and realised how unnatural everything was, the way they lived in the dug out earth of the garden beneath this tree, the temperature was cold and prickled their naked skin, they realised the world was different by realising that this bubble of Eden in which they existed was a model protected by Yahweh for his own amusement, that the love he gave was tempered by the worship they shared - that the two things existed in equilibrium with the other - that his love was not just or forever, it was bought and bartered by their desire for his shadow.

Eve covered her mouth and realised that she was nothing more than a toy to Yahweh for his son and that Lilith had been different, holier, purer, more powerful...

Eve could not believe her life had been so second hand.

Adam saw all of Lilith's pain and the love that she had for Yahweh she did not spare him, saw how he was seen as a bumbling fool, an idle idiot doting on the animals and the flowers, but vacant and sterile to her. He saw how little he meant to the world.

The two of them looked at each other and saw that the two were perfect for the other, because despite it all, they loved one another unconditionally, and the children in her belly were to be loved unconditionally, and as secondary as Eve may have been to Yahweh, she was everything to her husband.
"I love…" Adam started, but Eve silenced him with a sweet, sticky finger.
She smiled, and her head dropped to her chest, she looked up coyly, and Adam stayed silent.
"I know, husband. I know, I know, I know." And she kissed Adam deeply.
The apple fell from her hand, rolled to Zeus' foot. He looked down and reached for it.

The two humans kissed heavily, held the other, knowing whatever happened from here on out, they had love enough for them to survive this revelation and fire of life.
Zeus stood and made way to exit.
Before he did, he smiled at the two.
"West of here, is a land where more humans live. Scattered, just a few, a dozen of so.
The gods of the other lands have seen you two and the life you have created, they have witnessed your love and your service and your dauntless optimism, and they built lands and people after your design.
Go west and find them, and there, carve your own land and life. Away from this Eden, away from this land – and – if you do take your God with you, as I am sure you must, at least remember his vengeful, petty qualities as you must his love and his loyalty."
The two humans nodded.

Zeus left the tree and cut the air before him in two and stepped into his world through the portal, leaving a shimmer and a waiver upon the air in Eden.

His duty to this war appeased and complete.
He stepped forward to the future, and whatever lay ahead.
In his hand, the apple for Lucifer that he promised.

Zeus now waiting for whatever was to come excited to see how he would die.

* * *

Lucifer could not remember much from after his halo was ripped and torn from his body. The exquisite pain had knocked him out utterly, and he was a wrecked slab of meat for days, weeks, months – he could not tell you.

He could recall falling though. In fits and starts, blacking out as air rushed past his head, his back burning from where his wings had been torn from his body, his head aching with ferocious grandeur from where his halo was missing and the grace above now absent. His body was a wreck of crushed and smashed bone and flesh. He recalled falling and now and then, he would wake and then see the clouds and the heat rising from his body as he hurtled toward some unknown ground, before passing out again.

He never felt the impact into the building, but did remember hitting the wall hard, the air forced from his lungs, and slumping to the ground, as he came to a thudding halt his eyes opened fractionally, and he saw the hole from which he had made his entrance into this room suddenly stitched closed behind him, the stained glass window, like the one in Yahweh's hall and throne room, returned to colourful being above him. A weak light shone behind, and the window reflected back in broken, coloured glass the image of the archangel Lucifer falling, of him hitting a wall, and of the window shining down on him. It changed again, the glass moving like fluid to new shapes and images of the throne room of Yahweh, and the God moving from his chair, and spreading his arms out. The glass shifted again and spelled out three words, three words only.

"WELCOME TO HELL."

It shifted once more and spelled out the meaning of HELL.
"HERE EXILED LORD LUCIFER."

The window then changed again to a blank slate of colour patchwork, no images, and a dull, fading sunshine behind.
There was nothing there. This cold, monochrome, blank marble temple was empty, had no exit and gave no life or passion.
It was absent and devoid of any joy.

The only thing in the room was a table and a book.
The book was called – "The Old Testament", a note upon it made Lucifer aware entirely what was about to happen, and how he was to be part of it.

"This is the works that the men of Earth have come to expect of me, vengeful and judging, quick-tempered and furious. But, forgiving.
You have made this possible; you have made me have purpose in a wider world, beyond my garden and my isolated thinking. And in doing so, I have given you and your name new purpose.
You saw yourself as a God, well, you are now.

I suppose I should be grateful.
So... Read this now and then and see how our stories grow with each new human tongue. See how our lives entwine and meld as these humans build our future for us.
Who knows where it could lead...
You and I are now players in a wider game.
May the best god win."

Lucifer read the note a dozen times if he read it once, and he sat

339

cross-legged on the floor of his marble, white-walled, doorless prison
- and he smiled and he laughed and he screamed.
An eternity trapped from the grace of God, the light of the morning,
to think of his revenge and plot his retribution, tormented by the
notion of Yahweh's human children - tainted and lead astray by the
children of the gods of the West.

Lucifer embraced his future heartily.
And he waited.
Through the book and the window, he watched Earth turn and change
before his eyes, far from his influence or protection.
Waiting until his day came round.

* * *
- 8 -

Yahweh stood in the doorway.
Lucifer folded his wings back in close to his body. He took a sidestep
and beckoned the God into the house. Yahweh nodded his thanks.
"You are looking well." He said to Lucifer, looking him up and
down.
"Those wings have really grown on you. I like them. Black is a good
look for you."
Lucifer smiled with a sarcastic grin and shook his head, dumbstruck
temporarily with Yahweh nonchalance.
"Thanks, Dad. You look surprisingly chipper as well for a man who
is terminally psychotic." Yahweh smiled back at his son and nodded.
"That's a good one. 'Terminally psychotic.' Funny because it is true.
But, funny all the same."
He pointed at the lounge door.
"In there? I take it Lord Death and his posse are here? I only saw
three horses, so did he drive here?"
Lucifer laughed loudly at this. He slapped his hands loudly, Yahweh
visibly flinched at the noise.
"You are a comedy cavalcade this afternoon aren't you?"
Yahweh looked at Lucifer half sternly, half quizzically.

340

"What are you talking about?" Yahweh asked. Lucifer caught his gaze, something about the look did not sit right.

"Are… are you?" He looked at Yahweh with a fixed and penetrating glare. Trying to find the shimmer that Yahweh was kidding or playing around, there was none to see.

"Fuck off…" he said under his breath, in a scoffed exasperation.

"You don't know do you? You have no idea?" He asked of the God. Yahweh shook his head, confused.

"Know what? What is going on?" He asked of Lucifer; the fallen angel laughed again loudly. He called out for Death.

"Death. Baby, we have guests."

They entered the lounge and Death immediately stood and took up his scythe and the life and power flushed his muscles and his body coiled up in alert readiness.

"Yahweh." He said to the God.

"Lord Mort." Yahweh returned the greeting. He looked at War and Famine and nodded.

"My Lord War, Milady Famine…"

They dutifully returned the salute; Famine offered Yahweh a smile. Yahweh returned it generously and then turned his gaze to Death.

"So where is the other one, the sickly fellow? I assume he is vomiting somewhere out of sight or something?"

Wars face turned up in a vicious, unchained snarl, Death waved a hand to calm him – or hold him off – and looked at Lucifer, the Morningstar shook his head in answer to the look.

"You do not know?"

Yahweh stopped in the centre of the room and looked around the assembled creatures and entities of myth, scripture and legend.

"I don't know what?" He asked.

Death looked at him fiercely, took a step forward and each step made him seem a foot or so taller.

Yahweh shrank in comparison, as everything but War did in Death's full presence and grandeur.

"Pestilence. Our 'sickly looking fellow' is dead. He died and is done, never to come back." He bore down on Yahweh now.

"Come now, Lord Mort, remember your place in the balance, are you not supposed to witness and not pass judgment, are you not the

impartial spirit wandering and surviving? Is that not how it is?"
Death smiled and looked at his cohorts, War glowered and huffed, his breathing a ferocious heave of his barrel chest.
Famine stood staring at the God hungrily. She licked her lips and eyed his muscular, taut, meaty body as though it was a side of beef.
"Dead?" Yahweh said, quietly and confused.
"Dead. His purpose was extinguished. The world is advancing at a rate of knots."
Yahweh sat down his hand on his mouth. Shocked, silent.
"I told you. One day even I would face my oblivion, War and Famine too. This existence even for creatures such as we is fleeting and transient."
Yahweh nodded. He looked at Lucifer, who shrugged, held his mouth in a clutched hand, chuckled and scoffed a laugh and exited the lounge.
"Where is he going now?" Yahweh asked of Lucifer's speedy exit.
"My guess is to make a tea. He has become somewhat attached."
He sat down on his armchair and beckoned War and Famine to join, the four of them sat around in silence, looking at each other, no one speaking, exchanging awkward glances and glares as the only noise in the room was the tick-tick-tick of James' carriage clock that he had inherited from his grandmother, an ugly trinket heirloom worth pennies, but which he kept clean and wound and in fresh batteries out of habit if nothing more.
There was a banging and a clunking coming from the cupboards in the kitchen, Famine smiled and pointed at the door.
"Noisy units." She said quietly.
Lucifer burst through the door with a tray, upon which were five clean mugs and a teapot full of tea, a plume of steam rising from the spout.
He dropped everything upon the table and disappeared into the kitchen again, returning with sugar and milk and some more ginger cake on the tray.
Famine's eyes lit up.
Yahweh looked at the table and his errant, transformed son and smiled weakly and wondrously.
"Very civilised I am sure."

Lucifer looked at him bitterly, his hands and the empty tray falling loosely to his side.

"Shut up and drink your tea."

He left to the kitchen again; more banging and clunking could be heard.

Then over the top of all of this, as the four creatures of divine myth stood around the table helping themselves to tea and cake an almighty explosion was heard and a flash from the garden.

The whole room swung round to look, and the shed had burst into flame and bits of wood and debris scattered the garden, smoke billowing dark and black.

The backdoor was flung open by Lucifer, and he ran out, the shed was dust and ash and shards of wood now, nothing inside could have survived the explosion, bits of debris and smashed remains of knick-knacks and items from James' personal boxes were all over the garden, in the willow tree, fire was pitched here, there and everywhere. There was nothing left.

It was all gone.

As the smoke subsided, Lucifer was joined by War and Famine, Death looked on from the kitchen window, Yahweh by his side. Lucifer's hands were on his head, his jaw was slack and loose and open, War looked at the shed base, there was nothing there but a deep, burst hole.

"Where has his body gone?" he muttered to Lucifer.

"Where did you put it?" he answered.

"Right here... I lay him right here; there should be something here."

"Famine looked up in the tree tops, babies clothes hung forlorn and lonely from branches, some burnt, some singed, some blazing fire. She sighed sadly, and a tear ran down her cheek. She looked at a pair of baby shoes tied at the laces and hanging scorched and smoking from a branch, at shoulder height,

"So little." She said. She looked at Lucifer, and he noticed the tears.

"They are so little." She repeated.

Lucifer let his head drop.

343

"They were his son's. Never worn."
Famine's head fell to her chest as she held the shoes loose and gently in her palm, still dangling from the tree.

"Where is James Edmunds?" Yahweh asked Death.
Death turned and looked at the God with suspicious and questioning eyes.
"Why do you wish to know?" he asked, his voice full of doom and glower.
"Because he is to be my Messiah," Yahweh stated clearly and with confident arrogance.
From the lounge, a solitary voice rang out.

"Well, you can fuck that twice in the ear. That's not happening."

Yahweh and Death spun around and looked through the hallway door through to the lounge.
Death saw him first, Yahweh second.
Death asked the question.
"I beg your pardon?"
The voice said once again.

"I said 'you can fuck that twice in the ear. That is not happening' – uh uh. Not with me."
Death looked at the kitchen window and called loudly and high pitched for the others from the garden.
"Guys…" No one came.
"Guys…" No one heard.
"GUYS!" Death screamed louder still, and the three came to the window, Lucifer looked perplexed and raised his hands and shoulder in a shrug that said
"WHAT?"
Death pointed to the lounge, and the three creatures walked the short way across to the French window and looked into the lounge.

There, sat at the dinner table, sipping tea and chewing Jamaican ginger cake, covered in blood, but quite alive, and not injured in the

slightest...
Was James.

How he had got there, why and how he was alive were all questions
on the tongues and minds of the people assembled. However, no one
could ask, no one could speak.
The faces instead were blank, shocked and silent. Eyeballs intently
fixed on the man.

"What the fuck are you all staring at? And who the hell is the guy in
the golden pimp suit?" he pointed at Yahweh, who had walked
slowly forward looking at the man at the table.
Death answered.
"This is Yahweh, you may know him as God, or Allah or Jehovah.
He is the Old and New Testament deity."
James looked him up and down, chewing ginger cake; he scoffed as
he chewed some down and suppressed a sarcastic giggle.
"Oh, really. God are you?"
Yahweh nodded and offered his hand.
James stared at it.
"I was married. I had a child. My wife died from a bleed that the
doctors could not fix due to a ruptured placenta. She died on the
operating table, without even having the chance to see her... our...
Son.
My son died twenty-seven minutes later, in a plastic box. His lungs
had not formed properly, and he suffocated on fresh air – the doctors
could not do anything, every scan had been perfect, no warnings or
worries existed on the run up.
I was left alone, widowed, childless. I have never been so lonely,
never been so angry, never been so sad.
And you come in here and tell that you want me to be your messiah?
That you want me to work for your team?"
Yahweh tried to talk, but James cut him off sternly, spit flying from
his mouth, a teacup smashing right next to Yahweh on the wall
thrown by a ferocious, now standing, red-faced and teary-eyed
James.

"I'd sooner rub my hands in horseshit and then blend them in a garden strimmer than shake your hand."

Yahweh looked at him, cocking one ear toward James; a stutter formed awkwardly on his voice.

"I… I beg your pardon?"

"I think you heard me. Now do me a favour, you absent, cruel, murderous old cunt and get the fuck out my house. Before I throw you out."

Death's jaw slowly dropped. His eyes a lucid, wide-eyed stare of wonder.

War and Famine looked at Lucifer, who shook his head in awe, and said calmly, quietly beneath his breath.

"Oh, *James*. You brave, foolish dolt."

He put both palms on the glass and his head hit the window. He shook his head gently further, looking at James, furious, righteous and foulmouthed standing his ground, having the high road and right to do so in his own home.

Lucifer stared and thought admiration and pride at the man, how he could not help but love him. How much like his brother Jesus he was, and how different and brilliant besides.

Then he noticed it…

Lucifer pushed himself away from the window and ran into the house.

He pushed past War, who looked confused rather than angry, Famine was dazed and jumpy, Death looked at the Morningstar and raised a quizzical eyebrow.

"What do you see?"

Lucifer drew the shape of a box on the air, and Death immediately saw it.

"Oh."

"Yes, Oh."

Death looked panicked.

"Well. This changes things."

Lucifer nodded.

"Yes, it fucking well does." He looked at Death.

"I don't know about you…" Lucifer said. "But I am terrified."

Death nodded.

First the man was dead, then he was alive – neither thing Death could account for and now if Yahweh did not kill him again for his impertinence and vulgarity.

"Well." Death thought, "He is going to have wished he did."

And he began to sweat.

A new sensation, he had never experienced before.

Death did not like it one little bit.

* * *

CHAPTER SIX
THE PASSION

"Being his real brother I could feel I live in his shadows,
but I never have and I do not now.
I live in his glow."

- Michael Morpurgo – "Private Peaceful"

A dust of sand and blood and pity was being kicked up in the courtyard, as soldiers stomped and marched hither and thither. Each spear-carrier was on some important or unintelligible mission from someone who believed they were higher-up the food-chain barking orders while pretending to have importance above and beyond the common soldier.

The sand in the court was a clod hewn mess of dried and congealed blood and footprints, seen from the battlements and the tower where the guard was met and changed every 6 hours, the courtyard was a strange canvas of ever-changing vistas, had there been ways to document on papyrus or cloth it would have made a dazzling design, so many spirals and lines and scored marks from feet and the spray of arterial blood had made the small, horrific yard into a brutal and beautiful painting of life and torture.

Regulus marched into the yard, his short-sword by his hip tap-tap-tapping at his armour and providing him with the warmth of comfort for it simply being on his side, his helmet was tight and heavy, and the sweat trickled n floods into his eyes. He removed the helmet and went to the small trough of drinking water, took a ladle of the stuff and poured it over his head, then another he gulped down hungrily.

From the other side of the courtyard, by the giant wooden and iron gates, came Helio. The Greek soldier who had donned the Roman red and gold and had always been seen as a philosopher to the garrison, especially looked up to by Regulus, he was an older, wiser and more gentle soldier than Jerusalem had seen in centuries.

"How goes it, Regulus?" He called out, also removing his gold centurion helmet, the bristles of the red plume atop the gold cast of the helmet rested under his arm, he wiped a gold bangled wrist, wrapped in red cloth across his forehead and smiled at the younger soldier.

"Helio. All is well. Some disturbances in the villages bordering the city, word that the Messiah has been caught and dragged to the capital to face the Emperor himself are rife… Something is happening, you can tell that there is something afoot."

Helio took the ladle, swallowed down a gulp of the water and turning to Regulus he took his compatriots wrist and shook Regulus' arm strongly, the two men nodded approval at each other.

"The rumours are wrong, my friend, to an extent… anyway."
"Meaning?" The young soldier rubbed his neck with more water and sat down to adjust his boots.
"In as much as the Messiah is not in Rome. That is not correct."
Helio took a ladle of water down in one, and then poured one over his helmet, the gold and red feathers' bristles fizzed as the water cooled the surface, how these things had not cooked the soldiers' heads alive Helio had often wondered.
"He is here, in Jerusalem. Pilate has him."
Regulus looked at the man hard and sharply. "Here?" he asked, his hands absently rubbing the dust from his plume.
"Here." Helio smiled back. "So look sharp, I have a feeling we are to see history made this day. And history is seldom quiet, it roars like Daniel's lion, it growls and groans and it very rarely goes without scorching the Earth and its inhabitants lightly."
Helio replaced his headwear, and with his right hand on his heart, he saluted Regulus.
"Soldier. May the gods of old and new smile on you."
He returned the gesture, and the two men embraced with a strong hug.
"And on you too, my friend."
And he watched as Helio marched out the way he himself had entered.
The activity beyond the gates into the market was clear and obvious; something was happening out there, something big.
He put on his helmet and picked up his spear and exited the same way, back into the throng, hearing the whispers and the talk of this Messiah from the plebs and the downtrodden, the commoners and the

paupers… Each one excitedly chattering about the King who had been caught.

The King of the Jews.

* * *

- 2 -

Barabbas had been staring out of the hole that allowed him the rationed air to breathe; it also provided his only source of light. For an hour or two now, his eye and his mouth intermittently switched and swapped around to take advantage of the breeze or the light, never allowed both at the same time.

His hands were rough and broken, cracked from his futile pounding of the hard, heavy oak door. The wood imported by ships as big as buildings brought here from Europe.
Heavy Germanic wood, shaped and forged by slab-like Roman hands.

The blood had caked and dried in clusters and scabs on his ravaged knuckles; before today the knuckles had seen to the death of three Roman guardsmen and a whore who had not pleased him as he had paid and demanded.
He could close his eyes to remember the sound of flesh and bone popping under his effortless strength.
He could smell the bitter iron tang of blood as it splashed on his tunic and skin, the warmth in the cell he found himself in easily brought these memories burst to fervent life. Alas, they were only memories. As strong as he was, as powerful as his merciless will may have been, locked inside this box, stone and wood and heat – clammy, searing and claustrophobic his knuckles were as pitiful as the man himself.
One eye and a parched mouth moving back and forth from the hole, a heavy breathing cyclops, sharing the air and the light.

Never both at the same time.

He saw the activity of the guards and soldiers and watched the crowd cowing and hiding at their approach. He saw the children being gathered by their mothers, herded into huts and houses, the sense of something building on the streets of Jerusalem, way beyond the control of any one people or person.

The panic was like wine for him, and he drank it in.

Its deep, intoxicating allure was all he craved.

Barabbas waited. He knew there was something happening and that he would soon see the light again with both eyes, and drink in the air like it was honey mead, and he would be in the wine-house once more.

He closed his eyes again, and fantasized about the feel of his rough, angry hands grasping at the buttocks of the cheapest whore, one that bordered on the verge of ugliness, just as Barabbas had liked them.

His memory raging at the idea of the woman's leathery skin under his calloused fingers.

Meanwhile, the panic on the streets was palpable.

The chapped lips, cracked and dry and angry, they smiled lightly.

Broken teeth jagged and ugly were prominent in the dark.

Barabbas waited.

Soon. Everything screamed that his time was coming.

* * *

- 3 -

Herod had not seen fit to do anything with the Nazarene. His questions unanswered and his soldiers ignored. All of his kingly power was not enough to dent the silence or the stoic calm around the man.

Herod had heard so much rumour, had expected a king. He had expected someone resplendent and draped in the colours of position, power and authority. Instead he had been faced with a man of simple cloth, his hair a sun-cooked, blonde hazel colour, his skin a rich and spotless caramel, eyes of pure brown, the corona of fire circled the iris, a beautiful and magnificent beauty hidden behind such humble attire.

Herod had no idea that this man was the child who had escaped his father's grip, his mad father, whose power had weakened and waned and then finally sputtered to nothing in illness and corruption.

Augustus, the emperor, had seen fit to tear the empire of Judea apart and deal it out amongst the brothers Herod. Antipas had maintained his grip on Judea – the Bethlehem and Galilean alike had fallen under his jurisdiction, hence why Pilate had seen fit to send the Nazarene to him for judgment.

Not that judgment was able to be passed, no crime committed under the King Herod's belief, and so, back to Jerusalem and the Romans he had sent the man.

But.

Those eyes, the man's silent acceptance, the way he gently shook his head and smiled even in the face of possible death, Herod had watched the man and had been moved to a feeling of uncertain and ominous hopelessness.

He knew his domain as King was given by birth-rite and the good grace of Roman patronage, he knew all-to-well from watching his father's decline that he was not divine amongst the gods. Unlike his father, he was well aware the delicate balance of power and ego. The man who had stood in his presence had shaken him deeply with a feeling of utter emptiness for the first time in his life.

Looking upon the face of this other man, he had felt humble and worn to nothing, like a statue left in the desert, blasted by sand and wind and element, contours chipped and shredded away, his essence was peeled layer by layer by each ambivalent and silent nod or shake the Nazarene had made with his beautiful head.

His altercation with Jesus was less a footnote in the story unfolding, than a humourous and beguiling aside, he had sent the man away for no other reason than to be free of those eyes, the burning circle that lit fire around the iris, the faint look of abandoned fear in his mouth, as if the man knew exactly what was to come and had been stripped of any worry for its execution or coming to pass. The Nazarene had shaken him with how calm he was taking the events that were surrounding him, the accusations, the whispers on the people's lips, the evidence that supported the claim and followed him.

Herod had watched him keenly and with a growing unease had made his decision to get him out of his palace, and return him whence he came.

Herod had hated himself every second the man had stood in his sanctum, and now he was gone, sent back to Pilate to be dealt with elsewhere, and forgotten.

Herod found that he could not forget.

Could not let go of the lingering feeling he was destiny's fool.

The overbearing feeling of his father looking down in anger and the terrible feeling that something had been left begging and history, the daunting weight of his family's history, had been unfulfilled in its scream for closure...

As he sat alone in his throne-room, the sun burning a line like a dial on the floor, slowly ticking down the minutes and hours, counting down to something he could never comprehend, King Herod Antipas wept.

And the throne-room shook with his tears.

* * *

- 4 -

Pontius Pilate was getting tired of washing his hands.

The day was hot and humid; the city was buzzing with expectant rumour. Angry mobs stalked from street to street and house to house, the feeling of the mob was being filtered down through the ranks as one of hungry, desperate need – the Messiah born and walking amongst them, now a man, and spreading his gospel – names and deeds whispered and shared. Talk of the man reaching feverous levels and his name a virus spreading amongst the people.

A word that held power like a sickness; a name that infected and spread fast and deadly amongst such rampant, needful ears.

Pilate had been up since before dawn, as usual, he had taken his robe and his finery and hung it upon the hook on his mantle, and dressed in the rags and clothing of one of the cities miners, dusty and worn, torn and common, he threw the brown burlap cape over his shoulder and fixed the hood to it, pinned down with a simple wooden pendant. His leather sandals cracked and weathered.

The two Praetorian Guard dressed in similar fashion and waited by the fountain for the Prefect to make the short walk down to the garden. From there, they were tasked with walking sandwiched between the Roman councilman as he made his morning circuit through the markets and trade stalls, up through to the temple, where he listened, observed and gained a perspective of the city for which he was tasked with supervising, as only the poor and common man could.

From the ground up, he gained the insight and understanding of the mood of his people.

The morning sun was starting to get hotter and hotter, dust and scent and humidity rose in the atmosphere, and the sun became a mottled dot in a thick smog filled sky. The scent of the spices and meats began to become increasingly prominent as the stalls took shape in the bazaar around the marketplace. Swelling numbers of people poured out of houses and huts, flooding the street with curious faces and wandering need.

Pilate walked amongst them all every day - these were his wards and charges, and he needed to feel the pulse of the city to keep his position tenable.

A fact of life that his predecessor Gratus failed abjectly to understand.

He would return home to the counsel palace, and he would wash his hands scrubbing hard and deep with the oils and the sponge, scouring the dirt of the common man from his hands. As much as he wanted to understand and gain a feel of the people his hands were the one thing Pilate would obsess over. He would wash and clean a dozen or so times a day, specks of imaginary dirt ingrained and infected in his pores, he would scrub and cleanse and repeat whenever he could.

The street under his feet never bothered him, but the idea of life upon his hands terrified and upset him in equal measure and so... to the basin and the water and sponge he would go.

As he did this morning, washing before he left and knowing full well how futile it would be and how he would repeat the process again on his return, and not once or twice either, maybe a half dozen times before the end of his day and his bed and his stirring and restless wife.

Pontius kissed the forehead of his wife, Procula, as she lay sleeping in their bed. Cotton sheets and silks draped about the chamber, her left arm resting against her side, the hand on her other arm cupped tight against her cheek. She was warm, a fine film of sweat glistened on her skin and salted his lips upon the kiss.

Recently she had been feverish in dream, sleep disrupted and frantic, as her mind had come aflame with vision and image which she recalled in detail glorious and morbid over breakfast, Pilate drinking in her words greedily, seeing the patterns in her dreams and the whispers on the street that were undeniable and inextricable.

Links and patterns emerging that he could not ignore.

So, to his streets, every morning he had gone. Guard in front and Guard behind, to listen and to absorb and to soak in the street, the murmurs and to shape the tapestry of all of these individual stories and dreams and rumours into fact and negotiate its meaning and import.

With the taste of his wife's sweat upon his lips, and the call of the morning bird and crow of the rooster in his ears, he left.

The smell and sound of the city were already building, to a deafening and ripe fever pitch.

* * *

- 5 -

Lucifer sat upon the open portal of the arch by Pilate's window, watching as Procula slept, dividing his time between the sleeping woman and the husband who now exited the giant yawning arch that led to the garden and the fountain where two men waited, giant and huge, hands like shovels and faces that looked like they were barely carved from granite. Roughly dragged out as unfinished sketches in the rock, the edges of their jaws jagged and misshapen, the brows too big and ugly to exist in normal society with any job other than soldiering or hired killers.

He watched as the elegant Pilate strode across the yard to the fountain and flipping the hood he crafted from the rough material of his burlap and sack cape, he attempted to wander amongst the commoners like a chameleon changing colour in a forest, hiding his true nature from the masses.

Failing abjectly. His stride too sure-footed, his manner in the crowd too much like a man who has a mission rather than one of the droning, lost populace.

His skin too golden, his eyes too keen and awake, his soldiers too clear in the mass of bodies as dangerous individuals who should be avoided, and the people on the street did just that, walking around, giving wide berth to the giant cloaked men like they would to a hornet's nest or a raging river.

Pilate's intentions may have been good and pure, but his ego shielded him from how obvious he was amongst these common men.

It made Lucifer chuckle gently to himself.

If there was one thing that Lucifer loved more than anything, with no cruel intention or reason – just, because – it was the folly of man's ego.

357

It reminded him so very much of himself. A sad and lingering sting of truth mixed with a heady pride that man, like himself, was naught but a fool for destiny and fate and circumstance, guided by ego and driven by intentions almost never in their full control.

Procula, however. She was a quandary he could not account for. The dreams were not of this Earth, the visions not of her own creation, the fears she exuded in sticky sweat-laced nightmares and restless sleep that tormented the poor woman's mind and body, they were not hers to have and Lucifer was unhappy that this innocent was burdened with them, he was angered that they were so important and so ignored by all around her.
Procula was his prime curiosity right now.
And what she had seen was more important than anything else on this green and adolescent Earth.

Jesus had not spoken to him since the debacle in the desert. Where Lucifer had gone to him as a brother, older, wiser, more aware of the game and the rules and Jesus' place as prime King on the chessboard, his every move being manipulated by a lazy, angry, bitter father. The link between the two men that bound and conjoined them. Lucifer being Jesus' half-brother.
Same father, different mother.

May the gods old and new have bitter mercy on Mary's soul.

Jesus had sat in the desert, barefoot and dressed in nothing but a thick white tunic; he had wandered into the plains alone, without telling anyone. One morning he had woken up, his heart heavy and his mind full of noise and confusion, his gut screaming signals at him. So he ate well and hearty, drank down a jug of water and had left the warmth of the house and had started walking straight, without stopping, into the desert and then further, into the heart of the wilderness plains beyond the farmland, the sand banks and the free lands and into the arid, dry, dead landscape that had no man. No life and no shelter. Where he found his perch atop the cliff face and sat cross-legged, barefoot and naked but for a tunic to watch

358

the plain turn over minutes, hours and days.
For a month and ten days.

Lucifer had walked in his footsteps and had followed him,
and had sat down beside him and had lent him company, silently,
stoically for the first ten days.
Jesus was emaciated, his lips were broken and shredded from the
heat and the wind that blew out here warm and blustery. Sand picked
up and cried along with the whisper of the air, battering the flesh like
a weapon - scratching, scorching and scarring the soft skin.
Lucifer had attempted to shield his brother, but, the wind kept
changing direction, and he could not be in every place at once – he
was not their father after all – so his efforts were mostly futile. When
this had failed, he had tried to dissuade Jesus from this ridiculous
mission and to talk to him of the folly of his actions, the futility of
what he was doing. Advising him that as much as it would be
remembered it would change little and be a footnote in the story.

Jesus had ignored him.

After twenty days, Lucifer had tried to give him food he had
folded time and space and dimensions to get. A trick he had learned
from his father, a weak replacement for omniscience or omnipotence.
He thought about the market, the bazaar and the succulent apricots
and dates, the apples and the grapes. The juicy halves of chickens
hanging dry in the sun from hooks fashioned from bronze and iron.
Then he reached out and the space between the bazaar and the
clifftop touched and he passed through and back, in the blink of an
eye, existing in both spaces of time and both dimensional plains at
one and the same time.
He sat beside him, eating piggishly – despite his shame, busily
drinking from a camel hide full of water stitched and waxed tight into
a fine flask. Every now and then handing out toward Jesus, who
would ignore or raise a single hand with palm out, and wave away
twice, three times and then return to his sentinel watch over the
valley of the plain.

Lucifer had never forced the issue but had offered, this he was happy to admit.

A man who knew a thing or two about temptation, he had never gone to these lengths – he gained nothing from turning Jesus' head, instead, it was purely concern that made him want to stay here by his side.

Concern for his younger brother.

Same father, different mothers.

Same blood.

He watched the man shed weight, essence and life in front of him, constantly talking, constantly reassuring that he was there, and constantly reinforcing the issue he had tried to tell the man since he was a child in Galilee.

"There is no divine plan. Your life is your own. You can still be as good a man as you are now and NOT have to follow the footsteps in the sand left my our father. Why do you need to follow them so blindly walking toward the darkness?

I am simply telling you; there are alternative paths, full of light and clarity, which lead to the same result you are trying to achieve. Your blind loyalty to a man who you have never met, who has never bothered to even show himself to you, who is manipulating your every waking breath... It is irrational, it is ridiculous.

Why do you so unquestionably do this?"

Jesus had never answered, he simply turned his head, so briefly it was less a gesture than a twitch and flashed that ambivalent, calm smile at his brother.

Lucifer received it and returned it with a shake of his head, and a frustrated but gentle laugh. He never attempted temptation, because...

Why bother?

Why exude such effort on a wall that will not crumble.

Jesus was a wall.

A solid, unshakeable, unmovable, unbreachable wall.

His smile was serene, gentle and welcoming but never faltering.

His was the way and the path, and he would not be swayed.

So Lucifer had left him to see out the mission, forty days and forty nights, no food or water. He watched as Jesus staggered half-dead out of the desert plain, from the intoxicating, withering heat of the lifeless lands into civilization and let life once again fill him.

He sipped the water courteously, he broke a fragment of bread and chewed delicately and he smiled at Lucifer and left him on the edge of the desert as he walked back to his disciples to share the visions he had seen.
Lucifer watched him leave, and his head rested on his chest in sorrow, love and despair.

How he had loved his brother.

Procula groaned and stirred, a jolt of life, and a sigh of uncomfortable restlessness. Lucifer walked soft-footed to her side and lay on the bed beside her, with one elegant, long-fingered hand he drew circles on the warm, damp skin of her back and shoulders and with the other hand he ever-so-calmly, with love and with attention, pushed the hair from her brow and cupped her face in his hand, the pinky gently stroking her cheek. And, he sang songs of Enochian calm, patience and beauty.
As he listened to her dreams, his eyes closed and his heart deciphered the images within her mind.

As he had every morning for a month.
Her head so full of images of his brother.
Of Jesus.

A man she had never seen nor met.

* * *

The hill of Golgotha was a barren, dustbowl of grey and muddy brown. The ground was littered with blood and fibres from rope and wood, dried and shredded, strewn around with wanton abandon.

Men ran around rampantly trying to clean up space for the oncoming crucifixions. The hill was closed off to everyone else but them. Soldiers took the bodies of the dead from crosses and carried them down toward the waiting wagon, heaped high on top of each other, the murderers and thieves, adulterers and wilful, open apostates. Unclaimed upon death and left to rot and bake in the sun, skin as thin as gauze, hair as lank as river weed, and blood dried hard on wounds that were brutal reminders of successful judgment carried out and now complete..

Lord Death stood, silent and still, elegant and unseen amongst the throng of busy movement from the soldiers and slaves. His cloak billowing in the warm breeze that caught on the hill's top, ambivalent and oblivious of the men and the stench of the dead. Bowels emptied on arid, parched and untillable ground, human remains, shit and blood. None of this bothered him or made him turn up his nose, he stood, errant and majestic amongst all this, pondering the final cross that remained, soon to be returned to the bottom of the hill, given a wash of fresh varnish, and bestowed upon the shoulder as burden for the next prisoner.

Death would have smiled, had he known how, knowing full well whose cross this would be.

His dark blue cloak - almost black but for the inexplicable sheen and shimmer it contained, like moonbeams caught on the tide, was at terrific odds with his location. So beautiful and noble, so rich and fine, upon this hill that housed so much malice and anger, yet bore no life or plant or grass.

Sat atop of a horse, thin and grey skinned, pallid and waxen, ill-looking, shallow eyes set deep in an ugly skull, was Famine. She wore a white gown, with bronze stitched woven into the fabric, it caught sunlight and refracted it in bursts of secret messages, unreadable and unknown, but deadly and ill all the same.

She held in her hand two lead weights, which she expertly flipped and trickled from one knuckle to the other, as she watched over the blue-robed, white-skinned brother.

War was circling the cross, his stride around the mighty structure wide and booming, heavy footed and menacing.

His leather boots an oxblood colour, that was at the same time dull and rich and deep with life; his tunic was just above knee height, and gold fringed; his ankle boots resembled those worn by Roman nobility; his red tunic swept aside to show two giant swords, the smaller of the two still larger than a Roman broadsword by 6 inches or so. His wrists were adorned with thick, gold and ruby cuffs, that cupped over his knuckles like a duster or a half glove, and that would have inflicted horrendous damage on anything on Earth should it be used to make a blow against someone or thing.

He let out a belly laugh that was magnificently opulent and hungry, and turned to Lord Death.

"This is the final weapon then?"

Death nodded, once, a curt and final gesture that did not need repeating.

"Aye. This is the very same. He has an endgame unlike any I have seen him use before. This is the method with which he will release it upon."

Famine yawned one solitary, unhappy time and then patted the mount she was on absently, the horse looked tired, malnourished and on the verge of death, yet, fire was behind those eyes, and a steelish silver spark existed behind them.

"Steady now, steady." She rubbed the weak flesh of the horse below her.

The horse's name was Blight, and with her touch quietened down and steadied itself, she dismounted uneasily, her thin legs wrapped in the swabs of cotton and laced with bronze ribbons around her bare ankles.

"It seems to be somewhat an inauspicious end."

Death did not waver nor move, his eyes fixed heavy on the cross and the sky behind, as the clouds broke and parted and sunshine began to seep through to fill the quickening blue canvas of the air.

"It is an end at least. And, a beginning. As we have come to expect." War laughed again and slapped the cross, the wood gave a hearty shudder, it creaked and gave a groan and then it, too, was quiet.

"The chess pieces move even now, hey, brother? The rules are evolving daily… soon, we will not be playing the same game as the coward Yahweh."

Death was inclined to agree but kept his tongue, and he turned slowly to return to his mount tied safely against a pillar post.

The pale, beautiful beast took a knee at his approach, and Death easily took his saddle, gripping the reins tight and firm. His horse was a cream colour, mottled with pale grey patches, its skin's hue was a glorious contract to his rider's robes, and the fine black leather straps and fittings were connected via perfectly crafted silver buckles.

The horse was named Khlōros, and its eyes were dark and full of slithery movement, like quicksilver in water, a deep glint that seemed as though galaxies were being formed in clusters and bursts inside the orbs.

Death looked down at the bottom of the hill and saw Pestilence knelt at the side of a beggar, whose body was ravaged with sores and deep welt-like bruises.

He had a hand against the beggar's face, and his pale yellow robe was mottled and stained deep with blood, sputum and bile. His other hand held a corner of his hood to his mouth, hiding the bronchial cough he seemed unable to shake, his eyes were raw and pink, one a creamy white colour full of cataract and blindness.

Despite all this, he was a beautiful man, or at least the shadow of a beautiful man, an echo of a man once dazzling and blessed with beauty, now pockmarked and scorched with illness and infirmity.

Pestilence looked up the hill, and caught Death's eye, he gave a gestured nod to his brother – the beggars hand came up slow and arthritic, it cupped and patted Pestilence's neck in thanks for his attention and time. He noticed the man's gaze had been stolen by figures upon the hill. The beggar looked around at where the half-blind man in front of him was looking, caught sight of Death staring back at him and let go a stream of bloody vomit all over the ground and himself, shook in a rictus of pain and immeasurable agony, and then still holding onto Pestilence's arm, tight and heavy, his limbs gave up and snapped loose; he fell to the ground still and hot. Pestilence ran two pustule stained fingers over the man's eyes to close them. The sick man lay a final kiss upon the feverish forehead of the dead beggar.

"How I love to be here when they burn."

He walked toward a Roman soldier's horse, buckled against a post by a garrison hut, and kicked high upon the mount, as he did the flesh became cauterized in pox, sores and welts, the eyes faded into blindness, and the gait became unsteady and fragile.
It climbed the hill, slowly and with agonized steps, to where the other three were.
The horse's name was Nosus, and it was as sickly and diseased as the rider was. Lank and wet with decay. It brayed and whinnied as foam gathered at its mouth. Grey and red and wretched.

War came around the cross and gave one last belly laugh, his red hair bushy and thick and wiry. His beard flecked with blonde that streamed down from the corner of his mouth was in a permanent sense of joyful happiness as he laughed loud and harsh and cruelly. His hands rested on his waist as he turned and looked at the riders and gestured back toward the cross, shrugged his hand and shoulders toward it in a "Look at it!" gesture. His belly shook again with an uproarious and angry laugh.
He turned on his heel shaking his head in absent mood of humour and mounted his giant shire horse – scarred and regaled in the fruits of battle, its leathery skin was muscular and thick set, its legs had curtains of auburn hair around the hooves, which looked caked in blood and guts and human flesh.
The beast's eyes were bloodshot orbs of anger, it looked like it could kick a wall to dust, stomp a human skull to nothing but a memory. Its

mane was a deep rich auburn that looked like embers ready to burst into fire.

He mounted it with a single kick, and when he gripped the reins the horses mouth neighed and blood flecked spittle spat from his mouth.

The riders united on their steeds, War's horse named Conquest, bowed discreetly to his equestrian brothers and the four of them rode down the hill of Golgotha, toward the town, where they would wait and watch and let the day unfold.

War gave a half salute to the guard at the bottom of the hill, solitary away from the garrison huts or the dead beggar, facing the city.

The soldier returned the salute with a strong, steady arm, the spear in his hand unfaltering and strong.

War laughed heavily.

Booming and massive.

The riders departed the hill toward the town.

All except Death, who bore out toward the palace leaving his brethren to find their own way. Death needed to be somewhere else. On a day like this, it was not enough to let the universe maintain its usual status quo, there were people he needed to speak to and a man he needed to speak long and hard with.

So far the only man who had escaped his domain, and, who Death now wanted to finally sit down and break bread with. The endgame of this particular set was coming.

Death wanted to see what the universe wanted, wanted to let the chips fall and bare witness to the coming change.

Khlōros marched to the city palace, and the crowds parted as he approached like a tide splitting open for Moses and his exodus. His path clear and his mission begun.

Death carried on to his destination.

His robe, like a shard of the night sky. Its layers wafting effortlessly through the parched desert, sparkling with life and history.

- 7 -

The spear was heavy, and it hurt his hand. The sun was hot, and it burned his neck. His robe was brittle and dry from the heat, it rubbed and left a rash on his intimate areas that he was unable to itch for the sake of decorum and his standing in the guard. Such insolent acts would be punished with severity if he were seen as to be disrespecting the Roman red.
Despite this all he carried on his guard at the bottom of the Golgotha hill.

He watched as the workers came, the cadets and the slaves, moving the clods of kicked-up earth and stomping it back down into the ground, dusting the sand over the blood spatters and splashes as the crosses were removed and carried back down the hill, with the bodies of the last lot of prisoners.
Crucifixion was both a booming and messy business, the army of men and eunuchs who came and cleared up the space and ground only for it to be returned to a soiled and spoilt state again mere hours later did not think twice about the futile nature of their actions or work, the transience of the result of their labour.

Truth be told, they did not care.

He stood stoical and straight, despite the growing pain in his neck from the blistering heat, despite the itch and the pain in his crotch from the robe riding up and the friction burn he got every time he moved.
So, he tried to not move, and thought instead of other things – like his family's villa in Lanciano, his late wife's beautiful lips licking closed with the taste of olives, flicking her tongue out to steal the final remnant of juice from her cheek. His beautiful wife who died on her bed giving birth to their son. Of his late child Emilianus, who survived for a mere 20 minutes before dying in his arms.

He tried to concentrate on the good he remembered of his wife: her beautiful bosom, the laugh that made him blush with happiness, the way she kissed him and left his lips tingling for minutes after, the bright twinkle in her eye. But somehow these good memories always faded to tragedy, the strongest memories of them all. Of his wife crying with happiness as she looked upon the child they had so dearly wanted, before she just stopped, no breath, no life, her eyes fixed and a weak smile on her gorgeous lips. Dead as if with no effort or force, just as if the life was drained from her, and she was cut off from this world. His gasping child whose heart stopped as he gave his first smile, looking up through almost closed eyes and the flicker of happiness on his mouth before the life was stolen from him with no effort at all.

Tears ran down his face, and he turned his head, despite the discomfort from his neck. He coughed loudly and spat, and with a roughly wrapped wrist – a red ragged fabric bandage acting as guard from the sweat that poured in this climate - he cleaned his eyes and coughed loudly again before turning back to the statue that he once was.
One hand gripping the spear tighter and more fiercely than before. His eyes red, but focused, staring at the workers and slaves as they ran around preparing the slaughter ground.
He stood silent and severe, a picture of Roman force and nobility, a soldier hewn from clay and cooked in power fire, strong, forceful and elegant despite the climate and the uniform's myriad discomforts and flaws.
Longinus, Spear of the Garrison of Jerusalem, Soldier of Rome, son of Lanciano stood and watched as the killing grounds he was tasked with guarding came to be, shaping in front of his eyes, transforming from death-drenched carrion ground – with bodies dragged and carried from the mount down toward the miller's cart, in preparation for the horror that would unfold again that evening, ad infinitum, blood begetting blood, the soil at the top of Golgotha a soup of a thousand men's sacrifice.

Amongst the throng a man dressed in darkest blue walked unchallenged, noble lineage clearly, his skin an almost paper white, his hair as fine a blonde as Longinus had ever seen. By his side a lady of feeble age, her skin sallow and grey, thin and translucent, the veins prominent and the eyes deep set and empty. Her gown a pure white of beauty, with bronze trim and decal.

Behind, a giant of a man with hair as red and curly as a bramble bush dipped in bronze, his beard a thick and flowing red with two streaks of white down the mouth, his garb a form of Roman soldier he had never witnessed before, but so rich and fine, it meant he was clearly a commander, a prefect or a noble-soldier who had bought his commission… though it looked like this man could crush a head with his bare hand… Maybe he had seen action and earned the right to bare the gold and crimson.

Finally, a creature of some ugly beauty walked, his staggering gait was hypnotizing, his face obscured by a fine gauze, but clearly the man had some illness or disease.

Longinus did not want to know.

The red headed monster came to him, born on the back of a horse as big as Longinus had ever seen, he bellowed a booming-voiced "HOI!" at the guard, who with hand beating chest, returned with a gesture any Roman soldier would know.

The man in red bellowed again, but this time it was a spittle filled laugh.

"Inspection. We have come to see your killing grounds… we understand a crucifixion is happening today, we are here to inspect the grounds and the setup. Stay here, guard the hill, let no one come up and tell the slaves and workers to stay down here while we are up there.

Do you understand me, boy?"

Longinus yelped to the affirmative, and the red-headed man flipped him a gold coin that bore the head of some emperor even he did not recognize.

He turned his head to the coin and back to the red-headed man, who had already led the procession up toward the hill.

His laughter ringing out in giant echoes and swells all the way to the mount.

The sickly man turned to regard the spear on the way to the top. Longinus gripped it tighter and nodded as the man walked past, his face still obscured, and a tang of sweetness and decay wafted from his being as he passed.
Longinus breathed in hard and almost gagged, but his fear of the red man, in garb clearly Roman but of some untold expense and value, whose laugh sounded like a drawbridge slamming down - rattling and heavy and full of dreadful anger - stopped the gag in his throat, and there it rested like a ball of regret comfy in its discomfort, somewhere between a scream and a fit.

This was a long, strange and inexplicable day – and, Longinus thought,
"It feels very much like the very start of something more."

He sighed wearily and then clipped his heels together to show his rigidity and unwavering loyalty to the role. Inside, his every cell screamed with pain as the blister on his neck grew, his crotch tickled and became sorer and sorer, and his knuckles became white in response to the hold on his weapon.
But, he stood strong.

He was Roman, this was his guard, and he was Longinus of Lanciano.
Honour was as important as air to him and soon, soon, the guilty would come, and his guard would really begin in earnest.

He had a job to do, and he would do it.
Heavy spear or no...

* * *

The day was drawing on, later and later, the sun higher and brighter and hotter than it had yet been. Bearing down on the backs and necks of the people, no moisture in the air, humidity all but disappeared, the day was a dry and uncomfortable heat, people waved fans made of palm leaves in their faces and sipped from full cantinas formed from animal hides.

Pilate had seen and heard much on his hike around the city. The voices of his wards and people were loud and heavy with rumour of the Jew, who had been dragged to Herod. There had been laughter from some that the prophesized Messiah was returned to the son of his mortal enemy and returned free of sin to the city and to the Romans. There was rage at the incessant prosecution of his name from the Pharisees and elders of the Jewish Council, The Sanhedrin, the voices joked of revolution and rising up – some did not laugh and spoke of this as being a genuine concern, others actively supported the idea of striking out against the Pharisees and their corrupt stance on every aspect of the day to day lives of the cities population of Jews. Talk of the Nazarene overturning tables in the temple and throwing money-lenders out on their ear, his rampage through the house of worship screaming of the impurity of these actions.
The general consensus was that Jesus was at the very least a change that the city needed, whether it was good or bad was yet to be decided, but the status quo was due a change and a shake up and Jesus had gained enough of a momentum and a reputation to have been able to maybe make moves to begin discourse and discussion to start making changes that were for the best for everyone rather than the privileged few.

His arrest had caused genuine upset and a mixed storm of emotions. Pilate heard this clear and true as he wandered, listening to the public debate and argue amongst themselves.
He watched as temple guards broke up some such meetings and dispersed the people from such talk and public opinion, warning them against rabble rousing.
He had returned to the palace, shed himself of the rags and sack

clothing and gone to bathe the day off himself, before dressing in fresh cotton robes. Now he paced back and forth in his quarters, behind the desk that he sat and filled in numerous reports to return to Rome and his superiors, listening to the chatter of his day's meetings – half a world away and errant from the boredom of the scheduling and general chatter his men made amongst themselves and with the public who demanded his time and attention.

His second in command did most of the talking, Pilate occasionally dipped in with an affirmation or negation of others comments, but his mind was on the Jews, and the Pharisees and the Nazarene now sat in his dungeon, a prisoner and a possible martyr.

The day grew longer, and when the sun was at its highest point he took the last of his meetings with the chief amongst the Sanhedrin – Joseph Caiaphas – who had brought the case of Jesus of Nazareth to him. Outspoken, bull-headed and moderately repulsive, he was disliked by his own people for being a zealot of his own faith, his face was severe, and his forehead creased as though burdened by a thousand worries. When he spoke it was louder than necessary, and his passion aroused spittle to fly from him in frenzied showers with every spat word.

The Sanhedrin was a necessary evil Pilate had to work with, keeping the Jews in line with their own laws and instructions and institutions, the Council held the peace and general self-governed, but in this instance, The Nazarene had shaken something that was clearly already broken and from Pilate's own witness on the street amongst the throng – he had heard and seen the disillusionment rife and abundant amongst the people. Pilate collapsed into his chair. Four fingers - the index and middle finger of each hand - routinely worked in circles against his temples as he fought a growing migraine that had continued to build during the course of the day.

It was Passover festival, and the streets were bursting with life; loud with shouting and laughter, angry voices screaming at each other, people bustling and hustling to and from places, markets and homes and temples.

The money lenders and the fruit sellers. The tax men and the soldiers. They all stomped and started, ran and marched and busily kicked sandy dust into the air, so the hot, dry day was an arid and barren orange. A speck of yellow in the sky penetrating with a dull and insistent drill, skin crisping in its presence, eyes screwed and scrunched up and lungs heaving with the particles of the ground inside.

It was a busy, unbearable day, and Pilate was in no mood for the priests' usual brand of self-gratiating grandeur.

"Caiaphas. Good day." He said, half standing when the priest stormed into the office.

"Good day? Good day is it, Pilate? I dare say I do not understand how this can be the case when the firebrand is still in your cells and not in Judea rotting in a pit."

Pilate gave him a look of bored resignation and collapsed back into his chair.

He flung a signed document across the desk at the priest.

"Herod found no guilt. Neither did I. Far from him being outspoken and good around people – something you could well learn to emulate – he has committed no crime, he has broken no law and I cannot punish the man for doing nothing but speaking his mind, especially when the people – be it Roman, Jew, Samaritan, Greek or apostate wanderer alike – are listening. What would you have me do?"

Caiaphas stared at the Prefect with an intensity and hatred that had always remained a barely contained entity. Pilate did not care what Caiaphas had or had not thought about him, he was concerned more with being a fair guardian of this city that was crammed with faiths so varied and myriad that he was almost always having to sidestep certain traditions or beliefs or rituals – trying so unenviably to be a man of all people and a representative for his own nation of people – which already was hated the world over, whilst maintaining his own strict beliefs and ideals. Pilate was a good man, struggling, drowning in a world of ingratitude and growing unhappiness.

"I would have you order that the blasphemer be stoned. His claim to be the Son of God, his claim of being the Messiah born, his staked claim for the throne of heaven, that he is a 'King of the Jews' – these statements and false claims will not be tolerated, he is nothing but a man, of flesh and blood and human limit and his life should be forfeited to show this to the masses of idiots who follow and bare witness giddily and blank-eyed at his words… He is a blasphemous monster, no more the Son of God than any one of those other deluded street preachers and my church will not tolerate his constant claim to the contrary.

So, Prefect Pilate, I expect you to drag him to a circle and rain justice down on him and do your job."

Pilate slammed his hands on the desk and grasping the sheet of paper with which the charges were drawn, he crumpled it in his fist as he stamped angrily around the desk to where the priest, startled and shocked his face drawn into a surprised look of outrage, stood prostrate.

"I find no guilt, Herod finds no guilt – the people are listening to his words, I cannot see a single piece of evidence he has made these claims you say he has made, not a single shred of it. His actions in the Temple were – if anything – a minor act of sedition, the riot that was spurned by its happening was quickly quelled, and there is no lasting damage – and his words were not against the Roman people but against your own churches failings and methods… Yet, he still believes, he still follows the scripture and he still preaches your own church's teachings, whether you like these or not is your own problem, Joseph but I cannot find a single thing that will allow me to stone this man to death."

"Then crucify him," Caiaphas said, calmly, taking the document from Pilate's hand.

"What?" Pilate took a confused half step back.

"I said, if you cannot stone him for his blasphemy, I want him crucified for sedition. Against the law of Rome and the Law of Jerusalem, the fact people died in the riot after his action in the temple, the simple fact he called out a catalogue of charges against the church and the state – you said yourself, this was seditious. So crucify him, and make an example to other revolutionaries that uprisings will not be tolerated.

After all, isn't that what you Romans do? Kill revolutionaries on the cross?

Or do you so quickly forget Spartacus and his ilk and how quickly one man can turn the many?"

Pilate looked at the priest, his anger dissipating, and realization falling over him like a shroud, the priest saw the look in his eyes as the Prefect of Rome understand his own lazy mistake borne of exhaustion and the unstoppable heat.

Caiaphas smiled and dropped the document on the desk, turning heel he made to the exit as Pilate rested down on the desk, leant against it with resignation, a reserved sense of failure, his hands by his side and his head downcast toward the ground.

Caiaphas looked at him one last time before taking his leave.

"Do what you know needs to be done, Pontius. Before the capital hears of this, and you are dragged down in this mire with that man… he has damaged enough, and you need not be another victim to his actions.

Nail him to the cross and let us and history forget his name."

The priest left in a brisk trot toward his temple.

Pilate sat with his eyes fixed on the back of the man, his hand had found the charges, his fist gripped tight around them as he looked at the account laid out on the paper.

He took to his chair behind the rosewood desk, wrote one word:

SEDITION.

Pilate signed his name, slowly, deliberately and with a heavy sense of self-hate, he burned his seal onto the paper.

Pilate then fell back with his hand over his eyes and his heart heavy with this simple action's importance and weight.

He was suddenly so very alone, solitary in the office, the weak wind that occasionally stirred outside crept in pushing his net drapes and allowed a blade of sunshine to cut across the desk into his eyes. As it did, the Prefect of Jerusalem cried.

Saltwater tears falling from his puffy, tired eyes like rain down from heaven.

* * *

Procula watched as the priest Caiaphas went out – he had half bowed to her in passing her in the corridor of the palace, and he stopped and smiled before carrying his hurried exit from the building.

Procula waited for him to be out of sight when she made the move toward Pilate's office. The two guards at the door uncrossed their spears and then one opened the door for her to make her entrance in, un-announced, as usual, the guards well aware of her importance to the Prefect.

Inside, Pilate was sat with his hand still on his face. Procula floated as if on air, fast and effortlessly to his side, Pilate startled at her touch on his arm.

"Procula, my wife, what are you doing here?"

She had tears in her eyes, and was oblivious to his question, as if caught in some strange and hypnotic trance she dug around on the desk and found the charge sheet, and the warrant he had signed and sealed, and passed them to her husband.

"Do not kill this man."

Pilate sat up, his gaze flitting between the papers and his wife, unsure why she was so perturbed and moved so by his case.

"What do you know of this man? Why do you tell me such a thing?"

Her eyes were red and tired, the purple and grey sagging under them gave away all he needed to know about her state of mind. Her sleep disrupted for weeks now, the last few nights so full of fits and starts that Pilate himself had had to get out of bed to sleep sat in his study. She quivered, her lips were thick set and looked bitten and sore, her fingers shook as she held out the papers. He took them and placed them down and held her hands in his own, the shaking abated a little but was still alarmingly apparent.

"Do not kill this man." Was all she could say, the tears in her eyes fell in thick streaks down her cheek, dragging the kohl and makeup she had applied some days previously and never washed off.

Pilate lead her to the couch that lay by the window and sat her down on a long comfortable chair, often used by the Prefect when he needed rest, his substitute bed for the last few nights. She sat hurriedly, and she looked at him, and half smiled, he returned the look with a charming and loving grace, and knelt by her side, kissing her hand.

He asked again.

"What do you know of this Jesus?"

""I know all," Procula exclaimed, "I dreamt of a lamb being dragged through the streets, leaving a trail of blood and of tears, people were crying as it passed. There was a procession of men, six either side of a small pathway with stone steps that lead to an altar. The final man on the left side of the procession took the lamb the final few steps and then picking it up, bloody and scared, he gave the lamb to a Roman.

This man was flanked either side by two priests, the first priest – it was Joseph Caiaphas, he gave the man a bag and inside it was thirty pieces of silver, and the man left, leaving the procession and out of the arena where the altar lay. He made his way away from his brothers on either side of the procession, to go and hang himself and with his tears he scorched his own land. The Roman – it was you, and you held the lamb aloft, and the other priest held onto a leash that held a lion, salivating and blood flecked around his mouth, his claws long and deadly, it screamed terror at the crowd, and mauled the priest alive. This was when you said that we could choose the lamb or the lion – and you would free only one amongst the people. And the people – like people do – they brayed, and screamed and hollered and they demanded the lion – and you released it – claws and teeth and foamy, bloody mouth and all back into the crowd, where it caused horror, mutilation and devastation unknown – before you gave the lamb to the priest Caiaphas, who slaughtered it in one brutal swing of an axe, killing it as soon as he had touched it."

Pilate had disappeared into some vacant place that he had never been to before, the imagery so vivid, so stark, the idea he was handing lambs to slaughter, releasing lions into crowds to kill and maim at will, the implication that he was in collusion with the Sanhedrin in any way left a bad taste in his mouth, but, regardless, this – it was still nothing more than a dream.

"What does this have to do with the Nazarene?" he asked calmly, his hands now on his lap, as he looked at his wife, her face awakening to the idea her husband did not understand or... no, worse... did not believe.

She clutched at his arm.

Hard, sharp fingernails dug into his soft skin.

His face cut into a grimace of pure pain... but inside, with her touch, he saw it all, the lamb, the lion, the altar, the blood flowing through the streets, the axe falling and the lamb's head rolling across the alter into the gutter. Blood flowed thickly from the wound, dripping wastefully off the altar.

And the crowd smiled spastically, laughing and crowing as the lion sank its teeth into them and tore them apart.

As horrific as this was, in the midst of it all, was two men: Caiaphas smiling and stood in good humour drinking in the scene in bemused ambivalence, and Lucifer, sat atop the archway that led into the arena, hugging one leg, the other dangling loosely below, crying as the lamb is taken and butchered before the crowd.

Pilate's eyes were wide open and alive with the vision, his wife let go, and it was like someone pulling a blindfold off and he was back in his own reality, his hand raising slowly toward his mouth as he realized the visions meaning.

"You see?" Procula asked, her voice low and gentle, like a child whispering toward God.

"Y.. Y.. Yes..." Pilate stuttered, his voice broken with a growing well of tears.

"What do I do?"

Procula sat up, and held her husband's head, pulling him close, his breath and tears absorbs in her breasts, she lovingly caressed his head, one errant hand running through his hair.

"The Nazarene will die. This much is certain. But it does not need to be by your hand or your choice…"

She took his head in her hands, and pulled him back, soft palms on stumbled cheeks, her eyes an unfathomable green, staring at him deeply, he swam in her gaze like a salmon in a stream.

"This man is innocent. But, all the same he will die."

Pilate knew this to be true, his own stupid slip in conversation with Caiaphas had all but consigned the man to death – regardless how it was carried out – yet, he knew he was innocent.

"We need something. Pontius, we need something you and I."

Pilate pulled himself from the watery depth of her stare and put his hands to his wife's, which still held his face.

"What, my darling?"

Procula smiled weakly, but with a defiance that often burns through history and leaves legacies scorched into books and legend.

"Simple, my husband, my love." She said, tilting her head to kiss her beloved, a deep rich kiss, full of passion and emotion, full of love and desire.

She pulled away, her lip and his connected by a single strand of saliva that formed a rope of lust between the two.

With no more than a whisper, she gave answer to the riddle.

It was obvious really.

"We need a lion." She said.

And Pilate closed his eyes and nodded.
A lion he had.

* * *

The Iscariot had made it to the edges of the fields that he had been coveting for the last two or three years. The talk with the landowner who wanted to be rid of the wasted, unused land had revealed that it was prime soil for the growth of a vineyard, where Judas had wanted to grow grape and fruit to allow him to make the wine that would give him the reputation he so dearly sought.

His love of Jesus had grown as the vines would have had he been able to take the land and run with his plans. His ambition had been put on hold just as suddenly as his obsession with the prophet Jesus had bloomed. Every word clung to, gripped tight, shared and spread, his love had known no bounds for this man, his teacher, his master…

Then came the temple.
And… The garden.

Judas sat on the edge of the fields, parched and dry, nothing much to look at, a wasteland really – bordered on all edges with dry, raspy patches of weed and boulders, sharp stones dug out of the soil, rivets of lime and granite, jagged shards of dead trees, withered and burnt by sunshine and the arid temperature.

He stared out at his beloved ambition he had held so dear and wantoned in his own mind, and he cried thick, choked-back tears of disgrace and realization that the prize he had finally gathered up and held aloft as his and his alone was naught more than a barren wreck of the Earth, that would require ten lifetimes of work to fix or make useable.

The temple had made Judas realize that maybe this mountain of piousness and purity, this reader of parables and psalms, who cured the sick and infirm, who rose Lazarus from the dead, who fed the multitude with nothing but crumbs and scraps – maybe – he was a rebel, maybe he was a broken promise, doubt had set in his mind, and the actions of the man who he had blindly followed and who he had supported, stood for and fought for – was beginning to show the terrible signs of a man who was fading, losing his way and his mind and who was raging against the ideals that set him apart. Judas had seen the smears on the mirror, which so recently reflected his beliefs and needs – and these stains on the man were not to his liking.

And the wine kept creeping back into his heart, mind and soul.

The field was always there on the horizon, home now, in Jerusalem. Back to where his ambition had been borne and to the field where he had hoped to make his name.

A name now being dragged bitter to new lows by his supposed master's antics...

And the Pharisees, the priests, the lawmen, had noticed, and suddenly, Judas was not where he wanted to be, and he doubted and he hated his place amongst the twelve.

And so, he replaced his master for his mistress and returned again, silver in pocket, to the fields.

Lucifer stood, leant against the tree. He plucked the dead fruit from the branch, shrunken and dehydrated and it fell apart, like dust in his hands, throwing the fragments of the seed to the ground, his anger apparent to the whole of creation. His fury a smouldering inferno, barely contained under his fine, sun coloured skin, his perfect brown eyes which were circled with a line of fire, now incandescent and burning freely, his hands were strong and tense, veins on the back of the hand prominent and thick, his arms bare, golden-skinned and alive with untold muscular strength, deep strength, pure and righteous strength. Like what is unto Heaven.

He watched Judas, the Iscariot, the Betrayer, the Traitor. His teeth grit tight together, his mouth a thin line of disdain, and his eyes fixed pinpoint on the man sat by the edge of the rocks, crying into his own hands.

He watched the man silently, in fearless, hellish damnation and judgment – wishing the worst atrocities in creation upon him.

And then, allowed the ether of the other side to part, and manifested his life into prominent and lurid life, imposing his will on that of the fallen disciple.

"Judas, son of Simon. I judge thee, Traitor. Liar. Usurper of your master's trust."

Judas spun around, losing his footing; he tumbled off his perch, twisting his ankle harshly. The pain was instant and unrelenting in its insistence.

He shrieked, and tried to stand to escape the man who stood, dressed in fine green robes, and golden finery. Whose face was so at odds with his elegant and rich attire, whose eyes were burning him with the merest of gazes.

"Who are you?" he gasped in a bitten back, agonal bark. His ankle was at least twisted to the point just before breaking if it was not already in fact broken. He winced in pain as he tried again to move away from the stare.

Lucifer moved forward, his hands open and palms turned outwards, in the gesture of a man about to embrace someone. From his hand, dust from the pulverized fruit fell like snow and ash to the ground. "I am like you, a follower of Jesus. So recently you called him your brother – and he called you this back – well, this makes us brothers too. My claim to this title, of course, is bound in contract of blood and kin – but this matters not, for he said those who follow him will be brothers to him all. So call me brother, and let us embrace as such."

In a fluid, astonishing movement, Lucifer was upon him, one hand on Judas's throat raising him high and supernaturally from the prone position he had fallen to a foot or so above the ground, pinned against the side of the natural stone shelf that primed itself at the top of the field, forming a natural proscenium arch with the bowed branches of the fruit tree to form a gateway into the wasteland. Judas grasped at his throat, the man's arm, cold wet slaps against the incommunicable power in the muscle of the golden-skinned Lucifer.

Judas had no defence, no counter, he prized at the hand that squeezed his throat and pounded meaninglessly on the flesh of the arm, that did not move or show the slightest bit of retreat absorbed the heavy thumps with effortless and magnificent terror. His eyes a furious, orange hue now, fire licking from the iris, held captive by the pupils that now resembled a snake's eyes.

Judas knew then that this was the Devil. His hell had arrived and judgment as it had been told to them by John the Revelator was upon him.

"My name is Morningstar. Firstborn Son of God. Brother to the host and to the spirit of heaven – who you have sold into oblivion for the sum of thirty pieces of silver."
He squeezed harder at the words, spitting each word, punctuated with a definitive pause.

THIRTY. *Squeeze*
PIECES. *Squeeze*
OF. *Squeeze*
SILVER. *Release.*

Judas slumped throttled and nearly blue in the face, his lips a deep violet colour, his eyes red from broken capillaries, the neck red and sore, mottled with bruised fingertip marks, coughing and hacking and spitting froth and foam and blood.
Lucifer adjusted his robe, ran two fine, perfectly manicured hands through his thick, sandy coloured hair, the shimmer of galaxies and supernova shone in the strands.
He knelt gently, to meet Judas eye to eye, and clicked his fingers, as if he had remembered something.
From inside his robes, Judas watched in silent, gagging terror as the man pulled out two things – a leather purse, which he jangled and smiled at.

And a slither of perfect silver, with a jagged broken edge, dripping blue fire.

"I want to kill you, Iscariot. I want to kill you like I have never killed anything before.
And believe me, I have experimented and attempted every horror you can begin to imagine in that feeble mind you have. Any horror you can assume, invent or develop – I have done and a thousand, thousand times worse. Anything you have invented is already a page in my growing and glowing book, Judas. My brother." He spits.

The bilious wad smacked Judas square in the face, his startled
expression breeding the action of one hand to wipe his face, the other
rubbing his throat still to regain life.

Lucifer had already made his move and had grabbed the
man's hair, raising up and throwing him toward the tree, which he hit
hard and flopped motionless to the ground. The air left him with the
sound of a sack of flour hitting the floor with height and weight, a
dry and ultimate sigh, loud and broken.
Lucifer threw the purse at him, and the wallet hit the slumped,
lifeless Judas hard in the head, waking him and making him shoot
back to the tree.
He sat ragged and upright, the silver coins inside the pouch spilled
and lay shining in the late afternoon sun.
Judas stared at the coins in a panic-stricken fit. His legs kicking out
to raise himself up, the hands scrambling to gain leverage to the
trunk of the tree to push himself up and run from this maniac.
But it was all for nothing.
Lucifer was upon him again, and a wet, horrendous sense of release
suddenly washed over him.

There was no pain.
It was more a sense of relief.
A gesture of tightness suddenly allowed a moment of calm, relaxed
peace.
The sound – however – was another thing entirely.

The sound one of meat smashed hard onto a wet surface.

The sound of a damp rag, being beaten with a heavy paddle.

The noise of a fish; being slapped hard and stunned against a
fishmongers slab.

Judas's bowels fell from him like rain falls from clouds on stormy
mid-summer afternoons. The insides of the man left his belly like the
coins had left the purse, suddenly and with nearly no effort, the slice

across his stomach inches deep and half a foot wide, the sudden gash enough to allow the tightly packed human offal to slip and flow from him in a wet, starkly beautiful, utterly horrifying gesture.

Judas looked at Lucifer, whose arm was still extended wide, the pose of a ballerina proud of some pirouette and spin that had been perfectly executed.

In his hand held between pinched finger and thumb the silver blade spotless but for the tiniest drop of blood – deep crimson, and putrescent, dangling from the blade's fine sharp tip, fizzing and cooking on the white-hot, deadly edge.

Lucifer closed his eyes and said a silent internal prayer for the blade's action, and the sacrifice he had just made. Before folding the blade into his robe, and turning to the coins, and gathering them one at a time, slow and deliberate, the blood and intestines of Judas slowly flowing like lava toward the coins as if they were some doomed village in the flow of a volcano.

He clutched the final coin just moments before the blood touched its edge.

"Jesus of Nazareth is my brother. His father is my father. His kingdom is my kingdom. And you have taken him from me, and you have doomed him to the hands of man who does not care for you, nor him, nor anyone on this sodden ball of sorrow."

Judas was a pale white now, his lips turning a dark purple, his eyes shallow, bags under them now clear and heavy.

He looked down at his feet to the obscene sight of his own insides now all over the floor, red and black and sinewy, his stomach a gutted hole of devastation and death.

Lucifer took his head gently in his hand and raised it to face him.

"You mean Joseph Caiaphas?" Judas said quietly, calmly, and with conviction.

Lucifer shook his head slowly, his head bowed and his mouth a cruel line of a smile.

"No," Lucifer said, and raised a single finger heavenward.

"I do not."

Judas looked up from the finger and gave a weak, revelatory smile.

Lucifer nodded and kissed Judas's forehead.

"I deserve this and more." He whispered pathetically and absently.

"And a lot, lot more." Lucifer agreed.

Like he had done with the fruit and the water and the apples from the market on his forty days in the desert with his brother, Lucifer folded in and out of space between spaces and pulled forth a rope, clean and white and taut.

He threw it to the lap of the Iscariot. Who looked up at the Angel, and gripped it, fingering the material, toying the texture in his fingertips.

"I will leave you now. My brother loved you, he really did. I saw his love for you growing more and more each day, had you allowed it would have exceeded even that of Simon who he called Peter, more so than the Baptist. But... you could not be patient and allow passage to the light and instead the sins that stain and soak your soul mean that you will be my guest for the duration."

Judas knew what he had to do; it was his own thought, not spurred or compelled on him by any other influence or person, the thought was his and his alone.

Yes, he was a dead man, but, he would rather it be by his own hand than the blade of a creature who should not be.

"I understand, your Majesty." He said toward Lucifer. Who nodded quiet and with grace to the man.

Judas had already fashioned the noose and was already putting it round his neck.

"Would you help me to my feet?"

Lucifer leant him a solitary arm effortlessly hoisting him up and embracing the man, ignorant of the gore on his robe, indifferent to the horror that they stood amongst, he pulled Judas close and whispered into his ear.

"I will fashion hooks from these coins, coins I gathered from the priests and the Pharisees – men who will see their own reward soon enough for their part in this affair. I will fashion hooks and with each hook I will stretch and suspend you, on rope made of your own belly and insides, and you will stand sentinel over the gateway to my kingdom, so each guest who walks past that threshold will see what

Hell awaits the traitors and the betrayers of love in this world. And you will apologise to each and every man and woman and child who steps foot in my land for the sin you have created. And this will be their hell as well; this will be your punishment and your reward. I have decided and will not be swayed from this accord. Do you understand me Iscariot, Son Of Simon?"

Judas pulled his arm around Lucifer, and pulled him in tighter, and embraced the Morningstar as he would of Jesus.

"For what I have done, I take this gift and thank you from the bottom of my heart and soul. Thank you, thank you, thank you."

Lucifer held his face, and they shared a glance of honesty and poignancy, and Lucifer nodded, Judas returned it, and the rope pulled tight and Judas flung backward through the air, suspended by his neck, from a length of rope that now wound itself around the branches and trunk like a snake constricting an antelope. The rope alive with some magic not of this Earth.

Suspended from high, and his guts connecting him low to the turf, Judas resembled some twisted marionette, he spun and turned slowly in the weak and meaningless breeze, and from his hand fell the leather purse.

It was now quite empty.

The wages of sin awaiting him in Hell.

* * *

"I killed four of your boys. I ripped their filthy Roman throats out and fed them to street dogs. I gutted one with his own spear and smeared his innards over a half mile of the city, carried his tongue in my purse for a week. He cried like a child, wept like a whore. Do you hear me, you Roman bastard? Do you hear me?"

Four guards dragged Barabbas to the courtyard, chains around his ankles tied tight in robe a half inch thick were his giant hands, fingers thick and strong, the palm calloused and torn and marked with scar and gristle.

The guards dragged him, resistance from the prisoner the whole way. Kicking and stopping suddenly, half falling, dropping his shoulder, the guards nearly went over with him two or three times, the guard's leader only stopped the show when one guard was slammed hard against a wall as Barabbas shouldered hard into his chest, the soldier not expecting the blow crunched against the plaster, and sandstone, he let out a huffed breath, as the air left him entirely.

Winded and broadsided, he fell hard to his knees, and Barabbas followed the shoulder with a knee, which connected just below the soldiers chin.

The solder recoiled, and a teasing line of red arched up and splattered the perfect white of the wall, and he fell down hard and unconscious. The soldier in charge came forward and drew his sword hard and hilt first into Barabbas' stomach, the prisoner buckled to one knee, the guard leader then unleashed a harsh, brutal backhanded slap across the man's face that was accompanied by an absolute silence.

Barabbas was stunned and winded, he had found that the guards were not joking around, they were not toying, they meant business, and he had better started adjusting his mood and attitude around them in accordance.

He gasped for breath and was met eye to eye by the troop leader.

"I frankly don't care what the Prefect says, if you lay another hand on my men again, I will gut you here with a piece of slate. Dull and covered in dogshit. Do you understand me, Jew?"

Barabbas smiled weakly, but defiantly, nodded.

"Good. Now get to your feet because the Prefect has need of you."

The guard dragged him high to his feet and pulled him forward. Another guard came from behind and threw the gag around his mouth, and tied it tight, Barabbas laughed at being taken off guard and unawares. Choking back a cackle of surprise.

The guard leader caught the eye of a junior soldier, pointed at the slumped guardsman, and barked two simple words.

"MOVE THAT."

And they carried on to the palace. The guards and Pilate's lion.

* * *

Jesus stood in front of the Seat of Pilate. Beside him, shackled, bound and gagged was thrown Barabbas, who sneered heavily at the Jew next to him, and snidely laughed behind the gag at Pilate, who sat, head resting on arm, resting on the high wooden arm of the chair – as he soaked in the two men in front of him.
"Jesus, Son of Joseph, Of Nazareth and Galilee; Barabbas, of Jerusalem. This is the day your judgment is signed, sealed and delivered. One of you will walk away from here today a free man, and the other will carry the cross to the Hill at Golgotha and you will rest there till your dying hour. So it has been written, so shall it be done.
The Pharisees and the court have so willed it."
Pilate looked drawn and tired, his eyes were deeply bagged, his skin had gone pale and wane, the day had affected him, his wife's word, the vision, the walk and rumours – the voices of the populace so stirred and so angry, Caiaphas' chilling threat of allowing Sedition and telling the capital.
Pilate had washed himself and his hands a dozen times since his wife infected him with her vision as if he could wash the images away. As if they were a stain upon his skin.
Nothing came of it; his skin only became red and sore.

He knew before the day was out he would wash his hands once more at least.

Barabbas choked back hard on a laugh, phlegmy and rawkus; Jesus stood silently and serenely, his face passive and emotionless. The words had flowed by him, like a river parting for a feather, floating with no danger of damage or remorse.
"Do either of you have anything to say?"
The two men looked at Pilate, silent and still, even Barabbas, his breathing heavy and his laugh suddenly muted, his face just looked

on in patient impatience.

"Nor you, Jesus?" Pilate forced the question once more.

"I cannot say anything that would change this day even should I want. It has long been written and long been decided. Let the day unfold then as it may, we all have our part to play."

"... Meaning what exactly?" Pilate asked, standing from his chair and taking a step toward the Jew dressed in a simple white robe, his hands bound in front of him, his golden skin stained by the dungeon. The eyes of the man were as impassive and calm as they had ever been.

"Meaning, that the decision has been made, neither you nor I could change it if we wanted... Our roles will become clearer soon. Worry not, Pontius Pilate; history will remember you for your good. They will remember the lambs from the lions."

Pilate looked at the man, At first a feeling of panic set in and – then - a sudden urge to slap Jesus washed over him, his hand and arm tensed and the anger rose to astonishing proportions – he hated the piousness of his words, how calmly he had taken this decision, how quietly he faced almost certain death with no argument or fear. His words lacking any sense of judgment or mockery, but said with utter conviction and calm.

He wanted to slap some sense into the man – but – resisted, and swallowed the bile down, his eyes axing downward toward the floor as he stood on to the balcony and the courtyard below.

The faces of five hundred people or more met him, crammed into the courtyard; people were reaching out way beyond the far gate, and the numbers were clearly into the thousands.

Guards were posted at every entrance and vantage point. Roman legionnaire's armour sparkled gold and red in every direction – two hundred at least – either on the wall, the balcony or amongst the crowd and beyond the yard into the land beyond the palaces gate – where the throng poured further.

The rasping and caterwauling that greeted him onto the balcony was untrue, shocking, his ears rang, and he took a half step back before moving forward.

As he did, he raised a single arm, with one finger heavenward.

"Today is the day before Passover. And, as is customary on this day we release one prisoner from our cells to face the world, his crime expunged and his sin committed to dust, to live his days as a free man from our punishment and judgment.

As is customary, we have two men, which you will choose to free – one will walk out amongst you all and the other will away to the hill. You are his jury; you are his executioner… So you will choose."

The crow let out a massive cheer, and much chatter amongst themselves ignited, pockets of supporters for one or the other man, voices deep and angry screaming to release them both a solitary voice screaming for death to the Empire – quickly silenced with a spear handle to the back of the head before being dragged out by guards. Acts of neither rebellion nor rebel being tolerated nor their errant tongues.

"The choice is between Barabbas – arrested for his role in Stasis, and the intervening riot of the temple, for assault on women, children and Roman alike. Or Jesus of Nazareth. Accused of sedition against the state. Of blasphemy and of causing the stasis of the temple with his actions against the moneylenders. Two men with similar crimes. Both facing the same punishment. One can leave today expunged of crime with your say so, and the other will bear full punishment for himself and the other.

You can choose. As is your custom as is your right."

The crowd immediately set ablaze with voice and activity, dotted amongst them were the disciples James, Simon Peter, Andrew and John.

Thomas had abandoned the city to find refuge after the altercation on the garden, his faith shaken and dented and his bravery evaporated amongst the unease and rising tension, he ran north – to find a place of solitude and try and find his courage and belief again.

Bartholomew had been taken in by family in Jerusalem and had feared so much for his life he did not take another step in daylight until long after the events of this day. James and Simon Peter and Andrew spread out amongst the crowd, and all screamed for Jesus to be released, baying and goading the crowd to take up the call, and they did.

John watched from afar, by the entrance to the gate, as a gang of workers and tradesmen booed and cried out obscenities to the call for the Nazarene. Amongst their number a Pharisee of the Sanhedrin, who was handing out wine and bread, and coin.

The men taking what they were handed with greedy eyes and broken-toothed grins, calloused hands cupping mouths and booing harder, fingers slipping coin into the folds of wallets and purses tied to belts and robes, the chief amongst them screaming—

"GIVE US BARABBAS!"

So loud and angry, so clear and demanding, the voices of the crowd calling for Jesus outnumbered and out-paid, greed-infected and pockets warm with new coin, the Barabbas crowd began shouting a rhythmic and solid catcall for the beast Barabbas.

"GIVE US BARABBAS! GIVE US BARABBAS!"

The crowd began to bloat as the push from the space beyond the gate pushed and surged, voices drowned out who called for the Nazarene to be freed.

Pilate stared at the scene in bemused, confused agony.

Barabbas – who he knew to be guilty, who he knew to be guilty of more – but could not prove, smiled at him, his eyes belying the giddy pleasure he had from a crowd calling his name.

Jesus stood ambivalent and silent, his arms in front of him, his hands clasped as if in prayer, the look of serene comfort still on his face, no smile, but his eyes calm and certain, his mouth a line of stoic indifference.

Pilate shook his head and raised a hand to the crowd.

"Do you want The Nazarene?"

A yell of approval, hearty and pure, not angry, not forceful, but of joyful affirmation.

"Do you want Barabbas?"

The crowd pushed again, more violently, the surge from the back being translated amongst those at the front as a push of confirmation, and therefore, some who had just shouted for Jesus turned tail and called for the beast instead.

A scream of several hundred men and women calling "GIVE US BARABBAS!"

Pilate held two hands aloft. The swell softened, the voices began to quiet down.

"Then I must free the man Barabbas. Whose guilt I am assured of, whose innocence was proven untrue – who committed crimes hitherto unpunished and who will commit more I am sure. You want me to free this man, who I know and you know to be a prisoner of some reputation, and you want to commit the Nazarene – Jesus, whose innocence was proven and who has been cleared twice by court and council – brought to us by the Sanhedrin, with charges of sedition against the state that is tenuous at best, regardless the evidence I have seen...

You would have me commit this man to the cross to satisfy your bloodlust, and free the guilty party?"

The Sanhedrin Pharisees looked at Pilate with perplexed rage; Caiaphas stared hardest, and with his staff he aimed a curse at the figure of Jesus.

"He is a blasphemer, a seditionist, he caused the riot at the temple, and he claims to be the Son of God... There is no innocence here!"

The crowd pushed harder forward; the courtyard was fit to bursting now, the words of Caiaphas had influenced a new chant, and the guards took two steps forward ready for crowd control measures – spears raised.

On the balcony, either side of Pilate stood Regulus and Helio. They exchanged a glance at each other and the guards on the wall, the guards on the gate, and they too stood forward flanking Pilate, hands on sword, ready to draw.

Jesus looked at the anxious face of Regulus and gave a weary, relaxed smile, and lowed his hands in a patting motion – Regulus released his swords hilt, stood up straight and looked at Jesus, as he said six calm words.

"Do not worry. It will be fine."

Regulus lay a single hand on Pilate's shoulder – a move sure to come back to haunt him with a punishment he dares not imagine, laying a naked hand on a prefect of Rome – but Pilate did not look angry, instead, he snapped back to full alertness and turned to look at the soldier.

"Sir, this is seconds from becoming uncontrollable, one of our boys will make the first move and we are looking at a wholesale slaughter of innocent civilians – the swelling is becoming a danger to us and the Jews and the rest of the crowd – Roman, curious bystander and all… If you are to release a man, do it now before this situation worsens, and we are carrying out bodies to bury."

Pilate stared hard into the eyes of the young soldier; he looked at the rough-skinned hand on his clean white robe, and he looked at the fierce eyes, tempered with calm control. At the Grecian in Roman armour who stood to his left, and then at the two men who had been displayed to be bartered for freedom or committed to the cross.

And he nodded.

Regulus released his hand and returned to the side of the prisoner Jesus.

Pilate stood forward again.

Called for his aide, and demanded a bowl of water and a sponge.

"Fine. The decision is made. The prisoner Barabbas will be freed. He is yours now; I release him back unto you."

Pilate gestured to the Grecian, who drew his sword and swiped once cleanly through the ropes on Barabbas hands, then unpicked the knot in the gag, and released this too.

Barabbas spat heavy on the balcony floor and gave a laugh of pure darkness, tar dripping from his lungs, phlegm from his throat cracked the laugh in unnatural ways.

The noise was like a knife down a barrel's side.

He laughed at the guard, the Nazarene and at the Prefect and made his way down the steps, as the crowd silently let him pass, parting as he did, the realization on faces of what they had called out for too late and dawning with no hope of change.

The swell had stopped, and a hardcore part of the crowd started calling out for Barabbas and joined him, arms around his waist and shoulders, he was picked up and carried on hands above heads toward the gateway, he span on his perch of hands and saw the balcony one last time, at the innocent man Jesus who would take his place and then his smile momentarily left him as the man smiled at him and said quietly, so he could see his mouth make the words.

"Make your life mean something, Barabbas. Make this chance mean something."

Barabbas lost his smile entirely, his eyes cracked at the awakening of his counterparts innocence and the weight of his own sin he must now try and replace with life, and he collapsed onto his back and allowed the crowd to carry on lifting him as he lay toward the gate.

Above him, on the wall, as he went under the gateway and made his appearance to the other side and freedom, he saw the figure of a man – golden skin, glowing, green robes flecked with silver, hair as blonde and as golden as the morning sunrise, his eyes a bright orange and brown that shone like a reflection of sunshine on water. The man looked sad and angry all at once, and passed a little salute to Barabbas, and said "I'll see you soon." And Barabbas demanded to be put down. As soon as his feet touched Earth he ran as far from the man and the courtyard as he could, his heart racing and his mind afire with the words and the gesture of strength and purpose the man had given not blinking, not breathing, passing the comment in a way clearly threat and clearly warning.

His skin felt prickly with anticipation, and his strength and chutzpah left him, he was empty and dry and very, very scared of the largeness of the world, the size of freedom and so he ran, until he was just another face in amongst the multitude of the crowd.

Blood on his hands the rest of his days.

Pontius Pilate watched as he disappeared beyond the gate, and the crowd cheered and regaled his escape and run to his new life. The aide returned with warm water and a sponge, oil in a small urn, scented and fragrant and also warm. Pilate removed his bracelets and bangles, his wrist guards and finery, and rolled his sleeve up, and showed the audience present. He poured the water into a basin, and poured the oil onto his skin, and then dipped his hands in the bowl and sponged them clean, showed the hands to the crowd.

"I do this every day, after I leave those gates and walk amongst you and listen to your voices, your chatter and your talk... I buy from your marketplaces, and I eat of your fruit and I listen as you all talk amongst yourselves as though you are all scholars – talking of the coming Messiah, of the man they call Jesus, of the return of the King of the Jews, the man who will lead you to Heaven… Your happiness, your gratitude that he is walking amongst you and spreading a word you have long since been spoon-fed in ways that suit only the minority and never the majority – I listen to it all.

And I give you the chance to free this man, and then you turn tail and you betray him to the hill for the sake of a man that you all screamed and demanded and petitioned that I arrest – whose guilt is clear and sinister, whose terrorism of your own ways and freedoms you ordered me to stop.

Given the choice between the man Jesus, who I hear you talk of daily – who has done so much for your meager lives – compared to the Barabbas who caused nought but pain – you chose the latter, and gladly commit this man Jesus to the cross?"

The audience stood, the crowd silent, in guilty open-mouthed stupor as Pilate repeated the routine again. Oil, water, sponge, hands aloft and turning his palms back and forth to show the cleanliness of them, he ordered the aide to take the water and oil away.

"I have washed my hands clean of the guilt of this man's blood – I gave you the choice and chance to do what I could not do myself, and you threw him to the dogs.

I have no guilt for what will happen now; my hands are clean – I look amongst your number and ask you, are yours?"

The crowd murmured and started to rustle and move heavy again, the surge was not so bad, but the bodies turned and started moving out of the gates and exits, James and Andrew, John and Simon Peter stared at the figure of Jesus on the balcony, his head slightly stooped, his face turned toward the crowd in a way that was part curious observer and part silent witness – his eyes gently wet with tears.

He looked amongst the crowd and saw each of his disciples, and smiled briefly – before Pilate ordered the man away.

Regulus and Helio took an arm each and led him out of the balcony toward the back courtyard where the trough was, underneath the barracks, toward the guard tower and the cells.

396

Pilate stood, and then slumped into his chair, defeated.

The lion free to run amongst the men, the lamb dragged to the alter for slaughter.

The faces of the Pharisees, of Joseph Caiaphas and the Sanhedrin in the bull pit below smiling up at him, Caiaphas touching his head and bowing in mock graciousness to Pilate, and they left too, the courtyard soon empty but for one or two souls crying at what had occurred. Amongst them all, Simon Peter, who had denied his Master three times before the crow of the cockerel, who had done what he promised he would not.

Jesus was gone, and the courtyard was empty, and so was Pilate. Scorched of all his strength and purpose.

The vision burnt into his bones was all that remained.

* * *

Regulus and Helio lead Jesus calmly and judiciously into the soldier's courtyard, flanked by the cells either side, a small barracks hut under the guard tower where soldiers readied themselves before their guard and in the centre of the yard itself was the ravaged, well-worn flogging post.

Two soldiers were stripped of helmet and armguards, wrists wrapped in red cloth and blood flecked and dried on dirty skin, their faces were ugly, brutish, and they carried with them cat-o'-nine-tails. One in each hand, one soldier's whip slightly longer, flecked with knots along the leather strands, the knots each held a fleck of wire.

"We are to relieve you of this man. His punishment is to start immediately, it has been ordered." The first and biggest of the two soldiers said to Helio.

"Ordered by who?" He responded, holding Jesus' arm, and guarding him behind him and Regulus – out of reach of the two cruel looking soldiers.

"Under the order of the Pharisee and Chief of the temple Joseph

Caiaphas. Under decree of the Prefect Pilate."

Regulus stood forward – his hand resting on the hilt of his short sword, he removed his helmet with the other hand and measured the man in front of himself.

"We just left Prefect Pilate, and he gave us no such order. This man is to be prepared for the hill and to carry his burden as the rest of them. What punishment are you set to distribute, may I enquire?"

"This seditionist is to be scourged. His skin is to be whipped and flayed, and he is to take the lash for his crimes in the temple and the act of rebellion against the standard of Rome. No filthy commoner can claim to be royalty and overturn tables of money lenders in the city and not expect to be punished... Especially when he is peddling anti-Roman sentiment."

"This is not standard punishment," Helio interjected.

"This is not a standard prisoner... is it? We have the King of the Jews himself here today – don't we boys?"

A cheer of blood lust and cruelty bubbled from around the courtyard – Regulus gripped his hilt to draw, and Helio held a hand to his compatriot's own – as three other centurions stood and drew their own swords.

The smaller of the thuggish guards stood forward an inch away from Regulus's own face and cocked his head left and right, a smile wide and vicious broke open on his stubbled, scarred jaw.

"Your Greek friend just did you a favour; we will let it go and forget what you just gestured to do. Just release the prisoner to me, walk out that door" - a finger pointed to the far exit, under the portcullis – "... And let's forget this ugly encounter ever happened, we all have jobs to do at the end of the day don't we?"

Regulus held the man's stare, Helios' hand came from Regulus sword to his shoulder, and Regulus looked left at his ally.

"Helio?" Was all he could say.

"Regulus, there is nothing we can do. Not for this man... Not now."

Jesus looked at the two soldiers, Roman and Greek, and he smiled and held his hands out to them both, open palm and welcoming.

"This is how it is intended to be, you two are free of guilt, walk out of the gate and know you are clean of sin. This is my path and my burden, please... No one else need suffer for my sins."

Regulus looked as though he were to say something, Helio stood forward and Jesus held his hands out once more and patted to stop, he raised his hand to his mouth and a single index finger tapped gently on his lips as he smiled and looked at Regulus.

The two guards stood forward as well – and Helio gestured for Regulus to replace his helmet, meeting Jesus' gaze he saw the pleading look in his eye and nodded.

"Regulus. No. Our parts are done. Leave now."

Regulus looked at Jesus too, his gaze said, "Are you sure?"

Jesus nodded and closed his eyes gently and smiled weakly, Regulus touched his hands and held the grip for a few seconds. Jesus held his fingers and squeezed a thank you. Regulus broke the grip and left with Helio – through the gateway, neither one looking back.

"Welcome to the pit, Messiah, my name is Terio, and this is Istamil. We will be your chaperones." The larger of the two guards barked out a vicious laugh, and Jesus dropped his head. Terio caught it and raised it again.

"We have gifts for our esteemed royal guest."

Two more guards came over and grabbed Jesus on his shoulders and dragged him backward, Istamil grabbed the fabric of Jesus' tunic robe and ripped hard, pulling the clothing from him and leaving him naked for all to see.

The other two guards slammed him down into a wooden chair, hard, lay on the chair a red scrap of fabric, fat hands grabbed the side of Jesus' head and Terio came over with a circle of bramble branches, thorns thick and evil jutting from every angle and direction.

"What is a King without his crown?" Terio's massive fingers, his monstrous hands forced the ring of thorns hard onto Jesus' head, he screamed and cried in pain.

Blood flowed immediately from his scalp and temples, dripping into his eyes, his mouth. Blinding him, filling his palette with the tang of iron.

"And your robe, your majesty!" Istamil tied the rag of red fabric hard around his neck, choking Jesus, two more hands came and hammered staples into the shoulders, fixing the red rag in place more securely, again, Jesus lashed out in ferocious agony as the rough hands held him down.

When the rag was secure the hands lifted him from the chair, and a circle of Roman soldiers pushed and slapped and punched Jesus between one another, before a final meaty fist laid him down battered and exhausted from Terio's gargantuan fist.

Blood spattered on the dry sand, combed to hide the previous victim, so the new canvas of pain could be started for all to watch from on high on the guard tower.

Istamil dragged Jesus to the centre post by hand and hair; the crown fixed in place leaving a trail of blood lining the sand. A leather tether was lopped around one hand, twin barbs in the inside of the tether caught Jesus' skin and grappled the leather tight into his wrist. The tether was fed through a loop on the flogging post and round to his other hand, the barbs on this gripped and pinched and bit. He lay on one bended knee, the red rag laying loosely by his side, stuck to his chest, as the lash thunderous cracked the sky and the first gash appeared on his back.

Jesus screamed in anguish, and furious pain, and the lashes rained down harder and faster and more terrifyingly than before, every crack ripping another line into his back.

On the other side of the city, sat in tears on the Hill of Golgotha sat Lucifer, each whip of the Nine tails caused his whole body to jolt like lightning was scourging through him, his eyes were rolled tight into his skull, his mouth dry and full of the taste of blood. His hands balled tight into fists that pounded the rocky floor of the desert with each new lash across the skin of his brother – filtered through Lucifer, who shared each and every ounce of pain.

Tears pouring from his eyes even as he convulsed in muted agony, an avatar of his brother's punishment sharing the burden and the burn. With each drop of blood from his Jesus's veins, a single tear of blood dripped from Lucifer's eye.

Jesus lay slumped on the floor, his arms stretched in ugly contortions, his fists balled tight, blood congealing around his wrists from the barbed leather tether.

His eyes rolled deep in his skull and his mouth dry and parched and full of the taste of blood.

His skin a terrible canvas of punishment and bloody violence.

From the far gateway, Pilate came in just as the lash from Terio's unholy nine-tails scourged across Jesus back, now a torn fabric of ripped gashed skin and blood, his whole body, back, neck, legs and arms were ripped to ribbons.

The soldiers and guards were spattered with blood and flesh, their faces red with exertion.

"What the Devil do you think you are doing?" Screamed Pilate from the gateway, his White Robes were at odds with the red scene in front of him, the bleached white sand now a gory pattern of red lines and splashes.

"Who ordered you to flog this man?"

Terio stood forward, clicking his fingers a guard who had been watching and laughing came running over with a shred of paper.

"You did Sir." And handed over the sheet.

Pilate read the form, saw Joseph Caiaphas name – and the order, and screwed the paper into a ball and threw it at the soldiers face.

"I gave no such order. This man was to be taken to the hill of Golgotha, and his punishment was to be put to the cross, look what you have done to him, look at the horror you have unleashed. There is no man in creation who could carry a cross now in this man's state."

Istamil stood forward, his idiot features burst into a wide smile, and he laughed.

"You'd be surprised your honour."

Pilate's hand connected hard with the soldier's face, a backhand slap that span the man around and down, laying him to his knees in one movement.

Istamil reached to his clearly broken jaw spat out three teeth onto the red sand and his eyes welling in tears, Pilate reached down and grabbed a handful of hair and pulled hard toward him.

"Then maybe I will see you flogged and carry it for him, and we can see how surprised I will be then?" and he threw the man to the floor with a violent thud.

"I want him cleaned and dressed and out of that bloody rag. I want you to get someone from the outer courtyard and have him carry the man's cross, and I want him on his way to the hill NOW! Am I clear?"

Terio nodded quickly, snapped at two more soldiers to come, Istamil lay down on the ground with his jaw in his hand, a pool of blood dripping into them from his cracked bone.

"And put this one in the cells, he will take the punishment for all of you and I will see it will leave him sure that cruelty is no mistress worth keeping."

Pilate gave Jesus one last sorrowful gaze, Jesus returned it and reached out two fingers to him and then an open palm – Pilate hesitated, his hand twitched and moved as if to take the Nazarenes hand, he swallowed down the urge and turned on his heal – his eyes welling with pained shame. Jesus held his hand out in hope, his eyes a red mass of tears, watching Pilate leave hastily from the courtyard and then, as he realized he was alone, and this was going to be seen through to the conclusion, Jesus passed out.

Pilate, in the gateway, was breathing heavy and shallow breaths, his chest felt crushed by the weight of complete uselessness - his eyes and heart full of sorrow, his mind ablaze with guilt.

* * *

Simon of Cyrene was sat on the bank of the courtyard steps. Flipping a coin between his fingers, he watched the traders and market men go about their busy business. Listened to the city scatter and move in hectic patterns all around him and smiled as the sun bore down warm and bright lighting the sand and rocks up in glittering patterns.

He smiled absently to himself. Free and easy and full of gentle humour.

From the gate came Terio and two other Guardsmen, Terio pointed at Simon, and the guardsman shouted at him.

Simon turned around nonchalantly, his life had always been a simple one, and his needs and way through life was one that had little impact on his environment or his fellow man, so he had no fear.

"Are you calling for me sirs?" He asked with a simple smile.

"Yes. Come with us." And four rough, leather wrapped hands grabbed him and dragged him into the courtyard through the gate at the far side of the guard square.

Through two corridors and a portcullis fifteen or so feet high – Simon was half carried half dragged by the Guards before he was taken into a side room, and Terio begrudgingly offered him a chair.

"What's your name boy?" He spat impatiently.

Simon was scared now.

It took a lot to scare him, having been brought up as an honest man, a man who asked for nothing and demanded even less. Simon was never caught in even the smallest storms – he kept himself to himself and seldom involved himself in anything that could drag him under in the riptide.

The sight of this blood-stained Roman, whose hands were like two shovels, whose head was like a boulder with ears and eyes and a mouth carved into it, he sat nervous and scared.

"I am Simon; I am from Cyrene. May I ask what I have done, sir?"

Terio spat out a barked, anguished laugh, dipped in cruelty and mockery.

"You have done nothing... we have need of a man, and you are all we have... I have no time to quibble or scramble around for a better to you I just need a pair of hands and a shoulder. You are it."

"For what do you need such things, sir?" Simon asked, his voice weak and cracked with unsure nerves.

"I need you to bear the cross for one of my prisoners... I will pay you three coins for it, and then you are free to go. But it is needed to be carried from here to Golgotha on the hill. It's not a question, I am not asking, I am telling you. You are carrying it, so go with these men and they will give you your cross."

Simon stood, as two hands from two guards slapped hard on his shoulders, dragging him up from the chair and out into the courtyard.

In the centre of the yard, still slumped on the ground where he was now being cleaned down with damp sponges and washed clean of the whip's punishment, was Jesus. Simon saw the man and the blood and horror scattered across the yard, he spied the two cat-o'-nines hanging bloody and horrific from the far wall, he saw the guards around still smirking at the recent horror that was unleashed here and he immediately went to the man, shaking off the grasp of the two guards who had held his shoulders.

He shook them off him and staggered over and fell to bended knee as he took the man Jesus' hand and held it tight as he grimaced and groaned upon the water touching the wounds on his back.

"Sir, what have they done to you?" Simon asked, holding Jesus lovingly in his hands.

"I am here to be punished, worry not about me or my flesh… it was made for this day."

Simon looked at him and felt the man squeeze his hand tightly and with grace, Simon gently smiled, and looked at the guards.

"This is the man whose cross I must bear?" The guards nodded. He looked up and saw the face of Terio staring out at him from the window of his office.

Simon pointed at the man of the floor being tended to roughly and carelessly by two young guards.

"I carry his burden gladly… and may God above carry it with me as penance for allowing such brutality and terror upon this Earth."

Terio smiled. His lash had drunk thirstily today, no doubt it would again soon.

He imagined it licking at the skin of this whelp of a man in front of him…

Maybe one day, he thought, maybe one day.

And he waved Simon of Cyrene out of the yard toward the cross maker, and onwards toward the Hill.

Jesus was raised to his feet, and Simon helped him toward the Hill as well, carrying the man on his hip step by step as well as the Burden of the wood on his shoulder.

Terio watched them go.
He disliked the hill; he disliked the stench of the dead and the filth of
the flies and decay of the bodies old and new.

His love was the scars he scorched and scourged into the flesh of the
alive and living.
A signature he signed into each back before sending his masterpieces
off to the plebs and soldiers who walked the hills and its encampment
below.
His was the city, and as far as he was concerned it was just another
satisfied customer leaving his workshop to the cashier at Golgotha to
pay their dues.

He could not help but be happy this one was finally out of his hands.
Crown upon his head.
Signature prominent and raw upon every inch of his spine.

* * *

Lucifer fell back into reality and to life from his trance upon
the final whiplash snapping down on his brother's back. As he did
his eyes rolled back into focus, and the whites became spherical
globes pierced with thick brown and fiery orange iris, a trickle of
blood ran from his nose, he raised his hand and caught the first few
drops – looked down and examined the fluid.

It had been some time since he had seen his own blood.
It was a fascinating pearlescent red, oily and full of shimmery life.
He smiled a false smile, his eyes not convincing, his mouth betraying
the anger it stored behind itself.
As he looked up, knelt facing him was Death. From a
distance the two men could have been mistaken for siblings, both had
long blonde hair, Deaths was a bleached, aged white, his skin was a
finer, smoother and paler hue to Lucifer's golden radiance, his limbs

405

were a little lankier, longer, weaker looking. Lucifer's were taut with strength silently rippling throughout, the definition clear and concise. Deaths eyes were a pale azure blue, with a green halo, Lucifer's fiery brown with an orange corona. But… they held so much similarity you could have sworn they were of one blood.

And no one was to say they were not.

Lucifer smiled, Death gently let his head loll to one side, and he simply stared back, his eyes twinkling with curiosity and envy.
"I have never learned to smile. It bothers me even now to this day. Humour and mirth seem to escape me eternally… maybe they will be the only thing that ever escapes my grasp."
"Maybe Lord Mort. Maybe. Though… knowing you like I do… I doubt truly anything will ever get away from your gaze or grasp. If you were not named Death I imagine you would be named Determination, for never before has anyone had as much of it as your good self."
Death brought his head back up and lolled to the other side the slightest fraction.
"You are too kind Master Morningstar. I thank you." And he stood and bowed curtly, touching his forelock and temple and crossing a leg behind himself.
It was a genuine balletic gesture that was received with gratitude by the firstborn.
"My pleasure Lord Mort. You know how you have ever been in my favour."
Lucifer stood, and offered a hand to the elder paler man, who looked at it absently, a pause that lasted eons, before taking it and they embraced in a tight hug.
Lucifer grabbed Deaths back – who copied and followed the gesture, and then they parted still holding each other arms.
"It is truly good to see you," Lucifer said to his compatriot, the ferryman of gods and men to the world beyond this world.
"Aye. It is. Come, Morningstar, we have much to discuss."
"That we do cousin. That we do."

And the two men walked toward the mount.

* * *

The Cross had been taken from the cells through the streets toward the hill where over a dozen men had died upon its bough now. The rough splintered timber had been treated with wax and liniments and oils. It had been chiselled and carved and carried and borne on shoulders and backs, carried by cart and by soldier, slave and slaver too. Back and forth from the courtyard and the palace through the Jerusalem streets to the top of the Golgotha hill, where, on the mount – Fourteen men had died upon its wooden spine.

The busy activity today had seen the previous tenant taken down, dead and rotten, scorched and dried by the sun, to allow new occupants to take residency. The cruellest and most violent of Roman evictions; The most barbaric and brutal of all rentals in the city.

The cross had been unearthed and carried on cart dragged by two donkeys back to the palace to be treated and cleaned once more, and then to be designated to its occupant. This particular cross had, in its time, been home – albeit temporarily – to a murderer, a rapist, three adulterers and a plethora of innocent men who deserved much more than to die upon its wood, legs broken and sides pierced by Roman lance.
Still, its wood carried on and bore more bodies and blood and returned back and forth from palace to hill, palace to hill and palace to hill again.

Pilate had made sure that this cross was marked clearly for the man Jesus and had given to the cross makers a placard that stated the four characters INRI.

JESUS OF NAZARETH - KING OF THE JEWS.

Whether as a comment on the crime he was not committed for, or as

407

a comment on his Jewish underlings – or, as a concession to the Sanhedrin's power and influence, it was not clear nor did it matter, it rested in the sun, waiting for its owner to come and carry it, crown and sign and robe and all, to the hill once again.

When there the man would be nailed and bound to the skeleton of the cross, erected with their backs to the setting sun, so that they would catch it rising again the next morning and there to hang and to bake, cook and die in its radiant and heavy light.

Like Lucifer his brother had been born, so would Jesus die in the light of the Morningstar.

Lucifer could not stop the actions about to happen any more than he could stop the will of gods and men. His power was in influencing and enticement through negotiation and discourse. His greatest asset was an unwavering honesty, a break-neck ability to tell you the exact thing he was thinking with no fear of remorse or consequence. The men broke their own wills, Lucifer merely provided the hint of truth about how things could be better if only they were brave enough to take the step into mystery, the men were never pushed, they fell.

The wills here in play though were more powerful than any he had previously attempted to bend and influence with his unwavering confidence.

Most potent and inaccessible of them all; Jesus, himself.

There had been a time that Jesus had spoken to Lucifer and had listened to the words and musings he had to say – then, as if overnight – he stopped entirely. Lucifer never once tempted him beyond what would be reasonable by the situations standards, nor had he haunted or hurt, lay finger upon or betrayed anything Jesus had confided in him. Not once did the Morningstar speak or influence a Disciple or an Apostle.

Even as he sat in the garden of Gethsemane and watched as the lawmen came in and broke up the supper, Lucifer allowed it all to take place and happen. Tears welling in his eyes as he watched his stupid half-brother doom and damn himself to these cowards and liars.

Death, it had to be said, watched the happenings occur paying more attention to Lucifer than he did anyone else. In Lucifer, he had met someone of the Pantheon of gods and deities who was completely ambivalent to his fate. He knew exactly where he came from, he embraced his spirit and acted like one of the men he often walked amongst.

Death had long admired his brazen wit and passion. The way he had fallen with grace and landed with his feet very much on the ground like a cat. His doom at the hands of his estranged brothers – especially Michael, who had been such a cowardly, prideful boy – had long struck a chord with him.

Having walked countless gods into the ether between our world and the shadows – each begging and crying to be spared, he already knew that if his day came Lucifer would skip merrily into oblivion and make a joke as he fell in the spaces between spaces.

Such was his power.
Such was his way.

Death watched Lucifer crying in the garden for the man who he loved above all his other siblings, who was so clearly on a path of self destruction no voice on Earth could talk him away from – and he had felt a cold pang of sadness in his chest – a feeling Death had never experienced before, for a man he had never believed could inspire any feeling or emotion from anyone – let alone a celestial being of such infinite power as Death.
Yet… he did.

Death had a plan then and had intended to share it with the Morningstar at the first opportunity. Even as pieces of the chessboard were being set and lain out for the next game, even as this one was winding down.

Death had decided that this cycle of lies and liars was no longer worth his time and it was time to start a different game.

Throwing the cosmic chessboard across the ethereal plains and smirking down the infinite vortex of destiny.

Lucifer and Death had walked the short distance to the top of the hill and watched as the cross was carried on the shoulder of the Cyrenian. Watched as he held the burden on his back with gravity and silent effort, whilst still holding an arm around the waist of Jesus himself, staggering and tripping, bleeding and dying even as he walked toward the mount.
Lucifer and Death watched silently stood sentinel, and the procession of prisoners and soldiers paced and stomped the dusty trail toward the killing grounds.
Lucifer had a tear in his eye, the residual connection between he and his brother was still alive, and each step coursed through him,
Lucifer acting as a filter to draw some of the pain away and give his brother the help toward death he could not give him toward life.
Jesus, for his part, seemed unaware of this gesture – or – welcomed it with his usual silence when Lucifer was involved.
Without the help, without the support – Jesus would have been dead already.

"I want to change the terms of the game. For too long I have watched as your father makes mockery of the souls of this globe, the siblings who laugh and goad you from their pedestal in the heavens, the scriptures that belittle and spread untruths about you and your nature. I propose a new game – one with new rules, I would like to see you on the throne, the more I see you amongst these people, the more I believe that this is no kind of life or world for them... with you on the throne I can imagine a better place, a better life... I can imagine, for once, freedom."
Lucifer turned and looked at Death, his face blank and emotionless, not shocked not surprised, ambivalent to the core. The Morningstar way.
"I appreciate that you have such faith in me and my nature, Lord Mort, but I could imagine nothing more terrifying and terrible than that throne and its corrupting power.
If I had my way, I would see the whole damn seat on fire in the

garden for the entire world to see burn."

Death stood quiet and still, his arms behind his back, no motion or life in his skin or limbs.

"If I had my way, Lord Death – Shepherd of life. I would see you upon the throne if I had to see anyone on the thing at all.

I can see no one better.

You have never harboured any desire for it, you have walked and wandered and experienced every facet of the human condition, from opening breath to final sigh, and you have never once wavered in your duty.

There is no one more deserving of the throne and the crown and the seat on high watching over this mistreated flock than the man who is there at their start, their middle and end... someone who has power incalculable and yet never uses it for good nor bad. You are more a god amongst gods than I have ever seen, my lord."

Lucifer turned and pointed at the procession and the cross now rising high as Simon of Cyrene took it to his shoulder once more and shimmied closer and closer with Jesus at his side, staggering, bleeding, dying on his road to ruin.

"You are the true King of this universe, Lord Mort. And I can think of no one better to take the seat and rule this world and the countless others as it was intended, not like some ant farm that is boring you already."

Lord Death – Chief amongst the riders looked at the man stood next to him.

Lucifer smiled his wide, welcoming smile.

"I am not a King, sir. I am and always will be a servant fumbling my lines and stumbling through this life with good intentions I later use to pave my way back to hell. But you... You are a king."

Death looked at the man.

At this Demi-God.

This Golden-skinned, golden-haired Archangel – firstborn son to a hapless, errant father, elder brother to seven worthless and spoilt brothers and guardian to a half-brother who even now threw himself upon a sword of his Fathers creation.

He looked at Lucifer, then at the Nazarene bleeding and suffering, blistered and beaten, scourged and lashed, a crown of thorns stuck sharp into temple and bleeding into his eyes.

He felt the pain filter and flow from the first born son at his side, and swelled with pride and genuine love for the man and then… he held out a hand toward Lucifer, who took it without thinking.

"I accept."

Said Death.

And he smiled wide and openly.

White pearly teeth inside a mouth of Rose Red. His eyes twinkling in Azure Blue.

He smiled for the first time in his entire existence, and it froze the clouds in the sky and the winds in the treetops, and it dazzled Lucifer as though it were the morning sun rising out of the ocean.

"I will be your King."

And at this, Lucifer Morningstar, Firstborn amongst the host – disenfranchised, cast out and exiled rightful heir to the throne smiled as well.

His plan was coming together as he had hoped and expected it too. Each piece falling into place one after the other, after the other.

His influence and his pride panged as hard as the filtered pain from his half-brother's flesh.

His end game was almost here.

The Morningstar's day was dawning…

* * *

CHAPTER SEVEN
Nothing Lasts Forever...

"It's hard to be done a favor by a man you hate.
It's hard to hate him so much afterwards.
Losing an enemy can be worse than losing a friend,
if you've had him for long enough."

— Joe Abercrombie, *Last Argument of Kings*

The temple was dark and silent but for the creaks and the groans of the ancient rock being pushed by the winds. The night sky was a blue sea of cloud and occasional star, and – but for the flicker of the torches that lined the stone stairwell – the main hall was obscured by darkness and existed in a calm stillness.

Sat amongst the emptiness, in a chair that was made of a rich oak wood and bore a beautiful carved antler from the back rising high in the air two or three feet, casting a shadow like a crown over the room, was Zeus.

In the years since the garden, he had watched, as the Earth was carved and torn in new directions and shapes by the humans upon it. Each one pinning their hopes and dreams, their wishes and their prayers to the mast of one god or other.

Zeus looked on as Eden was taken in a great tide of fire, scorched and erased from the world by a God who did not cope well with losing at the game he had set in motion.

Adam and Eve had been driven west, exiled from the paradise and the isolation of the garden. She gave birth to twin boys and then a further son, she and her husband watched as they grew up and became strapping lads mingling with the flock of other gods, watched as desires grew, tensions became taut and frantic and one son fell to the other's hand – opening the world to a new concept called murder.

Zeus watched hungrily as this became an art-form that some humans excelled in much as their angel masters had before in the halls of Heaven and the garden exile. New and monstrous ways to kill developed and war became a wholesale industry.

Armies grew overnight, industrious in their creativity and flair for pain; the land soon became a savage playpen to vicious apes and violent wandering clans of killers.

Soon, Cain was worshipped by some as a god incarnate for showing the act and utilizing its power first, the progeny of Adam shared blood with the humans of the western gods, and the earth burgeoned and swelled with mouth and fist.

Zeus bore witness to it all.

From in his throne room, he had sat, idle, soaking up the adulation and the love and worship from his carved lands. He greedily sipped and swigged from his goblet, and voraciously ate from his table of worship and, for a time, he was the most powerful of the gods in the pantheon of Heaven.
His table overflowing with tribute and feast as his followers desecrated tribes and villagers of other non-believers, the lesser gods fell by the handful at a time as their buffets dried and festered, the people falling and the worship drying to a powdery nothing. He would leave his hall and he would lay in the beds of the women of Earth, creating in his union half god, half men who would bolster his legend by adventuring and taking odysseys and journeys throughout the land, their mythical progenitor always following spreading his power far and wide.
But soon – even these half gods fell. As all gods do.

In this time, Zeus and Death became well acquainted.
War would stride in and smile broadly, the undeniable madness behind his eyes clear for all to see, as he laughed and watched as whole nations fell and whole civilizations were wiped from the map.

During this time Yahweh had become deeper isolated from his brethren. Keeping to his lonely hall in Heaven, his remaining sons his bodyguard, delivering message and miracle to his small band of followers. Keeping to a single name, and allowing his existence the bare minimum to survive; not yet to thrive.
Zeus was unaware that Yahweh's plan was not in feeding his ego to the humans, but, instead, allow the humans to fight and create amongst themselves schisms in the belief.

A disagreement here, a difference of opinion there…

Soon, his table began to grow with tributes from varied and increasing numbers of people who would identify and pin their flag to his mast.
They alone had found ways to carve Yahweh's name into different ideas and thoughts – the isolated God realizing that the creative capacity of the human to kill and build walls and weapon against their fellow man was almost unstoppable.
Yahweh became the God of many names without ever having to call himself anything different. Just as he had coveted the power to be the God amongst gods, so did the humans and their ravenous need for knowledge, power, their insatiable hunger for war gave him everything he had craved – without him raising a finger to need to make it happen.

The Riders of the Apocalypse learned of their power at this time as well.
With War came hunger, thirst, need, desire and greed.
Those who had supplies had them all, those who did not, were barren, famished and stripped of dignity alongside the flesh.

From the ether, the mists of the eternity beyond, where her brother had journeyed, Famine appeared. Bedecked in a fine cream satin, her perfect, beautiful body soon taking ripples and creases in the skin, as she suffered alongside her charges, only to heal and bloat with the furtherance of their starvation.
Her flesh became obese and darkened red from tight corset and lace.
From bangle and belt.
The riders were three now – War, Death, Famine.
Soon their fourth came as Pestilence was passed into being from the domino effect of his three siblings.

These creatures who were not gods, but who walked amongst and rested upon the shoulders of gods were the middlemen between this world and the various constructed other worlds beyond the veil.
Worlds that humans had developed and designed.

One such world supposedly held Lucifer, welcoming everyone who had sinned unrepentantly into its doors and walls. Fallen angels, stripped of halos grace and wing, walked and lived and died amongst the humans, each one talked of the Hell that Yahweh and his many names had built to house and imprison the Morningstar.

The stories took shape, became legend, power grew like shoots on the vine, and the godhood of Lucifer truly began, as his name became synonymous with the heavens and the last days. Hell became a horror story of torture and of pain, a temple of vicious delights that satiated the fallen prince of heaven.

In reality, it was an isolation and absence of light. A prison no more or less.

Lucifer could not see the reality of the world outside, just had fleeting glimpses of the developments as painted on a stained glass window.

Seeing gods fall and be carried out to the door to the world beyond, watching the fall of islands and cities, towers and men as the Earth broke down into chaotic and bestial appetites. Much of which he was blamed for, and though this worship – as false as it was – swelled in his belly and his heart, it left him dull and powerless in his prison.

Zeus was in a prison too. Always ten steps and moves ahead, he saw the world turning, saw the humans falling into their idiot routines, and saw how Yahweh had bided and waited and how his sons – those who survived – were making moves and greetings, taking sojourns to Earth and influencing the people into his way and name, swaying the minds and hearts of the great unwashed against the ways of other gods and to the path of Yahweh.

The humans aware of his many names, and choosing to develop beliefs and traditions for this various aliases that Yahweh no longer used but had never relinquished.

His strength growing from trickled reserves to vast oceans.

His name complicit on the tongue of most monsters and leaders of the worst kind of armies on the land – each one pitted and spat against the other.

Even as his own people fought and brayed and killed the other for a tiny difference in the complexity of their worship or belief, Yahweh tasted victory with each fallen soldier, woman or child.
His star ascending even as Zeus watched his best-laid plans and greatest warriors and men die at the hand of the followers of Yahweh's many armies, many people, many factions. Zeus watched in righteous, hungry madness as he realized this was Yahweh's plan all along.

Not to force his name across the world, plotting to destroy the world by taking on his brothers and sisters in a violent and bloody confrontation.
But to slowly plant seeds of his defeat in Heaven, and watch as the whispers distort and change with each retelling, mutating and building into legends that acted as fodder for his ego and belly, each half truth and outright lie, each rumour and each whispered question about the truthfulness and correctness of the facts and stories going some way to feeding his vast desire and hunger. His plan all along to cover the Earth in those who did and did not believe who argued for and against his existence, watching the people tear themselves apart whilst denouncing old gods and building Yahweh into a new form of his old self.

Zeus and his gods of the Pantheon dying and dead, few remaining on scraps and morsels, others wiped from memory and existence escorted to the world beyond or the cells to await their sad, lonely demise.
Whilst the riders four grew in stature and in strength, and the many-named God of the East sat smug in his tower atop the world watching in boredom and ambivalence as war after war, battle after battle and death after pathetic death secured his place as the deity above all others.

Zeus watched and sat alone in his cold, broken, shattered palace. Waiting lonely for Death's hand to clamp down coldly to his

shoulder and whisper.
"It is time."

Hoping more and more day after the next that it would happen soon.
Ready for his goodbyes and his final walk to the edge of tomorrow.
Happy he had made a stand when he did.
Satisfied his legacy had been protected in Lucifer.
Sure his revenge would be one that would be unexpected and pure of
intention, and for the benefit of the greatest of the humans at large.

Zeus watched the clouds roll overhead, the sad, somber flickering of
the flames on the torches in the stairwell, and the stars popping from
behind the blanket above and making themselves known in the
heavens.

Zeus waited.
Beckoning and welcoming Death and his family for a final powwow,
before his inevitable demise.

* * *
- 2 -

Pestilence had walked the halls of the hospital invisible and
untouched for hours now. Countries were dying at a rate of thousands
per day from disease and famine, Pestilence and his sister mopping
up after his brother War had started great tidal shifts in these
backwater civilizations. One civil unrest destroying thousands of
lives in hours. Burning down homes and towns, throwing weak, poor
and hungry onto dirty, unkempt and violent streets. Infection taking
hold and boosting the famine, famine taking effect and feeding
infection.
Together they were a formidable team.
However, Pestilence preferred these quiet days where he could walk
undeterred, unquestioned through the halls of some small town
hospital, some inner city surgery, and spread his wares and his
influence on the building in small, personal flourishes.

Today he had sat in on an appendectomy, leaving a suture and stitch just a little too loose, allowing bacteria and germ to settle in and make home. He had stroked door handles and seat armrests – leaving streptococcal and MRSA on surfaces far and wide. He coughed into water filters and stroked the buttons to elevators and lifts leaving his gifts for mankind everywhere.

Sickness was spread throughout the building, if only 1% of his exertions this day gave return, it would be worth it.

He smiled and gagged back a laugh, a nauseating rattle of cough mixed with his laughter, the inside of his chest sounded like a stone sliding around inside a tin can.

A thick, raw, wet sound with a metallic rasp.

As he was walking from the building, he crossed paths with a couple going into the hospital. A young pregnant woman of about 30 years of age, and her beau, a shuffling man with glasses, fair auburn brown hair, his walk somewhat lazy and his feet never really leaving the ground, he waddled with a faint comedy as he held her hand, and they entered the hospital toward the prenatal wing.

There was an unblemished beauty to the woman: she was happy, her skin was untouched, unmarked, her teeth white and her thin pink lips were bursting with health and goodness, Pestilence was shaken by her presence and watched her go, the man turned and a second of eye contact – impossible he knew, but sometimes looking in the right place with no knowledge can lead to these meetings of minds and lives.

Pestilence saw the charm and goodness in the man, and within him an inexplicable anger rose. This perfect specimen of woman partnered with this shuffling, bumbling man felt like a gross waste of opportunity and life to the Rider.

He turned around and followed the two into the hospital, and into the prenatal unit for her ultrasound.

As she walked through the door with the man, Pestilence took heel and went to follow – until a hand was slammed hard and forceful into his chest and built a barrier to his entrance.

Invisible and unknown he may be, to all but one of his siblings. Even gods could not see or interfere, but, Death – the first and most powerful of the Riders, he could see and touch, question and stop anything.

The pale, anemic colour of the hand, the ripple of muscle, the strength behind the push – Pestilence knew immediately that his brother was here.

"Not that one." Death said, forcing Pestilence through the doors, hard and sharply he pushed him against the wall and applied further pressure to his brother's chest.

"Not her, not him."

Pestilence brushed his brother's hand away and went to walk toward the door once more, a half smirk on his face.

Death pushed harder back and the thin, lithe body of Pestilence slammed hard and loud against the wall again. Death's hand moved from chest to throat and wrapped joyfully, and with inarguable authority around the windpipe.

"And, not the baby." He shoved up harder and squeezed, Pestilence raised an inch or two from the floor and held his brother's thin, powerful arms trying to loosen the grip.

"Do I make myself clear, brother? You are not to touch, look or follow. You do, and I will see you walk the long way to the other side. Am I clear?"

Pestilence nodded, but his face still wore the awkward, hungry, leering smile.

Death squeezed harder still.

"Why do I not believe you? Why do I feel you are lying to me?"

Pestilence gagged, a dribble of spit flashed from his mouth to Death's hand and evaporated upon touching him, a puff of sulphur and smoke, and it disappeared.

Pestilence stopped smiling as the throat creaked and groaned as though it were to give up and collapse.

He tapped Death's hands and raised his in a surrender, and nodded again.

Death slowly released his hold of the creature, lowered him, and then tidied his brother up, wiping the lapels and fixing his brother's tie.

"You should leave now, and not come back to this place. Forget you ever saw her, or him, forget the baby in her womb. You leave, and you do not look to them again. Are we clear? Or so help me... I will allow War to cleave you clean through and throw your carcass to the oblivion of the void."

Pestilence coughed hard and thick, a wad of terrible fluid spat from his mouth to the floor, yellow and red, green and black.
He looked at his brother Death, and smiled weakly, an attempt at swagger and cockiness that was ruined by his weary legs and his crushed larynx.
"Good to see you too, brother." He managed to gag, a rasp of hard consonants and spat vowels.
"Well met." And as he turned around he exploded into a burst of green smoke, dark and acrid, as the world opened around him, and he took flight to one of his other theatres of illness.

Death watched the smoke fade and die, and turned to the window of the prenatal ward. He walked through the solid door, like a spectre on the wind; he floated through nurse and patient who stood in his way, a cold flutter shaking over each person's flesh, as though someone had walked atop their grave.
Death stood, facing down upon Kay and James, the man stroking his wife's baby bump, bigger now, wider, bursting with life, soon the child would be here.
Soon the game would begin again.

* * *

Death followed them for days. He mirrored their every movement, watching, witnessing. He followed the Edmunds family with one keen eye on the peripheral to see if Pestilence would do as commanded, or – as had been his way with countless other humans – his weak obsession had burst into a flowered bouquet, heavy and

422

thick with need and sick desire.

Thankfully Pestilence had never shown.
In truth, he was too ill to do so. Superbug resistant antibiotics had taken effect on MRSA, the new slow release of cancer treatments that were being drip-tested in Africa were showing amazing results and data, paving the way for new, fierce spin-off treatments that could be unwound to profit beyond dreams.
Ebola had proven to be beatable, AIDS research had taken a vast giant leap forward with preventative medicine now becoming so good that - though it did not kill the disease itself – it certainly aided with the victim's recovery and dealing with the effects, aiding a longer life with constant upkeep of the drugs.
Pestilence had taken to walking to halls of hospitals as a distraction from his own failing standard. The warzones that would be so fruitful and bountiful to him in recent memory were fast becoming overrun with peacekeepers and aid stations – new treatments and charity raised aid and medicine overflowed into these countries and the rider of sickness found his plate becoming less and less filling, and he had taken to consuming morsels from wherever he had been able to find them.

Death had seen something though in this degeneration of his youngest brother.
The game had been in stalemate for years since the cross on the mount. Everyone expecting Jesus to be some fierce warrior, instead, Yahweh had unfurled a new aspect to his game. Murdering the son he had lined to be his heir, as a cheap and tactless way to bolster word and legend of his own name.
Lucifer had stood and watched the murder of his brother – who he had held so dear, above even his twins from the host. The Fallen Lord of Paradise, now King of Hell had said to Death that the universe and all of creation needed new guidance, new leadership, and new direction.
Lucifer never wanted or desired the role of creator – he stumbled into the part through his choices and his need for independence from a father who was mad and angry and fighting every sane decision of a

423

council of his peers – his need and hunger for power and love undermining his reputation, Yahweh had been planning his final act for sometime. His son was to take his two thousand years upon the seat and reshape the world in his own image, but Yahweh was to unleash some madness before this took effect.

Death had designs on the throne himself.
But…

So many worlds had been and gone before.
So many cycles of life and death. Of fear, pain, war, famine and pestilence.
He had seen his brothers and sisters be born and die a thousand, thousand times. Had walked the beach as the same mistakes and egos took control and the world came to its crushing end - bit by bit by bit from the hands and desires, hearts and hungers of gods who did not deserve the crown.

Death was slowly plotting, and this family had been his key to tomorrow.
The throne was Death's should he want it…to do with as he saw fit, and to use as he so desired.
Lucifer refusing claim, no doubt with some plan of his own, some selfish reason for laying appreciation, worship and tribute at the foot of the Black Rider.
Death was not stupid and had seen every betrayal imaginable, but something about the boy had always given him a glimmer of hope he was different from the others, different from the players who tried and failed and fell before this world.

Death hoped so anyway.
He had plans for him in the endgame that was impossible without his power.

The Edmunds, soon enough, would be drawn into the board, moved into position, and the start to the end would begin.

The sunshine was warm and the skies blue. Once in a while a brisk gust of wind would bluster and blow and calm the tiresome heat down, adding much needed relief to the air, but, all in all it was a good, old-fashioned, British summer day.

James had packed up all his belongings, his books and his comics, his clothes and his toys. He had said his goodbyes to the few kids left on the estate he spoke too. Had made his way to Michael's father's house and said a final goodbye and an apology to him, Michael's father shaking away his apology and offering a hand to James – knowing full well how his son had grown into a loose cannon, obsessed with his own standing amongst the kids, selfish, arrogant and angry. The death of Poppy had been a bolt from the blue and had meant Michael was now in a secure home, being looked after for a time. His father had a sadness about him that was apparent from the moment the door opened. A grey jumper on and dark blue jeans, his hair had grayed thanks to the incident and aftermath, his eyes were baggy and heavy. He had been a fun, chirpy man before Michael brought this horror to his life, now, he was serious-faced and sad-eyed, and he had an air of distraction about him.
Michael had been in St. Joseph's Borstal for six months and he would be there for the foreseeable future, too young for prison, not insane so unable to be put in hospital for psychiatric care, so it was instead a young offenders' institute. His sentence was one of her majesties pleasure. His release entirely dependent on future parole hearings and psychological assessment.

Michael's crime of voluntary manslaughter – death through negligence and violent actions, not intended to kill, but leading to the death of an innocent party – was witnessed and seen by over a dozen children and one adult who had excised James from any involvement or blame.
Ruining more lives than just poor Poppy's - her parents were sad,

nervous wrecks – James' parents had decided to move and get as far from the estate as possible, and Michael's father was an exiled, pariah of a parent. Despite him being a good father, on the whole, and having brought Michael up properly, instilling discipline and drive in him. Ambition had taken care of the rest and turned his son into a killer, whether he had intended or not.
The act was still the act.

James shook Michael's father's hand and wished him well, and hoped that his world became calmer soon. The man thanked James and wished him well also, never blaming the boy for Michael's actions, nor his mistakes.
And James left to Poppy's mother's house to say thank you and goodbye to them as well. He was met with a tender hug and a small kiss upon the cheek. He shook Poppy's father's hand, took the playful ruffle of his hair and he promised he would say goodbye to Poppy one last time before he left – to which they thanked him and hoped he had a good time, settled in fast and enjoyed his new school. James nodded, and made his excuses, leaving behind the estate and his home for the last 15 years.
He made his way to the graveyard, walking the usual way through the fields, over the turnstile-like kissing gate, over the troll bridge and past the slopes to where St. Lawrence's church was – his backpack on his shoulder, and inside his usual picnic of orange juice and weak milky tea, biscuits and an apple. He also had a copy of THE SILVER CHAIR by CS Lewis, the one he had been reading on the horrible, fateful day. His intention was to leave it there for Poppy, as a thank you and a way of saying he would never forget her.
When he arrived he was met by a man, tall, thin and pale skinned in a dark suit, almost black but for a deep rich flicker of blue –like an ocean lapping at a beach at night – in the fabric. The man was stood over Poppy's grave, pale white blonde hair tied back on his head in a tight bun, he was talking to the grave.

James thought best to not pull attention to the fact, nor interrupt, and made way to walk around and sit down waiting for the man to leave. But. The man clocked him as he entered and called him straight

426

away.

"James, is it?"

James stood still, one hand on the gate post, a single foot in the yard itself, he was caught unawares and surprised, his lips moved, but no sound escaped.

"James Edmunds?" The man asked again.

James nodded and found his tongue again.

"Erm… Yes… That's me, sir. May I have your name?"

The thin man looked at James and smiled thinly and mirthlessly. His smile was not nice to look at; it was awkward and looked as if it hurt to make.

James' stomach involuntarily gurgled its displeasure.

"I thought so. The Reverend told me all about you. You look exactly as he said you would."

James nodded, not knowing whether this was a compliment or a good thing; he nodded agreement regardless.

"May I take your name, sir? And ask how I can help?" James mustered some courage from deep within and stepped into the graveyard.

"My name is Mortimer. I am the groundsman. Fix up these gardens, tidy these graves, and cut the grass and such. Do it to make the place look tidy like. But, rain or shine, whatever I do, young Poppy here always seems to have a lot of activity. Birds tend to like her gravestone, always has flowers or gifts on top, her parents have told me a young man comes quite often and reads to her, leaves gifts and morsels for the birds.

I assume it's you, as we don't get many kids in here with no reason."

James smiled. He liked his attention to the grave was noticed for the positive reasons, as the man had said, not many kids came in here if not for some mischief or other.

"That's me… Yes. I hope I have not left a mess or more work for you, sir."

Mortimer shook his head gently.

"No such fuss, young man. I just think it's nice that people still raise children to have manners, if not, on the whole, it's nice to know there is a minority of you."

James nodded. He took the compliment as intended and walked

closer to the gravestone.

"May I ask what you were saying to her just now, sir? You looked deep in conversation."

Mortimer looked at the grave, then at James.

"I was just thanking her for her patience as I cut the lawn. Makes an awful racket, and wanted her to know I appreciated her bearing with me. I say an apology to all the graves. If I can… some of the ones round the back I ignore now, been there so long they're deaf as a post. But, most of these fellows are good enough to be patient with me, and I feel I should be gracious to them in return."

He smiled again at James and raised his eyebrows comedically.

James smiled broader and let out a little laugh.

A raven flew down and landed on the grave, it chirped and cawed at James, impatient for its treat. Recognizing the laugh right away.

"You know what a raven is do you, James?"

"No, sir. I don't."

"The harbinger of death. Legend has it that ravens are round only when Death is. They carry messages for him, they act as a herald for his arrival, they guard his graveyards and cemeteries. Some call them the Angels of the Graveyard. Intelligent birds they are. Smart, loyal, good listeners. Some people of legend say that a raven carries secrets and stories to the good Lord Death for his ear only, and he knows what's happening all around the world in every graveyard and cemetery because of the ravens and their loyalty."

James nodded, he looked at the bird and then the man beside him fascinated.

"I was unaware of that, sir."

He held a hand out, rubbing his fingers gently together to the bird; it cawed loudly and rubbed its head against James' hand.

"The birds have grown accustomed to me, I think they recognize me and my laugh, my voice, I'd like to think so – it's that, or they can smell the biscuits."

He let out a little giggle that Mortimer mimicked and followed with a laugh of his own.

"I'd say the biscuits are a good factor, but, they are picky birds - given who their master is, if you believe that kind of thing - it makes sense that it's probably a good judge of who it does and does not want to be friends with."

He held his hand out, and the raven jumped up to his finger and cawed again. It looks at Mortimer deeply; the black, marble-like eyes shining. Its head turned this way and that, and then it looked as though it recognized some spark of similarity or something regal inside Mortimer and the bird curtsied low and graciously. It then took wing back to the treetops, to caw and chatter to its mates.

"He seems to like you too," James said.

"Loyalty," Mortimer said, winking.

James smiled, not sure what to make of the wink, but smiled all the same.

"I was coming to say goodbye to her for a while. I'm moving, you see. Quite far away. Dad has a new job, promoted, so we are going to be closer to his head office. But, means I will be studying hard now as exams come up next term and... well... I'm going to miss her. Poppy, I mean. I'll miss our chats and reading to her and the birds, I wanted to make sure she would be ok. Ask the birds to take good care of her for me." He looked forlornly at the gravestone, then to Mortimer.

The man smiled weakly, this time his smile was not scary or mean, not ugly or damaged.

His eyes were bright, steel blue.

His hair pulled tight and into a bun, a faint wisp of grey stubble on his face, a few wrinkles here and there. A striking looking man, to be sure, but the weak smile gave James everything he needed to know he was if not a kind man, at least he was an honest one.

"How about if I have a chat with her every now and then? Read a bit of my book to her. I'll look after those birds as well, don't worry. They are not nearly as bad as the pigeons we had at the last church I worked for, droppings everywhere, fat birds doing fat droppings on everything..."

James giggled, and he rubbed his eyes wearily.

"I'll take good care of her, and the ravens, and that sparrow or two I see down her sometimes."

James cut in. "And the bolshie robin!"

"Ah yes, the bolshie robin! How could I ever forget him?" Mortimer chuckled.

"He wouldn't let you forget him."

"That's for sure, young man; that is for sure." He laughed.

James looked at the man, and the gravestone, he tenderly stroked the grave and patted it twice, he rested his hand upon it and turned to Mortimer.

"Hear that, Pop? Mr. Mortimer will take good care of you when I am gone. I'm coming back, to see you, soon – but while I am away, for now, Mr. Mortimer and the birds will look after you. Is that a good deal?"

As if in confirmation, the birds all took wing from the tree and came down to the grave. The raven, the swallows, the blue-tit and the sparrows. And finally, landing on the grave itself, coming up and pecking at James' shoe, was the Robin.

A solitary raven fell from the headstone to the grave beside him, and the two birds butted heads fraternally.

"See." Said Mortimer. "Gangs all here."

James smiled. He took his biscuits out the bag, and crumbled them and placed the crumbs on the headstones amongst the birds, and the grave itself between the robin and raven.

He sprinkled the rest in Mr. Mortimer's hand and closed his hand over the man's.

"Take care of them for me, yes?"

Mortimer nodded quietly.

James took out his book and gave it a kiss whispered something inaudible beneath his breath, and then lay the book on the headstone at a lean, stroking the cover one last time.

"A little 'see you soon' present. Promise I'll be back in no time."

He paused and swallowed back a lump in his throat.

"Take care, Poppy. Thank you… and I am and always will be sorry. But…"

He stopped and wiped a tear from his eye, gave a manly little cough and swallowed hard.

"…You knew that."

He saluted at Mortimer and shook the man's hand. Saluted the birds who all gave him a caw and chirrup as way of acknowledgement, and he turned and made his way to the gate. As he did, the wings flapped and swooshed, and the birds all lined up on the gatepost offering him a salute and an honour guard as he walked out.

He opened the gate with a smile, and as he closed it behind him, the raven gave a final CAW! And James nodded dutifully, before walking across the road and making his way home. Walking at first, then picking his pace with a run as he cut into the field, tears in his eyes, he then ran the whole rest of the way back home, shuffled leg and lungs on fire.

Mortimer smiled his terrifying smile at the grave, and nodded. Smiling widely.

"No, you are right. He is absolutely the man I am looking for." He wiped his face, and the beard disappeared, the lines and features rubbed off as though painted on, and he ran his fingers through his hair and the bun fell down and released his fine, silver blonde hair in length around his shoulders.

He cracked his knuckles, and the lines disappeared from his hand as did the prominent veins of Mortimer and all that remained was the harsh and horrifying beauty of Death himself.

"Thank you, Poppy. You have done me proud."

He turned to the gateway, and the raven took wing and landed on Death's shoulder, the creature broke a piece of biscuit in his hands and fed to the bird, who squawked and flapped in appreciation loudly.

"He is definitely the one we need."

The raven nodded in approval, rubbing his head against Death, and gratefully received another crumb.

* * *

- 4 -

At first it was a minor wheeze, unlike his usual laboured breathing, which felt good, felt honest, real and raw – this was a painful endurance test. The more air he swallowed down, the harder it seemed to fill his mangled, decayed and diseased lungs. His eyes also hurt, the myopic glare that usually made his day, interspersed with bursts of blinding whiteness now only gave him a piercing white light all the time, he was practically blind and the pain it drilled into his mind and cortex was something indescribable.

Pestilence clattered into the council room, his calloused, pockmarked fingers could not feel the surfaces of the wall, door or table, instead he coughed a wad of dark viscous phlegm and spat to the floor, a bloody chunk of spit that looked ugly, angry and drenched in oily sickness.

He hit the floor with a sudden and violent thud, and his chest cracked, as ribs snapped under his sallow, paper-like skin.

His face was discoloured - an abrasive purplish pink, and his lips deep blue, heavy, acne marked, blemished bags were under his eyes, that were creamy, pearl white, and which gave no indication of his physical or mental state – suffice to say, both were annihilated and ragged.

Pestilence was dying.

Famine came to his side, at first, she had a strange distant look of curiosity on her face, her fine cream white dress and headscarf with bronze and gold finery were in stark contrast to Pestilence's stained, fluid speckled, forest green rags.

She knelt beside him and watched him without touching, silent and giddy with curious interest. She looked at War, who sat at the council table and smiled at this show from his younger brother. A creature War felt was below him, he had little time nor love for him, cared even less for what was happening, he merely was amused at the conflict of the man against his own body and nature.

War reached across the table, tore a leg from a chicken, and wrestled himself out of his chair onto the edge and ate while he watched the wretched figure of Pestilence choke and gag on his own insides.

Famine had put her hand on the least offensive part of his clothing, and gently rubbed, soon, even this was stained from pustules that popped and wept into the fabric.

She looked at War and shook her head.

"He's dying." She said, quietly. Wiping her hand on a napkin laid clean and glorious on the table.

War shook his head, his face suddenly serious.

"Dying?" he asked, biting down on his chicken leg, spitting a fleck of skin and meat toward Pestilence, which landed on his cheek.

War stood up and walked over, giving the choking creature a prod with his boot.

Pestilence wailed and his body arched in spectacular rigor, he grasped out and his other hand went to his throat.

Death came through a split in the air, touching two parts of creation; he strode through elegantly and the brief slit in space sewed shut behind him leaving a fizz of sulphur and smoke. He looked down at the choking sickness on the floor, at Famine looking confused and uselessly knelt at his side, and War stood prodding him with his boot tip, and his mood did not improve from his previous destination, which had left him angry and tired and needing some peace.

However...

Looking down at the frame and state of Pestilence did make him smile inside that the plan was slowly coming to be, his machinations, his toiling for the last two thousand years, and his efforts and ministrations were slowly coming to the point of no return.

Lucifer and he had made their blueprint, and soon his table would be vacant one seat.

"Pick him up. Don't just stare at him." He ordered of War.

War glowered at Death in the way Death had grown weary of, the younger brother, the Rider in Red always giving some glare or grimace as if to illustrate his desire to usurp and overthrow his standing at the head of the table.

Death was in no mood.

He pointed at Pestilence and stood forward, coming within a foot or two of War, no flicker of fear or pause of patience and hesitation, War rose to his full height, as did Death, and the two met nose to nose.

"I am tired of your shows of disrespect, brother." Death said to War.

"I am tired of your petulance, of your feeble acts of rebellion, of you petty little displays of arrogance. I invite and welcome you to take

433

the first move to do something about your standing and my own, I would enjoy you trying to switch the roles we have around...I really would."

He looked cold and dead into his angry brother's eyes.

War stared back, his lips turned into a ferocious flicker, teeth occasionally flashing from turned in lips.

"Make your move, War, or calm down your temper and take him to the chamber.

I have no time or patience for your ridiculous mood swings today. Make the fateful final move or pick your brother from the floor and take him out."

War looked hard in Death's blue steel coloured eyes.

This was the closest he had ever gotten to them before and staring down on them he saw the aeons of generations burned and brushed away from this tiny plain of creation, he saw slow exploding galaxies, deep nebula crashing together, he felt the cold, empty and violent, uncaring tear of space ripping whole clusters of worlds apart. And felt Death's presence on each and every world that died.

He realized his brother was more than he had ever given a hint at being, his unique and fascinating, mind-boggling massiveness.

His omniscient size, and a shiver of fear ran down his back, a tiny pinprick of sweat boiled and bubbled from the nape of his neck and ran down his spinal cord, and, tactfully and with no sense he was perturbed – though deep down inside he was – he lowered to a calmer height and smiled broadly.

"Not today, brother. Not today." He bowed theatrically and leant down and roughly lifted his sick sibling from the floor and carried him out of the room to the arched chamber.

Death watched him and the Rider in Green leave.

A smile on his carved lips, he nodded gently in amusement, cut a seam in the world and stepped through.

Famine was on the floor, alone, she noticed a crumb or morsel between two slabs of stone, picked it out and swallowed it down, looked up and realized she was alone, so she went back to the table and devoured the chicken on her own, greedily and with haste.

Smiling and chuckling as she gorged on the fowl.

* * *

In the countless cycles of this world. The million, million times that we have been born and destroyed and reborn again, the four horsemen have been the only constant.

Born into the world upon the advent of their name. Death exists from the moment birth is given, his need an opposite to the other, so his place secured forever amongst the stars. Even when the universe is taken to the point of no return and is reset with intention to begin again, one big bang after another, when the beach is remade, and new players are scattered amongst it all, two creatures were there from the beginning without contest or competition.

Time and Death.

Death is the black rider, the general of the apocalypse and the journeyman who carried the brave and bold, the weak and feeble and the old and young alike across the plain of life to the other side, the world beyond this, all matter becoming fodder for the next revolution of this creation cycle.

Some aspects of our world exist retained from the other; some figures are newer versions of older ideas and ideals. Some cosmic concepts repeat in new variances, but Death and Time remain unchanged, unsullied and unhampered.

Time does not ride with her brother, as she is an independent. She speaks to no one, she involves herself with no matters, she is not to be negotiated with, nor is she able to be manipulated or tricked. Science does not alter her, and man cannot bend her, she is the true and only through line in the universe.
Witnessing the timers restart countless million times, she always begins again on the beach as the next pantheon starts their game.

Death sharing rules and guidelines. Making his way with secrets and names, giving the new players their purpose.

Time watches from the peripherals.
Cutting her threads and making the lifelines for each of the people on the beach, her line of threads becoming bigger, thicker, more robust with each new line and life.
Her scissors are pitiless, and her cuts are unbiased, every person lives for the length of thread she cuts for you.
No other entity in creation influences or alters this fact.

Yet.
Even Lady Time was becoming weary with this world. With quarrelsome gods, with hungry appetites of uncaring deities, of the world falling apart and watching the threads become longer but thinner, lives lived in weak and unbalanced ways.
People surviving longer, but in agony and weakness, infirmity and poverty.
She cut her lines that would snap in her hands, she would cut children weak and despicable threads of life, her scissors rusty and old, the thread becoming weaker and weaker.

She had grown a sense of hatred for her job in this version and cycle of creation.
And she was no longer willing to play by the usual rules.
So, for the first time since the world and creation had been birthed from the ether of some unknown higher power's imagination – someone even Death and Time had no knowledge or understanding of – Time reached out to her eternal brother and spoke her mind.

The world, creation, this universe we see fit to inhabit, frozen for one whole hour, as Time, with her weak, barely whispered voice, spoke quietly of her fear for this world, her boredom and how she wanted to set it right.

And Death listened intently.
Realising that Time's plan was something he could enact and enable

with a limited number of associates if he sold the benefits well enough.

Before even Lucifer's turn at the foot of the cross at Golgotha, something was stirring that would be a new beginning in a meaningful way, and with one man, and a bitter, vengeful god, they could pull off the start the world deserved.

Pieces arranged and the chess board reset, the countdown had begun. Time slowly counted down the seconds, and had been doing so for so long that the dawn was upon her.
She counted these days with a smile on her lips.
Each second a step closer to the beginning and the end.

* * *

Three days after the crucifixion the rock was rolled away and the body was not there. Jesus, the Messiah, was not in his final resting place, and no one could account for his whereabouts.
Stories came in of the apostles seeing his body, seeing a man who was Jesus reincarnated walking amongst them, of his appearance by the river, helping fishermen. Of his walking on the road to Bethlehem, of his appearance to Mary Magdalene and the Virgin Mary. Of an angel rolling back the rock to his resting place and freezing Roman guards.
The country abuzz with talk and legend growing of the returned Messiah Christ. His spirit roaming the Earth spreading more gospel for the masses, his church gaining a word of mouth unlike any other church the land had yet seen.
One more church worshipping Yahweh and his contradictory, confused, angry rules. Apostles beginning the arduous task of writing down the teachings of Christ. The learning's, parables and stories, his truths and his follies, his life and his time.
A book so dangerous that it is reassembled by a council of peers and church elders who release what is now considered "THE HOLY BOOK" – a bastardized version of the truth, suited only for the

elevation of the few over the many, and therefore, feeding Yahweh all that he needs to stay powerful, relevant. Just enough paradoxes and schisms that the church of Christ is split into factions, each worshipping with different views and different approach. Orthodox and unorthodox, all personal and ceremonial, feeding directly into the stomach of the greedy, bloating god Yahweh.

Starving the gods of the West.

Mountains crack and tumble.
Deities fall and die, starvation leading them to the great walk to the world beyond.
More food for the fire for the next world.

Zeus sat across from Death and listened.
Death gave the silver-haired, emaciated god the whole story, the unabridged version of events. Every tell tale second. The silver god sat in silence and swallowed hard.

"Lord Zeus. Would you like to see the other side of the veil?"
Death sat with his hands folded in crossed pattern before him. Fingers entwined.
"I will tell you a secret, and I will ask you a question. Are you game to answer?"
Zeus nodded.
"Firstly, tell me. Do you remember the secret I told you on the beach?"
Zeus nodded.
"I do, Lord Mort."
"Good. Then I give you another secret, one not even Lucifer knows. Jesus is dead. His body was pierced in its side; he bled out and died upon that cross.
Yahweh took it upon himself to return the body to the ether; he absorbed his son inside himself and took his form. He walked the earth, fraternizing with Jesus' compatriots and followers, family and friends, and finally with all assembled, he ascended himself to his own throne having set the legend of the trinity to the masses.
Father, Son and Holy Spirit. What we see and what we know are

different, you see... but we see behind the veil. Behind the curtain."

Zeus nodded. He tensed his fists together.

"Is this why you asked me to remember my secret?" He asked.
"Yes, Lord Zeus. I need you to remember that I told you each a secret, one apiece, as I woke you on the beach. Well... I also said you can die, and I said you would be walked by me to the edge of forever, and you would see the door to the world beyond... do you want to see it?"
Zeus nodded.
"Is it my time, Lord Mort?" he asked earnestly.
"Zeus, my friend, you know it is not. This is my gift to you; see it as a favour, for when I ask you what I will ask you, I need to know you will say yes. Do you understand? This is the most precious thing I have to bargain with, and I wish for you to see the stakes."
"I understand, my lord."
"Then come." Death pointed to the door to the left of the temple at the top of the Parthenon. A Door that should not exist.
The mountaintop was ravaged and broken, shattered and torn apart by years of toil and of misuse. Zeus stood and walked toward the wall where the door stood, a black portal.
Upon it was a sigil unrecognizable to the god.
He ran his fingers across it and looked at Death.
"What does this mean?"
Death smiled – he put a hand on Zeus's shoulder and gave a gentle squeeze.
"It says 'the end' or 'the beginning' as whispered by the first God of the first universe, our creator and our builder. From whence he came – no one knows – as I was his construct, designed to live forever and guide the universe anew until we got it right."
Zeus delicately fondled the deep groove in the door, which was a heavy black wood, it smelled like marzipan.
"We have never got it right, Lord Zeus. The same mistakes and follies, the same idiots and idols, the same greed and hate and vengeance. I have seen it all.
And every time I return the ruined world to the place beyond this

door.

If I open – I need your solemn and righteous vow that what I ask of you afterwards will be undertaken with no questions – or I will strike you down and dead where you stand. Do we have an accord?" Death looked at the god, his hand extended palm open, welcoming a shake as a bond of trust.

Zeus looked at the hand and stopped touching the sigil.

He looked at the door, the hand and the sigil again.

"The beginning." He said. And smiled.

"Or the end… We have an accord, Lord Mort." And he shook the hand firmly and held the grip that second longer than necessary to make sure of the deal.

Death nodded, his smile broad and happy.

"Then look at what awaits."

Zeus opened the door and peered through. His hands rose to hold the frame of the door, and he leant in adventurously, gripping and holding on tightly.

He closed his eyes and soaked in the radiant warmth and the primordial light.

Tendrils of something magnificent and ancient coiled around his arms and gripped him tightly. The light permeated his skin and muscle and shone brightly illuminating him inside and out. A tendril slithered up his waist, coiling round his body and sought the softest spot, slithering up his chest; it found it by penetrating heavily and sharply directly through his temple and boring into his mind.

Zeus' eyes opened, and his mouth hung agape.

He groaned as the tendril became his psyche for a few golden burning moments.

Then the tendrils evaporated in a tug and a puff of smoke.

Zeus was left dangling in the doorway, a loose vacant stare on his face, his eyes drunk and heavy.

His grip loosened and he began to fall forward.

Death grabbed him by the midriff and pulled him back, closing the door.

Zeus looked at the rider in black and gripped his tunic tighter.

"It is beautiful. So very beautiful. What's beyond that door is the perfect world that you are looking for."
Death smiled.
"What is beyond that door, Zeus, is merely the gateway to the next universe. The beach lies beyond that, your beach, your ocean lapping. It is what is upon that beach that the portal decides."
Zeus looked at the door, and touched the sigil again.
His hands flattened out on the wood over the sign.
"Whatever you want, I offer my service to you, Lord Death. I offer my worship and strength to you."
Death bowed graciously, receiving the gift and swallowing hard on the imbibing power.
"Tell me your secret, Zeus." Death said. "The one I shared upon the beach. Tell me it now."

Zeus smiled.
"There is an answer to a question no one knows. It is but one pull of the string away."
Death nodded.
"Do you now what it means, Lord Zeus?"
The god shook his head, his face still bright with revelation, but his eyes glazed in confused wonder.
"No, my Lord, what does it mean?"
Death took Zeus by both hands and drew him close, hugging him.
"It means that your service to me begins right now."

And, he held him close and gently swayed with the god in his arms, crying softly into the blanket of Death's dark cloak, the colour and texture of the thick night sky.

* * *

Pestilence died.
His death was not as soft or as brilliant as his birth. Born forth from the void with a burst of smoke, upon the first poisoned cough and hacked glottal of the new world.

441

Adam and Eve's third child Seth born early, ill with fever and weak lungs, hacking and spluttering with every breath. His tiny organs full of infection and of sickness. Unlike anything that had been seen on Earth before.

Pestilence emerged and watched, slowly pushing the fever higher and higher.
Eve became sick with it, Adam too.
Sharing amongst other villagers in the small village in the west in which they had settled.

This illness spreading like wildfire amongst the population.
Not fatal to any at all.
But a start, enough to draw the creature from his sleep.

His entrance was a ballet compared to the wrestling match that he undertook now, his temperature spiking, and his joints aching, his eyes blinded by cataract and sore, his lungs coated with poisonous and foamy fluid, his heart blackened by smoke and tar, his kidney failing.
Every organ and muscle group dying and atrophying around him.
His life ebbing out one artery and muscle at a time.

He gave a final, violent rictus, heaving from the bed, arched back and seized joints, grit teeth and burst sore and boil.
He reached high for some invisible spirit, screamed high and violently, and then he died.

The rider vacating his saddle and seat, leaving behind an Earth that had cured all ills, in one form or another.
No final surprises left, no hidden virus or terminal infection hidden or biding time.

Pestilence had left the building.
All that remained was his lifeless, cold, ravaged body.

Death felt the twinge in his gut when the light finally dimmed on Pestilence's life. Some things defied even Death in the end, though gods came and went, lived and died, and Death walked them beyond – Riders were not gods, they were not people, they were constructs.

Tools.

When a tool lost its purpose, broke, no longer worked as intended, a gardener does not control if it lives or dies, he replaces it with something new.

Though he was sad his brother had met his end, last in and first out, he was glad that it had finally happened as it was intended.

Death had a clear run now to recruit again.

And though he had candidates galore waiting in the wings…

He wanted to make changes, and the rules never dictated that you could not hire as you saw fit.

Best man for the job.

Pestilence was dead. Indeed

But sorrow, sorrow was everywhere to be seen.

It was in three thousand men and woman falling from Two Towers, to the woman walking into the supermarket in some far off township where she blew herself to kingdom come. From the teenager with cancer dying before fulfilling his bucket list, to the college tutor who dedicated his life to God and his job, even at the expense of his sexual orientation and own happiness.

Sorrow existed as a physical force now, deep and rich and heady.

And EVERYWHERE.

Death knew what belonged at his side, in his stable.

And though it may only be a means to an end…

He knew he always got his man.

* * *

Kay was sitting in the kitchen, at the breakfast bar counter, sipping her morning brew. Unlike James, she enjoyed her tea strong, sweet, and with so little milk that the cup looked the same colour as He-Man's skin. A joke she made regularly to let people know how to make it right.
Often met with blank faces as she realized how much older she was than some of her friends and co-workers.
A fragile little wake up call when people missed out on such benchmark cultural moments.

She took a sip from her mug and broke off a chunk of banana from her breakfast muesli, she playfully nibbled at it, whilst watching James in the garden, he had gone to hang up some clothes on the line, when he had clearly been distracted by something in the shed, dressed in his casual jeans and a baggy shirt, he had gone out with arms full of wet washing, and then after hanging, looked at the house, looked at the shed – weighed it up for two or three seconds – and then gone in.
Kay loved Eddie deeply, all his little quirks and foibles; his gestures and his hesitations. She loved how he always looked worried by the tiniest thing, how he always fretted over inconsequential incidence – like spilling the sugar or ring marks on the table. He never made it anyone else's problem, he never blew it out of control, but he always gave a look around to make sure that he had not been witnessed and cleared it with a guilty haste.
Kay almost always saw, but went back to her book, or the TV show they were watching, or the knitting she had taken up for the baby boy they had coming.
She always saw and always smiled, a wry, happy smirk painted in the corner of her mouth, even while her heart grew ten times the size with love for her shaggy, shambling husband.

It was 11.23 am, and she was still in her pajamas and housecoat when she had come down, slippers on and hair unwashed

444

and tied loosely atop her head in a weak bun. Her belly was huge now, but she was still a month out from the date they were expecting Callum would be born. But, she looked ready to pop at any moment. She ate another piece of fruit from her muesli, which sat idle and dry in her bowl. She gulped another mouthful of her tea and smiled. What James was doing she could not begin to tell, his shed was a no man's land fit for exploration by no one but him; full of books and paints and tools and projects. As well as being where he kept his office computer and did all his work. Since learning of the pregnancy the spare box room had been turned into a nursery, so he was relegated to the shed.

Kay was certain he didn't mind.

Which was right. He loved it in there. Carpet on the walls, over plasterboard, covering insulation, it was warm, it had power, it was moderately soundproofed, so he listened to music loudly, usually old Beatles records or a George Harrison CD.

He loved having his own island of isolation he could go and crash in and escape.

Kay was just happy he was happy.

James' parents now lived in Reading. His brother and sister were busy raising their own families in the south coast and the Midlands, so he rarely saw them except at big family gatherings. But, mostly, he was happy to be away from his folks, always relieved to be living in the now not the past. Kay had never wanted to ask about his past simply because he would go quiet and have a sad look take over his usually happy face. Draining him of all warmth, making him cold and silent. She was aware of some incident when he was a child that had haunted him, and speaking with his parents and getting a gist of the story, she thought better than to poke and prod at the clearly still open wound.

Kay's parents, in contrast, only lived a twenty minute drive away and were always around. James had not minded at all, he found her father a source of constant amusement with his stories and his bad jokes, her mother had kept him in constant supply of good cake and baked goods – so James welcomed her and her biscuit tins and old chocolate tubs with open arms and flagrant affection that always made Kay smile and laugh. And in turn, her parents had fallen in love with him straight away.

His cheeky sense of humour, his shuffled walk, his stories, his jokes and his odd but loveable sense of humour.

Compared to the boys Kay had seen before, all muscles and bland humour, fast cars and no substance, a cavalcade of external shine and dull insides – they had positively loved this handsome, but awkward, funny but solemn young man.

Mostly it was just Kay and James against the world.
Add Callum to the mix and they would be a perfect trio.

Kay stood up, and went to the fridge for the milk, leant down to get it from the bottom shelf and stood upright immediately holding her side, a small grimace fixed upon her face. The twinge in her side throbbed somewhat.

She stretched out and turned side to side with her hips fixed straight, and shook out the discomfort. When the sudden pain dispersed, she leant down again, and then doubled back up in pain.

Her face now was a picture of worry.

A bead of sweat ran down her forehead, onto her cheek.

She cast a quick glimpse to the garden, and thought of calling James, but stopped herself and instead with slippers on her feet and housecoat flowing behind her she traipsed to the downstairs bathroom.

Holding one hand to her side, rubbing gently.

* * *

James had thought about whether or not he should show his wife the framed picture he had made. He had gone down and sketched the park, from the canal looking up, he sketched the copper-tinged soldier on the war memorial; he had drawn the clock tower at the top of the abbey, the bandstand and the pedalo pond.

He had drawn the park and the swings and roundabout, the climbing frame pirate-ship. And amongst all of this, had drawn in sketched

446

Disney characters. Winnie the Pooh on the bandstand reading a book. Tigger in a pedalo, Mickey and Minnie on two swings rocking with abandon and big smiles, Donald Duck was playing fetch with Pluto at the clock tower.

It was a beautiful mix of traditional sketch work and cartoons, and under the picture, central at the foot of the composition he had drawn a box and written inside in clear capitals – "Where Mummy and Daddy met."

He held it up and smiled.

He had been wanting to save it for just before Callum was born, but had gotten it back from the frame-makers the evening before straight after he had dropped off some work to a client, and he was so proud of it, pencils and inks and acrylic, so happy with how it had turned out – he wanted to give it to his wife now for no other reasons than to see her smile. The one thing that he wished he could see forever.

So, he gave a little laugh and putting the frame under his arm, he made his way out from the shed locking the door after him with its combination padlock, looked up to see grey skies rolling in from the edge of town, but blue skies everywhere else, decided to hedge his bets and leave the clothes where they were and headed back inside.

Kay was not in the kitchen. Her cereal bowl was there, with dry muesli inside, James picked at a raspberry and swallowed it down, he took a glass of water from the sink and then wiping his face he called out for his wife.

"Kay, sweetheart, you okay?"

There was no reply.

He stole another raspberry and wandered into the hallway, frame under his arm, and called again.

"Kay, babe?"

A muffled groan came from the downstairs bathroom in the hallway, opposite the dining room. James walked toward and saw the door was ajar, he knocked and pushed it slightly open.

The frame fell from his arm and hit the ground hard.

Glass shattered and splintered around the hall and bathroom floor,

447

and the picture flopped from one corner limply, resting torn on a shard of glass.

It hit the ground flatly, and more glass smashed but was muffled by the weight of the frame.

Lay upon the floor, vomit on the seat, flecked with blood, and holding her stomach, was Kay.

Her crotch was wet and sticky; her waters had burst, and she had bled. The smell was sweet and had a tang of iron and warm perspiration.

James threw his hands to his mouth and a moment of fleeting uncontrollable panic flushed him as he looked at all the parts that made the scene.

He then turned through the door and grabbed the hands-free phone on the wall beside the dining room door. Dialed 999 and fell to his knees by his wife's side.

"Kay, sweetheart, I'm here okay, I'm here, babe. You are going to be fine... stay with me, baby, okay?"

The phone connected.

"Emergency services, which service do you require?"

"I need an ambulance" James hurriedly said. "My wife is bleeding and unconscious!"

"Connecting you now." The calm voice said on the other end before another operator took over.

James held his wife's hand and squeezed her gently, her head now turned in to the side, recovery position, he explained and described the scene and told what had happened, and he sat when the call ended, phone on his lap, and wife's hand in his hand.

"Kick the door in." He had said. "Kick it down for all I care, I am not leaving her side."

Twelve minutes later the ambulance and paramedics arrived and had found the door luckily unlocked and open, they found James on his knees, kneeling in shattered glass, a frame broken and flopped ragged and smashed on the floor, the man holding his wife's hand and stroking her hair.

She had been responsive to a point; they took a sample of the sick from the toilet seat, and they wheeled her out to the car. A police car arrived seconds later, and the officer came in and sat with James and took a statement, and administered first aid to the cuts on his knees, and then said that he would drive to the hospital with James as his passenger, just behind the ambulance, as James was unable to go with her.

James had protested this… But, he had gashed his knee badly, and the paramedics had assured him Kay was fine, and that she had low blood pressure, and that he had called the services at the right time, they were in control and she would be fine.
The policeman in the car that followed had seen the lights and sirens and followed to the house on the off chance, the paramedics explaining the situation, and hurriedly leaving.
James hastened the officer to get him there too.

When he arrived, a nurse was waiting. Concerned look upon his face. He held his hands out to calm James and explain what was happening.

"Mr. Edmunds, Mr. Edmunds." James looked at him, stopped his frantic push to get past and on to wherever his wife was.
"Mr. Edmunds… You called the ambulance at the exact right moment. Your wife has suffered a bleed, it's not a miscarriage, but we think there may be a rupture in the placenta. We need to know if there has been any disruption, any other moments of pain or discomfort, anything that may have come before today that may be a factor in this bleed?"
James looked at the man, he saw his mouth moving, but after the word "Miscarriage" his ears stopped working except for a high, violent whine, he could not understand what was happening, he looked at the officer who escorted him in and then back to the nurse.
"Miscarriage?" was all he could say, tears welling in his eyes.
"Mr. Edmunds… James… Your baby is alive, but it is in distress, and considering how far along the pregnancy is, I need to know now, has there been any other issues until today?"

449

James shook his head. He looked over the nurse's shoulder at the entrance to the wards beyond.

"Where is Kay? Where is my wife?"

The nurse held onto James' shoulders and turned his head to face James.

"James... I need you to understand, this is serious, but we are doing everything we can. She is in surgery now; she suffered a heavy bleed on the way in, but you called the ambulance at the most crucial time, this could have been a lot, lot worse. I need you to understand, she is in good hands, and the doctors are with her now. Okay?"

James nodded, he looked at the nurse.

"Good hands?" he asked, vacantly. His eyes now flowing, but no noise escaped from him otherwise, his face was white with shock and confusion.

"The best, Mr. Edmunds, the absolute best. Now, please come with me."

The officer spoke something into his shoulder radio and shook hands with the nurse, James wandered toward the doors to the wards, and then was joined by the nurse guiding him, hands on his shoulders.

James could remember nothing of what happened when he walked through the doors, nothing that was coherent.

Just flashes and images and moments.

Of his bleeding knees, his jeans were cut and gash at the knee and dressing applied, but they stung.

He remembered his phone ringing and answering, but not who he spoke too.

He remembered looking at his wife through a window.

Waving as she lay in the bed with tubes helping her breath and her face clammy and pale.

He remembered the doctors running in and a lot of activity before being taken away where he remembers suddenly being surrounded by his mother and father-in-law.

Of being hugged and kissed on the cheek, of people crying.

Of...

Of...

Of silence.

Doctors spoke to him.
Nurses spoke to him.
His mother-in-law spoke to him.
He remembered nothing of what they said.
"Can I see Kay now?" he asked everyone who walked in front of him.
A doctor said yes, finally, and he was lead into a room, his father-in-law at his side, dazed and confused, he stood before a bed upon which lay his wife.
Still and quiet, eyes closed.
Her hands lay flat by her side; her hair was brushed back and tidy behind her ears.
She looked calm and relaxed.
James turned and looked at his father-in-law.
"What's wrong with her? Will she be okay? When can we take her home?"
Kay's father looked at James and covered his mouth with his big, aged, wrinkled hands. He put a hand on James' shoulder and shook his head gently.
"James. She's dead, son… Katherine is dead."

He looked at his wife upon the bed.
Took her hand in his, and shook his head.
She was so beautiful; she was so lovely, so peaceful.
He looked at the doctor and then his father-in-law again.
"She's… dead?"

The doctor, a young 30-something woman, barely nodded, her eyes toward the floor. Kay's father nodded heavier, and took James' arm gently and squeezed reassuring.
"Yes, son. She died."

James looked at his wife, her hand still warm in his, or so it felt.
Her chest was still, no movement. She was not breathing.

Her skin was pale and dry.
Her hair brushed back in a way she never wore it.
He looked at his father-in-law.
"But I never gave her... Her present... I never got to give her the present... The present. I never..."
He began crying, and his legs went out from under him.
Kay's father grabbed hold and squeezed him in close, bear-hugging him, the two men cried in a tight embrace.

The doctor left them, each holding and calming the other.
The doctor caught the eye of Kay's mother upon exiting the room.
She smiled weakly and padded her eyes with a tissue.
"When he is ready we can take him to see his son."
Kay's mother nodded again. "Thank you, doctor."
The sound of sobbing came from the room, and it echoed dull and low throughout the entire hospital.

* * *

- 6 -

The water lapped noisily at the sand. Coming in with a warm rush, then sucking back out again. The water ending on a horizon of nothing, forever waterfalling into a bleak, starless void, the tide – however – perpetual and heavy.

Upon the beach lay a dozen, dozen bodies. Still and lifeless, they were strewn about in random order, some face down, others on their back, yet more on their side. None breathed, none moved, the tide lapped around them and the beach was illuminated by a single dot in the sky, bright and warm, flickering fires danced across its surface, and around the corona, twinkles of new flame bursting into life.
A primordial sun.

The bodies were still and quiet, but, amongst them, walked a man in a thick black cloak that shimmered with a dark blue shine.

The sky above and his cloak shared more than just colour between them.

Indeed, it looked like the sky had dripped and draped itself around his frame, and this cloak was an awesome, liquid skin upon the man.

Death looked around and opened his eyes slowly breathing in the new universe as it had popped, quite literally, into a new and infant existence.

One second the door to the other side, the endless and churning void, upon which all matter was returned to be regurgitated and rebuilt existed. The next, the universe was burped out in a clean, new beginning.

Everything that may have existed before now primal matter from which this beach and water and the sun was built.

Death looked around and behind him was Time. His sister.

She looked at him. Her clean white cloak looked as though it had been grown from the sand itself, it was tight and surrounded her like a second skin, a large white hood the only exception.

She looked at her brother and gave no expression.

Instead, she breathed in deeply and closed her eyes and allowed the new oxygen to run circles around her lungs and heart.

She breathed out heavily and smiled, opening her eyes.

"Do you think this time will be any different?"

Death turned and looked at her, he saluted and bowed low. But, did not smile either.

"I cannot answer until I see what we have to work with."

He walked to the bodies around him, and saw one that stood out from the other, a golden-skinned creature, deep tan on his muscled body, his hair a chestnut auburn. He glowed upon the sand, and next to him was a twin, but silver-haired, and with a beard.

He leant down to the two, both striking and both beautiful.

He looked to his sister.

"There are more this time. Maybe this will mean a better cooperation. Unity, maybe they will work together."

"Have they ever before, brother?" Time mocked, a tinny, thin laugh escaped her lips.

Death shook his head heavily.

"Not once. But, still we persist."

"Still we persist." She repeated.

Death turned to look at her. He raised a finger and then mimicked a second hand falling, one tick at a time.

"Are you ready, sister?" he smiled to Lady Time.

She shook her head.

"No. But, do not let that stop you." She closed her mouth, started walking toward the far end of the beach, she raised her hand, and three fingers were extended.

Death smiled as she lowered them one at a time, and when they all fell, and she had nothing but a closed fist raised, he leant in and whispered in the golden skinned bodies' ear.

"You are Yahweh. You are a God... I have a secret for you."

The body stirred but did not wake. Its heart became alive and beat fast and furiously in its chest, his mouth gulped down a heavy breath of air.

"Do not trust the morning, for it will bring the end."

Yahweh's eyes opened, and then closed again.

He lay gasping for air, groggy and awake, but caught in a world of slumber, until his brothers and sister were awoken.

Death did not know where the secrets came from; he had no one he could ask.

He merely opened his mouth, and out they came, each one built for the body before him. He remembered them all.

But understood none.

He turned to the silver haired twin of the god before

"You are Zeus. You are a god. Would you like to know a secret?"

And so it went.

Body after body. God after god.

Name. Secret. Stir.

Finally, the gods were all awake, Yahweh stood first and helped Zeus to his feet, and they went around and raised everyone up and they stood, unsure, shaky, in front of Death.

The Rider in Black raised a hand and explained his place and his rules.

Every god looked at him and he smiled a vicious, horrendous gash of a smile, his lips thin and red, his skin too white and jagged to hold such an expression without it looking awful and ugly on his face.

"Good." He said.

"Now I will leave you. But, know I am watching, know I am paying attention – and - know I am waiting for you."

The gods all looked at him and nodded.

"Be good." He said before the cloak melted into the sky once more, and he was gone as soon as he had arrived.

Time watched on from the rocks; she counted silently to herself, smiling.

"Soon." She thought to herself.

"Soon." And smiled wider.

"The end will be here soon enough."

And her cloak seeped into the sand and took her with it.

The gods stood around looking at themselves and the others assembled, naked and new and alone with each other.

The beach was small now.

But it was a start.

"And…" Yahweh thought, "You always have to start somewhere."

How right he was.

* * *

- 7 -

The glow was strong, and it carried heavy with it a sound that resembled a deep, resonant whine. It shook the root, vibrating along

to frequency. The boxes lid chattered like an exciting mouth as the high pitch whine shook the silver. It looked like the box was jumping from side to side, and its lid rose and fell like a motorized mouth, jabbering away to itself.
From inside the box, a deep, sharp blue light emerged that illuminated the underside of the dresser and the floor of the shed. James' face was lit up in a clear and clean, blue white light, his one eye, still and fixed stared right back to the light with no reaction.

Inside James' head, a voice flooded and animated his quickly closing synapses, bringing a flow of life of sorts back into his brain and stimulating a movement of blood and sparks of intellect again. Even as his heart and body were dead, his mind clung on in the presence of this booming voice.

"In the beginning James, there was nothing.
A vast field of black and a resolute, arrogant, static bleakness.
Then, from beyond in some far off continuum or thread of existence the God who is above and beyond all gods, the one who began everything, he took the lid off the joke peanut can and the snakes inside, spring loaded and waiting, exploding into life and relevance.

I was one of those snakes, James, as was the God, who failed you and your family, the God of Adam and of Eve. This entire Earth is his plaything; humanity is his grand failed experiment he no longer cares for and will do anything to wipe out and start again… And he wants you to be his king while doing so.
From the south Lucifer Morningstar rises, prideful, resentful, full of anger and needing revenge for his mother and his brother.

The horseman ride as well.
One saddle empty in their troupe, Death wants to change the rules and shake the game up from top to bottom, he wants the throne and to beckon in a new age, defying his purpose and place in the universe. He could yet prove to be the brightest hope our world has, or its darkest enemy.

456

And then there is you.
A man amongst men. Wronged, widowed, childless. Mourning the perfect world you alone carved for yourself and which was stolen from you and burnt like so much salted earth.
The crux of the entire universe without even realizing.
And here you lay.
Dead. Expired. Broken and hidden.

Soon, the board will be full of players, and I will need you to make good your return.
Dead you will lay, three days hence, and then to return glorious and in control, awake and aware.
You will choose the endgame.
And you alone will victor."

James' eye reflected the light heavily.
For a second, just one second, his eye pulsed, and his pupil flared and he blinked.
Then… Stillness.
He lay dormant and dead for three days more.
Waiting to rise again.

* * *
- 8 -

James still had not cried. He was walked by his late wife's parents to the wide viewing window, overlooking the newborn babies. Inside next to the cots was an incubator where his son Callum had been lay.
Callum was tiny, fragile and the brightest pink he had ever seen. A beautiful little human, which was beyond perfection in James' eyes. An amazing miracle of life that he immediately poured every ounce of love he could muster towards from his warped, damaged insides.
His wife was beautiful, delicate and perfect too – but she was dead.
He kept thinking that the concept was alien and made no sense,

rolling the statement over in his mind over and over again.

"Your wife is dead. Your wife is dead. Your wife is dead. Your son killed your wife."

The last part coming from somewhere, not his own mind, and he baulked and shook, trying to dislodge the idea as he looked at the boy.
The nurses walked him in, and he stood over the incubator, looking down on his baby boy, shoving out the full absolute of his love toward him.

The voice in the back of his mind repeated again and again.

"Killed your wife. Killed your wife. Killed your wife."

James began to cry, silently, tears filling his eyes, his heart set itself on the boy entirely, and his mind taunted and raged and screamed obscenities at James for his betrayal of love toward this murderous little brat.

His heart shone a light, a beacon of pure adoration, his poisonous mind spat venom and hatred at the unfairness the boy lived and the woman to whom James gave his entire life and love, attention and soul was not allowed to be by his side enjoying this moment.
Dead.
Because of this child.

James cried, looked at the boy and whispered,
"I love you, murderer."
His eyes startled to full alertness, as he realized what he said.
"Hey, hey… Callum, baby boy, I love you… Callum, I'm sorry…"
James apologized loudly; he touched the glass that divided him from his son. His eyes were red and bloated from the tears now, as he apologized fully, pawing the glass and looking at this 27-minute-old child.
The baby cooed, looked up, kicking his fragile little legs and feet.

Waving his arms at his father.

"*Mur. Der. Rer.*" Said the voice inside. "*He is nothing but a murderer.*" It pushed.

"*He's not a murderer*" James argued.

"*Mur. Der. Rer*" It persisted.

"*Where is your wife? Hey? Where is Kay? Where is she?*"

The voice inside continued to jab away at the reason and sense.
James looked down, looked at the nurses and the other babies, his mother and father in law, stood holding each other, dabbing the tears from their eyes.

"*He is a Mur. Der. Rer.*"

The baby cooed, looked up, kicking his fragile little legs and feet. Waving his arms at James.

"HE IS NOT A MURDERER!" James screamed.

His hands hitting the temples of his head. He looked at the nurses, who stop and stare, mouths aghast, one dropping a folder she was holding.

He looks at Kay's parents, Callum's grandparents as they touch the glass and stare at James, shocked and appalled, Kay's father holding his wife tighter, a stern look of disgust in his eyes.

James turned and looked at his son, Callum looked up a faint smile upon his face.

The tubes coming into the cot, the airways and the ventilator, the wires leading to his heart monitor.

James stared down and one hand flat upon the glass, his eyes red and wet with sorrow.

He silently mouthed, "I'm sorry." And as James opened his eyes, his head gently shaking side-to-side, unable to believe what he just did, his babies' arms and legs stopped moving, his little arm falls slowly to the cot floor resting by his head.

His eyes close gently; his fingers curl in and then open loose and relaxed.

And the monitor stops its gentle pulsing, and instead it fixes on a high, persistent whine and a line as flat and as static as it was horrific gave the signal that James' boy, Callum. His first and only child. Was quite, quite dead.

Just like his mother.
Leaving James alone and fractured, forever broken beyond the day.

* * *

- 9 -

In the shadows of the ward, Zeus watched.
Hidden and concealed in the dark corner, somewhere between here
and some place beyond, he watched silently as the man collapsed to
the floor, crying, a nurse at his side, he screamed as his child was
taken in a rushed stupor to behind closed doors, doctors scrambling
to full alert.

He watched as James punched the wall and floor, and cried, wailed
and screamed at the doors, Kay's mother and father now by his side
as well, as he raged and screamed in sorrow and anger.

Zeus smiled.
His place amongst the board was now ready. His new master Death
had made his orders clear, and Zeus would not disappoint.
First the woman, then the child, then...

The world.

* * *

CHAPTER EIGHT
All is Fair in Death and Life

*"It is better to recognise that we are in darkness
than to pretend that we can see the light."*

— Hedley Bull,
The Anarchical Society: A Study of Order in World Politics

The characters were assembled in the lounge. James sat at the table, his face and clothes spattered in blood from his beating at War's hand.
Death and Lucifer had edged into the doorway, both staring at the man, Lucifer in open-jawed shock, Death more relaxed, but still reluctant to say or do anything in the presence of this strange enigma of a human.
War and Famine had opened the French window and walked in the back of the lounge by the garden, War had strode purposefully to the centre of the room and pointed at the man, accusatorily.
Famine, coyly smiled, sat on the sofa staring at the others one by one, and then rested her eyes on the miraculous human.

No one spoke, as Yahweh took a seat opposite James and rested his hands on the table.

"Would you mind repeating what you said? I do not believe I heard you correctly."
The God looked harshly at James. The man himself looked unimpressed and arrogantly back, holding the stare, neither blinking.
"I believe you did, mate." He answered. His voice was strong and did not waver.
Yahweh visibly cocked his head in a flick of annoyance.
Lucifer gulped down hard.
"Oh, goodness." He said, and walked into the room.
"James. Please, tread carefully. This is a very, very taut situation. The entities here, now, in this room have not been in the same room together for a long time. There are enmity and history layered with animosity, jealousy, hatred and need for revenge in here that you could never begin to imagine."
James smiled at Yahweh. He slowly moved over the silver box in front of himself, and patted the lid.
"I feel a bit stupid calling you God. What name do you call yourself, pal?" He said to Yahweh. Yahweh baulked again at the informal way

that the man spoke to him.

"I am Yahweh." He said deliberately and quietly with menace.

"I am the Lord God of this earth, James Edmunds; I am not your MATE."

James chuckled, mockingly.

"In my house, under my roof, I'll call you the whatever the absolute fuck I want, mate." He stroked the silver box. And slid it across the table.

"Do you know what this is Yahweh?"

The God regarded the box; he went to touch, and James slapped his hand.

Yahweh withdrew his hand sharply and stood up ready to act upon his rapidly decaying mood.

James stood up as well, hands resting on the box, smiling at Yahweh, leaning across the table.

"Do what you want to do. Take a swing. Smite me. I promise you pal, it will end worse for you than it will for me."

He stared deeply into the God's eyes, and smirked, something burned deeply behind his eyes. There was an inferno bursting inside the man, hungry for release.

Yahweh broke the staring match and looked at Death, Lucifer and then the box.

He slowly sat down. He looked at the box again.

"May I please?" he asked, beckoning for the box to be released for him to examine.

James nodded, and took his hands off the silver container, and slid slowly across to Yahweh. The god took it in his hand and immediately, his head snapped back, and his eyes rolled into his head, and he opened his mouth in a rattling gasp.

Everyone went to the God, but Death stopped them in their tracks.

"Stop!" he commanded, everyone froze, looking at the black suited creature.

"Leave him to learn."

Lucifer looked half-crazed with confusion.

He looked at James; he stared at his father whose hands were red-hot and burning onto the silver box.

"James, what are you doing?" he demanded of the man.
James smiled weakly at the angel.
"I am giving your father what he asked for."

God gently shook, a tiny rattle through the body that let a steam tendril squirm from his open mouth, as the box burnt into his core, sharing its secrets with the deity.
Finally, Yahweh let go of the box and pushed it back across to James.
He stood and walked away from the table, barging past War and Lucifer.
War looked angrily at the table and the human and his brother Death.

"What the hell is going on here?" he angrily asked, his voice a deep echoing boom.
"He was dead." He looked at James. "You were dead!"
James nodded, and stood, walking over to the Rider in Red.
"Wasn't I just." He stood before the red haired man.
"How short that temper of yours is. How close you came to ruining all of Death's grand plans." He smirked at the creature and let out a sigh-like laugh.
"Next time, don't hit like a girl."

War reacted on instinct, having never been spoken to by any living thing as he had been twice now by this man, he immediately swung his hand in a slap to knock some sense and knock the fight out of the man, instead, James beat him to the punch and War flew across the room and smashed into the French window, smashing through the glass and slid heavily in the grass to the stump of the willow.

Death held Lucifer back and looked at him shaking his head gently.
"No," he said. "Allow it."
Lucifer looked at the table at the box, he looked at the floor, at the parcel, singed but still unopened and then he looked at the God,

Yahweh, stood holding his eyes and his head, trying to take in what the box had done to him as well as witnessing James throwing War – the rider of the apocalypse, through a French window into a solid and ancient tree.

Famine carried on sitting silent, her eyes bouncing from one incident to the other, bemused, confused and as absent as ever.

James followed War outside, stepping over broken glass and splintered PVC framing.
He picked up a spade leaning against the wall on a hood, unused since Kay his wife had died, he looked at the flat, iron end and nodded, smiling, and swung it hard and low and smashed War under the chin with it, it clattered against the copper and white beard with a sound like breaking, rolling thunder and sent the creature sprawling backwards against the tree.
War landed with a thump and slid down into a crumpled mess at the foot of the trunk, his face had risen in a deep purple bruise, and the shovel had dented heavily from the impact, but not broken.
James looked at the dent, unhappy.
"My wife bought me this." He said, and span the shovel in a wide baseball spin and connected with righteous malice and frightful force against War's skull, the shovel snapped in two, the flat end ricocheted off into the bush, the handle was splintered and shattered in James' hand.
He gave a wholesome chuckle as he looked at the relic in his hand, and the smashed face of War, one cheek completely collapsed, an eye smashed in his skull, a fragment of bone sticking out from his cheek and fluid slowly dripping down his neck where he lay.
"James?" came a call from the hedge that separated his garden with his neighbour.
"Oh, hello, Yvette" he called out, a lonely eye peering through the hedgerow at him.
"Is everything ok next door, pet? Lots of banging and shouting, do you want me to call the police?"
James chuckled.
"No, Yvette love. Everything is fine… My BBQ had a wee gas leak,

and the bottle exploded. Silly accident. Don't worry, have some
friends round and they are helping me tidy up."
"Oh, okay, love." His aged neighbour said.
"Was ever so worried."
James smiled broadly through the hedge at her.
"Don't you worry, Yvette darling, I have everything under control
now.
Will try and keep the noise down."
He went to walk inside. Stopped and looked back at the hedge.
"Have you spoken to your son recently?"
Yvette looked at him and shook her head.
"Not for a few weeks. We had a falling out."
James smiled, it was warm, welcoming and full of love.
"Give him a call, eh? Tell him you love him. Never a bad time to say
you love someone. Never knew when you will never get a chance,
hey?"
Yvette smiled, "I'll do just that. You are a smart lad."
"Night, Yvette," he said and returned to the body of War.
James reached down and took grip of his sword, and unsheathed it.
Grabbed the scruff of War's neck and dragged him into the house,
where he slumped unconscious, possibly dead on the carpet,
bleeding.
The sword felt warm and welcoming in his hand, and he lay it upon
the table alongside the box.

Famine looked down at War and fell to her knees to stroke his face.
A single, unharmed eye stared back half closed and glazed over.
The rest of his face was an obliterated mess.

"Right," James said. "Let's talk shop, eh?"
And he picked up the parcel with ease, no effort required after days
of torture and stern resistance, the package moved with ease as he
lifted it and placed it with a groan on his dining table.
Yahweh shook his head, a faint line of silver blood ran from his nose,
only the second time he had seen his own blood in his life, the first
when Lucifer had head-butted him at the trial.
He sat with a slight stupor at the table, joined by Lucifer and Death;

Famine stayed by War's side, holding his hand.

James smiled at the assembled cast.

On the table lay the silver box, the sword of War, the package and an envelope that Lucifer immediately recognised as Littlehorn's three secrets. Unopened and untouched after all these years.
James sat at the head of the table staring upon his guest, his face a picture of alert, terrifying intensity.
Lucifer was confused at how the situation had found its way to this end.
He looked at James, his great white hope, and felt the tangle of heavy strings above himself, realising something had played him like he had assumed he was playing others, Lucifer now no more or less a puppet in this show.
He looked at the man, and a crack of a smile appeared on his lips, the Devil in him relishing this sudden shift in the story.

James toyed with the letter in his hand and smiled.
"Do you know what this is, Yahweh?" he held the letter up in two fingers and flicked it with his other hand.
Yahweh shook his head. James looked at Lucifer.
"You do, of course, Littlehorn." He chuckled.
"I realized immediately who you were when you stood there with your crown of flies and your black raven wings and your arrogant riddles."
Lucifer nodded.
"You never opened it?" he asked.
"I never had reason to. I have been curious for a long, long time. Think maybe I should open it now, what do you reckon?"
Lucifer nodded, "No time like the present."
James agreed.
"How long have you been playing me for a fool? Using me as a plaything. Leading me along like a piece of cattle?"
Lucifer shook his head.
"It was never like that. You were to be my champion as you reminded me of someone close to my heart. Giving, patient, calm,

loyal. After Poppy had died, I saw in you the reflection of my youngest brother and I needed to have someone like you on my side to make my final move.

You were to be the champion and change everything."

James tore the black wax seal open and pulled back the flap.
He slowly pulled out the piece of papyrus, upon which was scrawled the three secrets give by St. Leonard.
Death looked at the envelope and raised a hand.
"What is this?"
James handed it across to the pale man.

Lucifer answered the question.
"The legend says that every prisoner is visited by St. Leonard and given three secrets with which to barter or keep or use as they seem appropriate.
Inside that envelope are three secrets given to me. By the only visitor I ever had in my cell, a ghost of a martyr, leaving me stranded with three secrets I could never use.
So, when he was 14, I visited James at the grave of a departed friend, and I gave him them as a gift. His to do with as he saw fit."

Death looked at the paper.
And then to James.
"Poppy?" He asked.
James nodded.
"Poppy. Mr. Mortimer." He said quietly.
Death smiled, as usual, without meaning to be it was a horrific thing to behold.
Yahweh was glaring at the table in silence; he stared at the man before him, and the box. He had an impatient grimace upon his lips.
"What has this to do with anything?" He spat.
James stood, and his hand wound around the hilt of the sword.
"It seems to me that having been dead for three days, and with each of you coming here to woo and steal me for your own nefarious means…"

James started talking, and then Lucifer interrupted him looking at Yahweh sternly.
"It has everything to do with everything you old, mad fool."

James continued walking round the table, his voice was authoritative and strong, he stopped behind everyone as he talked.

"Once upon a time, I was a lonely, isolated boy. Disregarded by my siblings, brought up by parents who did not understand or get me. On an estate hidden behind walls and a deep circle of fields and woods. A plain of nature separating me from the rest of humanity."
He looked at Yahweh as he stood behind Lucifer.
"One day, I was almost killed by a vicious and angry boy named Michael, a bully, an arrogant and stupid child who thought himself better than everyone else and wanted to do nothing but prove it to satisfy his father."
He laid a hand upon Lucifer's shoulder.
"I was visiting the grave of a friend who took the bully's wrath in place of me, and I met a man who told me secrets and stories and who opened my mind to a new world of possibilities and legend."

He walked to Death.
"Another man met me at the same graveside, sharing with me details of ravens and robins, telling me how the ravens guard the graveyard and report all happenings to the Lord Death himself. Curious and hungry, he took strides to meet the boy and see why he would be of such interest to the Morningstar. So he took the opportunity to learn of him and his worth so that he could advance his own agenda."

He walked to Yahweh and rested the sword heavily against his neck, on the God's shoulder. Yahweh looked down at it, a slight smirk on his lips.
"And me?" He said to the man.
James smiled. He pointed to the parcel, wrapped in brown paper, tied with a simple string bow and with the scrawled postage label.
"I thought that was from you," James said. "I thought that had something to do with you and your overblown theatricality. Of

course, I did not know what it was before the red man over there killed me... But... Three days of being dead does something to a man and shakes something hidden inside him that only gods and monsters can reach, is that not true?"

Yahweh nodded.
"Yes. I allowed you to be killed. Three days was what it took for Jesus to be returned, and as my Messiah, I thought it only fitting that you share the same destiny, history and fate."
He looked at the red man on the floor, bleeding and broken.
"I didn't know it would be one of these idiots that killed you."
Death stood angrily, James flicked the sword around and held it to the creature's sternum, and pushed gently, Death looked down at the blade and then quizzically to James.
"Be sure you know what you are doing, Son of Adam."
James smiled, broad and sarcastically.
"My dad's name is Roger."
He pushed Death back into his chair.

James took his seat again, resting the sword against his chair. He looked at Famine and then to Death. The Black Rider looked behind him and clicked his fingers, the thin woman came over.
"Put the kettle on."
Famine looked dozily at her elder brother, and shook her head, confusedly.
"What?"
Death held her hands, and pulled her closer.
"Put the kettle on. We need tea. Our host is thirsty, weary and tired, and your brother made him so, therefore, tea. A pot, a big pot, now."
He released her hands, and Famine walked out of the lounge, into the hallway towards the kitchen, looking quizzically behind herself.
James placed his hand on the silver box and turned it slowly toward Yahweh, James lay a calm hand, heavily on top of it. .
"When I was dead in the shed, lay quiet, thinking of nothing but meeting my wife and son again – the people who you took from me – who you stole and killed in front of me. A voice came and spoke to me. Even as my thoughts faded and burned out one by one, I could

471

hear the voice talking to me telling me secrets and histories. All about the garden, the waterfall, the lagoon. All about the host and the fall of Eden, all about the tree in the centre of the plain and the fall of creation to the madness of men. He told me of murder and mayhem and how you wanted nothing more than to watch this creation burn. How each of the men and women who walked this earth was just ants in your massive farm, which you idly watched, bored and broken and waiting until you could wipe us out and start again. The last god standing, free to rebuild and pillage your perfect creation."

He looked at Lucifer.

"I was told this by your friend Zeus."

He looked at Death.

"I don't think he likes working for you."

He slid the silver box to Lucifer.

"He says that you would be expecting this."

And picking up the root from the floor, polished and clean, he handed it over to Yahweh. A tight, half meter tangle of wood that he had clean and polished.

Yahweh refused to touch it.

"He also said this was for you. He also said you would not want it."

James took the parcel, and as he touched it, he was overcome with the wave of dizziness and nausea. He vacantly stroked the string despite the ill feeling it gave him and toyed with the knot – a desire overcoming him to give in to one simple tug.

Yahweh looked at the root. He stared at Lucifer holding the silver box delicately.

And looked at Death greedily staring at the parcel as the string came off loose and fell to the table.

"Where did you get this? What am I supposed the do with a tangle of deadwood."

"It is far from dead, Yahweh. Dormant, resting, embers remain within the core. I can feel her even now. I saw her last, so brave, so proud of her boy, so in love with her child. Then I let her rest within the roots."

472

Yahweh looked at the root once more.

Lucifer could no longer beae it, and he opened the box, a brilliant burst of white light exploded from the box, and then just as quickly, having illuminated the whole house, it faded, and all that remained inside was a half eaten apple, brilliant and red, two bites taken from it.

He took it from the box and held it up to the light of the window, and he started crying.

"So fulfilled. The promise." And he took a deep bite, his mind flooding with images, truth and knowledge, things he knew that he had learned himself over time away from his father's influence, and things he never knew, not even shared to him by Zeus who would never have known the extent of the lust within Yahweh's heart and would never have understood the sickness that had been running through the veins of Eden from the start.

Lucifer raised himself from the table and pushed himself back, his hands to his head, and his chair falling hard to the ground.

He looked at Yahweh, and lunged forward, his hands aiming for the god's throat.

Death trying weakly to intervene and stop the attack, Lucifer slapping him away.

"You murdered her. You drove her bleeding into the plain, ripping her from the children she bore from your lust, and you drove her pitilessly into the desert to die.

All that remains of her is a root and a rotten apple."

Lucifer spat in Yahweh's face and threw the apple at him. His hands wrapped around his throat; the two men collapsed on the floor spilling chairs and knocking over ornaments and picture frames. Lucifer on top of his father throttling him, Yahweh slapping and pushing into his son's face to get him off.

James sat at the table, looked at Death and asked the question that Death had wanted.

"Lord Mort, Mr. Mortimer. Do you want me to open my package?"

Death looked at the parcel, at War lying on the floor, the two god's strangling each other. He nodded, looked at the parcel and nodded.

"I think now is the time to do so."

James pulled the string, and the knot flapped free and allowed the brown paper wrapping to unfold. It unveiled a simple plain brown box, as he pulled the paper away he saw a simple brass clasp, and unhooked it, and went to open it a voice rumbled and the clasp slammed shut.

"Not here, not yet."

There was a burst of thunder, a flash of lightning the blinded the whole room and shook the lounge and the whole house was lit up and the room, its inhabitants and the contents therein were swallowed in a sphere of perfect silver and imploded in on itself, folding into a space between spaces and emerging fully formed, under open blue skies, on a deep, scorched, barren plain. The lounge of James' house stood alien with no walls and no ceiling, just the furniture and carpet and the ornaments and the people within – all, except Famine, stood vacant in this warm, humid, desert plain.

Before them stood a throne.

And upon it, a god.

* * *

Famine walked into the lounge carrying the tray with the teapot and china cups, a tiny pot of sugar and a jug of milk. Her head was down watching the tray as she stepped wearily and weakly into the lounge. Looking up she saw the circle of the room ripped from reality, scorched from the house, and the outside world now very much peering into the remaining part of the lounge.

A gash tore from the brickwork from the window to the hedgerow, and back toward the patio doors, everything that would have stood there gone, and a black burnt hole now taking its place. The table, the presence of Death, James, Lucifer, Yahweh and the prone and broken body of War now all gone.

The other half of the sofa sat with a deeply scorched burn running the width of the fabric and left it looking like an art installation. The house was decimated, only the sofa, the shattered door way and a

474

five or so foot portion of upstairs bedroom and hallway was all that was left of the front facade.

Sparks flew from plug sockets torn apart by the sudden teleportation of the room, and there were tiny fires here and there. Famine walked in, looked around in bemusement, rested the tea on the floor by the sofa, and looked at the singed hole and suture of where the room had been torn apart.

She sat down gingerly on the sofa's smoldering remains and looked out at the garden where the horses of the apocalypse looked in, confused and haphazard.

She picked up her tea and supped noisily.

Cutting a slice of ginger cake, she ate it whole, and sat back waiting for whatever was to happen next, even as the horses came into the house and started chewing the carpets burnt and smoky remains.

* * *

There was an almighty crash as the top level of the house that was dragged and teleported with them to the plain materialized and fell down hard to the barren dusty plain, spreading a thick glaze of dust on everything and everyone there.

Lucifer let go of Yahweh, who pushed him hard away, the two men struggling to their feet and spinning on the spot looking to gain bearings and understand what had happened.

Death was stood. He smiled at the man James who was sat on the floor, thick in dust, his chair collapsed upon hitting the floor of the plain. Death had eased out his chair and stepped sideways upon appearing on the soil, aware how transubstantiating worked, prepared and ready for the alienating and queasy pop as the world opens and closes around you.

Before them, sat on a tall wooden throne was Zeus. In his hands, he held a plain wooden box. The one James had been sent through the post, which brought them here.

It was closed. The god held it loosely in two hands and looked at it resolutely.

War was on the floor, brick dust and masonry had collapsed on him from the falling upper level. The same masonry had flattened several chests and the table, as well as crushed the TV cabinet, TV and video player that James had previously had in his lounge.
Zeus smiled and gave a weak laugh.
"Apologies, James, the first time you do it, I appreciate it can be a little strange, but, believe me – it is the only way for us gods to travel."
James vomited heavily and loudly into the pile of bricks beside where his window once stood. He heaved hard and everyone looked at him.

From behind them, War suddenly bolted up into a sitting position, shaking the dust and broken bricks off of him. He growled and roared as he snapped back to full consciousness. He pointed at James; his one good eye fixed upon him.
He took to his feet and screamed.
"YOU!"
And he strode toward the man, James tried to summon some strength, but all at once, the travel between realities had wiped him out, and whatever had been driving him at the house was now gone and unleashed, Zeus sitting on this spectacular oak throne, looking over the empty plain – empty but for the crashed and ruined scene before him.

James tumbled backwards and tripped over some bricks and landed awkwardly onto his back, and War was almost upon him.
Zeus left his throne and threw an arm out at War. The red rider immediately flew backward sliding on his heel. He came to a sudden stop and looked at the new god in their midst.
"What do you think you are doing?" War said through a thick slur, his mouth missing teeth from James' unexpected, and incredible beating.
Zeus looked at Death, and the black rider nodded. He lowered his head and turned slightly toward his brother.
"I am sorry, War. But, this is how it must be." He let his head lower and looked away from the red man.

"What are you talking about, Death? I am kin!"
The giant man took a step forward, and his path was blocked by a cushion of invisible force. He rested a hand out and a pop and sizzle of static lit around his palm, he snarled and pounded on the force, and nothing gave.

Instead, he was pushed backward further, sliding onto the plain, further from the debris of James' house.

The more he pounded and fought, the further he was pushed, until he stopped, gasping for air and with two balled fists, he rested head and hands upon the wall that pushed him, and watched, imprisoned behind this invisible field.

Yahweh looked at the rider, and then to Zeus. He recognized the force and realized it was for his own person entertainment that Zeus had employed this rather than anything else against the red haired powerhouse.

"Very quaint, Zeus." He said, and picked up a chair, dusted the material down and sat down, looking at the silver haired god before him, who strode forward into the wreck of the house, picking James up and dusting the man off.

"I thought you would like it, Yahweh. After all, it was once your party trick with people you no longer cared for."
Zeus looked at Lucifer.

"Your mother for instance." He said gently.
Lucifer looked at Yahweh and spat.

"You are a bastard." He said to Yahweh.

"It seems so, it also seems that it runs in the family, boy." Yahweh responded. He chuckled as Zeus threw a hand into Lucifer's chest as he charged toward his father.

"No, son. There will be a time. Not right now." He whispered to the angel, his back toward his golden brother.

"Calm now. Calm." And Lucifer backed down, breathed deeply and pulled up a chair as well.

James looked around and surveyed his smashed and broken belongings.

He picked up a fractured, broken frame. The silver one War had smashed upon killing him. Lucifer had demanded he fix it, but the

photos inside were creased, torn and ripped. His wife ripped in two and fixed with a crude piece of tape on the underside.
The man clutched it to his chest, and he cried.
"Why am I the one you all want?" He sobbed.
"Why have you done this to me and my life? Taken the only ones I have ever loved and left me ruined and so utterly broken... Nothing but a shell that holds uncompromising sadness, full of sorrow, full of loneliness and anger."
He fell to his knees and held the picture tightly.
"Why are you all torturing me?"

Zeus looked at the people in the room.
He looked at Yahweh sternly, cold, his eyes blazing with malice and ill wishes.
"You look surprised to see me, brother?"
Yahweh smiled slightly, a sneer more than anything else.
"I'll admit I thought you were dead. Seems the rumours were exaggerated."
Zeus shook his head.
"Not so much. I am very dead, Yahweh. I died, and I was scorched and wiped from the Earth. Death took me to the portal to the world beyond, and I was allowed through, but, somethings are incomplete here and, therefore, the voices and whispers, the sound and the light on the other side said I was to stay and fix this world.
I was told to go back and was given a gift."
He leant into Yahweh's ear.
"I was told secrets that you will never be able to comprehend, brother."

Zeus walked to James and sat cross-legged by his side, under one of Zeus' arms was the box that had arrived in the parcel.
He lay it down in front of James, and on top he lay the envelope containing the three secrets.

"You were chosen, James, because Death needed someone who would make the hard decisions for the last of us, someone who had lost everything and had nothing else which he could lose to make

478

decisions that were impossible, act on desires too horrifying for us weak, selfish gods and monsters."

He took James' head in his hands and raised it, looking at the man with calm, beautiful, silver eyes, his soft pink lips, peering out from a perfect silver beard smiled.

"You are the apocalypse, son. It is with you that the world will end."

Zeus pointed to Lucifer.

"The Antichrist."

To Yahweh, who turned and looked at the man.

"The Messiah."

And to Death.

"The Final Horseman."

He turned James head back to himself.

"Remember what I told you in the shed?"

James nodded. He wiped his eyes.

"When I was dead?"

"When you were dead, my boy. Yes." Zeus nodded, closing his eyes he rested his head against James'.

"You told me that the world would end. You said that I had been chosen, and I was the one who would decide what would happen next.

You told me that creation was meant to be perfect, and I could help you make it so."

Zeus smiled and held James' head in a loving embrace.

"And what did you tell me?"

James cried again.

"That it would never be perfect, as it had been stripped of its most beautiful thing."

Zeus nodded, he lay a kiss upon James' head.

"It had been stripped of its most beautiful thing," Zeus repeated, staring at Yahweh.

Zeus split the world before him, reached in and pulled through the root of the tree, the final remains of Lilith. As the seam closed, before he had even finished pulling the wood knot through, he had thrown it, and it had penetrated heavily and with a sickening thud

479

through Yahweh's chest.
Yahweh looked down in disbelief, the speed in which Zeus moved was beyond his comprehension, the pain in his chest, unlike anything he had felt or experienced before.

Zeus smiled broadly, and pirouetted in a ballet of movement and astonishing fluid speed, with his other hand he tore a seam and pulled through the apple that was discarded by the debris of the broken table, and before Yahweh was aware or able to do anything Zeus had landed upon him, knocking him over, and the air from his godly lungs, sat straddled over the golden-skinned God's body.
Yahweh clutched his chest and tried to pull the root out, but Zeus pushed it down further and pinned his arms down heavily.

Death threw out a hand and held Lucifer back, Lucifer looked at the black rider with panic-stricken eyes, and Death held a handful of Lucifer's suit tightly and held a finger to his lips and stared him down hard.
"Wait. Watch… Do not tell me you have not dreamt of this yourself. Believe me when I tell you, this revenge is not for you, not for Zeus, it is something much, much more primal, significant.
Just watch."

Lucifer struggled to no avail, and glared toward his father, Squirming in agony as Zeus sat atop of him, pinning him down, Yahweh's arms under Zeus' heavy knees, he lay prone, prostate and crucified. Pinned to the floor under the weight of Zeus, the silver god playfully pushing the root in deeper, and toying with the final remains of the apple.

Yahweh was screaming, as the root slid in deeper, and something squirmed and moved under his skin, the root taking shape and form and filling the God's arteries and veins, wooden splinters sliding down capillaries and into muscle, fusing his body - the more he struggled, the more the wood took hold.
He became a petrified puppet of his former shape and grandeur.
Zeus, Lucifer and Death could see the skin fading into a natural

pigment, and the blue veins becoming more and more magnificent as the wood seeped and flowed into the bodies' nervous system, He screamed and gagged, and soon, only his neck and head were able to move as he spastically gasped for air.

"I loved her. More than you could ever have known. I told you that I would one day have my say, and you would pay for your sins.
It is only now that you lay here I realize that it will not be me who kills you, dear brother." Zeus raised in his free hand the apple, and smiled at Yahweh.
"It will be her. Her revenge upon you and yours."
Yahweh shook his head; the tiny motion was weak and unable to stop Zeus from his next action.
The silver god forced his hand into Yahweh's mouth, pulled it open and rammed the apple home hard.
Yahweh gagged and spat muffled cries, the apple slowly sucked into his mouth as he turned a deep purple colour, then a choke blue, before the apple was in entirely and out of sight. Yahweh spluttered and choked, spittle flew from his mouth and landed on the ground around him, tiny, weak blades of grass grew and withered and died in seconds. The golden-skinned God, now frozen with the brittle splintered roots in his every fiber of his body lay prone and rigid to the ground,, then his eyes rolled white into his skull, and the rest of his face and neck, his hair and his eyes and sockets slowly became a wood veneer, and he was entirely encased and frozen in wood.

Lay out on the floor as a human-shaped crucifix.
His arms stretched out and wooden, his legs flat and tighter together, his head the stock of the cross, dead and gruesome, grim and haunting.

Everyone, James included, holding his picture frame limply in his hand, watched on as the ground slowly shook and vibrated, and from the partly opened mouth of Yahweh, a hand burst free, holding in its palm a perfect red apple.
The hand pushed and an arm emerged, and then, splitting down the centre of his entire body, Yahweh burst in raw, wet wooden glory,

splinters of what was the God, now just rotten and dead wood scattered violently and damply all around, Lucifer and Death, James and Zeus shielded themselves for fear of blindness from the splinters, and when they looked back, stood naked and perfect amongst the debris of the former God, stood Lilith in all her perfect spirited wonder.

She stretched and cracked her bones in a serpentine shake, and then opened her eyes and looked upon the people and creatures before her. To Lucifer, she smiled and threw him the apple.
He caught it with a slap against his palm and began to cry. Lilith beckoned him closer, and he collapsed hard into her arms her hand in his hair, holding him lovingly.

"I'm home, son. I'm home."

Zeus looked at James and pointed to the envelope.
"Open it."
James picked up the envelope and broke the seal gently.
"And, read it."

James looked at the card and began to cry.
"Number One: a double revenge will be unleashed, reuniting long lost family."
He looked at Lucifer and Lilith, holding each other tightly, the woman kissing her son's forehead and the son crying with thankful release.
"Number Two: There can be no perfection while there is Chaos, War and Famine."
Death stood forward and pointed to War.

The red-haired man kept pushing against the invisible force and screaming vile, vitriolic rage, he was barely audible, the wall pushing and silencing his screams.
He suddenly turned, and his hand went up and pushed to his left, then his right.
He turned and pushed backward, and he was trapped in a cage of

482

invisible violent energy.

The rider in red turne, looked at his brother and mouthed one word. "Brother...?"

It was a half question, a half begged plead. It fell on deaf ears as Death simple shook his head.

"I am sorry, brother. But I am tired. And it needs to end."

He shook a hand in an open palmed gesture toward the red man, and the force pushed harder, and for a second there was a great huff of anger and pain, then nothing but a burst of red mist and gore that quickly burst in a puff of wind and drenched the plain.

As the four walls of force pushed in and crushed the rider of War into a dust and wet cloud of nothing.

James' hand clapped to his mouth.

He looked at Death, who pointed at James' TV, dragged through with the rest of the lounge, lay on its side in a pile of stone and plaster.

The TV lit into powerful, static life. Upon the screen was Famine sat upon the half sofa, and before her stood a shadow of another entity.

It was Lady Time.

* * *

Famine dunked the biscuit into the tea, a weak milky cup; she dunked three times and bit into the soggy digestive. She picked another out of the packet and vacantly dunked again. Upon the third dip the shadow of a creature seeped from the ground and appeared before her, its shadow a slippery dark liquid that flowed over Famine, and shrouded her in a darkness, made the biscuit snap off and fall into her tea, it sank with a bubbly gulp to the bottom of the cup.

Famine looked up and was face to face with her elusive, silent, secretive sister.

483

"Famine, my love."

Famine dropped the cup, and it shattered noisily to the ground, china flying every which way.

"Lady Time. Well, met."

Time nodded and smiled a thin, appreciative smile. Her hand pointed to the hole in the wall overlooking the garden and the hedge and the street beyond.

"Do you see, sister?" Time asked the thin, emaciated rider in white. Famine nodded. She smiled weakly, but graciously.

"I see, sister. I see it is time."

Lady time shook her head.

"No, darling sister. There is none left."

She held Famine by the shoulders and tore fiercely as Famine ripped straight down the centre, and the insides spilled out dusty, grey and ashen. Her body decayed fast and fell to powder in Time's hands. She looked over the street, and a wave of pure, brilliant white washed across the road and poured into alleyways and drains, gutters and side roads, it rushed toward her like a tidal wave, and it covered her in a white hot flash of nothing.

The channel changed, and there were hundreds of angels, at the forefront of them all in silver chest plated armour stood Michael, all staring out of the stained glass window in the great throne room of Yahweh. Rushing toward the window was a pure white wave of heat. Michael took wing and tried to flee, but the window exploded inwards, and the hall and throne and every angel assembled there was swallowed and eaten by the wave of white. Michael scorched, disappeared into the pure absence of colour and was gone.

The channel switched again, and the archangel Gabriel was hung from chains, wingless and beaten, bleeding and near death, tortured by his own brothers, he looked up and directly out of the screen, and smiled as a line of white painted and burned into his skin from the thin portal of a window in front of him, the wall and window exploded and evaporated and Gabriel was swallowed as well.

The channel switched once more, and the vast marble castle of Hell was washed over and crumbled and sucked into the light white wave, and was gone, and then the light rushed toward the TV screen, and it too exploded outward, smoke quickly bellowing from its broken shell.

"What... What the fuck was that?" James asked, pointing at the
screen and flushed, sweating and scared.
Death stepped forward.
"That was my sister Lady Time. Only she and I can step forward into
the new world. And we no longer want the job. I am tired of this
imperfect world, of its idle faults, its constant failings, it broken
spirit. Time has run out for this world, and we have decided it is time
for something new.
I do not want to do this again.
I want to die."

He gestured to the card.
"Read on."
James looked down. The last secret remained unread.
He read silently, and looked at Death, at Lucifer and Lilith, who
stood before him, he looked at Zeus who smiled delicately and
quietly, he picked up the box and held it in front of him, toward
James.
He nodded.
"Read on, James."
James looked at the papyrus and swallowed hard, and read the final
secret. To his unaware mind, it made no sense.
Number Three: It remains untouchable, Unusable, Unknown until
given to new hands, new eyes and new minds."
He looked at the box.
"What is in the box, Zeus?" he said.
The silver-haired god smiled broadly and held the box out.
"Your final gift. Deserving of a loyal and humble servant. Who has
been mistreated and abused, manipulated and lied to – and yet, who
persevered despite his every loss."
He pushed the box out again.
"Open it."

James tentatively touched the clasp, unfastened the lock, and
slowly opened the box and looked inside. He reached in and stroked

a thin, perfect piece of material, softer than silk, it was warm to touch, but cold as well, it felt to his fingers like water, but it was solid matter, and it was more elegant and beautiful than anything he had ever seen or felt.

He pulled it out, and his hand went to his mouth.

Tears streamed from his eyes.

He peered into the box, and it was as if he was staring down on a room from a window, spying on a couple on a doctor's surgery. The woman was lay upon a gurney bed; her stomach exposed as a man held her hand and stroked her arm and kissed her hand lovingly. They both stared at a screen, a small black monitor, as a doctor squeezed a clear oily liquid to the woman's belly and ran a scanner over the belly, and slowly a picture formed on the screen, and a baby, crude and speckled, but beautiful – appeared in the cloudy picture. The man gasped and held his mouth, and then kissed his wife deeply, his wife smiled broadly and let out a giggle, and she looked at the picture and then the man, the two of them cried joyfully.

As did James, witnessing the moment.

It was an aerial view of the day he first saw his son. He was looking down on himself and Kay at their first scan together when they discovered that they were having a boy.

He took the box from Zeus' hands and cried happily.

He watched more, as the doctor asked if they wanted to know if it was a boy or a girl.

The woman and man nodded and agreed they wanted to know.

The doctor saying it was a boy, asking if they had any names.

And Kay saying yes.

"Callum. It means Dove."

James said this alongside his wife.

And he closed the box as his other self kissed his wife's stomach and the two laughed and embraced.

Death put a hand upon the box, and the other he took James' hand, holding the fabric.

He closed his hand over James' and smiled, for once, his smile was

486

genuine and earnest, and he leant into the man.

"I coveted the throne for a time. Thinking I could right the wrongs of this world after removing Yahweh's influence. But I was wrong. This world is done for; it is broken beyond repair and, therefore, is dead and will shortly be consigned to the ether as the cycle begins again."

He looked at Zeus, who came over and placed a hand upon the box also, and took the hand of Death and James, pushing the fabric closer to James' heart.

"This is the time to rebuild, James. It is time to wipe the slate clean and start again.

And you are all that is left of the world before."

Lucifer and Lilith stepped forward, and Death looked at them.

"I want you, Lucifer to take up my scythe and carry on my duty. You wear my wings already, and they will do you well in the world beyond this, You, Lilith – will take the place of Time – Your bond and blood is thicker than mere mother and son, you will be the drivers and guides of the next world... You will live on, forever trying to attain perfection, forever to try and build the perfect world."

Lucifer nodded and placed a hand upon the box.

Lilith smiled at the man James and wiped a tear away from his eyes, she laid a kiss upon his cheek.

A door opened brightly in the ether, carved from the very air, and stood pensive and daunting before them.

"It is here." Death said. "Are you ready, Zeus?"

The silver god nodded and looked deeply at James.

"This fabric is the last remaining remnant of this creation. Carved and cut from the fabric that made your world. It carries within it unlimited potential, and from this fabric you came, and Kay and Callum. It is everything, and it is nothing.

I give it to you as a gift, and I ask you use it wisely."

He smiled, and raised the head of the human, and looked him in the eye deeply and lovingly.

"Don't fuck it up." He chuckled and turned to Lucifer.

"Look after him, and your mother, and take care to make the next world count."
Lucifer nodded.
Zeus took Lilith's hand and kissed it gently, and bowed.
"Milady." Lilith bowed back.
"I loved you dearly, would that your were mine."
Lilith blushed, and he bowed again.

Death handed the scythe to Lucifer and shook his hand.
"Remember. Death is not the end. It is a means to an end."
He smiled his usual ugly, terrifying scar of a smile and patted Lucifer upon the shoulder.
"Good luck."

He turned and opened the door, looked over the vast blank and spectacular expanse of everything and nothing beyond and, with a final look back, at the human the angel and the Nephilim. He nodded a final goodbye.
He shed his cloak, and naked, pale and beautiful, he saluted Zeus, who returned his tribute, and watched as Death fell backward through the portal, bursting into specks of dazzling, fluorescent and potent light as he dissipated and became one with the primordial nebulae soup.
Zeus watched and turned toward the final remaining creatures of the dying creation, he spoke directly to James.
"Everything and nothing, All within your hands, carte blanche."
He smiled at them all, and he too fell backwards into the door.

Lucifer picked up Death's cloak and held it tight, inside was something solid, it jangled and fell out into his hand, it was a pocket watch. Made of solid silver, delicately and beautifully engraved, its chain long and completed with gold embellishments, the winder and a ring on the face lay in perfect, precious gold.
The clasp and fob were dotted with gold finish as well.
It was exquisite.
He popped the face and looked at the hands spinning in errant chaotic spins.

He handed it to his mother, the beautiful, nude Lilith.

She inspected it, smiled and kissed her son on the forehead again.

"Shall we?" He said to her, holding the cloak tightly in one hand and the scythe in the other. She nodded and looked at the Lucifer.

"No time like the present." She giggled and smiling she said to James.

"Untouchable, Unusable, Unknown. Except to new hands, new eyes and new minds."

She blew him a kiss and took her son's arm. Clutching the pocket watch in her hand.

"Make it better."

And the two of them fell into the portal, caught by tendrils that carried them on into nothingness; they burst into pure light, effervescent and beautiful.

James was left alone on the plain.

He noticed the horizon was a quickly rushing wall of white all around him.

He sat cross-legged and held the box close to himself and opened it one last time.

Looking in, he saw his wife. Looking out onto him as he hung out his washing, she sipped a cup of tea, and she laughed and smiled and stared lovingly outside at James.

She whispered under her breath.

"I love you so much, Eddie."

He stared at her for a moment or two.

Then closed the box, knowing what came next.

"I love you too, Kay, darling. See you soon."

And he threw the fabric high into the air and looked up as it unfolded and parachuted down upon him as the wall of white closed in.

He looked up and in the dark, infinite brilliance of the material he saw stars and planets, moons and comets, nebula and galaxies. He saw the past and present and future, and he saw his wife and baby.

"I love you."

He said, closing his eyes. He smiled, and the blackness hit him cold

and inescapable.
Drowning him like the midnight tide, dark and beautiful.
Wiping out the light and halting the push of the burning, scorching whiteness.
Darkness ruled and darkness prevailed.
A powerful emptiness ebbed out and returned the world and all of creation to a blank state of nothing.

Nothing.
Yet Everything.

Carte Blanche.

* * *

EPILOGUE
Seeds.

* * *

There was a ripple upon the water's edge.
A hand lay stretched out as the water flowed around it, it bobbed and floated idly, under a perfect blue sky, and a warm yellow sun.

The arm lead to the body of a young man, whose perfect auburn hair was shaggy and unkempt, he was naked and sleeping, unmoved by the brief, brisk wind that flowed over him.

Beside him, holding his other hand was a woman, she had thick brown hair, chestnut coloured, and she was inexplicably beautiful. Her thin frame was laid out on its side, and she held the hand of the man beside her tightly.

Under them was a perfectly green patch of grass that went on for some distance, arching up into a hill, upon which was a bandstand, made of perfect marble and that stood solitary and alone, its surface warmed by the sun overhead.

Beside it was a bench, made of what looked like a single piece of carved and beautiful oak, and beside this was a giant weeping willow which bowed and gave a perfect shade to the bench, allowing it to overlook the river that the two people lay beside.
Just next to them was a bridge, also carved from marble, and perfect in every detail, it had thin veins of blue and red throughout, grey line reflected madly in the sun.

The dark clad entity walked calmly and quietly over the bridge and came to stop in the centre, as a beautiful, cloaked woman, with a silver and gold pocket watch in her hand clasped to her cloak met him at the half way.
She smiled to the man, who ceremonially bowed in return and then the two embraced.

"Lord Death." She said.

"Milady Time" he answered.
"Well met."
"Well met, my son."
They looked at the two people lay still and quiet, holding hands as the water lapped and gently rippled around the naked man's hand.

"What are their names?" she asked.
"I think you know." He smiled.
"And what are their secrets?" she probed.
"I have decided to make a change, mother."
She looked at the man in black, and he removed his hood, his beautiful golden blonde hair fell about his ears and neck, and his brown eyes burst into fiery life.
"What change is that?" she enquired, in awe of this magnificent man before her.
"Simple." He said.
"No more secrets." And he laughed and walked toward the man and his sleeping wife.

Death looked back at his mother.
"Carte Blanche. He said. Carte blanche."
The woman nodded, and smiled.

"In this world, we will make perfection."
He knelt beside the two sleeping humans, and when he lay a hand upon them, they both woke to startled and animated life.
The two humans looked at him, then each other and they flung themselves together and kissed hungrily and passionately.
Each kiss was deep and full of love.

"James!" The woman said.
"Kay!" The man responded as she lay a single kiss on his forehead after a loving, passionate embrace.
"You found me." She said.
James nodded. He kissed her cheek, her lips and her hand, gently, and looked as Death stood and walked away toward the bridge.
He smiled at the shadow of the man in the cloak.

At the beautiful woman stood beside him on the bridge

James returned to his woman and laughed.

"My love." He said.
"I never lost you."

He held her tightly, planting a kiss upon her lips, and smiled over her
shoulder, tears rolling down his cheeks, as the two entities in black
smiled and saluted him. They turned away and walked one step and
faded deep into the ether.

James cried again; happy tears streamed down his face.
"Everything and nothing," he said, quietly to himself, as he held his
wife.
He closed his eyes, kissed her deeply, she looked at him with
wondrous eyes.
He opened his and looked back in awe and joy.
He held her head in his hands and stroked her cheek.
They both laughed wistfully.

"I choose everything."
He said, kissing her once more. Surveying the scene of the park,
perfect and pure and full of love.

"I choose everything."

* * *

- THE END -

496

-AFTERWORD-

It was supposed to be a comedy.
It was never meant to be a novel...

ONE MAN AND HIS DOGMA started life as the second chapter in a trilogy of stage plays I wrote whilst studying Theatre in sunny Stratford Upon Avon back in 2002.

The main character of James Edmunds began life as an awkward Deliveryman, a minor player in a bigger story.
His presence only brief and fleeting in the grand scale of the whole story, making a bigger impression in the second instalment, as an Atheist who is chosen to be the incarnate avatar of Jesus and The Antichrist, as well as become the new fourth Horseman after Pestilence sprained his ankle...
The Apocalypse is averted (*it was a theme of all three chapters*) when James uses his atheism to disbelieve God and Lucifer out of existence with stubbornness and bad logic alone.

Some elements of the story stayed, others disappeared with each new rewrite. New moments and life born from the idea of loneliness and tragedy... But...
I struggled to make it work.
Six failed and aborted versions of the play exist, each more ridiculous and silly than the last.

It was my best-friend James Edwards (*after whom our protagonist James Edmunds is based*) who told me the story should be a book. Who made it apparent that the idea was more than a silly throwaway comedy; it was he who said the story had legs but was missing a spine.

The play was shelved, and I started working on the idea for a book - writing the prologue in late 2003. Where it stayed, incomplete and archived until the November of 2013 when the NaNoWriMo started and as a challenge with my cousin Daniel we both set out to complete a 50,000 word novel in 30 days - I found it out, dusted it down and got to writing.
Remembering James' words that it was worth more than silly comedy.

(SIDE NOTE: Dan Chamberlain, my cousin, wrote the beginning of an amazing Science Fiction story in the mould of Robert Heinlein and Joe Haldeman, called "ORBITAL". I really hope he finishes it, as it was an astounding, epic idea, which was a gripping page-turner. Maybe I'll find out what happens, one day, side by side with all of you.)

Between November and February of 2015 I wrote in bursts, taking an original plan for 50,000 – 75,000 words, it spiralled and spiralled and it became hungry for more words and – before long – my story was a novel.
But what do you do with a novel?

There were many influences who helped me along the way, some who I had to try and avoid comparing myself with and some which drew obvious comparisons I must recognise and acknowledge– in this instance, I doff my cap and thank the masterful and sadly missed Terry Pratchett (*for no one knows Lord Death better*) the wonderful Adam Roberts, Dante Alighieri and John Milton. Some who I had used as blueprints for how I wanted to craft a huge tapestry of story – but whom I had to try and stop idolising, - here is where Neil Gaiman is thanked.

I met him briefly at the Hay Festival this summer (2015) and I shook his hand and thanked him for being him, and apologised that I may have emulated his style – and he told me something in the flash of the moment I had with him that will stay with me forever...

"We all sound like others when we start, it's only by doing this that we find ourselves."

He patted me on the shoulder, wished me luck and rushed off with his wife for another lecture.

And I stood there with a huge grin on my face and a tear in my eye, dazzled at how elegant and sincere he was, how brilliant and genuinely sage he is – just like I had always hoped he would be.

I hope I did not walk his path too heavily, and carved a trail of my own somewhere along the line…

When I realised what I had, that I had created a genuine novel I asked my friends for help with a Kickstarter campaign to allow me to have the thing published.

76 Backers helped me raise £2060. That was £1060 more than my target, and allowed me to do everything myself to begin my journey as a fully-fledged, genuine author.

Without these 76 people this novel would not exist, and I would not be where I am writing this today. Please take a moment to read their names in the Acknowledgements; each one is a hero and a legend.

My profoundest of thanks goes to Paul Martin who worked genuine magic onto my manuscript as my editor and collaborator. His constant updates, his tips and advice and his deft handling of a dense story involving multiple timelines was calm, calculated and honest – with an eye for detail and continuity and allowed me peace of mind to get on with the boring admin work knowing the book was in good hands.

He was invaluable and inspirational.

Thank you mate.

My girlfriend Vix gave me nothing less than perfect encouragement, time and space and a helluvalot of patience… Also her insistence on not reading the work in progress meant that I had to really work hard to make the first time she read it really worth it!

Paul Minehane and John Hughes were my guinea pigs. They read the unedited novel before anyone and their opinion and advice and eye for detail helped me repair silly continuity errors and plot points that had gone begging or unseen.
I cannot put into words how valuable and amazing their contribution and help has been.

Liam Hesslewood was an incredible source of religious knowledge and translation of scripture. His help – particularly in Chapter Six – allowed me to write the story I had trapped in my head without fear of upsetting any people of belief and without disrespecting any religions or historians with bad translation of historical and spiritually significant events.

My dad has supported me every step of the way. Reading each and every short story – each chapter, each version of this story, being honest and critical, infuriating and brilliant.
As only Fathers can be.

Were it his story the dedication at the beginning of the book would be for him – because his influence in my journey to become a writer has been nothing short of sensational.
The dedication for him is waiting...
For a different story. A different time.
But soon.

Finally – Matt Young and Gareth Chamberlain, who took my mad scribbling's and turned them into proper works of art. Whether with the stunning photo-shoot my brother Gareth undertook which captured the exact images I asked for and more, or, the stunning graphic design that adorns my novels cover that Matt created from a scrap of paper and a photo sent via text message.
My book breathes and lives in the colours and shades you both lent it.

This has been a hell of an adventure. I have loved every single step, the good and bad. And now, the book is here and in people's hands, minds, hearts and imaginations.

So, mostly – and with complete sincerity – I want to finally thank each and every reader of this story.

I hope you enjoyed James' world. I hope you were rooting for Lucifer each step of the way. I hope you saw the colour and the shadows, the scents and smells of the world I created.

There may be more stories from this cast...
Who knows what the future may bring.

For now, know I am so stupidly grateful for your support and for reading. Keep your eyes peeled on my website - www.andijameschamberlain.com - for more future work.

Now... On with the next story.
And on and on and on.
But what genre to choose...
What genre to choose.

To quote James...

"I choose everything."

Andi James Chamberlain
Stratford Upon Avon – August 2015.

KICKSTARTER

Thanks to those without whom this book would not have been printed.
Thank you one and all.

James "Milo" Miles, Keith Nickless, Bo Davies,
James Edwards, Vix Sturdy, Jack Prentice, Laura Jones,
Sarah Tulk, Alex Caithness, Will Bennett, Tom Woods,
Matt Bell and Wolfshoulder Films, James "Lanky" Rea,
Gareth Chamberlain , Charlie Stanley, Annie Elizabeth,
Debbie Joynes, Kate Vassalos, The Brothers McLeod,
Christopher Booth, Lewis Copson, Garrett Monroe,
Gareth Bernard, Stephen Peel, Mark Waters
Laura Vincent and Darrell Greenway, Josh Stanton,
Patrick Monroe, Sophia Vassalos, Simon Chester,
Tom Eardley, Charlie Brind – Winnen, Dan Lee,
Graeme Davidson, Naomi Macdonald, Debbie Smith,
Gems Walker, David Piccone, Dan Booth, Chris Wright,
Andy Walker, James "Bling" Billingsley, Josh Melling,
Richard Neil, Calum Stansfield, Michaela Leszkovich,
Ellie Hopkins, Pete Hurst, Oliver "Rev" Taylor,
Matthew Scott Higgins, Paul "Hug-junkie" Waters,
Oliver "BoBo" Pawsey, Caroline Curtis, Jordan Hackett,
Scott Jessop, Abi Howard, Melvyn Chamberlain,
Mike McGreal, Mykael Barr, Dec Lynch, Luke Costin,
Charley Jocasta Venefica, Liam Brady, Ollie Gallant,
Stevo "Doc" Doccerson, Lydia Litton, Ian Trebilco,
Amy Smith, Kat Ward, Craig Valentine, Amy Keyes
and Kirsty Gouveia

An environmentally friendly book printed and bound in England by www.printondemand-worldwide.com

PEFC Certified

This product is
from sustainably
managed forests
and controlled
sources

www.pefc.org

This book is made of chain-of-custody materials; FSC materials for the cover and PEFC materials for the text pages.